Praise for *Up to No Gouda*

"Masterful misdirection coupled with a pace that can't be beat, Linda Reilly has grilled up a winner for sure!"

—J. C. Eaton, author of the Sophie Kimball Mysteries, the Wine Trail Mysteries, and the Marcie Rayner Mysteries

"A well-crafted and fun start to a new series! Carly and her crew serve mouthwatering grilled cheese sandwiches while solving crime in a quaint Vermont town. Plenty of twists and turns to keep you turning the pages and guessing the killer to the very end."

—Tina Kashian, author of the Kebab Kitchen Mysteries

"A delightful and determined heroine, idyllic small town, and buffet of worthy suspects make this hearty whodunnit an enticing start to a decidedly delectable new series! This sandwich-centric cozy will leave readers drooling for more!"

—Bree Baker, author of the Seaside Café Mysteries

T0015018

UP TO NO GOUDA

A Grilled Cheese Mystery

LINDA REILLY

Poisoned Pen
PRESS

Copyright © 2022 by Linda Reilly
Cover and internal design © 2022 by Sourcebooks
Cover design by Dawn Adams/Sourcebooks
Cover art by Brandon Doorman/Lott Reps
Internal design by Michelle Mayhall/Sourcebooks

Sourcebooks, Poisoned Pen Press, and the colophon are
registered trademarks of Sourcebooks.

All rights reserved. No part of this book may be reproduced in any form or by
any electronic or mechanical means including information storage and retrieval
systems—except in the case of brief quotations embodied in critical articles or
reviews—without permission in writing from its publisher, Sourcebooks.

The characters and events portrayed in this book are fictitious or
are used fictitiously. Any similarity to real persons, living or dead,
is purely coincidental and not intended by the author.

All brand names and product names used in this book are trademarks,
registered trademarks, or trade names of their respective holders. Sourcebooks
is not associated with any product or vendor in this book.

Published by Poisoned Pen Press, an imprint of Sourcebooks
P.O. Box 4410, Naperville, Illinois 60567-4410
(630) 961-3900
sourcebooks.com

Printed and bound in the United States of America.
LSC 10 9 8 7 6 5 4

For Dad

CHAPTER ONE

CARLY HALE LADLED TOMATO SOUP INTO A CERAMIC CUP, THEN placed the cup on the oval plate next to a grilled cheese sandwich. "Order up! One Party Havarti with tomato, extra pickles, hold the chips." She set the plate on the section of the counter reserved for table orders.

Suzanne Rivers, Carly's part-time server and all-around wonder woman, grabbed the plate off the counter. "Hey, Carly, how's that coffee coming? Almost ready?"

Carly smiled and held up a finger. "Ten seconds. That's the fifth pot I've made in an hour!"

"I'll have a fill-up too," someone called from a counter seat.

"Be right there, Buck," Carly trilled.

A retired fishmonger with a passion for anything from the sea, Buck Heffernan was one of Carly's favorite regulars. His order never varied—one Farmhouse Cheddar Sleeps with the Fishes, Carly's version of a tuna melt on thick ciabatta bread with a dash of spicy mustard.

She refilled his mug, then set the coffee pot on the warming burner at the far end of the counter. Suzanne immediately removed it and went over to serve her table customers.

Carly paused for a moment. She'd opened for business five months earlier, but sometimes she still couldn't believe it was real.

In a moment of sheer indulgence, she allowed her gaze to skim the grilled cheese eatery she'd dreamed of owning for so long.

Along the exposed pale brick wall opposite the counter, customers sat in cozy booths upholstered in muted aqua vinyl. Atop the gray-marbled tables were clusters of faux daisies arranged in vintage tomato soup cans. Carly had made the "vases" herself in one of her more creative moments. The counter area was designed likewise, with eight vinyl-covered stools stretching along a chrome-edged counter. Using overhead pendant lights reminiscent of lamps hanging in an old barn, she'd created exactly the look she'd been aiming for—a style Suzanne had jokingly dubbed "cow barn chic."

The restaurant, a former ice cream parlor, was a perfect fit for the picturesque town of Balsam Dell, Vermont, the town where Carly was raised. Carly's eatery sat in the town's center, directly across from the square patch of land known simply as the town green. Graced by winding walkways, curved wooden benches, and massive concrete flowerpots, the green also boasted a monument honoring the brave souls who perished during the Revolutionary War. In one corner of the green stood a solid oak post with a metal ring slung through it. Up until the late 1800s, a farmer could bring a dairy cow into town, hitch it to the post, and sell it to the highest bidder.

These days, Balsam Dell was still a farm town, although its quaint center, which had changed little in decades, had earned it the reputation of being one of New England's coziest villages. Carly loved being home again, as she thought of it. College, and later marriage, had taken her to the northern region of Vermont, but her roots remained firmly planted in the southern part of the state.

"How are those two Classics coming?" Suzanne's voice pierced Carly's wandering thoughts.

"Two Vermont Classics, coming right up!" Carly grabbed her metal spatula and flipped over the sandwiches sizzling on the griddle. They were perfect—golden brown and plump with tangy melted cheddar. Although Carly's menu offered a variety of grilled cheese combos, the good old Classic was by far the favorite.

When she first moved back to Balsam Dell, she'd felt more alone than ever. Still recovering from her husband's tragic death, she'd hoped that returning to her hometown might help her find solace. Opening her grilled cheese restaurant was a solid beginning, but it was her decision to source her ingredients locally that gave her the connection she was hoping for. Her delicious breads came from a local bakery owned by Colm and Sara Hardy, two former technology execs turned artisan bakers. A nearby cooperative farm that practiced sustainable methods supplied her quality cheeses.

Carly slid both sandwiches onto her cutting board, sliced them diagonally, and transferred each one to a plate. After adding pickle rounds, chips, and cups of tomato soup, she carried them over to the end of the counter and set them down.

"Thanks." Suzanne snagged the plates and went off to deliver them to the ninety-something twin sisters, Maybelle and Estelle, who ate at Carly's Grilled Cheese Eatery every Tuesday and Friday. One garbed in bubble-gum pink and the other in screaming purple, the white-haired sisters waved at Carly as Suzanne delivered their meals to their table. Carly returned their waves with a smile.

From the day she first opened, Carly had thanked her lucky stars for Suzanne. She'd interviewed two other possibles for the part-time position, but Suzanne had impressed her the most. An almost-divorced mom with a young son, Suzanne needed the part-time job and appreciated the tips. Carly's working relationship with her had morphed into an easy friendship, the kind where one could almost read the other's thoughts. Carly's other employee, Grant Robinson, was a nineteen-year-old who was saving his earnings to attend culinary school. Six days a week, Grant spent his mornings doing prep work for a local sub shop, then hightailed it over to Carly's to work from 2:00 p.m. until closing at 7:00 p.m. When his suggestion for improving Carly's homemade tomato soup proved over-the-moon amazing, she'd happily crowned him the soup king. He'd celebrated with a fist pump and a "Woot! Woot!"

The lunch crush passed by quickly. Carly felt as if she'd been working at warp speed to keep up with orders. Word of her delectable grilled cheese creations was getting around. Every day brought in new faces, along with those of old friends and acquaintances from her high school days.

As a teenager, Carly had been more studious than popular, but she'd made friends easily and involved herself in school activities. Shortly after graduation, she'd left town to attend college in northern Vermont, a two-hour-plus drive from Balsam Dell. Her plan was to earn a degree in hospitality management, work in the restaurant industry for a few years, and then open an eatery specializing in grilled cheese sandwiches—preferably back in Balsam Dell. All that changed when she met Daniel Brownell, a husky engineering student with a bellowing laugh and a soft spot for the underdog. They married and settled in Johnson, Vermont, where Daniel took a job as a lineman for the power company. Carly, meanwhile, worked her way from server to the top management position at the historic Ivory Swan Inn. Though she loved her job, visions of opening her grilled cheese eatery never left her mind—or her heart. Starting a family was also on her radar, but she and Daniel could never agree on the timing.

It wasn't until nearly a year after Daniel's death that Carly felt ready to move on and chase her own dream. She'd loved her husband dearly, but nothing was going to bring him back. When she learned that Bingley's Ice Cream Parlor, a long-time fixture in Balsam Dell, was closing up shop, she'd pounced on the opportunity to move back to her hometown and open her dream eatery. Its location in the center of town was ideal. Bingley's occupied the lower level of a restored brick building, so quaint that it appeared on postcards of the downtown. Harold Bingley himself was old and ailing, and his vegan son had no interest in either selling or eating ice cream. Added to Bingley's troubles was the fact that his landlord had mortgaged the building and was now facing foreclosure. After weighing the risks, Carly opted to take over Bingley's lease before someone else snatched up the prime space. Though she knew its expiration date was looming, she was prepared to work out a lease renewal with whomever ended up owning the building.

By 2:00 p.m., the eatery was quiet. Carly was wiping down her work area when Grant came in through the front door. Broad-shouldered and slender with a close-cropped Afro, he always wore a sincere smile that made every customer feel special. "Hey. How's it going?" He joined Carly behind the counter.

"Hey yourself, Grant," Carly said. "Getting hotter out there?"

"Like the third circle of Hades. *Way* too hot for mid-June, but it feels great in here. The AC is definitely cranking."

Suzanne looked up from the table she was wiping and jammed a hand into one hip. "Whoa. You're looking spiffy today in that red polo shirt. Gussying up for anyone in particular?"

"'Spiffy'? 'Gussying up'?" Grant laughed and rolled his dark-brown eyes, deftly avoiding her gaze. "Okay, now you sound like my mo—Um, never mind. Forget I said that."

"If you were going to say I sound like your *mom*," Suzanne said, winking at Carly, "then she must be one smart woman."

"She is. Hey, um, Carly, shall I start a new batch of soup? I noticed yesterday there's only one gallon in the freezer."

"You read my mind. That would be great." One thing she loved about tomato soup was it always tasted better a day later. "And can you help me make a list of supplies we're running low on? I'm going to call in an order this afternoon."

"You got it."

Grant pushed through the swinging door behind the eatery's

work area. Carly followed him into the kitchen, where stainless-steel shelves stacked with supplies lined two walls. A commercial oven with four gas burners rested against the far wall, next to a heavy-duty dishwasher.

It was her husband's life insurance money that paid for her restaurant's high-end furnishings. That and the proceeds from the sale of their home, the cozy chalet Daniel had fallen in love with the moment they'd spotted the *For Sale* sign back in Johnson. They'd lived there together for nine years, until the night Daniel's pickup skidded across a frozen roadway and tumbled down an embankment.

Carly went over to the far end of the kitchen, where her pine desk sat beneath a tall window. Sunlight gleamed through the panes, throwing a checkered pattern onto the desk. Two wooden chairs sat kitty-corner to one another. The desk served as a home for Carly's laptop, as well as an informal table where they could scarf down a sandwich during lulls. On the adjacent wall, a narrow shelf boasted vintage doodads of a cheesy nature—treasures Carly had collected over the years to remind herself of her goal.

"Before I start the soup, you guys ready for a sandwich?" Grant set a small container on the counter and tied a crisp white apron behind his back.

"I am!" Suzanne called out from the dining room. "And add some bacon this time, will ya?"

Grant chuckled, then went back to the work area and returned five minutes later, Suzanne trailing at his heels with two mugs of coffee. He set two plates on Carly's desk, each bearing half of a grilled cheddar and bacon sandwich on thick-sliced sourdough. "There's mayo on the inside, but I added something else. It's only a smidge, but I wanted to see how you'd like it."

Suzanne took a massive bite, chewed, and swallowed. "Mmm. Something tangy. I can't put my finger on it." She sipped her coffee and took another bite.

Carly was grinning. "I know exactly what it is. But where did you get it? I know we've never ordered any."

"From my folks' fridge. They eat it all the time on salads. I hope you don't mind that I tested it on you two." He looked pleased and worried at the same time.

"Grant, this is yummy. I don't know why I never thought of it before."

His smile stretched the length of his face. "It's not typical grilled cheese fare, but it tastes awesome, right?"

"I've got it! It's blue cheese, isn't it?" Suzanne asked him.

Carly nodded around her third bite. She swallowed and said, "Exactly. I think we need to create a new sandwich with it."

"Totally," Suzanne said.

Grant's eyes lit up. "You guys rock, you know that?"

"We know," Suzanne mumbled over a mouthful of food.

The bell over the front door dinged from the dining room. "Customer," Grant said and shot out of the kitchen.

After he left, Suzanne said, "Man, you lucked out the day you hired him, Carly. It's hard to believe he's only nineteen. He's so mature for his age."

"He is, but I also lucked out the day I hired you. I honestly don't know what I'd do without either of you."

Suzanne batted her eyelashes playfully, then grew serious. "Sometimes I can't read his mood, though. I've caught him staring into space a few times, like he's got the weight of the world on his shoulders. Do you think he has problems at home?"

"He speaks glowingly of his mom and dad, so I don't think so. I suppose it could be something in the *romance* department." Carly popped a pickle round into her mouth.

"Nah. A good-looking dude like Grant? He should have his pick," Suzanne stated with authority.

"It's not all about looks, Suzanne. Deep down, I sense Grant is inherently shy. And you know what? We're being gossipy for talking about him this way. If he wants to confide in us, he will."

Suzanne sighed. "Yeah, you're right. If something *is* bugging him, though, I just wish we could help. Big question is, what are you gonna do when he goes off to culinary school some day?"

"I don't know. I'll cross that scary bridge when I come to it."

"I keep meaning to ask you." Suzanne pointed to the shelf that displayed Carly's vintage collection. "Why is that can of pineapple up there? Did you forget you put it there?"

Carly followed Suzanne's gaze, and the comforting old memory washed over her. As a kid, she'd been the pickiest of eaters, unlike her older-by-two-years sister, Norah, who happily devoured a plate of slimy steamed clams when she was eight years old. Back then, Carly's favorite meal had been a grilled cheese on plain white bread, and her mom made her one nearly every day. Pretending she was on a TV cooking show, her mom would make a production of setting the sandwich in a cast-iron pan, placing a sheet of foil over it, and weighting it down with a can of whatever was in the cupboard. One day, her mom discovered that the pineapple can worked best because it was shorter and less likely to topple than the others. After joking that the can was her new grill press, she saved it and used it every time.

Watching her mom's grilled cheese ritual had inspired Carly. She swore to herself that one day she would make her own grilled cheese sandwiches and serve them to everyone she knew. The fact that her childhood dream had come true and she was earning a living from it never ceased to amaze her.

"But that can't be the same can, right?" Suzanne asked after Carly related the story.

Carly smiled and suddenly missed her mom more than ever. Despite her claim that she'd never leave Vermont, Rhonda Hale Clark had relocated to Vero Beach four summers earlier with her new hubby, Gary. Carly had been crushed to see her mom move so far away, but Gary was a sweet man who loved her mom dearly, so she had no right to complain.

"Actually, that *is* the same can," Carly confirmed for Suzanne. "I keep it as my good luck charm."

Suzanne devoured the last bite of her sandwich, then slid her hand into the pocket of her beige slacks and pulled out an envelope.

"Hey, what's this?" Carly said, taking it from her.

Suzanne shrugged. "I heard you talking to your sister on the phone the other day. Today's your birthday, right?"

"It *is* my birthday," Carly confessed. It was almost unthinkable that she was thirty-two. How did the years pass so quickly?

She pulled the card out of the envelope, grinning at the image of a pink candle stuck inside a golden sandwich oozing with cheese. *Hope your birthday oozes with fun!* the message read. It was signed simply *Suzanne.*

"Oh, Suzanne, this is so sweet. Thank you. It's almost like... like this card was made just for me."

Again, Suzanne shrugged. "Maybe it was."

With that cryptic remark, Suzanne took both their empty plates, rinsed them, and stuck them in the dishwasher. "I'll go out and wipe down the tables."

She started to push through the swinging door, but it swung inward as Grant burst into the kitchen. "Sorry," he said, his expression anxious. "Carly, there's a man out there who says he needs to talk to you right away. He looks...serious. I mean, *seriously* serious."

Carly's pulse sped up a beat. "Okay. Would you tell him I'll be right out?"

Grant went back to the dining room, and Carly washed her hands at the sink. The man was probably selling restaurant supplies or something. Nothing to be concerned about. Except that salespeople were usually jovial and upbeat, not *seriously serious*, as Grant had described.

Carly pulled in a calming breath and stepped into the dining room. She recognized the man immediately. He was the attorney for the bank that held the mortgage on the building. His expression told her something was up. For once, Carly was grateful for the absence of customers. Had the man intentionally timed his visit that way?

"Hello, Ms. Hale. It's good to see you." His grim expression said otherwise.

"Um, hi, Mr. Warner. Is everything okay?"

"I need a few minutes of your time. I'm glad I caught you during a lull." He glanced around, then set his briefcase on the counter in front of the nearest stool.

"Okay, now you're scaring me."

He puffed out a weary sigh. "I'm afraid I have some news that's, well, rather difficult to deliver. As you know, this building has been the subject of recent foreclosure proceedings."

Carly nodded. She'd gotten the certified mail notice from the bank four weeks earlier. At first, she'd gone into a full-blown panic. Until Mr. Warner had assured her the high bidder at the foreclosure sale would undoubtedly work with her to sign a new lease, something she'd counted on all along.

"Of course I know. We spoke about it, remember? You told me I had nothing to worry about."

Mr. Warner winced. "I know, and I'm so sorry, Ms. Hale. As it turns out, I was wrong. The high bidder at the foreclosure sale has expressed his intention to, um, *not* offer you an extension."

Carly felt her stomach twist into a knot. How could this be happening? How could her dream be ending after only a few short months?

Suzanne, who'd been fussing over the tables, came over and dropped onto the stool next to where the lawyer was standing. She set her spray bottle on the counter. "Wait a minute, are you saying we'll have to close? I'm sorry, but that is so totally unfair. Isn't there anything we can do?"

Mr. Warner gave her a helpless shrug that made Carly feel sorry for him. It wasn't his fault he had to be the bearer of bad news.

"I—I don't know what to say, Mr. Warner," Carly said. "There must be something I can work out with the new owner. Maybe I can call them and—"

Mr. Warner was already shaking his head. "I'm afraid the new owner is dead set on getting you out of here, to put it bluntly. He has plans for this space, quite substantial ones."

Carly didn't know how to respond. The news felt like a punch in the stomach and a slap in the face at the same time.

From the kitchen, the pulsing sounds of the food processor reminded Carly that the news wasn't only a blow to her. Closing the eatery would put Suzanne and Grant out of their jobs. She looked at Mr. Warner. His discomfort was reflected in his pale-gray eyes.

"Again, I'm so sorry, Ms. Hale. This was not the news I'd hoped to deliver to you today. I must remind you, though—you took over Harold Bingley's lease when it was nearing its termination. There was always the risk of it not being renewed."

"I understand," she said, but she didn't. Not really. She'd been sure she'd be allowed to renew. "I appreciate the heads-up, painful as it is."

Before the lawyer could form a response, the door opened and a man stepped inside the restaurant. Almost instantly, a pair of ice-blue eyes latched onto Carly's green ones, and her heart dropped to her stomach.

The span of years since she'd last laid eyes on him had done nothing to diminish his looks. With his sandy-blond hair tousled and gelled, his face perfectly tanned, he'd grown from a teen heart-throb into a devastatingly handsome man.

Hands in the pockets of his white golf slacks, he hovered for a moment near the entrance. Then his lips turned up into the tiniest of smiles as he walked slowly toward her. "Hello, Carly. It's been a long time."

"Lyle Bagley," she said, feeling the color drain from her face. "I haven't seen you since we graduated high school."

She and Lyle had dated when they were both high school seniors but only for a short time. What he'd wanted from Carly she hadn't been willing to give. After they split, Lyle set his sights on Carly's bestie, Gina Tomasso, a relationship that ended in marriage and later in divorce. Carly had tried to warn Gina that Lyle was bad news. Unfortunately, Gina thought she did so solely out of jealousy and never spoke to her again.

Taking Carly's greeting as his cue, the attorney raised a hand, muttered a hurried goodbye to everyone, and made a fast exit.

Lyle flashed the trademark smile Carly remembered from all those years ago. Back in the day, that smile had the power to melt hearts. Carly suspected it still did. A single gem winked from his left earlobe—a diamond stud, no doubt.

Lyle nodded at Suzanne, and Carly thought she saw a flicker of recognition in his eyes. He quickly turned his attention back to Carly. "By the way, you look great," he said, his grin displaying a mouth full of over-whitened teeth.

Carly glanced down at her white flowered tee, with its butter stain on the front and a splotch of tomato soup on the sleeve. While she normally prided herself on neatness, working over a hot grill all day definitely left its mark, or rather *marks*, on her attire.

"What can I do for you, Lyle? Would you like to see a menu?" She offered him one from the metal holder on the counter, but he made no move to take it.

After a long hesitation, he lowered his voice. "Look, Carly, I know you only opened for business a few months ago, but—"

"Five months, four days, to be exact," Carly corrected.

His face reddened, and he shook his head. And suddenly, Carly got it.

"Don't tell me—"

"I own the building now. I bought it at the foreclosure sale. Two other people bid on it, but my bid was the highest."

If her heart had sunk before, it was now down to her knees.

"Listen," he said, "I can see you've made a ton of improvements to this unit since the days when old Harold Bingley was slinging ice cream cones in here. But—"

"It's not a *unit*. It's my restaurant. And those improvements, as you call them, did not come cheaply."

"No, I'm sure they didn't." Lyle leaned over and tapped the fingers of his right hand on the counter. "By the way, I heard through the grapevine what happened to your husband. I'm very sorry." For the first time since he'd come into the eatery, he actually sounded sincere.

"Thank you, but can you please explain to me why you're kicking me out? I'm a good tenant who keeps her place spotless, and I pay my rent on time. Usually a day early, in fact." Carly knew she was sounding desperate, but with so much at stake, she had no choice.

Lyle hesitated, then cleared his throat and looked away as if to buy himself time to respond. It was an old habit, one Carly recognized from their younger days. "All right, listen. I'm going to come right out with it. I assume you know Tiffany Spencer, the woman who lives upstairs from you." He pointed a finger at the ceiling to indicate the apartment above Carly's restaurant.

"I'm acquainted with her but only slightly. Our paths don't cross very often. I know she works at one of the stores in the Manchester outlets. My sister shops there a lot, and she's seen her behind the makeup counter."

"She doesn't just work there, Carly. She's the assistant manager for a beauty supply shop, and she runs a tight ship. As capable as she is, she gets no appreciation, or compensation, for working her butt off every day."

Carly couldn't help wondering why he sounded so defensive. "I'm sorry for her troubles, but what does that have to do with my restaurant?"

Lyle's tanned face took on a slight flush. "I—Look, Tiff and

I have been seeing each other for several months now, and we recently got engaged. It's one of the reasons I bought this building, so she could open her own fashion boutique. She's been wanting to do it for a long time, and this is the ideal location. Besides, this town could use something like that, don't you think? It's been living in the past for too long."

Every nerve in Carly's body jangled. Did he seriously think she was going to agree? Balsam Dell's historic downtown was the main reason tourists flocked there, especially during the summer and fall seasons.

Before she could come up with a snappy retort, he said, "Listen, Carly, I just happen to know"—he winked at her—"there are two rental units available in the new shopping plaza in Bennington. One of them would be perfect for a small restaurant. If you relocated—"

Carly was already shaking her head, frustration growing inside her like a rampant weed. "I'm sorry, Lyle, but right now I'm not interested in your suggestions. I'll do my own reconnaissance, thank you very much."

"Have it your way. I was only trying to help." He glanced toward the door, and Carly suddenly realized that Tiffany Spencer was peeking in through the glass. Carly's first instinct was to rush over and lock the woman out. Instead, she stood there, frozen, as Lyle gestured to Tiffany to come inside.

Carly had only seen Tiffany a handful of times, and each time, she'd been dressed to the nines. Today was no different. Clad in a satiny white halter top over skinny red slacks, her face made up to perfection, she strode toward Lyle on red stiletto heels that echoed off the diamond-patterned tile. Looking slightly embarrassed, she opened her purse and pulled out a legal-size envelope. She gave the envelope to Lyle.

Lyle took it from her and set it on the counter in front of Carly. He slipped his arm around Tiffany's tiny waist and gave her a little squeeze. "This is your official notice, Carly. You need to be out of here by the end of July. If you need help removing the fixtures, I can get a crew in here. But the date is firm. Anything left here on August 1 will be demolished."

Carly swallowed back a huge lump of pride. "Are you sure I can't have another month or two?"

"Sorry, Carly. No can do. This place has to be gutted and all the restaurant fit-ups removed."

Gutted. The word made Carly's stomach turn.

It was then that Carly realized Suzanne had been glued to her stool, glaring at Lyle as if he were the devil himself. She hadn't spoken a word, but her face had gone a scary shade of gray. She stood, snatched up a metal napkin dispenser, and slammed it down on the counter. Lyle flinched and Tiffany let out a startled squeal, while Suzanne's pointed finger hovered about an inch from Lyle's nose. "One of these days, Lyle Bagley, you're going to get what's coming to you, big-time. You can *bet* on it."

CHAPTER TWO

AFTER LYLE LEFT WITH TIFFANY ATTACHED TO HIS ARM, Suzanne slumped on her stool. "I'm sorry, Carly. I didn't mean to snap like that. The whole thing just made me so...*mad*, you know?" She pushed a strand of dark blond hair behind one ear.

Carly came around the counter and slipped an arm around her shoulder. She understood Suzanne's frustration. She'd been tempted to lash out at Lyle herself. A bop with a spatula on his perfectly shaped nose would have given her a good deal of satisfaction. Fortunately, years of working as a restaurant manager at a popular inn during her prior life—her life before Daniel's death—had taught her patience and restraint.

She remembered the spark of recognition in Lyle's blue eyes when he first sauntered over to the counter and saw Suzanne. Did they share a past? Suzanne's parting words to him had sounded personal. And she'd called him by his name, his *full* name, when she told him he'd get what's coming to him.

Carly wanted to press her on it, but she decided to wait. Suzanne had always been open with her. She'd probably tell her eventually. Besides, did it really matter? Was it any of Carly's business?

Suzanne glanced at the wall clock. It was nearly 3:00, the end of her shift.

"Why don't you go ahead and head home?" Carly suggested. "And try not to worry, okay? I'll figure something out, I promise. Things aren't always as dire as they seem." *Except they seem pretty dire right now.*

"I suppose. What did you think of Bagley's idea about checking out the new strip mall? Those places do get a lot of foot traffic."

"I know, and I'll probably check it out. I'd rather see if anything is available in the downtown area first."

Suzanne was silent for a moment, then she said, "Listen, Carly, I gotta be frank. This job has kept me sane; plus, it helps me afford my son." She gave out a wry laugh. "I swear, Josh's feet grow an inch every week, and his father sure as heck isn't going to buy new sneakers for him. Jake's idea of child support is taking his kid to the bowling alley every Saturday."

Josh was Suzanne's nine-year-old son. The two lived with Suzanne's mom in a cape-style home not far from downtown Balsam Dell.

"I hear you," Carly said, "and I'm going to do everything possible to find the right space for us so we can move by the end of July."

"It's just that…I need the work, you know?" Suzanne went on. "My mom's been great, but I can't mooch off her forever."

"And you won't. Although I'm sure she's loving having the two of you bunking with her." Carly had met Suzanne's mom. She was caring and kind, and she adored her grandson.

"I know. She is. *Most* of the time." Suzanne gave up a weak smile and slid off her stool. "Hey, you'd better let Grant know about this. He's going to be bummed, for sure."

The thought of breaking the news to Grant made Carly's insides twist. He loved his job at Carly's eatery as much as Suzanne did. With his culinary bent, maybe even more.

"Let Grant know what?"

Neither of them had seen Grant slip silently through the swinging door. Suzanne looked down at her shoes, but Carly met Grant's questioning gaze head-on. "We just learned that a new owner is taking over this building. He's kicking me out so his girlfriend can open a boutique."

"*What*?" Grant's dark eyes blazed. "I knew something was

going on in here. I would have come out sooner, but I didn't want to look like I was eavesdropping."

"It's a shock to me too," Carly said. "Like I told Suzanne, I'm going to do everything in my power to relocate to a good space. We have until the end of July to vacate. If you hear of an available rental place, will you let me know?"

"I will, but—" Grant shook his head. "Are you sure you can't fight it, Carly? My dad has this really good lawyer. I can get her name for you."

"Thanks for the offer. For now, I'm going to make some calls, but the bank's lawyer gave me the news in person, so I'm pretty sure it's all legal. I knew my lease was on borrowed time. I just didn't think I stood to lose my restaurant altogether."

"This really su— I mean, it's so unfair, you know?" Grant waved his muscular arms in a sweeping motion. "Look what you've done with this place in a few short months. You turned a fading ice cream joint into a super fun place with an awesome vibe."

In spite of her heavy heart, Carly smiled at him. "That was a wonderful description. Are you sure you don't want to major in marketing?"

"I want to be a chef," he said firmly.

The tension and finality in his deep voice surprised Carly. Grant was normally so easygoing. She was relieved when three teenaged girls strolled into the restaurant. Patsy, Amber, and Olivia came in at least two afternoons a week for grilled cheese dippers. The dippers were made by grilling habanero cheddar between slices of asiago bread and then slicing them into half-inch wedges. Cheesy and spicy, they were ideal for dunking into Grant's yummy tomato soup.

The girls waved hello to everyone, but their eyes were fixed squarely on Grant. Olivia nearly tripped over her purple flip-flops gawking at him. The three slid into their favorite booth, their youthful faces illuminated with huge smiles.

"Hey, Carly, I'm gonna head out," Suzanne said quietly. "I'll see you tomorrow, okay?"

"Sure. And try not to worry. I'll figure something out."

Waving her car keys at Carly and Grant, Suzanne left through the rear door.

The remainder of the day was busy. Carly tried to stay upbeat, but as the hours passed, she was losing the battle. If she didn't find a suitable space to relocate to, and soon, she could kiss any hope of running a successful grilled cheese eatery goodbye. Was this her punishment for using Daniel's life insurance to fund the startup costs for the restaurant? Although she knew it was what her late husband would have wanted, the uneasy thought had nagged at her all afternoon.

Around 6:30, Grant came up to her with a sheepish expression. "Carly, I know this is lousy timing, but I wondered if I could leave early. My mom just got promoted to full professor at the college, and we're taking her out to dinner to celebrate."

Carly smiled at him. "Oh, Grant, how wonderful. What an honor that is. Please give her my congratulations. Of course you can leave. With my blessing."

"Thanks. You're the best." He gave her a grateful smile, but his eyes were sad. "I hate leaving you to close up alone. Especially after today."

"Don't be silly. I'll be fine. I might shut down a few minutes early."

"I'll try to come in early tomorrow to make up the time. I made two batches of tomato soup today and put them in the freezer, so we'll be in good shape for at least the next few days. And...don't stress over the eviction, okay? You'll think of a solution. I have total faith in you."

Fighting back tears, Carly watched as Grant left through the front door, his glum expression reflecting the ache in her heart. He always parked his car behind the sub shop on the opposite side of the town green.

By 6:45, she was ready to close. After checking to be sure everything was locked up and turned off, she left through the rear doorway. It led to the small, paved lot where Carly parked her aging Corolla.

She had just started her engine when a flash of fur caught her eye. A scruffy beige dog was poking around near the dumpster at the back of the lot. She'd seen the small pup a few times before, but every time she'd called to him, he'd run off.

"Poor little guy," she murmured. "I hope you know where your home is."

As if he'd heard her, the dog bolted in the opposite direction. Carly watched him trot along the sidewalk for a few moments, then shifted into Drive and headed home.

～

Her apartment was only a mile or so from downtown Balsam Dell. Within a few minutes she was pulling into the driveway of a well-maintained two-family home. Painted pale yellow with gray trim, the house sat on a half-acre parcel of land that had a wooden fence running along each side. Mature oaks lined the street, providing shade at critical times of the day.

Inside her second-floor apartment, Carly kicked off her flats, dropped her tote on the table in her hallway, and slipped on the orange flip-flops she kept near the door. Only mid-June, and already her apartment was too warm for comfort. Nevertheless, she was grateful to be home, even if it did feel a bit like an Easy-Bake Oven. She'd been meaning to buy a window air conditioner but hadn't yet found the time to shop for one.

Carly went over to the fan that rested on an end table next to her sofa. Flicking it on to the highest setting, she dropped onto the cushion beside it. Her husband had jokingly called the sofa their "girly" couch because of its flowery, lilac pattern. Despite his teasing, they'd spent many a chilly evening back in Johnson snuggled up on it, an afghan draped over their legs and a bowl of popcorn between them.

A sudden wave of melancholy crashed over her. The night Daniel died had been the most terrible of her life. It was mainly to escape the reminders of her loss that Carly had sold their chalet home in northern Vermont and moved back to her hometown. That, and learning that Bingley's Ice Cream Parlor was closing for good. She'd grabbed at the chance to take over its lease and open her dream restaurant. What would she do if she lost her restaurant too?

Taking a deep breath, Carly went into her kitchen and poured herself a glass of ice water. Glass in hand, she walked around her living room and drew down all the shades.

She'd no sooner drawn down the last one when her cell rang. She went over to her hallway table and retrieved it from her tote.

"Hey, birthday girl, what's cookin'?" It was her landlady, Joyce Katso, who lived in the apartment below Carly's.

"Hi, Joyce." *Darn, why did I tell Joyce today was my birthday?*

"Uh oh. I can tell from your voice something's wrong."

"Am I that transparent?"

"Like a sheet of Saran Wrap. Now get your pretty patoot down here and give me and Arlene the scoop."

Carly smiled to herself. Nothing got past her landlady. The seventy-something Joyce was sharp as a switchblade, even if her MS kept her largely confined to a wheelchair. She was lucky to have a devoted, live-in caretaker like Arlene Timson.

"Besides, Arlene has a surprise for you."

"Okay, I'll be down in a few."

Carly headed into the bathroom, ran cool water over her face, and patted it dry with a towel. A glance in the mirror reminded her that her wavy, chestnut-colored hair, which she normally kept pixie-short, was way overdue for a trim. Unfortunately, she'd have to shove getting a haircut to the back burner. Finding a place to relocate her eatery was now her top priority.

A minute later, she was tapping on Joyce's door.

"It's open!" Arlene called out.

Carly stepped inside the apartment and went directly into the living room. As she passed by the kitchen, the enticing aroma of chocolate nearly made her swoon.

The apartment was laid out the same as Carly's, minus the narrow balcony that jutted out over the front porch. An air conditioner crammed in one of the windows was pumping out frigid air, making the room almost too cold.

Directly opposite the forty-inch television, Joyce sat in her wheelchair. Garbed in a "Woodstock 50th Anniversary" T-shirt and seersucker shorts, coils of gray hair framing her face, she pointed to the chair beside her. "Sit."

"I'll get you some iced tea," Arlene said, hopping off her rocking chair.

Joyce turned and studied Carly's expression with her piercing gaze. "You've had a rotten day. I can see it in your face."

"It's been a day, that's for sure," Carly admitted. "I'm afraid I got some bad news." Arlene returned with her iced tea. Carly thanked her and continued, "My new landlord is kicking me out of my restaurant. I got an official notice this afternoon." The words came out quietly, but a voice inside Carly wanted to scream.

"What?" Joyce sputtered. "Well I'll be a son of a badger. Who's your new landlord?"

"A guy I knew from high school. Lyle Bagley."

"Hah! I should have known. He turned out to be as scheming as his father was. Ned Bagley never did an honest day's work in his life."

Arlene frowned and looked at Joyce, her eye twitching. "Lyle Bagley. Isn't he some sort of wheeler-dealer in town?"

"More importantly," Joyce huffed, "why would he want to kick out a good tenant like you?"

Carly took a sip of her iced tea. "I'm being evicted because Lyle is going to gut the entire building. His girlfriend is going to turn it into some sort of boutique. I've only got till the end of July before I have to move out."

Joyce sat back and drummed her fingers on the arm of her wheelchair. "Carly, I don't like the sound of this. You sure this is all legal?"

"I'm sure. The bank's attorney stopped by first and told me about it."

Joyce reached over and squeezed Carly's wrist with her long, bony fingers. "Listen, darlin', whatever happens, you're gonna be just fine. But in the meantime, you let me know if there's anything I can do. If you need the name of a lawyer, I can give you one. I've known a few in my day." She winked at Carly.

Carly managed a tiny smile. That was the second time today she'd been offered the name of a lawyer. "Thanks, Joyce. I'll keep that in mind."

Arlene rubbed the side of her right eye, then smiled at Carly. "I made something for your birthday. You can probably guess…"

"I bet it's chocolate cake."

"You guessed it exactly. Stay right here, okay? I'll bring us each a big slice."

"Yeah, let us eat cake!" Joyce crowed.

Carly wasn't sure her stomach could tolerate a big slice, but she loved cake—no matter the flavor. Plus, she'd never hurt Arlene's feelings by refusing. "Can I help you carry anything?"

"No! You stay right there and talk to Joyce. I'll only be a few."

Carly chatted with Joyce for a while. After several minutes, Arlene reappeared carrying three huge slices of cake on an oval tray. She handed out napkins and forks and gave each of them a slice.

It wasn't long before Joyce's favorite port wine replaced the iced tea in their glasses. They toasted Carly's birthday.

Joyce added a final toast of her own. "May Carly thrive, and may tyrants be denied!"

"I'll drink to that," Arlene said and tossed back a mouthful of the port.

The cake was unbelievably scrumptious, right down to the pink pastel flower that graced her slice. But after several minutes, Carly began to feel light-headed. Between the sweetness of the cake and the richness of the port wine, her brain was beginning to float.

After finishing her slice, she set down her plate and glass and rose from her chair. "Ladies, this was truly a treat. Arlene, thank you for baking me such a delicious cake."

"I'll pack up another big slice and bring it up to you tomorrow," Arlene promised.

Both women hugged her, and she promised to keep them updated on the status of her eatery.

Yawning, Carly climbed the stairs to her apartment. Her sugar high was fading. A deep weariness was beginning to slither into her bones.

After a quick trip to the bathroom, she shuffled into her bedroom and tugged off her clothes, slipping into a cotton nightshirt. The moment her head connected with her pillow, she was sound asleep.

CHAPTER THREE

THE FOLLOWING MORNING, CARLY AWAKENED WITH A jackhammer drilling through her head. She peeled back an eyelid, glanced at her bedside clock, and bolted upright.

"Holy jumping grasshoppers! It's after eight!"

She leaped out of bed and went into the bathroom, her legs wobbling, her stomach roiling. Why, *why* had she eaten that massive slab of cake the night before? And why had she agreed to drink a glass of Joyce's favorite port wine?

For a birthday toast, that's why, she reminded herself. The strong port had played havoc with her stomach. Lighter wines, like white zinfandel or champagne spritzers, were more her speed.

She wasn't sure if the sugary cake or the wine had gotten to her first. She vaguely remembered dropping into bed the moment she got back to her apartment. Obviously, she'd slept well. Her normally reliable internal clock had overslept along with her.

After swallowing two ibuprofen with a glass of orange juice, she took a record quick shower and dressed for work. Then she locked up her apartment and headed outside.

At 8:45 a.m., the air already felt muggy. She'd heard it might climb into the nineties today. Luckily, the AC worked fine in Carly's Grilled Cheese Eatery.

Carly groaned when she saw how close she'd parked to Arlene's dark blue Fiesta the night before. But in the state of mind she'd been in, it didn't surprise her. She eased open her car door carefully so as not to ding Arlene's, then lowered herself into the driver's seat. She was putting the key in the ignition when it struck her like a blow—in a little over a month, her eatery would be history. She pictured a *Closed* sign hanging on the door, her beloved grilled cheese restaurant dark and empty.

The idea of uprooting and starting over again felt unimaginable. The cost alone would be a nightmare. Plus, she hated giving up her prime location in downtown Balsam Dell.

During the summer and fall seasons, tourists prowled the local shops, and the picturesque town center teemed with visitors. Many detoured to nearby Bennington to view the historic Silk Bridge, then returned to Balsam Dell to dine at one of its myriad eateries. On Saturdays throughout the summer, area vendors peddled goodies and crafts on the town green, while music students from the local college gave impromptu performances. Carly had already imagined the uptick in customers she'd enjoy once the season got under way. Now, with summer just beginning, her business might be ending.

No, not ending. I will find a place to start over!

Forcing herself to breathe so she wouldn't cry, she started her engine and backed out of the driveway. The sky was a dazzling blue, the distant hills a lush, vibrant green. It was no coincidence that Vermont had been dubbed the Green Mountain State.

Driving along the main drag, Carly couldn't help feeling her spirits lift. Kids were already riding their bikes, parents pushing strollers. A ponytailed woman walking three dogs at once trotted briskly along the sidewalk, a plastic bag dangling from her arm. At the corner of Main and Silver, the owner of the used bookstore was hanging out his *Open* flag. Carly waved. He flashed her a big smile as she passed.

In spite of her current troubles, Carly felt, deep in her bones, that returning to Balsam Dell had been the right move.

A minute later, she turned right onto Liberty Street, then swung a quick left into the paved lot behind her restaurant. She parked close to the building and shut off her engine. Tiffany Spencer's snazzy red Nissan was parked there, the sun gleaming off its rear window.

As Carly was getting out, she noticed a midsize blue sedan parked beside the dumpster near the corner of the lot. She'd seen the same car there on a few other occasions. She assumed it belonged to someone who lived in one of the charming older homes on Liberty Street—someone who didn't want to leave their extra car parked on the narrow residential street. She certainly couldn't imagine Lyle Bagley driving a nondescript car like that.

Carly unlocked her back door and went inside her restaurant. First things first: she flicked on the lights and turned on the central air, then went into the kitchen and stuck her belongings under her desk. When she returned to the dining room, a face peeking through the glass front door caught her eye. She jumped slightly, then relaxed when she recognized who it was.

Ari Mitchell, the thirtysomething electrician who'd installed her lighting, was tapping on the glass. His eyes, the color of dark rye bread, beamed at her from beneath a cluster of short black curls.

Smiling at her unexpected visitor, Carly hurried over to unlock the front door. "Hey, come on in. What are you doing here so early?"

He stepped inside but hovered near the doorway, his hands shoved inside the pockets of his khaki cargo pants. "Sorry to bother you," he said, a slight hesitation in his voice. "I just wanted to say that I heard what happened yesterday with your lease. Carly, I'm so sorry. You're the last person in the world who deserves this. If there's anything I can do..."

Carly swallowed back a lump. "Why don't you come in and have a seat at the counter? I was just going to make a pot of coffee."

"Actually, that would hit the spot." He smiled, and Carly noticed, not for the first time, how perfect his teeth were.

Ari followed her over to the counter and slid onto a stool. Carly went through the motions of preparing her first pot of coffee for the day, but her heart was heavy. How many more times would she have the privilege of opening her doors to customers?

"So, where did you hear about my lease being canceled?"

His expression dark, Ari folded his suntanned arms over the counter. "Unfortunately, everyone in town's jabbering about it. Word sure got around fast." He shook his head, his jaw hardening into a firm line. "I've never been a fan of Lyle Bagley. What he's doing to you is just plain wrong."

Carly turned away and made a point of fussing over the coffee pot. She knew her face was a road map of her thoughts, and she wanted them to remain private.

The coffee made, she poured each of them a mugful. "You take yours black, right?"

"You remember that?" Ari smiled. "No wonder you have such loyal customers."

Carly felt a blush creep up her neck. "I have a good memory, that's all."

"By the way, you make the best coffee in town. It's strong, but not bitter."

Carly added a splotch of milk to her mug. She inhaled the wonderful smell, then took her first sip. Heavenly.

She set down her mug. From the fridge beneath the counter, she pulled out a package of frozen biscuits, along with a bag of shredded cheddar and a container of cooked bacon. Since she never ate lunch till midafternoon, she always treated herself to a breakfast snack to start off her morning. Every few weeks she made a batch of buttery biscuits and stashed them in the freezer.

"Ari, would you like a bacon and cheese breakfast biscuit? I make one for myself every morning."

His dark eyes brightened over a broad smile. "You sure it's no trouble?"

"It's just as easy to make two as it is to make one."

"Then count me in."

Carly popped two of her homemade biscuits into the microwave, thawed them for ten seconds, and sliced them in half lengthwise. She layered each one with bacon and cheese, then grilled them in sizzling butter. The combination of bacon and butter was a culinary fragrance she never tired of. When the biscuits were golden brown, she slid each one onto a separate plate and gave one to Ari.

"Oh man," Ari said after swallowing a large mouthful, "this is out of this world! You should open for breakfast and serve these every day."

Unwittingly, Ari had hit on a sore spot. When Carly first opened for business, deciding her eatery's hours had been the one thing she'd agonized over. But when push came to shove, she'd settled on the lunch and dinner hours. As it was, she was working twelve-hour days. If she opened any earlier, she'd have to live on a cot in her kitchen.

After swallowing his last bite and draining his mug, Ari wiped his fingers on a napkin. "Hey, I'd better get going. I'm installing some new lighting at the card shop today. You ever been in there?"

"I've seen the shop, but I haven't had a chance to stop in," Carly said. It was on the list of about a hundred things she'd been meaning to do since returning to Balsam Dell. "It's called What a Card, right?"

"Yep. I bought my sister a birthday card there last week. Prettiest card you ever saw. The owner designs them herself. You should check it out when you have a chance."

"I will. Thanks for the tip."

After an awkward pause, Ari said quietly, "Are you going to reopen the restaurant someplace else?"

"That's my plan, yes. Where, I have no idea. I'm going to start looking for another space right away."

"But you'll want something downtown, right?"

"I would love that, but it probably won't be possible. I can't even think of a space that's vacant right now. Can you?"

He shook his head. "No, but if I hear of anything, I'll let you know." He hesitated, then said, "Carly, whatever date Bagley told you to be out of here by, be careful. He's likely to try to push you out sooner, whether you're ready or not. And whether your lease is up or not."

Carly felt her color drain. "But…how can he do that?"

"He's conniving and cunning," Ari said. "I've seen him do things you wouldn't believe. When it comes time to move, I'll help you all I can, okay?"

Carly nodded. "Thank you."

Ari tried to pay for his breakfast sandwich and coffee, but Carly adamantly refused. He was a good customer, and he always left generous tips. He'd also done an amazing job installing her lighting, and at a price that'd been more than fair.

In spite of Ari's attributes, Carly breathed a sigh of relief after he left. She wasn't sure why, but she always felt a bit nervous around him. Was it the intensity in his gaze? The kindness that seemed to radiate from him like bottled sunshine?

Good gravy on a goat farm, where had that come from?

Pushing him out of her mind, she began her morning ritual. Her first and least favorite task: making sure the bathroom was clean. After that, she went around to each of the tables and tidied up the tomato soup vases. Then she gave the Formica tables and vinyl benches a once-over with a clean cloth until everything smelled fresh and lemony.

In the kitchen, she pulled a dozen tomatoes out of the fridge, then rinsed, dried, and sliced them. She set the slices in a covered container and stuffed them back in the fridge, pulling out a new block of cheddar at the same time. She set the cheddar on her work surface and was reaching for a sharp knife to remove the outer wrapping when she heard knocking coming from the dining room. Was someone banging on the back door?

"Just a minute!" she called out, wiping her hands on a dish towel.

The pounding was growing louder. Carly's first thought was Suzanne. Had she shown up early for work and forgotten her key? She hustled into the dining room, unlocked the dead bolt, and opened the back door.

Standing in the doorway was Tiffany Spencer, her normally creamy skin the color of spoiled milk. She swayed slightly and grabbed the doorjamb for support.

"Tiffany, what's wrong. Are you hurt?" Carly asked her.

"No, but it's bad. Really bad. I think someone…someone…" Tiffany shook her head and choked out a sob.

Carly took Tiffany's arm in a firm grip and led her inside. She steered her over to the nearest booth and pushed her down gently onto the bench seat. "Alright, now tell me what's wrong. *What's* really bad?"

She shook her head. "Oh God, go out there, Carly, please. He… he's by the dumpster, and he…he's not moving. I think he might be—" She broke into sobs that shook her thin shoulders.

It must be the poor little dog, Carly thought.

She fetched a glass of water and set it down in front of Tiffany. "Stay right here, okay? I'll check it out and be right back."

Tiffany nodded, but her pale-brown eyes had gone dull and unfocused.

Leaving the back door slightly ajar, Carly went into the parking lot. The blue sedan she'd seen earlier was still there. It partially blocked her view of the dumpster.

On legs that felt as sturdy as melted cheddar, she moved toward the sedan. Despite the warmth of the day, a chill crept down her spine. She stopped short and heaved a sigh of relief when she spotted the scruffy little dog. The poor baby was probably hungry.

Who knew when he'd last eaten? He was darting between the car and the dumpster, his tail flicking excitedly.

So what had Tiffany seen?

More slowly now, Carly approached the sedan. The dog gave out two short yips, ran over to sniff her shoes, then dashed back to the other side of the car. She followed him, her heart in her throat.

As she drew closer, a humming sound rang in her ears. It grew louder and more insistent until she reached the source.

On the pavement, between the car and the dumpster, a swarm of flies buzzed feverishly around the lifeless form of Lyle Bagley.

CHAPTER FOUR

CARLY CLAPPED A HAND OVER HER MOUTH, HER INSIDES gurgling. Lyle Bagley lay facedown on the pavement. The back of his head was caked with blood. His left arm was outstretched, his wrist encircled by a gold watch that gleamed in the bright sun.

She knew she should check for a pulse, but her feet felt like two stumps frozen in place. She finally managed to push them forward, but the thought of pressing her fingers to Lyle's carotid artery made her head swim. Instead, she reached down gingerly and slid two fingers underneath his wrist.

Nothing.

His skin was cool to the touch.

Please let this be a bad dream. Or a hangover effect from that awful port wine…

Only yesterday Lyle was kicking her out of her restaurant. Now he was—

Before she could complete the horrible thought, the little dog raced past Carly and made a beeline for the restaurant. He disappeared through the open back door as fast as his short legs would carry him.

Carly spun around and followed him, stumbling a few times before she reached the back entrance.

Inside the restaurant, Tiffany was still sitting in the booth where Carly had left her. Her streaked blond hair had gone limp, and her puffy eyes were fixed blankly at a spot on the wall. Without turning her head, she said in a hoarse voice, "He's…gone, isn't he?"

Carly swallowed back a lump of bile. "I'm so sorry. I have to call 911 now. Tiffany, do you know what happened to him?"

Tiffany shook her head. "He…left last night and didn't come back. And then this morning, I saw his car—" She broke into another round of tears. Carly touched her shoulder lightly, wanting to comfort her, but first she needed to call the police.

She hurried toward the kitchen, where she'd left her cell in her tote. As she pushed through the swinging door, something brushed her ankle. She let out a squeak, then saw it was only the dog.

With shaky fingers, Carly dug out her cell and punched in 911. In a rush of words, she told the dispatcher what she'd discovered and rattled off the address. After she hung up, she dropped onto her desk chair. Sobs threatened to erupt from her chest, but she forced them back. The police were on their way, and she needed to keep her wits about her.

In the next moment, Carly felt something lick her ankle. She looked down to see the dog gazing up at her with soulful brown eyes. His soft whimper squeezed her heart.

"Oh, you poor sweetie." She reached down and rubbed between his ears.

It suddenly struck her that having a dog in the kitchen was a major no-no for a restaurant. What was she going to do with him? She didn't really have a good place to hide him.

Carly removed a wedge of Havarti cheese from the fridge, cut it into small pieces, and gave it to him on a paper plate. She filled a bowl with fresh water and set it down next to the plate.

She started to head back to the dining room to let Tiffany know the police were on their way when the kitchen door swung inward. "Carly." Tiffany's voice wobbled. "The police are here."

Carly followed Tiffany into the dining room. Two uniformed officers had already entered through the back door. "Ms. Hale?" one of them said, looking directly at Tiffany. He was young and fit, with a swatch of dark hair that curled at the back of his neck.

"*She's* Ms. Hale," Tiffany sniffed, aiming a manicured finger at Carly.

"I'm Officer Palmer. Which one of you called 911?"

"I did," Carly said, hating the tremor in her voice. "I'm Carly Hale, the proprietor."

The other officer came up behind the first, this one a woman with stick-straight red hair and a gaze sharp enough to puncture iron. "And you are?" she said to Tiffany.

Tiffany swallowed. "Tiffany Spencer. I live in the apartment upstairs."

"Come with me." She directed Tiffany to a booth at the front of the restaurant. Carly was escorted into the kitchen by Officer Palmer. She cringed when she saw the dog slurping from the bowl of water.

"You keep a dog in here?" Palmer said sharply.

"No. I do not." Carly's voice shook. "He's not even my dog. He followed me inside the restaurant after I…after I found Lyle. He seemed hungry, so I gave him some cheese and water."

A look of amusement flashed in the officer's eyes. "Cheese and water. What dog wouldn't love that?"

Was he being flip, or was he only trying to lighten the tension? "Officer, may I please sit down? This has been a terrible shock, and I don't know how much longer my legs are going to keep me upright."

Palmer nodded toward her desk. "Be my guest."

Carly sat, and he pulled up a chair adjacent to hers. He removed a small notebook from the pocket of his short-sleeved blue shirt, along with a slender pen. "Ms. Hale, you obviously knew the victim. Was he an acquaintance of yours?"

"I—Wait, how did you know I knew him?"

"You called him Lyle, didn't you?"

Carly felt heat creep into her cheeks. "Oh, right, I did. Yes, I knew him. But before yesterday I hadn't seen him since high school. That was fifteen years ago."

"So where did you see him yesterday?"

"Right here, in the restaurant. He came in to tell me he bought this building at foreclosure and that he was kicking me—I mean, evicting me."

"Hmm." He furrowed his brow as if to empathize with her. "I'm guessing that didn't sit too well with you. I'd be pretty PO'd if that happened to me."

Carly pulled in a slow breath. He was baiting her, trying to get her to admit she'd been angry over the eviction. From there it would be a slippery slope to a confession. She'd seen it on TV crime shows dozens of times.

Except that Carly wasn't guilty of anything, unless you counted letting a dog sneak into your restaurant a crime.

"To answer your question," she said evenly, "no, of course it didn't sit well with me. I opened only five months ago, and I've been a model tenant. Nonetheless, I knew my lease was going to expire at the end of July. I wrongly assumed it would automatically be renewed, but apparently Lyle had other plans for the building. It wasn't my place to question him."

Palmer thought about that for a moment, then something outside the window caught his attention. He closed his notebook and tucked it, along with the pen, into his shirt pocket. "Ms. Hale, I'm going to let you off the hook for now, since the investigation is at a very early stage. Once we know the cause of death, we'll have more questions for you. You'll need to come down to the station either later today or early tomorrow to give a statement. Are we clear on that?"

"As clear as fresh rainwater. And speaking of water, would you like a bottle of spring water to take with you?"

For a moment he looked nonplussed, but then he graced her with a faint smile. "Actually, that would be great. I heard it's going to hit the midnineties today."

Carly gave him a bottle of water from her fridge. The idea of the police having to labor over the crime scene all day in the sizzling heat made her feel terrible. "If all of you folks, you know, working out there today would like refreshments, I'll be glad to provide sandwiches and drinks for everyone. My treat, of course. I'm guessing it's going to be a long day."

"You can bet on that," he said grimly.

His words tickled a memory, but then the kitchen door swung inward and Carly lost the thread. An imposing man with a lined face and a head full of thick gray hair stood in the entrance. "Carly."

At the sound of the man's voice, Carly sagged with relief. Fred Holloway was Balsam Dell's police chief, but he was also a family friend. His son had gone to school with Carly's sister, Norah, and his daughter, Anne, was a local veterinarian. His wife, before she passed, had been in a book club with Carly's mom.

"Thank heaven you're here, Chief. I can't believe this is happening."

The chief glared at Palmer. "The medical examiner just got here. Why don't you go outside and help with crowd control? We're beginning to attract some looky-loos, and it'll only get worse."

"Yes, sir." Water bottle in hand, Officer Palmer nodded at Carly and swept out the door. He looked as if he couldn't get away fast enough.

The chief shot a glance at the dog. "Did Officer Palmer ask you any questions, Carly?"

"A few. Mostly about my eviction and how I felt about it."

Holloway's jaw tightened. "He was instructed to sit with you until I got here. Period. The guy's kind of a wannabe Columbo, always overstepping his authority. Let me know if he pulls anything like that again, okay?"

"I understand, Chief." She didn't like the idea of tattling on someone, but the chief obviously had his reasons. With any luck, Officer Palmer wouldn't cross her path again.

"May I sit?" Holloway said.

"Sure."

Carly sat at her desk while the chief dropped onto Officer Palmer's recently vacated chair. A sheen of perspiration dotted his upper lip, and gray bags hung beneath his eyes.

"Carly," he said quietly, "I know all about the eviction, but I want to hear what happened in your own words."

A sudden blade of fear poked at her. Would the police try to connect her eviction with Lyle's death?

As calmly as she could, she related everything that'd happened, from the time the bank's attorney came into the restaurant, to Lyle's departure with Tiffany after he'd delivered the bad news.

"What about this morning?" he went on. "Run me through your actions from the time you got here."

Carly told him about seeing the blue sedan in the parking lot, and how, because of the car's angle, Lyle's body hadn't been visible. She went on to tell him about Ari coming in, and her making breakfast sandwiches and coffee for the two of them. She explained how Tiffany came banging on the back door while Carly was in the kitchen doing food prep.

"Can you describe her demeanor?" the chief asked.

"Tiffany's? Well, she was distraught. Pretty shaken. She didn't tell me exactly what she saw in the parking lot, only that it was bad, really bad. I was afraid she was going to pass out, so I made her sit in one of the booths. Then I went out to the parking lot, and"—she swallowed hard—"and I found Lyle on the pavement near the dumpster." A lump formed in her throat. "I'm sorry, this is all starting to get to me."

Holloway patted her forearm. "You're doing fine, Carly." He asked her several more questions, and just when she thought her head was going to explode, he slowly rose from his chair. "You don't need to give an official statement until later, but I want you to be prepared. Once the state police step in, they'll pretty much take the lead. The main thing is, tell them exactly what you saw. Don't put your own spin on it. Just relate the facts."

Carly folded her hands on the desk to keep them from trembling. "Chief, you know I had nothing to do with this, right?"

He stared at her for a long moment, then looked away. "Carly, at this stage it doesn't matter what I think. Our job is to figure out what happened so we can arrest Lyle's killer."

"Are…you sure it was murder? Couldn't he have fallen in some weird way, or…" She knew she was grasping, but she had to ask.

The chief was already shaking his head. "I wish I could say that was possible, but based on the severity of the head wound, Bagley's death was not an accident. By the way, is it typical for Ari Mitchell to come in for breakfast before you open?"

Wait. *What?* That came out of the blue. "Um, well, no, it's not. In fact, that was the first time." She explained how he'd knocked on the door, and how she'd invited him in for coffee. "I was making a bacon and cheese biscuit for myself, so I offered him one. Is there a reason why you're asking?"

He shook his head and gave her a crooked smile. "No, just curious."

Something about the question irked Carly. Was he being nosy? Protective? Implying that she had a boyfriend? She looked at him and noticed the obvious fatigue in his eyes. It was her turn to be nosy. "You look exhausted, Chief. Is something else going on?"

The chief ran his hand over his face. "I don't know if you heard, but we've had a rash of burglaries over the last several months. All high-end homes, mostly in Lilac Hill. Whoever's doing it is a pro, not your run-of-the-mill burglar. We're getting a ton of pressure to catch the culprit, or culprits, but to be honest, we're stumped."

Carly had read something about the burglaries in the town's free newspaper, the Balsam Dell Weekly. Lilac Hill was an older section of town, populated by historic mansions and exquisitely manicured lawns. She recalled reading that some of the items stolen had been extremely valuable.

"And now this murder will be taking top priority," he added grimly. "I just hope we can solve it quickly."

The sound of angry voices erupted from the dining room. Holloway went toward the swinging door, but Carly got there first. She stormed into the restaurant, halting in her tracks when she saw the cause of the commotion.

A few feet from the back door, Suzanne was being restrained by two uniformed officers. One was Officer Palmer. The other was a burly fellow with meaty arms and a hard scowl.

"Let me go!" Suzanne demanded.

"Good grief, what's going on?" Carly said.

Suzanne's eyes looked wild. "Carly, they said I couldn't come in here! What the heck is going on? Why are all these cops here?" She tried to pull her arms free, but the officers only tightened their grip.

About ten feet away, Tiffany stood beside the red-haired officer. Her streaked blond hair was askew, the pupils of her brown eyes dilated with fury.

"It was you, wasn't it?" Tiffany hissed, pointing a finger at Suzanne. "I heard you threaten him yesterday."

Suzanne's eyes dimmed in confusion. "Threaten who? What on earth are you talking about?"

"As if you don't know," Tiffany said coldly. "Lyle's dead, and it's all your fault. You're the one who killed him!"

CHAPTER FIVE

WITH THAT PROCLAMATION, A DAZED SUZANNE AND A furious Tiffany were escorted outside. Carly sank onto the bench of the nearest booth. She'd thought things couldn't get any worse, but she'd been wrong. Suzanne's arrival and Tiffany's crazy accusation had added fuel to an already blazing fire.

"Where are Suzanne and Tiffany going?" Carly asked the chief in a shaky voice.

"To the station, for questioning. *Separately*," he added. Eyebrows raised, hands on his hips, Chief Holloway shot Carly a questioning look. "Is there anything else you want to tell me, Carly? Did you hear Suzanne threaten Lyle? I need you to be honest with me." He slid into the booth opposite her.

Carly felt every muscle in her body tense. She disliked the implication that she might *not* be honest with him. She also felt weird talking about Suzanne behind her back.

Forcing her limbs to relax, Carly raised her chin and looked directly at him. "I heard what Suzanne said to him, yes. But in my opinion, it wasn't a threat. It was more like 'Someday you'll get what's coming to you. You can bet on it.' That was pretty much it."

"Do you know *why* she said it?"

"No. I didn't even know Suzanne knew Lyle. He never comes into the restaurant, and she never mentioned him to me."

"After he left, did you question her about it? I mean, you had to be curious, right?"

"Yes, I was curious, and no, I did not ask her about it. I didn't feel it was any of my business."

Holloway nodded but remained silent. He stayed that way for so long Carly squirmed in her seat. "Besides, even if I repeated what she said, wouldn't that be hearsay?"

He sighed. "Hearsay applies in court, Carly, and it's for a judge to determine. This is a preliminary investigation. We need to gather as much info as we can, as quickly as we can. Anything you know, or heard, can help lead us to the person who committed this crime."

But Suzanne wasn't a killer. She wasn't!

Still, she could see the chief's point. To get to the truth, you had to tell the truth. How many times had her mom drilled that into her head when Carly and her sister were growing up?

"Then I apologize for not telling you about it. It's just…everything happened so fast this morning, you know? Finding a dead man in the parking lot wasn't exactly on my to-do list."

He relented with a grim smile. "One last question. Who else has keys to the restaurant?"

"Suzanne does. Oh, and Grant Robinson does."

"Both of them have keys?" He sounded surprised.

"I trust my employees completely, Chief. If I didn't, they wouldn't be working here."

He nodded absently, then tapped the table with his hand. "Okay, why don't you shut everything down here and grab your belongings? You'll need to give a statement, so I'll drive you home to drop off your dog. Then we'll head to the station."

"But Chief, he's not my dog." Carly explained how he'd gotten there, then peeked under the table. The sweet little pup lay at her feet, his nose resting on the tip of her shoe.

"Say no more." The chief pulled his cell phone out of his shirt pocket. He tapped out a message and seconds later got a response. "I just texted Anne. She said we can bring the dog over to her clinic and she'll see if he's chipped. Maybe he's lost and someone's looking for him."

Relief washed over Carly. The chief's daughter, Anne Holloway, or Dr. Anne as everyone called the veterinarian, could feed the pup some proper dog food and help find his owner.

Holloway accompanied Carly into the kitchen, where she collected her belongings and made sure everything was shut off. With the chief eyeing her every move, she felt like a bug under a microscope. He had to be tremendously stressed to be acting this way. So much for family friend status.

Hoisting her tote strap onto her shoulder, she flicked off the lights and went into the dining room. Holloway followed her through the swinging door.

The little dog scooted over to Carly, sniffed her shoe, and gave out a high-pitched yip. *Poor little fellow.* "We'll find your owner, sweetie. No worries." She reached down and scratched between his ears, and he licked her fingers.

"Chief, can't I just follow you in my own car? I can drive the dog to Dr. Anne's myself and then meet you at the police station."

"Sorry, Carly. I can't let you drive your car yet. Even if I could, the side street's been blocked off. My car is parked out front."

"But I have to get back here later to open up!"

Holloway avoided her gaze. "Carly, you won't be opening up today. Tomorrow's out of the question too. By morning we'll have a warrant to search inside the restaurant."

Carly felt her world crumbling. How did all this happen in less than a day?

"But why?" she asked in a shaky voice. "Lyle...died in the parking lot, didn't he?"

"As far as we know, yes. But we need to preserve the crime scene."

"But my restaurant is not a crime scene. Why do they have to search it?"

The chief paused at the back door, his hand on the doorknob. "Because we haven't recovered the murder weapon, Carly. Judging from the wound, it was something heavy and solid. The dumpster was emptied early yesterday, so there's not much to search through. But if it doesn't turn up there, then whatever the killer used to murder Bagley is officially missing."

Something heavy and solid? A shard of panic went through Carly. She could name several things right there in her kitchen that fit that description to a tee.

~

The scene in the parking lot was nothing short of bedlam. Several police cars lined the side of Liberty Street, and traffic was being diverted away from the area. Official-looking types in outfits resembling space suits milled around near the dumpster. A massive truck emblazoned with the words *Vermont State Police* took up most of the lot. At the corner of Liberty and Main, Officer Palmer waved his arms and screamed at drivers who were slowing down traffic with their gawking.

A length of crime scene tape stretched along the sidewalk to the front of the building. Behind the tape was a line of people, all angling for a better look. The chief was right; the looky-loos were out in full force.

Carly clasped the dog tightly in her arms, grateful she'd insisted on holding him. Otherwise, in all the commotion, he might have run off again.

Suddenly, a skinny young man with a ginger goatee climbed over the crime scene tape, a camera thrust out in front of him. A uniformed officer promptly ordered him back behind the yellow tape. Undeterred, the pushy cameraman continued to snap photos of the scene.

Chief Holloway cupped Carly's elbow and steered her swiftly

around to the front of the building. His car was running—he'd started it remotely—and Carly hopped into the front seat.

The cool air blowing from the car's vents did nothing to dispel the tension. The chief stared through the windshield and drove as if he were on autopilot. Carly wasn't sure if he was mad at her over the Suzanne thing or just overly focused on the murder. He also made the dog ride in the back seat, despite Carly's offer to hold him in her lap.

On a good day, Anne Holloway's veterinary clinic would have been about a six-minute trip. But tourist season was ramping up, and cars clogged every downtown intersection. As annoying as it was, the summer traffic brought throngs of diners and shoppers into town—diners and shoppers who kept merchants in business so they could survive the leaner months.

Since the chief knew all the shortcuts, he detoured off the main drag and wove along the side streets to avoid traffic. They passed homes where some of Carly's old friends had lived.

As they approached the stop sign at Baker and Brigham, a pretty, pale-green ranch with white trim and a fresh-cut lawn came into view. Carly's heart skipped. She couldn't count the number of sleepovers she'd had in that cheerful little house. Her former bestie, Gina Tomasso, had lived there with her dad. Carly and Gina had done everything together—peas in a pod, Gina's dad had called them. Their long-time friendship soured after Lyle took up with Gina. Despite Carly's warnings that Lyle was trouble, Gina married him straight out of high school. Although the marriage didn't last, Gina never spoke to Carly again.

When they arrived at the veterinary clinic, Carly retrieved the dog from the back seat and handed him to the chief. "Don't worry, Havarti," she whispered in his ear. "Dr. Anne will figure out where you belong."

The dog licked her nose and gave a slight whimper. Holloway tucked the dog in the curve of his arm and smiled. "Havarti?"

A knot forming in her throat, Carly shrugged. "That's what I fed him at the restaurant."

She waited in the car while the chief carried the dog into the clinic. Holloway returned several minutes later.

"Anne's taking good care of him, Carly," he assured her. "He wasn't chipped, but she's going to put out an APB of sorts and see if anyone's looking for him. I gave her your cell number so she can call you with an update."

"What happens if nobody claims him?"

"Then I guess he goes to a no-kill shelter."

Holloway was slightly less formal on the ride to the police station. "I'm sorry for all this, Carly. I hate this as much as you do."

"It's just...surreal," she said and cleared her throat. "Only yesterday I was standing in my restaurant, talking to Lyle. And in the blink of an eye, he's gone. Forever. It's hard to wrap my head around."

A sudden thought occurred to her. With Lyle out of the picture, would she still be evicted? She wondered if he had any family in the area. She vaguely recalled a brother and a dad but had no idea if they were still around.

As they pulled into the parking lot behind the police station, Carly's pulse went into high gear. The lot was clotted with cars. Three state police cars were parked near the back entrance. Two uniformed troopers leaned against the trunk of the closest one. Arms folded over their chests, they swiveled their heads in her direction and peered at her through the windshield.

Carly recalled the chief's advice. *Just relate the facts. Don't put your own spin on it...*

"Carly, one last thing," the chief said, "if you'll consent to a search of your car, you can probably get it back later today. Otherwise, we have to wait for a warrant."

"A search?" She frowned in confusion, until it dawned on her what he meant. "You want to look for the murder weapon, don't you?" Her voice crackled.

"Unless it turns up before tomorrow, yes. I'm sorry, it's standard procedure. It's nothing personal."

Overcome with a growing sense of dread, Carly rummaged through her tote until she found her keys.

"I'll also need your key to the restaurant."

Blinking back tears, she tore both keys off her key ring and plopped them in his hand. She was tempted to ask if he wanted her to sign away her firstborn child, but she knew it would sound juvenile. He was doing his job, pure and simple. She had to respect that.

"Is that it?" she asked him.

Holloway nodded. "I'll take you inside."

Great. Just how she wanted to spend her day. Being interrogated for a murder she didn't commit.

CHAPTER SIX

It was close to 3:30 p.m. by the time a Balsam Dell patrol car dropped off Carly at her apartment. They'd kept her waiting for what seemed an eternity before ushering her into a stuffy room dominated by a huge, two-way mirror. The interview itself had lasted over two hours, but it felt more like ten. She was tired, drained, and more than a little cranky. On a normal day she'd be starving by this time, but the *grilling*, as she thought of it, had demolished her appetite.

The state police detective had been cordial enough, but his interview style was tricky. Over and over he'd asked her the same questions, each time phrased a bit differently. Carly was sure he'd been trying to catch her off guard. Like a boomerang, his questions always came back to the same subject.

Suzanne.

Despite the heat, a chill slid down Carly's arms. It was obvious the police were focusing on Suzanne. The image of her friend wearing prison orange and doing hard time for a crime she didn't commit made her stomach do a triple cartwheel.

Once inside her apartment, Carly rubbed the grit from her eyes and donned her flip-flops. It was a relief to be home. Since she'd never gotten a chance to raise the shades before leaving for work that morning, the temperature in the apartment was almost bearable. She'd have to remember to leave the shades down every day. And, more importantly, buy herself an air conditioner.

She tossed her tote on the sofa, dropped down beside it, and fished out her cell phone. At the start of her interview with the detective, she'd been instructed to turn it off. The instant she powered it back on, it rang in her hands.

"Carly, I've been trying to reach you for hours!" Grant bellowed into her ear.

Carly groaned. In all the turmoil, she'd forgotten about him. "I'm sorry I couldn't call you, Grant. I was at the police station for most of the afternoon. They made me turn off my phone."

"Yeah, I saw all the craziness at the restaurant. Are you okay?"

"I'm not sure. I'm still rattled. You heard about Lyle Bagley, right?"

"Did I ever! It's all anyone's talking about. Is there anything I can do? I feel sorta helpless right now."

"I do too," Carly said glumly. "The police seem to be fixated on Suzanne. I'm terrified they're going to accuse her of killing him."

Grant was quiet for a long moment, while the notes of a classical music piece played softly in the background.

"Grant? Are you there?"

"Yeah. Sorry. I was just thinking. Are we going to be able to open tomorrow?"

Carly reached over to her end table and turned on her fan, aiming it directly at her face. "Chief Holloway says no. They're getting a warrant to search the restaurant."

"Oh man, that is so unfair. Listen, just so you know, I've been asked to go to the police station for an interview."

Carly gulped. "You too? Did they say why?"

"No, but I'm guessing they found out I was there yesterday when Lyle came in to evict you. They probably want my version of what went down. Don't worry. I'll be fine," he added quickly, but he sounded nervous. "My dad insists on going with me. I'll check in with you later, okay?"

After they disconnected, something stuck in Carly's mind.

Despite Grant's reassurances, his long silence at the mention of Suzanne's name made her wonder if he was hiding something.

~

After a cool, refreshing shower that helped scrub the image of Lyle's body from her mind, Carly changed into shorts and a pink tee. Her stomach started to rumble, finally showing signs of hunger. Nothing really appealed, so she settled for a bowl of oatmeal topped with shaved parmesan cheese. She poured herself a glass of iced tea and carried everything over to her kitchen table. While she ate, she skimmed through her missed calls.

Her sister had called, probably with a day-late birthday greeting. Norah was currently vacationing in Montreal with her latest beau, someone she'd met through her job as an employment recruiter.

There were several missed calls from Grant's number, followed by one from—oh no, from her mom! Had news of the murder already reached her in Florida?

She was still scanning through her missed calls when her cell rang again. "Hey, Carly, it's Anne Holloway."

"Hi, Dr. Anne. I've been hoping you'd call."

"Listen, Dad told me what happened this morning. I am so, *so* sorry. I can't even imagine what you're going through."

"Thanks. I have to admit, it's been a pretty stressful day."

"Not to be an alarmist, but you know Erika is a lawyer, right?" Erika was Dr. Anne's partner. Although Carly had never met her, she knew she had a law practice in Bennington.

"I do know that, yes."

"I'm not saying you'll *need* a lawyer," the veterinarian was quick to add. "Just that she'll be glad to help if you, or anyone you know, needs legal advice."

Anyone you know. Was she referring to Suzanne? What had the chief told her?

"Thank you. That's good to hear. Did you find the dog's owner?"

"I'm afraid not. I checked around, and no one's put out an APB on him. He's been fed, he had a bath, and I treated him for fleas and other nasties, although he didn't seem to have any. Right now he's sleeping like a baby in his cage."

Cage. Carly swallowed. "Thank you, Dr. Anne. Do I owe you anything?" The least she could do was offer to pay.

"Nah, don't worry about that. One of the shelters is going to pick him up tomorrow, unless…" She paused.

"Unless?" Carly prodded.

"Unless you'd like to adopt him?"

"Me?"

Dr. Anne laughed. "Don't sound so surprised. Dad told me you already named him Havarti. With lots of love, he'll make a great companion."

"But I'm gone all day, and I work in a restaurant." *If I still have a restaurant.*

The veterinarian sighed into the phone. "I was afraid you'd say that. But keep in mind, a lot of working folks have dogs. There are ways to make it work."

"Dr. Anne," Carly said before they disconnected, "do you know what kind of dog he is?"

"I'm glad you asked," the veterinarian replied, a smile widening her voice. "The little guy you rescued is a Morkie!"

After ending the call, Carly Googled Morkie. The breed, or crossbreed, was a blend of Maltese and Yorkshire Terrier. The article she pulled up described them as sociable and energetic. They adapted nicely to apartment life and did especially well in one-person homes.

But I still can't adopt him. Especially not now, not with my life turned upside down.

Carly was putting her cereal bowl in the kitchen sink when she heard two sharp knocks at her door. Were the police back with more questions? It could also be Arlene returning with another slab of birthday cake. Except that Carly's car wasn't in the driveway, so it wasn't obvious she was home.

She padded over to her door and opened it, then took in a sharp breath. Standing on her doormat was the man with the auburn goatee she'd seen in the parking lot. A faint odor of perspiration drifted from him. His camera dangled from a cord around his neck—a very sunburned neck, Carly noticed.

"Yes?" she said, her hand on the doorknob.

He flashed a mouthful of crooked teeth at her in a lopsided grin. "Carly? Carly Hale?"

A sliver of fear trickled down Carly's spine. Not that he looked threatening. But after the horrible events of the day, the sight of anyone she didn't recognize hovering in her doorway made her nerves jumpy.

"Why don't you tell me who *you* are," she said, gripping the doorknob tighter.

"Aw, come on, Carly. You're kidding me, right? I can't believe you don't remember me." He pushed out his lower lip in a childish pout.

Carly stared at him. A spark of recognition tripped through her brain. But no, she still couldn't place him. While he looked to be in his late twenties, something about his mannerisms made him seem younger.

She pushed the door closed slightly, leaving about a foot of space between them. "I'm sorry, but I honestly don't. You need to either identify yourself or leave. This is a private residence." She tried to sound braver than she felt.

His grin collapsed and he placed one hand on the door. "That's no way to treat an old friend, now, is it, Carly? No way to treat one at all."

CHAPTER SEVEN

THAT DID IT.

In a tone she hoped proved that she meant business, Carly said, "Either remove your hand from my door or I'll be forced to call the police."

The hand, tipped with five chewed fingernails, dropped like a lead weight. The man's lower lip pushed out to almost caricature size. "You know, Carly, I'm really insulted. I can't believe you don't remember me, a kid you used to babysit."

Carly stepped back slightly and stared at him. Then light dawned on the man's titian-colored hair, which stuck out at odd angles from his head. "Oh my gosh," she said. "You're little Donny Frasco, aren't you?"

His lips widened into a grin. "In the flesh!"

"I *did* babysit you, but only once." A shudder ripped through her at the memory.

Donny Frasco had been the most overactive, rambunctious kid Carly had ever babysat. It had only been the one time, but it was memorable, and not in a good way. She could still picture him, tromping across his mom's dining room table in his cowboy boots—a stunt for which Carly got blamed. She'd thanked whatever angels were listening that day that his mom never called her again.

"By the way, no one calls me Donny anymore. It's just Don." He puffed out his skinny chest. "Um, anyway, can I come in? I want to interview you for the Balsam Dell Weekly. I heard you were right in the thick of things when Lyle Bagley was murdered."

Carly groaned. She knew the editor of the town's weekly free paper was a *Donald Frasco*, but she never connected him with that antsy little kid she sat for. "First of all, that's not true. And second, how did you know where I lived?"

"Easy. When your restaurant first opened, you paid for an ad, remember? I got it off your check."

Carly sighed. "Let's talk outside on the porch instead, and only for a minute. I've had a very long day."

With a disappointed droop of his shoulders, Don turned and loped back down the stairs, the rubber soles of his sneakers loudly slapping the risers. Another image of the goofy, bright-eyed little monster she babysat flashed into her head. His mom had instructed Carly to give Donny his lunch. When Carly began preparing a grilled cheese for him, he'd howled as if she'd stuck hot pins into his head. He didn't stop screaming until a peanut butter and jelly sandwich and a glass of chocolate milk were placed before him on the table.

With a wrinkle of his freckled nose, Donny pulled out his cell phone from his shirt pocket. "Sure is hot out here." He swiped a hand across his forehead.

All the faster to get rid of you, Carly thought.

He pushed a few buttons on his phone, held it up, and began peppering her with questions. "So, how did you happen to find the body? Did you see a murder weapon anywhere? Did you notice any peculiar odors?"

"Wait a minute. Put that phone away. I never said I'd give you an interview."

"Yeah, but—"

"Donny. Don," she said, eking out her last ounce of patience, "I only took pity because you helped me with my advertising when I first opened. Right now, you need to turn off the recorder on your phone. Either that or I go back inside. Alone."

Don looked deflated. He tapped a few buttons on his phone

and stuck it back in his pocket. "I'm disappointed in you, Carly. You're not looking at the big picture here. Think of it. If you and I teamed up, we could solve the murder before the cops do. We'd be local heroes!"

Carly looked him straight in the eye. "Listen to me carefully. We're not going to team up, and the police will solve the murder. And now I think it's time for you to leave."

She knew her mom would be appalled at her bad manners, but Carly was already dealing with more than she could handle. Tomorrow, *maybe*, she'd have a fresher outlook, but today, not one thing had gone right. Except, possibly, the rescue of a little dog—a dog who was now stuck in a cage waiting to be sent to a shelter.

Don's face hardened. "You might change your mind when you see yourself on the news tonight," he said slyly.

"*I'm* in the news?"

"Your restaurant is. Same thing," he said with a shrug. "There's a TV van parked right in front of your grilled cheese place. That reporter with the helmet hair is having a field day, blathering on about the grisly murder and how the police are questioning a person of interest."

A person of interest. Carly swallowed. "Did they say who it was?"

"No, but everyone knows it's Suzanne Rivers. Besides, I have a cop friend who gave me the lowdown."

Carly's thoughts swam. Between the stifling heat and Don's tidbit about Suzanne, she felt as if her head was going to float off into space. "Don, I'm sorry, but you really do have to go now. I need to make some calls."

It was a fib, but she wanted to get rid of him so she could gather her thoughts and figure out what to do next. Someone murdered Lyle, and it wasn't Suzanne. If Carly had to find the murderer herself to prove Suzanne innocent, then that's what she'd do.

After some coaxing, Don left. Carly went back inside her apartment. Almost instantly, her cell phone rang.

"Oh my God, honey! Are you all right?"

Carly turned the fan toward her rocking chair and dropped onto the padded seat. "I'm fine, Mom. Nothing happened to me." *Except for finding a dead body in my parking lot.* "How did you hear what happened, anyway?"

Rhonda exhaled loudly. "From Fred Holloway's sister, Deirdre. Remember, she was in my book club? Fred's wife was in it, too, poor dear, before she passed. Anyway, Deirdre didn't have my phone number so she got a hold of me through Facebook. She told me that…that Lyle Bagley creature was found dead behind your restaurant and that you're the one who found him!"

Her mom obviously remembered Lyle from Carly's high school days. Her "creature" comment reminded Carly that her mom had never approved of him.

As calmly as she could, Carly went through the events of the day, backtracking to her eviction by Lyle the day before.

"Oh, my poor darling," Rhonda said, sounding distraught. "And here I am, over a thousand miles away, just when you need me most!"

Carly wished her mom were there, too, but she had no intention of dumping a guilt trip on her. "Honestly, Mom, I'm safe and I'm okay. The police are handling it. I'm sure they'll find Lyle's killer very soon." That last part was a slight fib. She wasn't sure at all, but she didn't want her mom to worry.

"Do you want me to fly up there?" Rhonda sounded breathless now.

"No, of course not. Isn't Gary still having physical therapy on his elbow?" Her mom's husband had broken his elbow on a friend's sailboat.

Her mom took a breath. "He is. It's coming along, though. It'll be a few more weeks before he can drive."

"You stay right there with Gary," Carly insisted, "and give him my best."

They chatted for a while longer, and Carly promised to keep her mom posted on developments.

After she disconnected, she felt tears filling her eyes. A day like this made her miss her mom way more than usual.

When Daniel died unexpectedly on that awful winter night, her mom and Gary had immediately flown up from Florida to be with her. They'd stayed for nearly three weeks, helping with funeral arrangements and other sad tasks Carly hadn't even thought about. Norah had helped, too, in her own flighty way, but she was never a constant.

Which reminded Carly: Norah didn't know about the murder.

Carly debated texting her sister, then decided against it. Norah was on vacation, exploring a budding relationship with a new beau. Carly didn't want to spoil her fun, assuming she was having any. In the next instant, her phone buzzed with a text from the chief.

I'm in your driveway.

She felt her heart pound. Was he here to tell her Suzanne had been arrested?

Carly went to the front window and peeked outside. A patrol car was idling in the driveway behind Carly's green Corolla. The chief was leaning against her car. He waved at her and motioned her outside.

She hurried down the stairs. "Hey, you brought my wheels back. Thanks." She tried to sound grateful, but the words came out flat.

"I insisted your car be searched first," Holloway said. "You'll be happy to know nothing was removed. The key's in the ignition." He handed her a sheet of paper to sign, along with a pen. "If you'll give the inside a quick look-see and sign this, I can get out of your hair."

Carly slid onto the front seat and glanced all around. She first checked the glove compartment, then turned and scanned the rear seating area. Nothing seemed to be missing. She got out and closed the door, signed the paper, and gave it to him. "Chief," she said, nearly choking on the words, "is Suzanne being held?"

"No. We don't have enough evidence to hold her. *Yet*. We're getting a warrant to search her mom's home tomorrow, as well as her ex's. Plus, her car's been impounded. She's been warned not to leave the house, for any reason. We'll have a patrol car parked in front, just in case."

Carly shook her head. The situation was going south on a fast track. She wanted to proclaim Suzanne's innocence, but what could she offer as proof? Nothing, except for her firm conviction that Suzanne was not a killer.

"Carly," Holloway said wearily, "I think you need to prepare yourself. It's likely Suzanne will be arrested for murder some time over the next few days."

"Then they'll be arresting an innocent person," Carly said fiercely.

After he climbed into the patrol car, she turned to go back inside. Standing on the front porch staring at her was Arlene, her hands cupped around her elbows.

"Oh, honey," Arlene blurted. "We heard on the news. We're both so, so sorry. Is it true they have a, you know, a person of interest?"

"They have a suspect in mind, but it's the wrong one." Carly's voice wobbled, and without warning she burst into tears. She allowed Arlene to fold her into her arms, where she cried on the woman's shoulder for at least a full minute.

Arlene patted her hair. "Come on, now. No more tears. Besides, it's too hot out here. Let's go inside and have some iced tea and a slice of birthday cake. After all, we can't let it go to waste, can we?"

Carly shook her head. Arlene was so motherly. "No, we can't.

Besides, I'll need to fortify myself if I'm going to find Lyle's killer and save my restaurant. But no wine this time, okay?"

Arlene's smile faltered. "No wine this time, I promise. Just a good old-fashioned chocolate fix."

CHAPTER EIGHT

THURSDAY MORNING DAWNED HOT AND MUGGY. CARLY PADDED over to her bedroom window and lifted the shade, squinting at the already blazing sunshine.

After taking a tepid shower, she threw on shorts and a jersey tee and slid her feet into her flip-flops. Her stomach grumbled, and she realized she was ravenously hungry.

Today is going to feel strange, totally weird, Carly thought. She wasn't accustomed to being home on a weekday.

Supposedly the police were going to execute a warrant and search her eatery, but when? Would she be able to return after they were done? The idea of investigators pawing through her utensils and handling her appliances made her stomach do cartwheels.

First things first: food and coffee. After starting the coffee pot, she pulled eggs, butter, precooked bacon, and cheddar out of her fridge, and two slices of sourdough bread from a loaf in her freezer. Since she was accustomed to working quickly, it took only a few minutes to grill it all up. Depending on how things went, it might be the best meal she'd have all day.

Munching on her breakfast sandwich, she mulled over what to do next. If she had to stay home this morning, she'd probably go crazy. All she'd do was worry. She knew in her heart Lyle's murderer was still out there, even if the police were putting all their investigative eggs in the Suzanne basket. The question was, who disliked Lyle enough to want him dead? Carly was willing to bet there was more than one candidate for that position.

She pulled her cell phone over in front of her. In the Google search box, she typed Lyle's name. A short list of links popped up, the most recent being those related to his untimely demise.

She skimmed past those, looking for links with earlier dates. The farther down she scrolled, the more discouraged she became. Lyle certainly didn't have much of an online presence. A brief mention of him appeared in his dad's 2014 obituary. Other than that, the only other link was related to a small claims court case, several months earlier, in which Lyle was named the defendant. The plaintiff was—Oh good gravy on a gadfly. It was Sara Hardy!

Sara was one half of the Colm and Sara team, the bakers who supplied the fabulous breads for Carly's eatery. While Colm handled the deliveries and the sales, it was Sara's artisan breads that kept the bakery's orders flooding in.

Carly clicked on the link. The article was a short post about a claim against Lyle Bagley d/b/a Pine Grove Mobile Homes, by Sara Hardy. Lyle had apparently refused to refund a security deposit to Sara on one of his mobile home rentals. The judge ruled against Sara, to the tune of sixteen hundred dollars. According to the article, Sara failed to prove that the property had been left clean and undamaged, and Lyle had produced photos showing the place had been left a mess. As the article stated, the judge had no choice but to "find for the defendant."

Strange, Carly thought. Why would Sara rent a mobile home? Didn't she live with Colm in their nineteenth-century farmhouse?

With a sigh, Carly closed the link. In any case, Sara wouldn't commit murder. She was a peace-loving bread baker with a heart of gold.

Although…what harm would it do to talk to Sara? She might have some insight into who else at the mobile home park had run-ins with Lyle. Carly mentally added "chat with Sara" to her agenda for the day.

After cleaning up the few dishes in the sink, she slung her tote over her shoulder, exchanged her flip-flops for her denim flats, and headed out to her car. Five minutes later, she was driving past her restaurant. The crime scene tape remained stretched along the sidewalk to the front of the building, an ugly reminder of Lyle's brutal death.

With the eatery off limits, at least until early afternoon, she decided it was the perfect time to look for an air conditioner. Quayle's Hardware, only a few streets past the downtown intersection, had been advertising them in the Balsam Dell Weekly.

The building was a red, barnlike structure with a weather vane atop its roof. The moment she stepped inside the store, a blast of arctic air hit her square in the face.

The place was busy, which was not surprising given its huge inventory of, well, just about everything. A salesperson, a middle-aged woman with owlish glasses and parrot-shaped yellow earrings, escorted her over to the aisle where scads of air conditioners were stacked on shelves.

"I'm not sure where to begin," Carly said, frowning at some of the prices she saw.

"I know. It's daunting, isn't it?" the woman agreed.

"Can I help?"

Carly swerved at the voice that came from behind her. Hands shoved in the pockets of his blue cargo pants, Ari Mitchell stood there, smiling at her.

"Ari," she said. "I–I didn't realize you were in the store."

The salesperson clasped her hands and grinned. "Oh my, Ari's one of our best customers. We stock a huge selection of electrical parts. He refurbished a mini fridge for my son's college dorm room, and it works better than new!"

Carly knew Ari had a small shop, Mitchell Electric, opposite the town green. She'd never been sure quite what he used it for, since most of his business involved on-site work.

With the salesperson's and Ari's help, Carly chose the same

model AC unit that Joyce had in her living room window. Ari remembered, because he'd installed it for her two summers earlier.

"If you'd like, Carly, I'll be glad to install it for you," Ari offered. He flashed that smile again, and this time she detected a twinkle in his dark-brown eyes.

Carly felt her cheeks heating. She was becoming more certain that Ari had a crush on her. What scared her was the growing certainty that she felt the same toward him. Daniel hadn't even been gone two years. How could she already be developing feelings for someone else?

"I'm sure I can manage it, but thank you, Ari."

"Okay. But let me know if you change your mind. That unit isn't exactly lightweight. It helps to have two people to lift it into the window."

Carly thanked the salesperson, muttered a quick goodbye to Ari, then went to the checkout to pay.

After she supplied her credit card and the purchase was rung up, the checkout clerk plucked a vinyl decal out of a box on the counter. "Take one of these," he said over a wad of bright orange gum. "We're giving 'em out free all month."

Carly took it from him, smiling at Vermont's beautiful flag—the state's coat of arms depicted against a vast field of blue. "Thanks! I'll put this on my car window."

A stockroom clerk wheeled her air conditioner out on a dolly and loaded it into her trunk. She gulped when she saw the size of the box. Maybe she should have accepted Ari's offer.

Too late now.

The sun was beating down like a flaming torch when Carly slid in. Before she started her engine, she pressed the decal to the inside of her window, displaying the official flag of her beloved state. She liked this type of decal—it attached by static cling and was easily removed.

After leaving Quayle's parking lot, Carly decided it was the perfect time to pay a visit to Sara Hardy. The chief hadn't called with a status update, so she probably couldn't get into the restaurant anyway.

With the AC in her car cranked to the highest setting, Carly cruised south along Main Street toward her next destination. She'd visited Hardy Breads only once before, when she contracted with them to supply the artisan breads for her restaurant. The facility was about a twenty-minute drive from Balsam Dell, which meant weekly deliveries were prompt and special orders could be obtained with ease.

When she was almost at the turnoff road that would take her to the bakery, she spotted a large rectangular sign announcing *Pine Grove Mobile Home Park* with an arrow pointing down Grove Street.

Pine Grove. Wasn't that the mobile home park Lyle had owned? The one Sara Hardy had sued him over?

She turned at the next street and headed west, on the road leading to Colm and Sara's antique farmhouse and bakery. As she drove, the scenery morphed from a quiet residential area into rolling pastureland. Cows grazed in the distance.

Within minutes, a rustic-looking sign that read *Hardy Breads* appeared on the right. Beyond that was the paved driveway that led to the bakery building. The farmhouse itself—a sprawling white structure with a wraparound porch—sat about a quarter mile up the hill from the brick bakery.

Carly parked in the lot adjacent to the bakery and went inside through the front entrance. A young woman stood behind a wooden counter, loading several baguettes into a customer's canvas bag. Sara was probably in the adjacent room, where breads were baked in brick ovens and transferred onto metal racks for cooling.

As if Carly had conjured her, a petite woman with thick brown hair encased in a hairnet came through a door behind the counter. "Pam, someone from the Purple Gorgon will be picking these up this morning," she told the clerk and plunked a bag of dark rye loaves on the counter.

Carly waved to Sara, whose face widened into a smile when she noticed her. "Hey, what a nice surprise! I didn't expect to see you here. Do you need an emergency order?"

"No, but I was hoping you had a minute to chat."

"For you? I have five minutes."

Sara led her through a separate doorway, into a small office where a surprisingly modern desk was stacked neatly with papers. She grinned at Carly. "It looks worse than it is. Believe it or not, I know where everything is."

"I'm sure you do."

"Have a seat." Sara pointed at a padded chair opposite her desk. "I heard about what happened. I'm so sorry. It must have been quite a shock."

"That's putting it mildly," Carly said. "My restaurant is being searched this morning. The police got a warrant."

"That's awful! But why?"

"The police think my employee, Suzanne, might have killed Lyle. The motive isn't clear, but the murder weapon is missing. They think she might have hidden it there."

Sara's hazel eyes filled with sympathy. "I've met Suzanne. She's a love. I can tell from your expression you think she's innocent."

"I *know* she's innocent," Carly said, her throat growing tight. "Sara, I know you're really busy, so I'll get to the point. Last night I was Googling Lyle. I found an article about a small claim you filed against him a while back. I feel strange asking this, but…since you had a bad experience with him, do you know of anyone else who had a grudge against Lyle?"

Sara folded her hands and smiled. "You want to know if I could have been angry enough to kill him."

Carly felt herself flushing. "No. That's not what I meant." *But I did, sort of.*

Sara's smile faded. "Last year, I rented one of Lyle's mobile homes for my younger sister, Lori. She was finishing up her last year of college, and she was going nuts living in the dorm. She's a real serious student, and the noise and the distractions interfered with her studies. I offered her a room here, but she's allergic to our cats. I ended up renting one of the trailers at Pine Grove for her so she'd have a quiet place to live and study until she graduated. It was only meant to be short-term. She was moving to Colorado right after graduation."

"That was so generous of you."

"Yeah, well, I love my little sis. Anyway, after Lori moved out, I asked for my security deposit back. Bagley refused. Said Lori left the trailer in a deplorable condition. It was a lie. Lori and I cleaned that place ourselves. It was spotless when she turned in her key."

"Why would he say that?"

Sara blew out a breath. "I'm sorry to defame the dead, but Lyle Bagley was a sleazy landlord. I found out afterward that he *never* gave back security deposits. Most times the tenants gave up and didn't fight him, but this time he messed with the wrong woman." She pointed at her own chest. "I took him to court, and, lo and behold, he produced photos of Lori's trailer looking like a total pigsty after she moved out."

"That's terrible. What happened after that?" Carly remembered the article from the internet but wanted Sara's account of it.

"Long story short, the judge ruled against me. The photos had been doctored to look recent, when they'd actually been taken after the *prior* tenant moved out. I didn't think to take photos after Lori moved out. It didn't occur to me Bagley would blatantly lie just to keep my deposit. Bottom line, I was out sixteen hundred dollars."

This new revelation about Lyle boggled Carly's mind. Had he been so fixated on profit that he cheated his own tenants?

"As to your question," Sara said, "I'm sure Bagley made plenty of enemies over the years. Unfortunately, I can't think of anyone in particular. Colm wanted to confront him in person, but I talked him out of it."

Carly mulled over Sara's story. Even if Sara wasn't a killer, could her husband have attacked Lyle in anger? Maybe gone too far and killed him?

"Luckily," Sara said wryly, "Colm was out of state the night Bagley was killed. His mom needed a wheelchair ramp built, so he stayed with his brother in New Hampshire so they could get it done together."

Sara was quick to give Colm an alibi. Almost as if she read my thoughts.

"Sara, I've taken enough of your time," Carly said, rising from her chair. "Thanks for being open with me. If anyone comes to mind who might have been angry with Lyle, would you give me a call?"

"I will, but honestly, I didn't know any of the tenants there, other than my sister. Are you...investigating?"

"Not officially, but I'm kind of poking around. I know the police are doing their job, but I'm worried they'll be too quick to charge Suzanne with murder."

Sara came over to hug Carly. "I'll be sending positive vibes her way."

"Thanks." As Carly rose from her chair, a greeting card resting on Sara's desk caught her eye. The design, made from narrow strips of paper curled into tight rolls, was a peace sign superimposed over loaves of bread.

"Isn't that cool?" Sara grinned. "Colm gave me that for our tenth anniversary. He got it at What a Card. The owner makes them herself. Maybe you know her. Gina Tomasso?"

Carly sucked in a breath. "Gina owns the card shop?"

"You do know her! If you see her, give her my regards, okay?"

"I will."

Gina owns the card shop.

Gina, whose unhappy marriage to Lyle ended in divorce. Was it possible Gina could shed some light on who might have wanted him dead?

Carly hurried out to her car, started her engine, and headed back into town. She'd already wasted too many years.

It was time to face the ghost of her past, head-on.

CHAPTER NINE

CARLY HAD ALMOST REACHED THE CENTER OF TOWN WHEN HER cell pinged with a text. Pausing at the next traffic light, she glanced at it. It was the chief, giving her the go-ahead to enter her restaurant. Her keys—the ones he'd confiscated from her—were being held for her at the front desk of the police station.

Her plan to visit Gina would have to wait.

Minutes later, expecting the worst, Carly unlocked the eatery's back door and stepped inside. Hot, stuffy air assaulted her senses. It smelled as if the restaurant had been locked up for days instead of just over twenty-four hours.

She flicked on the lights and took a quick glance around. Her heart tumbled in her chest. On the counter where her customers ate, packages of napkins, trays of flatware, and unopened bottles of condiments had been plunked in disorderly fashion. The shelves beneath the counter had been emptied, presumably to search for the weapon that killed Lyle.

Carly pulled in a breath. *Stay calm. It can all be fixed.* She went to the thermostat and switched on the air conditioning, then pushed through the swinging door into the kitchen. She turned on the lights and skimmed her gaze over the room.

Pots and pans were stacked haphazardly on countertops and on her workspace. Her nonperishable foodstuffs, once neatly lined along her stainless-steel shelves, were in total disarray. Nothing was where it belonged.

Had the investigators confiscated anything? If so, it wasn't obvious. Carly plunked her tote on her desk and returned to the dining room.

Everything that could possibly touch food had to be washed, she decided. She'd start in the dining room and then move to the kitchen.

Armed with coffee, Carly worked nonstop for the next few hours. By 2:00, everything was spotless and in its proper place.

Gina's card shop was on the south side of the town green, a two-minute walk, at best.

Tomorrow Carly would open for business. She needed to regain a sense of normalcy, even if the status of her lease was unknown. Officially, Lyle had terminated her tenancy, but now Lyle was… well, gone. What would happen next?

After one last glance around, she locked up the restaurant.

The Ghost of Friendships Past was waiting.

~

A bell jingled when Carly stepped into What a Card. The shop was more spacious inside than it appeared from the street. Circular display racks of greeting cards sat strategically throughout the store. One entire wall was devoted to more conventional cards, while the opposite wall boasted eye-catching and unique gifts.

Behind the sales counter, in the center of the shop, a woman with a round face and espresso-colored curls was ringing up a sale for a customer. Carly's heart pounded.

Gina.

Fifteen years ago, she and Gina had parted on terrible terms. What would her reaction be when she saw Carly?

For a few awkward moments, Carly stood off to the side and stared at her old friend. Clad in a lace-trimmed coral top over flared, drawstring shorts, Gina looked as fit and trim as she had in high school. A few inches taller than Carly's five foot four, Gina had always been the more athletic one. In gym class, when they'd had to climb that blasted rope, Gina had clambered up to the top without a hint of effort, while Carly thudded to the mat after the first three feet.

A few months before, Carly had spotted Gina in Telly's Market wheeling a cart down the frozen foods aisle. The urge to steal up behind her old friend and tap her on the shoulder was overwhelming. She'd stood there for several long moments, debating with herself whether to take the risk. Ultimately, Carly had lost her nerve. She'd ducked down a different aisle and scooted out of the store.

The smiling customer strode off holding a brown paper bag, and in the next instant Gina spotted Carly. When her face froze, Carly feared the worst. Until Gina rushed over and wrapped her in a suffocating hug. "My God, you finally came in. I was wondering if you ever would." She pulled back, and Carly saw tears perched on her lashes.

A warm swell of sheer relief swept through Carly, and her throat clogged. She'd half expected her former bestie to shun her. Instead, Gina had welcomed her with a bone-crushing embrace.

Carly caught her breath. "I only found out today that this was your shop!" she defended. "Why haven't you come into my restaurant? I've been there since January."

"I was chicken. Afraid you'd tell me to take a hike. Or worse." She squeezed Carly again. "Hey, want some coffee? We can go out back for a few. I can hear if a customer comes in."

"Coffee would definitely hit the spot," Carly said. "Remember what we used to say? Human beans—"

"Need coffee beans!" They recited the words together, then broke into giggles.

"Seriously, though," Gina said soberly, ushering Carly to a small wooden table in the back room. "It's all over the news about Lyle. Even though I'm long over him, I cried when I heard what happened. No one deserves to be murdered, not even a jerk like him." She popped a coffee pod into a single-serve machine and pressed a button.

"I'm sorry, Gina." In a circular way, their friendship had been destroyed by Lyle. Did Carly dare question her as to who else might have thought Lyle was a jerk, or worse?

She had to. If she was going to find his killer, she'd have to dig in the dirt and root out information about his enemies, whoever they were.

"It's okay. I moved on long ago." Gina handed Carly her coffee cup, along with a packet of powdered milk, then dropped a pod into the machine for herself. "How are you doing with all this? Are you closed today?"

"Yes, but not by choice. The police got a warrant to search my restaurant this morning." Carly's voice cracked. "They think Suzanne, my server, might have killed Lyle and hidden the murder weapon in there."

"Oh boy," Gina said, under her breath.

"What do you mean?" Carly asked, then sipped her coffee. "Do you know something?"

Gina fetched her own coffee, added three sugars, and sat down with Carly. "Stuff gets around. Lyle used to pal around with Suzanne's husband Jake, then Jake got in some trouble. They hate each other now. I mean, *hated* each other," she added softly.

"What kind of trouble?" Carly pressed.

Gina hesitated. "Mostly stemmed from gambling."

Gambling. Carly felt something pinch her insides. Although gambling had never appealed to her, she knew for some it could be addictive. If Jake had been bitten by the gambling bug, had it led him to steal, or worse? And how did Lyle fit into the picture?

She wanted to ask more, but Gina deflected the conversation.

"Speaking of Suzanne, did you like your birthday card?" Gina asked her.

"My birthday... Did *you* make the grilled cheese card? I love it!"

Gina grinned. "When Suzanne said she wanted a nice card for her boss at the grilled cheese restaurant, I knew she meant you. I told her if she came back the next day, I'd have something special for her. I didn't have time to use the quilling technique, so I free-styled it with some textured paint."

Carly felt her heart swell. This was the Gina she'd always known and loved—generous and kind, with a strong artistic bent. A massive wave of regret washed over her for all the years they'd missed. Why hadn't she reached out sooner? Why hadn't they both acted like adults and contacted each other a long time ago?

"You've always been the creative one," Carly said. "And I love this shop. How's business been?"

"Good, but it's a lot for one person. I have a salesclerk who works mornings, but I handle things solo the rest of the day. I make most of my income on custom cards, wedding invitations especially. I've been known to burn the midnight oil." She smiled, and then lowered her gaze. "Carly—"

"Gina—"

"That's okay. You first," Carly said.

Gina sucked in a shaky breath. "That day, that awful day you warned me against hooking up with Lyle, I said some ugly things to you. I thought you were jealous that he picked me over you."

Carly remembered. How could she not? Gina had accused Carly of being a traitor, of trying to sabotage her relationship with Lyle because she wanted him for herself. Gina had used some rough language. Over time the memory had softened, but it never went away.

"I learned the truth pretty quickly," Gina went on sourly. "You warned me because you cared, not because you were jealous. You said Lyle was bad news, and he was. He was brash, immature, wild. I stuck with the fool for three years—three years of feeling rotten about myself—before I finally smartened up and called it quits. I feel bad saying that now, because he's dead, but it's the truth." She rubbed her fingers over her eyes. "I am so, so sorry, Carly. I've wanted to tell you that for a long time, but I didn't have the guts to call you."

Carly looked at her old friend. Except for the fine lines around her eyes, Gina looked as youthful as she had in high school. "Let's cut the past loose, okay? It's water under the bridge. For gosh sakes, we were seventeen-year-old kids."

Gina gave Carly a sideways smile. "I was eighteen, remember? You always teased me about being older."

Even with Lyle's unsolved murder hovering over her, Carly felt lighter than she had in days. Seeing Gina again, having coffee with her... It was something she thought would never happen.

"So, how's your dad doing?"

Gina's smile was sad. "He finally retired, but he's got health issues. He's moving into assisted living in the fall, which means I'll be looking for an apartment. He feels like he's abandoning me, but assisted living is expensive so he needs to sell the house."

"I'm sorry to hear that. Give him my love, okay?"

"You bet I will."

Carly smiled at her friend. "Hey, remember when he called us two peas in a pod?"

Gina laughed. "No, don't you remember? He called us two *pea-brains* in a pod. It was right after we got in major trouble for liberating those frogs from the science lab."

"Gosh, you're right. We got two weeks detention, but it was worth it. Principal O'Connor was apoplectic, remember? They never did find those poor frogs."

"Nope. We gave them a new lease on life in a peaceful pond." Gina grinned, and then her shoulders dropped. "God, I've missed you." She drained her coffee cup. "You know, Carly, when I first heard about your husband, I felt sick. I wanted so badly to be there for you, but I was afraid—" She swallowed, her brown eyes filling again with tears.

The memories resurfaced, and Carly felt that familiar pang. During those first awful days, she remembered wishing Gina would call or even send a note. Her mom told her to give it time, and she did. But still, nothing arrived.

"I had a card ready to mail to you," Gina said in a rickety voice. "I don't know why I didn't send it."

"It's okay. Honestly, it is."

Gina sat back and pulled in a long breath. "What was he like?" she asked softly.

"Daniel? He was husky and tall, with blue eyes and a reddish-gold beard, and a heart so big it's a wonder it didn't burst out of his chest."

"Sounds like he was perfect for you. Did he mind that you kept your maiden name?"

Carly laughed. "He said he'd have been surprised if I didn't."

"I wish I'd kept my mine," Gina said darkly. "I couldn't wait to take it back after my divorce."

"Gina, now that we're back on the subject of Lyle, can we talk seriously about him?"

Gina shrugged. "Sure."

"Do you know anyone who hated him enough to murder him?"

Gina sat back and squared her shoulders, then stared hard at Carly. "I've thought about that. When I first heard what happened, I figured one of his sleazy business deals went wrong and someone decided to get revenge."

"Didn't he have any legitimate businesses?"

"He had the mobile home park, but he ran it like a slum landlord." Gina sighed. "It's hard to explain. Lyle's dad was a terrible role model. He taught Lyle that being in business was all about sticking it to someone before they stuck it to you."

"That's sad." Carly shook her head and took a sip of her coffee.

"Lyle was always dreaming up get-rich-quick schemes," Gina went on, "most of which failed. If he'd used his brainpower to build genuine business relationships, he could've done a lot of good for himself and for this town. He had a sharp mind, never forgot a face. It was one of his superpowers. But as to your question, I can think of two people who weren't too pleased with him."

Carly sat up straighter. Was one of them Sara Hardy?

"The first is his half brother, Matt. When Lyle and I first got married, Matt was bummed. Their dad never stuck around much, and Matt's mom was sort of an absentee mother. Lyle was all he had, and suddenly Lyle was gone from the house. To pacify him, Lyle told Matt that as soon as he graduated high school, they'd start a business together. It was a vague promise he tossed at Matt to get him to stop bugging him. Problem was, Matt had been counting on him keeping that promise."

Carly vaguely recalled Matt Bagley from high school. Thin, with a gaunt face and deep-set eyes. No resemblance to Lyle whatsoever.

"About eight years ago, their dad died. He'd promised his vintage Cadillac to Matt, but Lyle drove off with it before Matt could stop him." She took a long sip from her cup. "Matt wanted that car, badly. He was furious with Lyle."

"Does Matt live around here?"

"No. He moved to New York years ago. Somewhere near Albany."

Close enough, Carly thought. He could have driven to Balsam Dell, killed his brother, and zipped back home, all in the same night.

"You said there was someone else who was mad at Lyle," Carly prompted.

Gina pushed aside her empty cup. "Yeah, but it was more like a love/hate thing. Her name is Janet Moody. She lives in that house on the corner of Second Street and Windsor. The one with the pretty flower beds and the painted stones in the front yard."

"I've seen that house. There's a huge giraffe in the front."

Gina nodded. "That's the place. For years she's been the manager for Lyle's mobile home park. Pine Grove used to be a nice place to live, until Lyle took it over. Janet's been handling the leasing, the rent collection, even the evictions for him. I'll cut to the chase." Gina lowered her voice. "Janet was crazy in love with Lyle. I mean, crazy to the point of obsession."

Obsession. "Did Lyle know?"

Gina shrugged. "He'd have had to be a fool not to. When Janet got wind that Lyle was serious about Tiffany Spencer, she went ballistic. She located Tiffany's car in the lot where she works at the outlet stores and smashed the bejesus out of her taillights. Let the air out of her tires too. She might have gotten away with it, but she forgot that malls have cameras everywhere. The next day, Tiffany watched the security video and ID'd her on the spot."

"Was Janet arrested?"

"No, Tiffany agreed not to press charges. I suspect Lyle talked her out of it because he needed Janet to keep working for him. It ended up getting swept under the rug."

A bell jingled in the outer room. "Excuse me." Gina dashed into her shop and returned a minute later. "Two browsers. I told them I'd be right back out to help them."

"I'll get out of your hair," Carly said, "but I'm so glad I came in. Can I ask you one more question before I leave?"

"Of course," Gina said. "Anything."

"Do you know what Janet used to vandalize Tiffany's car?"

Gina frowned at the question, then shook her head. "It never really came up. Why?"

"Because whatever was used to kill Lyle, the police haven't found it yet."

CHAPTER TEN

IN THE PARKING LOT BEHIND THE EATERY, THE SUN WAS BROIL-
ing the pavement. Waves of heat shimmered off the asphalt as if
trying to escape their fiery fate.

Tiffany Spencer's red Nissan wasn't in its usual spot, Carly
noticed, but the sedan that had shielded Lyle's body from view the
day before had been removed—towed by the police, no doubt.

Would Tiffany have gone to work the day after Lyle's body was
found? Carly couldn't imagine her doing that, but then, everyone handled grief differently. Maybe work was the best thing for
Tiffany right now. Or maybe she'd gone to stay with family, or with
a friend, until all the hoopla died down. It struck Carly that she
knew next to nothing about the woman living above her eatery.

Slipping on her sunglasses, Carly was unlocking the door to
her Corolla when she saw a shiny blue sports car swing into the
lot. She couldn't make out the driver through the tinted windshield, and for a moment she panicked. What if it was Lyle's
killer, returning to the scene of the crime to retrieve the hidden
murder weapon? Would he—or she—dare to do that in broad
daylight?

Her heart thudded as the car approached, its driver's side
window gliding slowly down. A musical sound reached her ears, a
haunting, classical piece she'd never heard before. Almost immediately it exchanged places with a rhythmic rap number.

"Carly!" The driver hopped out and jogged over to her, and she
sagged in sheer relief.

"Grant, I didn't know who you were! I've never seen your car before."

"Are you okay?" Grant asked her. He gave her a brief, uncharacteristic hug.

"I am, just a little discombobulated."

"Yeah, I can imagine." He frowned and glanced toward the sidewalk. "At least that ugly yellow tape's gone. Have you heard anything from the police?"

"No, nothing. They searched in here this morning, that's all I know. Everything was topsy-turvy when I arrived, but it's all cleaned up and put away now."

"Darn, Carly. Why didn't you text me? I'd have come over to help you." Grant pulled off his sunglasses, his brow creased with concern.

"That's okay. Doing cleanup helped keep my mind off things. How did your interview with the police go?"

His expression clouded, and he looked away. "Um, it went okay, I guess. I was there for over an hour. They like to ask the same questions over and over." He rolled his dark-brown eyes and stuck his sunglasses back on. "What about tomorrow? Are you going to open?"

"I'm planning on it," Carly said. She wanted to prod him further about his interview, but he'd seemed uneasy when she asked about it. Was there something he was holding back? Something the police warned him not to discuss?

"Great," Grant said, flashing an anxious smile. "I'll try to get in early to help you with prep work."

"Thanks, Grant. I'm heading home now. I bought a new air conditioner, and I have to figure out how to get it inside the house and into my living room window." She gave him a wry smile.

"For gosh sakes, I can help you with that." With a comical grin, he flexed his muscles to indicate how strong he was. "Want me to follow you to your apartment?"

Carly hesitated. Much as she wanted to take him up on his offer, she didn't want to take advantage of him. After all, he was nineteen. She was sure he had better ways to spend his free time, especially on a hot summer day.

"Grant, I'm sure you have better things to do. Friends, fun, that sort of thing."

"I have nothing planned. Come on, with the two of us pitching in, it'll be a breeze. In this heat you're gonna need it. I'll bet your apartment feels like a sauna about now."

"More like a bread oven." Carly smiled. "Okay, but I'm adding something extra to your paycheck this week."

"Don't you dare. I was raised to be a gentleman. I'm happy to help."

They hopped into their cars and Carly led the way. Minutes later, in Carly's driveway, she popped open her trunk. She started to reach for the box, but Grant immediately moved in and lifted it with ease. "Let's do this!"

Carly rushed to the front door and held it open for him. They went upstairs, and within fifteen minutes the air conditioner was blowing cool air from Carly's living room window.

"Oh, what a relief," she said. "Grant, thank you for doing this. You're a life saver."

"Hey, you're welcome. Any time."

Carly swept a lock of hair away from her face. "Funny thing. Ari Mitchell was in the hardware store when I bought it. He offered to come over and install it for me, but I didn't feel right letting him do that. I don't know him *all* that well. I'd have felt weird accepting."

Grant nodded. "I hear you there. Women can't be too careful. Gotta tell you, though, Ari's a great guy. One of the best. He does things for people no one knows about, and he'll never talk about it, either."

"Really?" Carly said, feeling another telltale flush creep up her neck. She hoped Grant wouldn't notice it.

Without explaining further, Grant looked around the apartment. "You have some cool digs here. I like this place."

"Thanks. I lucked out when I saw the *Apartment for Rent* sign in Joyce's window last fall when I was scouting out places to live. She's a dream landlady. Hey, can I get you a cold drink?" Carly asked him, going into her kitchen. "Iced tea, lemonade, water?"

"I wouldn't mind a water."

"Want a glass?"

"Nah. Just the bottle." He accepted the water from Carly and unscrewed the cap. "Have you, um, heard anything from Suzanne? I mean, like, has she texted you or anything?"

"Not today," Carly said glumly, "but I'll try to call her later. I've been worried about her."

Grant took a long swig from his water bottle. "Yeah, same here. There's no way she committed that murder, Carly. *No way.*" His voice was fierce with indignation.

"I know," Carly said quietly. *Something's up with Grant.* She wanted to ask him again about his police interview, but before she could, he whipped his cell phone out and glanced at it. "Oh, shoot. I totally forgot. I told my dad I'd help him clean out the garage. I better go." He shoved his cell back in his pocket.

Hmm. Wasn't that convenient?

"Sounds fun. *Not,*" Carly joked, wrinkling her nose.

Grant smiled, but there was no warmth behind it. She thanked him again for helping her with the air conditioner. The room already felt cooler by a few degrees. Once she got accustomed to the settings, she should be able to keep her apartment comfy without turning it into the North Pole.

Grant capped his water bottle, and Carly walked with him down to the front porch. She couldn't help admiring the sleek sports car parked behind her Corolla. "Those are some nifty wheels," she said in a light tone. "Your dad's car?"

"Nah. It's mine. See you tomorrow!"

Carly waved as he backed out of the driveway. Unfortunately, she now had something else to worry about.

Deep in her bones, she felt certain Grant was hiding something. Either that or he was protecting someone.

If only she knew which one it was.

~

With a frustrated sigh, Carly left yet another message in Suzanne's voice mail. "Hey, just checking to see how you're doing. Wasn't sure if you got my other two messages. Let me know if there's anything I can do, okay? By the way, I'm opening for business tomorrow as usual. Hope to see you then."

Was it wishful thinking to believe Suzanne would show up for work on Friday? Probably. If only she'd return Carly's calls!

A short while earlier, Carly had spoken to Chief Holloway. He'd confirmed one thing: Suzanne was not being held on suspicion of murder. Though she'd been relieved to hear it, she knew it didn't mean Suzanne was off the hook.

Carly made herself a quick grilled cheese. With her apartment beginning to feel soothingly cool, she made herself a cup of hot tea to accompany it.

As she munched on her sandwich, she thought about the one thing that had gone right that day—her unexpected reunion with Gina. Carly had expected their conversation to start off awkwardly, but instead she and Gina had slipped right into the groove that had always been so natural to them. The core of their friendship was still intact; Carly felt sure of it. She wanted more than anything to get to know Gina again. They might discover they had little in common, but it was worth a shot.

Carly jumped when someone knocked loudly. Crossing her fingers that it might be Suzanne, she started to unlock it when it occurred to her she needed to be more careful. "Who is it?" she called out. *Darn, she needed a peephole.*

"Don," said a muffled voice.

Carly groaned. Donny Frasco. Hadn't she gotten rid of him once?

At least he wasn't dangerous, she thought. *Only terminally annoying.*

She unlocked the door and gave him a fierce stare, one hand jammed onto her hip. "What can I do for you, Donny?"

"It's Don," he reminded her, then flashed a hopeful smile. "I think you and I can help each other, Carly. Can I come in?"

"You mean *may* you come in?" She didn't want to let him off too easily.

"Okay, yeah," he said impatiently. "*May* I come in?" He peeked around her into her living room.

"Before I let you in, what is it you think we can help each other with?"

Dressed in knee-length shorts and a short-sleeved plaid shirt that reminded Carly of vegetable soup, he looked a bit more polished than he had on his first visit. "For criminy's sake, Carly, can't we sit down for five minutes? I'm not going to bite you."

At that, Carly felt bad. She *was* giving him a hard time. Memories of that nightmare babysitting gig still resonated in her head.

She opened the door wider. "Come in. Have a seat in the living room. And do *not* pull out your cell phone to record our conversation. Would you like a cold drink?"

He flushed and his freckles darkened, as if she'd thwarted his intentions. "Um, sure. Do you have any root beer?"

"Sorry. I have lemonade, iced tea, water, and about three drops of OJ. Take your pick."

"Lemonade," he said.

Carly poured him a glass and returned to the living room.

She sat in the rocking chair opposite him and clasped her hands around one knee. "So, for the second time, what do you think we can help each other with?"

Don gulped noisily from his glass, grimaced, then set it down on the table beside him. "No small talk first, huh? Okay, here it is. Word around town is that Suzanne Rivers, is numero uno on the police suspect list."

"You already told me that, remember?"

"Yeah, okay, but listen. I know Suzanne. You do too, right?" He looked at Carly expectantly. When she offered a single nod, he added, "Before Suzanne started working for you, she was slinging hot dogs at Dot's Diggity Dogs down on Poplar Street. Everyone loved her there. She doesn't have a violent bone in her body."

Carly studied Don carefully. His eyes, almost the same color as his auburn goatee, were ablaze with conviction. She couldn't help wondering if he was crushing on Suzanne or if he had some other personal connection to her.

"Okay," Carly conceded, "I agree with you that Suzanne is not a killer. Hence, she did not kill Lyle Bagley. But that doesn't help her, does it?"

"It might, if we work together." He squirmed on the sofa and moved closer to the edge. "You and I both know that the *real* killer is walking the streets of Balsam Dell, free as a freakin' bird, right?"

"You're putting words in my mouth," Carly said. "I don't know where the killer is or who it is. I only know that it's not Suzanne. Period." *And I don't have a shred of evidence to prove it.*

His eyes glittered mischievously. "Well, what would you say if I told you I overheard a conversation this afternoon with the very person who probably killed Lyle Bagley?"

Carly felt her heart jump. Was Don yanking her chain, or did he really have solid information? Feigning nonchalance, she said, "Explain, please."

He slugged back another gulp of lemonade and swiped his

fingers over his lips. "Okay, get this. Every Thursday when my paper comes out, I leave a short stack of them at the front desk at the Peacock B and B."

Carly knew the establishment. Before she moved away from Balsam Dell, the Peacock had been a popular inn, hard to get a reservation at during the busy season. When she'd driven past it a few months ago, she was surprised to see it looking tired and careworn. She'd heard a new owner had taken it over, but she didn't know any of the details.

"Anyway, as I was leaving, I saw this guy who looked weirdly familiar sitting on a chair in the lobby. He was talking on his phone, and I was sure I heard him say 'my brother Lyle.'"

That got Carly's attention. She sat up in her rocking chair and dropped both feet to the floor. "Go on."

"He was sitting next to the soda machine, so I strolled over real casual, like I wanted to look at the selections. Soon as I got that close, I knew. He was four or five years ahead of me in school, but I remember him from the neighborhood. It was definitely Matt Bagley, Lyle's little bro."

"Keep going," Carly said.

"It gets way better," he said with a sly grin, "'cause then I heard him say 'ninety-one DeVille' and I knew he was talking about Lyle's Caddy. You ever see it?"

Carly shook her head. She saw no reason to tell him Gina had told her about it.

"Anyway, then he said—I swear, Carly, I heard it plain as day—'yeah, my brother had to die before I could finally get it.' And then he laughed, like it was a real joke."

Carly felt her heart race. Hard as it was to believe, Don might have stumbled onto something. "Who do you think he was talking to?"

"I don't know, but right about then Matt looked up and glared at me, like he knew I was eavesdropping. I threw a buck fifty in the machine, grabbed a root beer, and hightailed it out of there."

This was big, Carly thought. Or potentially big. Was there a way to find out when Matt checked into the Peacock? Had he been registered there the night Lyle was murdered?

"Don, you have to tell the police what you heard," Carly insisted. "Go down to the station right now and ask for Chief Holloway."

Don's freckled face paled. "No way! If the cops haul him in, it won't take Matt long to figure out who the squealer was."

Carly gritted her teeth. "Then why did you bother coming here and telling me this?"

"Carly, don't you get it? If you and I can get enough evidence to nail him, then the cops'll have to arrest him for murder. Between the two of us, we can ask questions, do a little snooping. If I just go to the cops and report what I heard, they'll question Matt and let him go, and then my you-know-what is grass!"

Carly almost laughed in his face. She hadn't seen Donny Frasco since he was a pesky kid, and suddenly he shows up at her door, wanting to recruit her to find a killer.

But when she caught his worried gaze, she saw that he was dead serious. She softened her tone. "Don, why do you want to bestow this dubious honor on me? What did I do to deserve it?"

"Lyle Bagley was killed behind *your* restaurant, Carly, and it's *your* employee who's being blamed."

Carly wasn't buying it. Something else was going on.

"Tell me the truth. Why are you so anxious to defend Suzanne? Is it personal?"

He swallowed and his eyes shifted sideways. "She came to my rescue when no one else did. That's all I'm gonna say."

"All right. Fair enough. But any snooping we do has to be discreet. I want to check out the Peacock myself, but I'll need a valid excuse."

His eyes lit up. "Cool! Maybe we can go there and—"

"Not *we*," Carly corrected. "I need to do it alone. Otherwise, we'll risk attracting attention. That's the last thing we want, right?"

Don's face drooped. "I guess."

"Tell you what," she said, hoping to appease him. "I'll buy an ad for next week's paper with a 'free soda or coffee with any sandwich' coupon. Make the expiration date the end of the month. I'll let you design it. You did a pretty good job on the first one."

His entire demeanor changed. "That's great! You want the quarter-page?"

Carly gulped. The quarter-page ad was a tad pricey, she remembered. After negotiating a slight discount, she added, "But make sure the design is good."

"Oh, I will," Don said, almost bubbly now. "At least *you* pay your bills. D'you know Lyle Bagley never once paid me? I ran those dumb ads for his mobile home park every week, and he never paid a single invoice."

Somehow, that didn't surprise Carly. "So why didn't you cut him off?"

Don shrugged. "He kept telling me he was gonna get after his assistant to pay me. He made it sound like it was all her fault. I figured if I cut him off, I'd never see a penny."

Hmm. The assistant had to be Janet Moody, at least according to Gina. More than ever, Carly wanted to talk to Janet.

"So, we're teammates now, right?" Don said hopefully.

Carly winced. "Not quite. Let's just say we have the same goal—to figure out who really killed Lyle Bagley."

CHAPTER ELEVEN

CARLY SPENT A CHUNK OF HER EVENING GOOGLING POTENTIAL suspects. Not that she expected to share her thoughts with the police, but in her own mind she needed to get her so-called ducks in a row.

Based on the one-sided conversation overheard by Don at the Peacock, she plunked Matt Bagley at the top of the list. That was assuming, of course, that Don had been factual in relating what he'd heard. He could have gotten it all wrong, or Matt could have been joking about his brother's death as a way of dealing with his grief. Anything was possible.

One thing Carly wanted to know: How long had Matt been staying at the Peacock? Had he driven to Balsam Dell after being informed of his brother's death? Or had he been in town before that, trying to finagle a way to get his hands on Lyle's Cadillac?

Carly was surprised to discover Matt had a Facebook page. He lived in Troy, New York, barely an hour from Balsam Dell. His posts were few and far between, but mostly they were about old cars. All the more reason he fit the bill as a prime suspect, in Carly's mind.

As for Janet Moody, the name came up about a dozen times on Facebook. None, unfortunately, had been the one Carly was looking for. She did find an online link to an article about Janet's role in last year's Garden Art Competition sponsored by a local nursery. From the photos, it was clear that Janet had a distinct talent for painting colorful garden stones. She'd placed second in one of the categories, winning a fifty-dollar gift certificate. Carly studied Janet's photo. Full-figured and tanned, she sported bright purple slacks and a white, boho-style top. She wore a hard expression, as if life had given her lemons and she'd returned the favor by crushing them under her heel.

By the time she shut down her laptop, her lids were drooping from fatigue. With the air conditioner blowing cool air throughout the apartment, Carly slept exceptionally well.

An idea must have come to her in a dream because at 5:00 a.m., she awakened with a plan.

Unfortunately, it meant including Don Frasco in her scheme. She'd hoped to keep his involvement to a minimum, but since she wanted to act quickly, she'd need to beg a favor from him.

Oh happy day.

~

At 8:30 a.m. on Friday, Carly unlocked the back door to her eatery. She flipped on the lights and turned on the air conditioning, then went to her desk in the kitchen. All her scrubbing the day before had infused the air with a clean, lemony scent.

She made a quick call to Don. He agreed to help, and Carly was grateful he could do a rush job for her.

Coffee prepared, Carly made herself her usual morning breakfast of bacon and shredded cheddar in a grilled, buttery biscuit. Instead of eating at the counter as she normally did, she brought everything over to the third booth from the front. Back in the days when the eatery was Bingley's Ice Cream Parlor, she and Gina had sat in that booth nearly every summer day, scarfing down hot fudge sundaes or banana splits. Being with Gina the day before had brought back that pleasant memory.

Carly was reminiscing about those days when she heard someone tapping lightly on the glass front door. She smiled when she saw Grant peeking inside. She jumped up to let him enter. "Hey, I didn't expect you this early! Why didn't you let yourself in?"

He came inside, closing and locking the door behind him. "No key. The police didn't give it back to me."

Carly stepped back and grinned at him. "You got a haircut this morning, didn't you? I thought you were going for short dreads on top?"

Grant made a face. "I was, but I decided to keep it more trimmed for the summer. Plus"—he waggled his hand—"my dad wasn't thrilled about the dreads idea. He's super conservative about stuff like that."

Carly knew Grant was close to his mom and dad, but there was an undercurrent of tension she couldn't quite get a handle on. She'd been hoping they'd stop into the restaurant one day so she could meet them, but so far it hadn't happened.

"Anyway," Carly said, switching topics, "aren't you supposed to be working at Sub-a-Dub-Sub this morning?"

Grant went over behind the counter and poured himself a mug of coffee. "I asked for the day off for personal reasons. I wanted to be here in case you needed extra help today."

"Grant, that's so sweet of you," Carly said, although his ominous tone made her nervous.

He waved off the compliment. "I'll tell you something. The way they prepare food over there is totally different from what you do here."

"Different good or different bad?" Carly refilled her coffee mug.

"Different bad. Stuff like, leaving mayo out all morning, not cleaning utensils with soap and water after they've touched raw meat." He shook his head. "If I mention it, the boss just laughs it off with some half-baked explanation and thanks me for pointing it out. I'm not sure how much longer I want to stay there."

"I don't blame you. It doesn't sound very sanitary," she agreed, although she didn't like dissing another restaurateur.

Carly's phone pinged with a text. "Excuse me for a sec." She read the message and felt her heart drop. Suzanne had texted in sick. Not that Carly was surprised, but still, it was disappointing.

She set her phone on the counter. "Suzanne won't be in today. She said she doesn't feel well."

Grant sighed. "That's what I was afraid of." Holding his mug aloft, he shifted his gaze toward the door with a faraway look in his eye.

"Grant," Carly said quietly, "is there something about Suzanne that you know, that I don't?"

He looked at her with a pained expression. "I'm sorry, Carly. I can't really discuss it."

After a long pause, Carly said, "Okay, I respect your privacy. But remember, I care about Suzanne as much as you do. If there's anything I can do to help—"

"Message received," he said, cutting her off. Then, "Sorry, I didn't mean to snap." He smiled apologetically. "If you don't mind, I'm going to make myself one of those biscuits you're eating. Then we can both get to work."

"I'm all for that," Carly said.

They worked together for the next two hours, Carly performing her own tasks while Grant made tuna salad, fried two pounds of bacon, and defrosted a container of homemade tomato soup over low heat.

By 11:00 a.m., Carly was ready to turn her *Closed* sign to *Open*. She'd gotten as far as the door when she saw Don Frasco standing outside, a grin plastered on his face. He waved a sheaf of papers at her.

"Come on in," she said and opened the door.

"Thanks. Hey, mind if I snag a root beer from your cooler? I *did* rush these for you." He handed her the stack of papers.

"Sure, go ahead." Carly examined the sheets of paper. She had to admit, Don had done an excellent job. The "free soda or coffee with any sandwich" coupons had been printed on bright yellow card stock to make them stand out.

Now she had the perfect excuse to do some snooping at the Peacock B and B.

"Just to confirm," Carly said, "this is exactly the same as the ad you're putting in next week's paper, right? Same expiration date?"

"Yup," he said after swallowing a mouthful of root beer. "I did 'em just the way you said. They're about four by five." He jabbed a finger at one. "Do you like the little sandwich I added?"

Carly smiled. Don had sketched a tiny grilled cheese sandwich in one corner of the coupon. "Actually, I like it very much. You outdid yourself, Don. Can you add the cost to my invoice?"

"Already did." He reached into his pants pocket and pulled out a folded slip of paper. "There you go."

Carly unfolded the invoice, cringing when she saw the total. "Yikes!"

"It was a rush job. You said you'd pay extra."

Grinding her teeth, Carly fetched her checkbook and wrote him a check. "There you go. Make sure the ad goes in next week's edition."

"You betcha. Want me to distribute some of those coupons for you?"

"Not if I have to mortgage my soul to pay for the service," she said wryly.

He shrugged. "Okay, but don't say I didn't offer. And don't forget what we talked about last night in your apartment. I can be a much bigger help if you'd let me." He winked and wagged a finger between the two of them. "Think about it."

Watching him leave, Carly shook her head. She jumped when she realized Grant was standing directly behind her. "Oh!"

"Sorry. I didn't mean to sneak up on you."

Carly showed him the coupons. She decided to confide in Grant, at least partially. She explained that Don thought he should work with her to find Lyle's killer. As for the conversation Don overheard when Matt Bagley was sitting in the lobby of the Peacock, she skimmed over it quickly, keeping the details light.

"Yeah, but…what was the big rush in getting these coupons printed?" Grant asked.

"I want to deliver a bunch of these to the Peacock B and B this afternoon, if you won't mind covering for me for a half hour or so?"

"You know I won't mind," Grant said, then chuckled. "You're hoping to run into Matt Bagley, aren't you? Either that or you want to ask questions about him."

"Kind of. Mostly I want to find out when he arrived in town. If he was staying at the Peacock when Lyle was murdered—"

"Then he's a viable suspect." Grant suddenly looked animated.

In Carly's mind, Matt was a viable suspect anyway. But if he'd been staying in town, that gave him a big boost straight to the top of the list.

"What I don't get," Grant said, "is why this Don guy is so interested in the murder."

Carly chose her words carefully. "I think he considers himself a reporter, even though his weekly paper is mostly ads with a few local stories thrown in. Let's say, just for argument's sake, that he could dig up enough evidence for the police to arrest someone for Lyle's murder. Maybe Matt Bagley, maybe someone else. Either way, he'd make a name for himself, wouldn't he? And then he'd get more local recognition, and more people would be inclined to buy ads from him. Honestly, I don't even know how he survives on the income from a free newspaper."

Grant shrugged. "Yeah, but he must charge enough for the ads to get by. Maybe he's hoping one of the big newspapers will take him on as a staff writer."

"That's probably it," Carly agreed, though she wasn't sure Don had that much ambition.

Grant excused himself and went back into the kitchen. He returned carrying a large, stainless-steel pot of tomato soup. He set it on the burner next to the grill. Lifting the cover, he inhaled the aroma, his eyes closing around a wide smile.

"Smells delicious," Carly said. "As always."

"Thanks. By now I could make it in my sleep." His smiled fading, he looked as if he wanted to say something else. Relief flooded his face when the door swung open, and the ninety-something twins, Maybelle and Estelle, ambled in. He hurried over to take their orders.

After that, only a few regulars trickled in. By 2:00, the restaurant was as quiet as a mausoleum. Carly removed her apron and shoved a stack of the coupons inside her tote. "I think it's time to execute my plan," she told Grant.

"Good luck," he said, glancing around with a sober expression. "And take your time. It's obvious that murder has been bad for business."

CHAPTER TWELVE

THE PEACOCK WAS ONLY A SHORT DRIVE DOWN THE MAIN DRAG, located on a side street of well-kept older homes. The inn itself was painted salmon pink, with white trim in dire need of refreshing. The front steps sagged. One stair had been propped up on the side with a slab of unfinished wood to keep it from listing any further.

At one time, Carly recalled, the inn had been painted sapphire blue, with trim a shade of sage green that complemented it perfectly. Hence the name "Peacock."

The condition of the house aside, the small parking lot was nearly filled to capacity. Many of the cars were from out of state. From the outside, Carly guessed that the inn had five or six guest rooms. A faded *No Vacancy* sign sat crookedly in the front window—another subtle indication of neglect.

Carly made her way carefully up the front stairs and entered an air-conditioned lobby. A shabby runner led to a reception desk at which a girl with thick brown pigtails, who looked barely eighteen, was jabbing away at her cell phone. A nameplate in front of her read *Hailey B.*

"Hi there!" Carly said brightly, "Hailey, is it?"

"Yes," the girl said without much enthusiasm. She set down her phone and tapped away at the laptop in front of her. "Um, we don't have any vacancies right now, but there's one opening up tomorrow. You need a single or a double?"

"Thank you, but I don't need a room," Carly explained. "I'm

Carly Hale, and I own the grilled cheese restaurant in town. I wanted to leave a short supply of coupons here, if that's okay with the manager. I thought your guests might enjoy using them." Carly handed her one of the bright yellow coupons.

The girl looked at it with suspicion, then shrugged. "I guess it's okay. But let me get my dad. Dad!" she shrieked at the top of her lungs, making Carly's heart pole-vault over her rib cage.

After several seconds, the girl huffed out a sigh and said, "I'll go get him. Wait here." She snatched up the coupon.

"Thanks."

The girl disappeared around a corner, and Carly heard her clomp up a set of stairs somewhere at the back of the house. She set her coupons in a tidy stack on the desk, then glanced around the edges of the ceiling. If there was a security camera, it wasn't obvious. She craned her neck to get a peek at the girl's computer screen, but the angle was wrong.

No one was in the lobby. The place was quiet. Carly reached over and swiveled the laptop toward her. On it, a document had a makeshift chart labeled *Suites* at the top. Each row had a room number, and in the column beside that was a surname, followed by a comma and an initial. In the right-hand column were the dates reserved by each guest.

Carly scanned the names. When she got to Room 5, she saw the name *Bagley, M.* Her pulse raced.

Could it be this easy? She was trying to see the dates reserved by M. Bagley when she heard footsteps galumphing down the stairs. She quickly swung the laptop back in place, positive her face was tomato red.

Trailed by his daughter, a thickset, balding man in his forties lumbered toward Carly with an extended hand, the coupon in his other hand. "Hey, I'm Artie Bradstone. How ya doing?"

Carly shook his hand and felt her shoulder shift from the force of his meaty arm. "I'm great, thanks."

"So, I hear you're looking to leave some of these coupons here."

Carly smiled. "I am, if that's okay with you, sir. I want to take advantage of tourist season while it lasts."

"Sure. Sure. And none of that 'sir' stuff. It's Artie, okay?" He slapped the stack of Balsam Dell Weekly papers that Don must have left there that morning. "Well, you can leave 'em right next to these, if you want. We'll be sure our guests see them. Can I keep this one for myself?"

"Oh, of course you can. I hope to see you in the restaurant soon," Carly gushed.

"Hey," Artie added, "if you know anyone looking for a place to stay in town, be sure to steer 'em our way, okay? Place might not look like much, but the rooms are clean, and we serve free coffee every morning."

"You got it," Carly said. "Um, actually, I think a friend of mine might be staying here. He was supposed to call me when he got into town, but I haven't been able to reach him. Is there any way you can check?"

Artie's brow furrowed. "We don't give out our guests' names. Sorry."

"What if I give you his name?" Carly offered. "Can you at least tell me if he checked in?" Without giving Artie a chance to refuse, she blurted, "His name is Matt Bagley."

Suspicion hardened Artie's gaze, and he stroked his chin. "Bagley, huh? Funny, the police were here looking for him too."

"The *police*? Oh, my." Carly tried to look shocked.

Artie's expression softened. "Look, if this guy's in trouble with the law, you don't need him, okay? Girl like you, you can have your pick of dudes. Take my advice and forget about him." He turned and plodded in the direction from which he'd come, the coupon still clutched in his hand.

Boy, did he jump to conclusions, Carly thought. He'd obviously assumed Matt was an old boyfriend who'd jilted her.

Hailey looked at Carly and shrugged. "Sorry."

"Me too." Carly hung her head, trying to appear dejected. "If he's here, I just wish I knew what day he got here, you know? He told me he'd be getting here on Tuesday."

Hailey shot a look behind her, then leaned closer to Carly, lowering her voice almost to a whisper. "Then he's a liar, because he got here on Monday. I remember, because he gave me a hard time about his room not being ready. The people who checked out of that room on Sunday left a huge mess, and it took a while to clean up. That guy, Matt, acted like a total jerk. Don't tell my dad I told you, okay?" She made a pleading motion with her hands.

"My lips are sealed," Carly said. "Thank you, Hailey."

"Yeah, well, us girls have to stick together."

Carly hurried out to her car, her heart pumping so hard she thought it might jump out and plop onto her shoulder.

She'd never done anything like that before. She felt mortified and euphoric at the same time. Mostly, she felt bad for tricking Hailey into revealing the date Matt Bagley checked in.

It had helped, though. Immensely.

If Hailey was right, it meant Matt Bagley had been staying in town when his brother Lyle was murdered.

CHAPTER THIRTEEN

WHEN CARLY RETURNED TO THE RESTAURANT, ONLY TWO customers were seated at the counter. The booths were empty.

Great.

Carly stashed her tote in the kitchen, then returned to the dining room. Grant was busy preparing a Sweddar Weather, a grilled sandwich made of swiss cheese and extra-sharp cheddar on marble rye bread.

She felt a pair of eyes on her, then realized one of the men seated at the counter was Ari Mitchell. Heat rushed to her cheeks.

"Hey, Carly," Ari said, smiling in her direction. "How are you today?"

"I'm okay," she said. "And you?" She cringed at how awkward she sounded. Why did she always feel so nervous around Ari?

"Doing okay, as well." He lifted his coffee mug and took a sip. "How's the air conditioner working?"

"Oh, it's great. Really cooled down the apartment. Actually—" She looked at Grant and he grinned. "Grant helped me install it. As it turned out, it was way too heavy for me to carry into the house and up the stairs." *Oh, sure, admit you didn't have the muscles to do it yourself, after you refused Ari's help.*

"Grant's a good man," Ari said, eliciting a huge smile from the young man in question.

Carly's mental antennae shot up. Why did she have a sneaky suspicion that Grant and Ari had been talking about her while she was out?

The man seated at the other end of the counter had finished eating his lunch and was pulling his wallet out of his pants pocket. Muscled and heavily tanned, he sported a tattoo of something slithering out of his short-sleeved T-shirt and curling around his wrist. Carly shuddered.

The man paid in cash, leaving a generous tip for Grant. On his way out, he winked at Carly, then clapped Ari lightly on the shoulder and said, "Take it easy, man. Don't do anything I wouldn't do."

"No fear of that, Kevin," Ari said genially. "See you around."

After he left, Carly said, "Who was that? I've seen him in here before, but I never knew his name."

"That was Kevin O'Toole," Ari said. "He moved here from Kansas a few years ago and started a commercial cleaning company. He does a lot of the office buildings in town. Has his hands in a few other pies, too, from what I hear."

Grant removed Ari's sandwich from the grill, sliced it in half with the slam of a sharp knife, and slid it onto a plate next to a pile of chips and a cup of tomato soup.

"Ah, that looks great. Thanks, Grant."

"I'll leave you to eat your lunch in peace," Carly said, then dashed into the kitchen. She sat at her desk, contemplating what she'd learned at the Peacock.

If Matt Bagley had been in town since Monday, he clearly had the opportunity to murder his brother. As for motive? Well, he wanted that old Cadillac badly, according to Gina. Carly couldn't imagine anyone killing for a car, but then, people had killed for much less. As for the means, he could have used any blunt object, assuming it was heavy enough to kill Lyle.

One thing bothered her. Why would Matt get a room in town if he lived only an hour's drive from Balsam Dell? Not that the Peacock was the lap of luxury, but it still seemed like a waste of money.

Another thought struck her. If he killed his brother, why would he still be hanging around? Wouldn't he want to put as much distance as possible between himself and the scene of the crime?

The kitchen door swung open. Grant came over with a grilled half sandwich oozing with golden cheddar, a pile of chips beside it. "I know you usually share with Suzanne," he said, "so I made you a half sandwich."

"You're a godsend, you know that?" Carly said. "Was everything quiet after I left?" She took a bite of her sandwich.

"Yeah, too quiet," Grant said edgily. "Have you heard anything from Suzanne since this morning?"

Carly shook her head. "No, nothing."

Grant returned to the dining room while she finished her sandwich. By the time Carly joined him, he was standing at the grill, preparing one of the eatery's most popular sandwiches. Smoky Steals the Bacon consisted of smoked gouda and crisp bacon grilled between slices of asiago bread.

A solitary man was seated in a booth, a magazine open before him. His black T-shirt depicted a cartoon-style muscle car with a grinning grille. He was drinking from a bottle of Moxie. Carly started to go over to greet the lone diner but stopped short when she got about ten feet from his table.

It was Matt Bagley. She was almost sure of it.

She hadn't seen him since he was a freshman in high school, but he had the same deep-set eyes and painfully thin face.

She changed direction and instead went behind the counter. The sandwich was just coming off the grill. "I'll deliver that to the customer for you," she said quietly to Grant.

"Sure thing. He wants extra chips, but no soup." Grant plated the sandwich, added a huge pile of chips, and gave it to Carly.

"Hello," she said, strolling over to the customer she was sure was Matt. "Smoky Steals the Bacon?"

"Yeah, whatever. Long as it has bacon."

Carly set down his plate, and the man closed his magazine. On the cover of the mag was an old car—a Chevy, from its front logo. "You're into classic cars, I see." She pasted on a big smile.

He nodded. "Yup."

A *real conversationalist*, Carly thought dryly. Talking to this man was like pulling teeth from a statue.

"Well, I'm Carly, the owner. Please let me know if there's anything else I can get you."

He looked up sharply at her, as if her name had struck a chord. Then he lifted one half of his sandwich and stuck the end in his mouth. Chewing, he nodded with appreciation. "It's good," he mumbled over a mouthful of food.

"Excellent." Carly scooted away and went behind the counter, but barely a minute later he raised a hand to signal her back over.

"What can I get for you?" His sandwich and chips had already been devoured, and his napkin was crumpled on the plate.

"I knew your name was familiar," he said brusquely. "I'm Matt Bagley. Didn't you used to date my brother Lyle?"

Carly almost choked at his bluntness. She couldn't believe he remembered that. "Only for a short while, in high school. That was a *very* long time ago."

His skimpy brows drew together over a deep frown. "Yeah, well, I want to know what *you* know about his murder. Seems like a major coinkydink that he got offed in your parking lot. Didn't he kick you out of this restaurant, like, just a few days ago?"

Struck speechless, Carly just glared at him. She started to respond, but then Grant came around the counter to stand beside her. His expression was placid, but Carly knew better. He was furious.

"I'm sorry, sir," Grant said calmly, "but you're being discourteous. If you have something meaningful to offer to the investigation, please visit the local police station. Thank you." Grant reached over and removed Matt's plate, leaving the man to gawk, openmouthed, at his retreating form.

"I'm outta here," Matt grumbled, throwing a ten-dollar bill and a crumpled yellow coupon on the table. "Soon as I get my change."

He already had one of her coupons. Had he been in his room at the Peacock while she was there?

Carly rang up his bill and returned to Matt's table with his change. "Matt, if there's anything I can do to help, please let me know. I truly am sorry about your brother. I know his death must've been a terrible shock."

He nodded but said nothing. As he strode toward the door, Carly noticed he'd forgotten his car magazine. She grabbed it and followed him. "You forgot this."

He snatched it from her. "Thanks."

Standing so close to him, Carly took the opportunity to study his face. His faintly stubbled cheeks were drawn, his eyes slightly bloodshot. She wondered if he'd been crying over his brother's demise.

"Are you in town to settle your brother's affairs?" Carly asked him.

Matt narrowed his eyes at her. "Not that it's your business, but I'm in town to collect my father's car, which Lyle stole from me. Once I get that, my work is done." He grasped the door handle.

"Do you know if there's going to be a service for Lyle?"

"Don't know. Don't give a flippin' hoot." With that, Matt opened the door and stalked outside into the steamy day.

Carly caught Grant's look, and he slowly shook his head.

"So," Grant said, "that guy who just left was Lyle's brother?"

Carly nodded. "Surly, wasn't he? I can't get a bead on him, though. He has a lot of anger. It seeps from him like sewage. But I learned one thing when I was at the Peacock. Matt checked in on Monday."

Grant's eyes widened. "That's the day before Lyle was murdered."

"Exactly."

"How'd you find out?"

Carly squirmed a bit. "I'm not proud of it, but I did a little snooping. Plus, I sort of…tricked the young clerk at the desk into telling me."

Grant gave up a weak smile. "My boss, the spy." His expression clouded. He lowered his gaze as he scraped the grill absently with a spatula.

"Grant, I know you're troubled over Suzanne, but I get the feeling it's more than just worry. Is there something else?"

He turned to Carly and swallowed, then shook his head dismally. "I did a terrible thing, Carly; I threw Suzanne under the bus. I turned her into the police!"

CHAPTER FOURTEEN

CARLY STEERED HIM OVER TO A BOOTH AT THE BACK, AND THEY sat down facing each other. "Tell me."

"I was eating dinner with my folks at Casa Margherita Tuesday night. Remember I told you we were celebrating Mom getting a full professorship?"

Carly smiled. "I do."

Grant blew out a breath. "Anyway, my dad had paid the bill and we were getting up to leave when I saw Lyle Bagley with his girlfriend heading toward the front door. They must've eaten right about the same time we did."

They were probably celebrating kicking me out of my restaurant, Carly thought bleakly.

"Turned out Lyle had parked only a few spaces away from my dad's car. All of a sudden, this woman gets out of another car and goes running up to Lyle. She gets right in his face, screaming and ranting at him and waving her arms. Lyle finally grabbed her wrist and shoved her away. When she turned to go back to her car, she was sobbing. That's when I saw her face under the light. God help me, Carly, it was Suzanne." He lowered his head into his hands.

Carly's stomach dropped. "Oh no. Did Suzanne see you?"

He nodded miserably. "I think so. I felt so bad for her. I wanted to run over to her to see if she was okay, but before I knew it she'd torn out of the parking lot."

And the next morning he learned that Lyle had been murdered. No wonder he was so distraught.

"Now I understand why you've been so quiet," Carly said. "You told the police what you witnessed, didn't you?"

"I did. My dad was adamant that I tell them the truth. He came with me to the interview, mostly to give me moral support. Gosh, Carly, I felt like the worst kind of traitor."

"I know it wasn't easy, but you did the right thing."

"Did I? I wish I could take it all back."

Carly was quiet for a moment as she mulled over everything. How did Suzanne know Lyle would be at that restaurant? Had she followed him? Stalked him?

Something occurred to Carly. "But Grant, if Tiffany was in the car, she must have witnessed it, too, right? Which means you can't be the only one who told the police about it. She probably reported it too."

"Yeah, but Bagley's car windows were up, so I doubt she heard much of anything. I, unfortunately, heard every word."

Carly tapped the table with her fingers. "Okay, listen. You and I know that Suzanne would never kill anyone. Right now, I think Lyle's little brother makes for a dandy suspect."

"Yeah, me too. I didn't like the way he spoke to you. I hope you weren't mad that I put him in his place."

Carly hesitated. "I wasn't mad, Grant. The way you rushed to my defense was admirable. But I do know how to handle myself in situations like that, even if Matt had me too stunned to respond for a few seconds."

"Okay, I get it." He folded his hands on the table. "It's just that my dad taught me not only to respect women, but to defend them, as well. Sometimes it's a fine line, you know? I'm sorry if I jumped in too quickly."

"Don't be. I totally get it. Besides, in my head I was yelling, 'Yes! Go Grant!'"

He laughed, then his expression sobered. "What are we going to do about Suzanne?"

"Keep our eyes and ears open, for one thing. Looking on the positive side, at least the police didn't detain her."

"Yeah." Grant's eyes brightened. "That means they don't have enough evidence against her, right?"

"That's how I see it. I'm going to try to talk to her later, if she'll take my call."

She debated telling him what she'd learned about Janet Moody's obsession with Lyle and the vandalism to Tiffany's car. For now, she decided to keep it to herself. It was a big leap from vandalism to murder.

~

Later that night, Carly glanced at the wall clock: 6:35 p.m. She groaned. The last customer had left about forty minutes earlier.

Grant was right. Murder was definitely bad for business.

"Maybe we should close up early today," she said to Grant. "I'll put out the *Closed* sign."

He sighed. "Okay. Sure you don't want me to do the floor first?"

"No, we're both drained. I'll do it in the morning when I'm fresh."

Carly went to the door to turn the sign when a face jumped into her vision. "Suzanne!" She opened the door and pulled her inside, then locked the door and turned the *Open* sign to *Closed*.

Suzanne was shaking. She looked wretched.

Carly hugged her, hard. "We've been so worried about you. Are you okay?"

Suzanne nodded, then switched directions and shook her head. "No. I'm...I'm terrible. I feel like the whole town's gossiping about me." She cried into the crumpled tissue she was clutching.

Grant came toward her but halted several feet away, his hands shoved in his pockets.

"I know my hair looks like a chicken's nest, but I honestly don't care. I've been trying to keep it together for Josh's sake, but it's so hard. I finally let him go to his father's. That way he won't have to see me like this. Plus, Jake thought it would be best to take him out of the limelight for a few days, and I agreed." She started to cough uncontrollably, her sobs making it worse.

Grant flew behind the counter and returned with a glass of water.

"Thank you." She drank several gulps and gave him the glass. "I'm not going to stay long, but I have a few things I need to say. Grant, I know you talked to the police about seeing me Tuesday night, and I want you to know I'm not mad. Honest, I'm not. If you were my son, I'd have told you to do exactly the same thing."

Carly glanced at Grant. His face looked ready to crumple. "Suzanne—"

"You guys are the best boss and coworker I ever had, and I've had a lot. I only came here to give my notice so you can hire someone to replace me. I can't turn in my key because the cops have it, but you can get it from them."

"Not a chance," Carly declared. "I won't accept your notice."

"You have to. I can't come back. I *can't.*"

Carly looped her arm through Suzanne's and walked her over to the closest booth. It felt like déjà vu all over again. She pushed her onto the bench and sat down beside her. She motioned to Grant to sit opposite them.

"Tell me what happened at the restaurant that night. How did it all start?"

Suzanne sniffled hard. "That day, Tuesday, after I got home. I couldn't stop thinking about Lyle evicting you for that stuck-up twit of a girlfriend of his. It ate at me, like a…a disease. I came back here after everyone was gone, thinking maybe I could talk to her, make her see reason. Which was totally stupid, right? People like that only care about themselves. That red car was the only one here, so I figured she was home alone, if she was there at all. I was thinking about what I'd say, how I'd approach her, when I saw Lyle drive in. For someone who thinks he's such a big shot, he drove a pretty boring car. He didn't even look my way, so I slumped low in my front seat and waited while he went inside. A few minutes later, they came out together, dressed like they were going to the queen's palace."

"So, you followed them?"

Suzanne nodded. "I don't know what I was thinking. I was behaving like a stalker. After they got to the restaurant, I left. I told myself to drop it, to leave it alone. I drove around for a while, but then I went back. I–I couldn't stop myself."

Carly squeezed her shoulder.

"I waited till they came out of that fancy restaurant. Tiffany got in the car first and Lyle closed her door. He was walking around to the driver's side when I went up to him and let him have it. I called him every nasty name I could think of, told him what a piece of trash he was. And now...and now..." She broke down into sobs again.

Grant looked helplessly at Carly.

"It's okay, take your time," Carly soothed.

After another minute or so, Suzanne pulled in a long, calming breath. "I know you're both wondering why I had such hateful feelings toward Lyle. I want to explain."

"It's not really our business," Grant said hoarsely, about the first words he'd spoken since Suzanne had arrived.

"No, it is." She pushed her hair away from her face. "Because I caused a lot of trouble, for both of you, and it's only fair that you understand the history." She took another gulp from the water glass Grant had set down in front of her. "My ex-husband, Jake, used to be an occasional gambler. Ten scratch tickets a week, maybe. Betting on football cards, that sort of thing." Her gaze darkened. "And then one night, he met Lyle Bagley at a buddy's house. They got playing poker, and one thing led to another. Lyle let him win a few times. It was all part of his plan. He knew a sucker when he saw one. Pretty soon Jake was losing game after game, throwing away hundreds every week. I didn't know it at the time, but Jake had started dipping into our savings to cover his losses, money we were saving for Josh's college fund."

Carly felt sick to her stomach. "Suzanne, I'm so sorry."

"Oh, but wait, there's more!" Tears filled Suzanne's eyes. "Once Lyle had Jake hooked on poker, he introduced him to the joys of offtrack betting. Jake got totally immersed in it. By the time I realized how bad it was, he'd siphoned thousands from Josh's college fund. And then the final straw—the reason I kicked his sorry behind to the curb. Jake found someone willing to forge my signature and took out a second mortgage on our home. When we started to get dunning notices in the mail, I was shocked. I confronted Jake, and he confessed. We ended up having to sell the house to avoid foreclosure. Guess how much equity we ended up with? Zero! It's what the bank calls a short sale."

Grant looked horrified. He started to say something, but then shook his head and remained silent.

"That's when I called it quits. I took Josh, moved in with my mom, and told Jake not to darken our lives ever again."

So many pieces clicked into place for Carly. Suzanne's animosity toward Lyle. The vague threat she issued the day he evicted Carly. Chasing him down at the restaurant and confronting him. Her loathing of Lyle was the result of a long, sad history.

Suzanne let out a shaky sigh. "Listen, I better go. My mom will worry if I stay away from the house much longer." She slid out of the booth and got to her feet. "I–I'm sorry, Carly, but I won't be coming in to work anymore. You'll need to find someone to replace me."

"I won't allow you to quit," Carly insisted. "Grant and I will hold down the fort until you're ready to return. Take as long as you need."

Suzanne shook her head. "That might be a long time, Carly. You might have to wait till I get out of prison."

CHAPTER FIFTEEN

CARLY RETURNED HOME FRIDAY EVENING TO AIR-CONDITIONED comfort. After the grueling day she'd had, she wanted nothing more than to flop on her sofa and indulge in some mindless television, followed by the late news. After that, she planned to crawl into bed with a book and read until her eyelids refused to stay open.

By 10:00, though, she was too tired to stay up any longer. She changed into a summer nightie and dropped into bed.

Despite her fatigue, her sleep was broken by fractured dreams and strange images. The only face she remembered from her dreams was that of a little beige dog, his big brown eyes gazing up at her with something close to devotion.

On Saturday morning, she awakened with a new resolve. In spite of her current troubles, she felt more hopeful than she had in days. She needed to take control of her situation, and that meant being more proactive.

First things first: call Dr. Anne about the dog. Her dream had triggered a whole new set of worries about the pup she'd dubbed Havarti. Had his owner finally claimed him? If not, was he in a safe place, like a no-kill shelter? After leaving a message on the veterinarian's voice mail, Carly showered, dressed, and drove to her restaurant.

On the way, she took stock of what she knew so far and, more importantly, what she didn't know. She knew that Matt Bagley had a motive for killing Lyle, and that he'd been in town the night of the murder. Was that enough? Would he really kill over an old

Caddy? Or did Lyle have something else Matt coveted enough to murder for?

Then there was Janet Moody. Carly desperately wanted to talk to her. If the restaurant got as busy today as she hoped it would, there wouldn't be much time to seek her out. Besides, what excuse could she use? Maybe Gina could help her come up with a plan.

The temperature felt cooler today—a blessed relief from the heat of the past few days. The skies were a cerulean blue, and a mild breeze stirred the trees. Temps in the mideighties were predicted, with nary a raindrop in sight to spoil the summer activities on Balsam Dell's town green.

Tiffany's red Nissan was the only car in the parking lot when Carly arrived at the restaurant. She hadn't seen Tiffany since the day Lyle's body was found.

Carly unlocked the back door to her eatery, turned on the lights and air conditioning, and went to work. By 11:00 a.m., the floor had been cleaned, the bathroom was spotless, and she'd gotten a solid start on the day's food prep.

Now all she needed were customers.

She was disappointed, but not surprised, that Suzanne didn't show up. Carly had hoped she might change her mind overnight, but…no such luck. She went to the front door and opened up for business. The sight of the town green, bustling with activity, made her heart sing.

Balsam Dell's Saturdays on the Green always began on the third Saturday of every June and continued through Labor Day weekend. Today was kickoff day, as Carly thought of it. Vendors had already set up booths and tables and were busily hawking their wares.

She pushed the front door slightly open to take in the sounds and smells. Laughter and chatter rode the breeze over the delectable scent of fried dough and the tangy aromas from the hot dog cart. If she got a chance around midday, she'd take a short break and check out the offerings. By then, Grant should be there to cover for her. She was keeping her fingers crossed for a cotton candy machine.

Carly was delighted when a mom, dad, and two teenage boys came in. All were dressed as if they'd just come from playing a few rounds of tennis.

She led them to a booth and handed them a set of menus, and they made their choices quickly. "We're, like, starving," one of the teens announced, flashing a mouthful of clear braces.

"I'll have your orders in a jiffy," Carly promised, already missing Suzanne.

As Carly was preparing two Classics, a Some Like It Hot, and a Farmhouse Cheddar Sleeps with the Fishes, more customers entered the restaurant.

Don't freak out. You can handle it.

In between grilling sandwiches, she scrambled to get everyone seated. She noticed that several customers were clutching her yellow coupons. Were they all staying at the Peacock?

The front door opened again, and a sudden feeling of panic gripped her by the throat. When she saw the familiar face smiling at her from the doorway, the feeling subsided and she blew out a gust of air.

"Hey." Grant scurried around the counter. "I begged off early again at the sub shop."

"You can't imagine how happy I am to see you."

He went to the kitchen and returned a minute later wearing a clean apron and vinyl gloves. "You want me to take over the grill or be the server?"

"The grill," Carly said.

"By the way, if you see a lot of people come in with those coupons," Grant informed her, "I dropped bunches of them off early this morning at my barber, the grocery mart…" He started to recite all the establishments he'd visited.

"That's great," Carly interrupted. "Tell me later."

For the next three hours, they worked together like a well-oiled machine. By 2:30, things had quieted down. Carly was in the kitchen eating the half Sweddar Weather Grant had made for her when a welcome visitor pushed open the kitchen door.

"Hey, what's cooking? You taking a break?"

"Gina! What are you doing here?"

"I've got a table set up across the street," she said, her brunette curls bouncing around her full cheeks. "My cards are selling like the proverbial hotcakes! I'm afraid I'll run out of inventory."

"That's great, I think," Carly said, as they returned to the dining room. "Do you want a sandwich? A cup of coffee?"

"Not right now, even though I'm starving. Carly, I *reaaally* think you ought to take advantage of the crowds. There's lots of hungry shoppers out there. Can you whip up a dozen or so sandwiches and wrap them? I'll make some room at my table and you can peddle them there. I'm telling you, you'll sell out in no time."

Carly laughed. "Gina, I'd love to, but I can't leave. Suzanne isn't working today so it's just Grant and me."

Gina made a face, then her eyes popped wide open. "Do you have a basket? You can make the sandwiches, wrap them in parchment or something, and I'll sell them at my table."

Before Carly could protest, Grant was at the grill lining up six Classics for grilling.

Gina squealed with delight. "I gotta run, but hurry over with those sandwiches, okay?" She gave Carly a sideways hug and dashed out the front door.

Carly was still chuckling when Grant said, "What if we wrap up half sandwiches instead of whole ones. With all the other food out there, people might be more inclined to buy a half over a whole."

"That's a smart idea. Let's do it."

Grant flipped over the sandwiches sizzling on the grill. "Can you dig up a basket somewhere? I think I saw one in the coat closet in the kitchen."

"You're right." When she first opened the restaurant, her sister had sent her a congratulatory fruit and chocolate arrangement in a beautiful wicker basket. Carly had saved the basket.

She went into the kitchen and found it, exactly where Grant had seen it. After wiping it with a damp cloth, she lined it with two clean dish towels and returned to the dining room.

Grant was ready with the sandwiches. He slid them onto the cutting board, sliced them crosswise, and wrapped the halves in parchment. Carly tucked them inside the basket and hurried across the street.

The noise level had risen, in part because of the swingy notes of a jazz tune being played at the far corner of the green. Carly wended her way around the myriad booths and tables, her senses tantalized by all the amazing foods. At one table, a crafter was selling animal face door decorations. A whimsical cow with a pink bow caught her attention, but she needed to get the sandwiches to Gina's table while they were still warm.

Carly spied the cotton candy machine—yay! She'd definitely stop there before the day's festivities ended. The vendors were supposed to be gone by 6:00, but Carly knew that some were inclined to linger, especially if they were experiencing brisk sales.

She finally spotted Gina. Her table was behind the Revolutionary War monument that dominated the center of the green. Gina waved excitedly when she saw Carly. Carly waved back and wove her way over to her.

Patting the corner of her table, Gina took in an exaggerated breath. "Man, oh man, I can already smell those grilled cheeses. Put them here."

Carly set down her basket, her attention drawn to the stunning array of cards Gina had displayed in neat rows. Designs made from minuscule scrolls of tightly rolled paper depicted various animals, flowers, and mountain scenes. "Gina, these cards—I'm speechless. Is this the quilling technique you were telling me about?"

"It is, and thank you," her friend said, a blush tingeing her cheeks. "How much you want to sell the sandwiches for?"

"They're only halves, so maybe…three bucks?"

"Sounds good to me." She pulled a blank note card from a box on the ground. In elegant calligraphy, she wrote *Grilled Cheddar Halves*, and below that *$3*. She stuck it inside the basket where it would be clearly visible.

"Perfect," Carly said. "Grant's covering for me and he's alone, so I can't stay long. I'd forgotten how much fun Saturdays on the Green are, especially with the music!"

"Yeah, today there's a band from the college playing swing tunes. One of them used linoleum tiles he found in his garage to set up a tiny dance floor. The old folks are having a blast!"

"I can tell," Carly said and glanced toward the bandstand. Two couples were kicking up their heels, literally, as they boogied to a jitterbug number.

"A classical trio is supposed to replace them later to wind things down, I heard. There's a lot of competition for that spot. But I like the swing music."

Two twentysomething men came up behind Carly. One poked his head around her and bleated, "Hey, look—grilled cheese! I'll take one. You want one, Ben?"

His friend nodded, and they each paid for their own. They strode off wearing blissful expressions as they inhaled their sandwich halves.

Gina smiled and rearranged the basket. "These aren't going to last long, are they?"

"That's okay. It was kind of an experiment, anyway." Carly looked around, regretting that she couldn't stay longer. "I'll try to stop back later. I'm hoping to score some cotton candy from that wagon. But right now, Grant's alone—"

"I know," Gina said wistfully. "What's happening with Suzanne?"

Carly sighed. "She hasn't been arrested yet. At least that's a positive. She thinks the whole town is talking about her, so she's not planning to come back to work for a while." *Or ever.*

"Poor woman," Gina said, shaking her head.

Customers were trying to look at Gina's cards, and a young girl and her mom were reaching for grilled cheese halves. Carly stepped aside. "Hey, I'll get out of your way. But stop in after you close up, okay?"

Carly crossed the street and went back inside her restaurant. More customers had come in, and it was obvious Grant was having to juggle duties. She hurried into the kitchen, scrubbed her hands, and returned to the dining room wearing a crisp apron.

Three booths were occupied, and two men were seated at the counter. "It got busy," Grant said. "Glad you're back."

Way to make me feel guilty, Grant.

"I'm not blaming you, Carly," Grant added, as if he'd read her mind. "You deserve a break. It's just...hard without Suzanne, you know?"

"I know it is."

He dropped a Some Like It Hot onto the cutting board, sliced it in half, and set it down next to a cup of soup. "That's for Kevin." Grant lifted his chin toward the end of the counter, where Kevin O'Toole was engrossed in reading something on his cell phone. Carly took the sandwich and went over to him. "There you go. Enjoy your meal."

"Well, thank you!" he said, a little too loudly. "Nothing like a sandwich from a grilled cheese lady to make my day." He set down his cell phone and rubbed his hands over the dish.

Carly smiled, but something in his tone creeped her out.

He lifted a corner of one of his sandwich halves, examining the melted pepper jack cheese and coating of Tabasco layered between the slices of sun-dried tomato bread. "Excellent! Extra Tabasco, just like I ordered. My man Grant knows how I like it—hot and heavy. Right, Grant?"

Grant glanced over and raised his spatula in a halfhearted acknowledgment, then immediately turned back to the grill.

Eager to get away from Kevin, Carly was moving toward the booths to see if anyone needed anything when a guitar riff from an old rock number blared from his phone. For a moment Kevin froze, then he winked at Carly and cut off the call. "The lady can wait," he said in a suggestive tone and took a bite of his sandwich.

After giving out coffee refills, Carly was putting the coffee pot back on the burner when a man sauntered in. She knew the face from somewhere. If only she could remember—

That was it! Officer Palmer, a.k.a. Columbo.

His black hair slicked back into a curl at his neck, Palmer's biceps bulged from beneath a forest green polo shirt that hugged his muscled chest. A gold medallion of some sort, possibly a religious medal, dangled from a heavy chain around his neck. He smiled at Carly, said, "Nice to see you," and then went over and slid onto the stool next to Kevin O'Toole.

Kevin grinned and slapped him on the back. "Hey, there's my favorite boy in blue."

"Hands off the merchandise, Kevin," Palmer said tightly. "In case you haven't noticed, I'm not your boy and I'm not wearing blue."

Carly's ears perked. *Sounded like Columbo was getting his dander up.*

Kevin's face flushed, his grin collapsing like a spent balloon. "You don't have to get your shorts in a knot, copper. It was only a joke."

Carly waited until the air settled, then asked Palmer, "What can I get you, sir?"

"Anything he wants," Kevin blurted, looking almost angry. "My treat."

Palmer ordered the Vermont Classic and a cup of java. She relayed the order to Grant and poured the man a mug of coffee.

"You don't remember me, do you?" Palmer asked her, a genuine smile returning.

"Sure, I do. You questioned me about a murder in my kitchen. How could I forget that?" With a smile so sugary sweet it almost gagged her, she walked away to let him ponder her words.

Almost instantly, she chided herself for acting snarky. Palmer was an officer of the law. He'd only been doing his job that day, or what he'd thought of as his job. As for Kevin, he was turning into a regular, paying customer. She needed to cut them both some slack. Whatever their personal issues were, it was between them.

Both booths emptied around the same time. Carly refilled Kevin's and Palmer's coffee mugs.

"Hey, whatever happened to that dog?" Palmer asked. He gave her an exaggerated wink, as if he were doing her a favor by not revealing where he'd seen the dog.

"As far as I know, he's at a shelter waiting to be adopted." She pictured Havarti's sweet, furry face and big brown eyes, and her heart clutched. "The vet thought I should adopt him. But working in a restaurant twelve or thirteen hours a day makes that impossible."

"What you need," Kevin said, after swallowing the last bite of his sandwich, "is a real pet, like mine." He stuck out his right arm and rotated it slowly.

Carly jumped backward a step. "Good gravy on a rolling reptile! What the heck kind of pet is that?"

Kevin laughed, but Palmer just shook his head. "Meet Slinky, my boa constrictor," Kevin said. "I had the tattoo artist make an exact replica of him. Did you ever see such a beautiful snake?"

Carly knew her face registered her horror, but she couldn't help it. The thing was orange, gray, and brown, mottled together in a twisty pattern that made shivers run down her spine. In her opinion, the words *beautiful* and *snake* didn't even belong in the same sentence.

"Do you seriously have a pet boa constrictor?" she asked Kevin.

Looking disgusted, Palmer tossed his crumpled napkin on his empty plate and pulled out his wallet.

Kevin's hand shot out and grabbed Palmer's wrist, his eyes narrowing. "I told you, Cuz, it's on me. Now put that wallet away."

Palmer pulled his arm back and shoved his wallet back in his pocket. He drained his mug and said to Carly, "Thank you for the delicious lunch, Ms. Hale. For what it's worth, I think you should adopt that dog. Life is short. Don't waste a minute of it."

He swiveled around and strode out, leaving Kevin to pay the bill.

A big smile returned to illuminate Kevin's face. Carly had to admit, with his even features, tanned face, and full head of sandy hair, he was good-looking, in a weirdly unappealing way.

"Don't mind him," Kevin said casually, waving a hand at the door. "He gets testy sometimes, but we're close buds. We always have each other's backs."

Her question about the snake apparently forgotten, Kevin paid the bill, including a hefty tip for Grant, and left. Carly breathed a sigh of relief as he disappeared through the door.

The booth customers had already paid their bills and left. As it neared 4:00, the eatery emptied out again, but Carly knew it wouldn't last.

At the ping of a text, Grant dug his cell phone out of his pocket. He peered at it, looked up at Carly, and tapped out a quick message.

"Um, Carly, that was a friend of mine. Do you think I can take a twenty-minute break? I'm going to meet him across the street on the green."

His mention of a friend surprised Carly. Not that he shouldn't have friends, but she'd never heard him talk about any of them. "Well sure, Grant," Carly said. "You haven't taken a break since you got here. Take all the time you want."

His face brightened and he removed his apron, folding it and tucking it under the counter. "Thanks, Carly. I'll be back in twenty! Hey, Chief," he said as he sailed out the door.

Chief? *Uh oh*, Carly thought. Was he here to deliver bad news?

Holloway glanced around, then removed his hat and strode up to the counter. Without preamble, he said, "Carly, how did you know Matt Bagley was staying at the Peacock?"

Carly grappled for words. "Um, now that you mention it, Chief, Don Frasco told me. He goes over there every week to leave his free newspapers, and he saw him sitting in the lobby."

"I see. And what led Frasco to share that with you? Are you friends?"

"Not exactly," Carly said. "I babysat him once when he was a kid, and he remembered that. Now he's nagging me about us solving the murder together."

Almost instantly, Carly regretted her words. Much as Don could be a pain in the posterior, she didn't want to get him in trouble.

"He didn't do anything wrong, Chief. You should know that Matt came into the restaurant yesterday and blurted out that he was only in town to collect Lyle's vintage Caddy. He acted pretty smug about it too. He had the nerve to suggest *I* was responsible for his brother's murder because Lyle evicted me. Doesn't that sound like a classic case of trying to deflect guilt?"

Holloway looked mildly amused. "I'm not going to comment on that, but I'm telling you now, don't go playing detective. I saw those coupons you left at the Peacock, so I knew you were up to something."

"I was just doing a little advertising, Chief. Those coupons were distributed all over town, not just at the Peacock." That part, at least, was true, thanks to Grant.

He looked dubiously at her. "About your friend Suzanne Rivers. Someone came forward and gave her an alibi for the time of the murder."

Carly felt her jaw drop. "Yes! I knew the truth would—"

"Unfortunately," Holloway interrupted, "it turned out to be a false one. She didn't do herself any favors having someone lie for her."

"I…can't believe she'd do that, Chief. Can I ask who it was?"

"Never hurts to ask, but I've already said more than I should've. Now, just one last thing. Has Officer Palmer tried to question you again?"

Carly almost laughed. "And you call *him* Columbo? No, he came in for a sandwich earlier, but he never brought up the, you know, murder."

"Good. Something's up with him, but I can't quite pin it down. I'm telling you that in confidence so please keep it to yourself." Holloway put his hat on. "The main thing is, no more playing spy games, are we clear?"

"I understand."

Three teenaged boys strolled in, all sporting ball caps and sunglasses. They made a beeline for a booth near the back. "I'll be with you in a jiffy," Carly called to them.

Carly breathed out a sigh of relief after the chief left. She took the boys' orders and was preparing their sandwiches when Grant rushed through the door. "Sorry, I'm about five minutes late."

"You're not late. Did you meet your friend?"

Grant beamed. "Yeah, a couple of them. It was great."

Carly wondered what had given Grant such a mood lift in the short time he'd been gone.

They started to get busy again. Carly was pleased that things had picked up so much since the day before.

By 6:00, things had quieted down. Across the street, on the green, most of the vendors were packing up their tables. Many had already left. Carly tried to see if Gina was still there, but the monument blocked her line of vision.

Taking a break in the kitchen to check her messages, she saw that she'd missed an earlier text from Gina. *I'll be there by 7, but watch this* was all it said, right below a video. Carly tapped the arrow for the video.

At the corner of the green, on the makeshift bandstand, three young musicians—two violinists and a cellist—were playing a familiar classical piece. One of the violinists was a young woman with chin-length, strawberry blond hair. The other two were men, one playing a violin and—

Oh goodness gracious.

The young man playing the cello was Grant.

CHAPTER SIXTEEN

CARLY WATCHED AND LISTENED, HER HEART POUNDING. THE sheer beauty of the sound reaching her ears astounded her.

The video played for about a minute, and then she tapped the arrow and watched it again. It wasn't until she felt tears rolling down her cheeks that she realized Grant was standing beside her.

"Pachelbel's Canon in D Major," he said quietly.

Carly stopped the video and pressed her hand to her damp eyes. "Grant, that was…stunning. I'm in total awe." She turned to look at him. His eyes were more animated than she'd ever seen them, and yet he wasn't smiling.

She swallowed, her mind snapping the puzzle pieces neatly into place. "Your folks want you to be a professional musician, don't they? That's why they're against you going to culinary school."

Grant went over to the desk and pulled up a chair opposite Carly. He straddled it and sat down. "You're a smart woman. You guessed it exactly. My mom and dad are both classical musicians, and they both have PhDs. Dad teaches music history at the college, and Mom teaches musical composition and orchestration. Dad's a brilliant violinist. If you could hear him—" His eyes grew damp. "Sorry."

Carly touched his arm. "Why didn't you ever tell me? Aren't you proud to be such a gifted cellist?"

"Yeah, of course I am. But try being a nineteen-year-old Black male who'd rather listen to classical music than rock or hip-hop. One of my friends sneaked up on me once when I was in the car waiting for Mom. I was listening to Yo-Yo Ma play Bach's Cello Suite No. 5. Know what my friend said? 'Hey, Grandpa, did you bring your cane and your dentures?'"

Carly shook her head. "Some people will never get it, Grant, but that's on them, not on you. If those two young musicians I saw in that video with you are any indication, I'd say they think you're pretty special."

"Thanks." His dark-brown eyes danced a bit. "I was named— well, partly anyway—after William Grant Still. He was a composer and a conductor, the first African American to conduct a major American symphony orchestra. I think Mom and Dad had already envisioned my future when they bestowed that name on me."

"And I'm sure you've already fulfilled that vision."

"All the more reason they're against my going to culinary school. If I study music, they'll pay my full tuition. One of the reasons they bought me the car is so I could commute to the college. If I choose culinary school? They won't pay a penny. They're adamant that it would be a waste of my time and talent." Grant glanced toward the swinging door. "Maybe I'd better get back out there in case—"

"Wait, I want to ask you something. Aside from your obvious flair for flavors and recipes, why is becoming a chef so important to you?"

Grant linked his hands together over the chair. "When I was in middle school, I used to sit at lunch with a kid named Trey. His folks were on a health food kick, an excessive one. All Trey ever had in his lunch box were cut up raw fruits and veggies and whole grain crackers that tasted like compressed sawdust."

Carly grimaced. "Poor kid."

"Every day, I'd see Trey almost choking over his lunch. Kids have about double the number of taste buds that adults do, and veggies—especially greens—often taste bitter to them. In Trey's case it was extreme, but his folks were blind to it. One day I told my mom about it, and she said his parents only want what's best for him. But I could tell that it bothered her too."

"So, what did you do?"

"I got thinking about what I could do to make his food taste better and still be healthy. I experimented with tofu-based dips and mild spices and managed to whip up a few that came out pretty decent. I brought some to school the next day with my own raw veggies and gave Trey his own separate container. When he tasted it with his carrot sticks, his eyes almost burst out of his head."

"Success!"

"I gave him a list of the ingredients and asked him to share it with his folks. He came in the next day with a sealed envelope addressed to Mr. and Mrs. Robinson. He said I had to give it to my parents."

"Did you do it?"

"Yeah, but I was terrified. I figured I was in big trouble. Inside the envelope was a letter from Trey's mom. Dad read it first, then gave it to Mom. When I finally dared to look at them, they were both smiling. Trey's mom praised me for being such a caring friend. After that, they made their own dips for him. Over time they got more lenient with food, but that was a rough period for Trey."

Carly rubbed her eyes with her fingers. "You know, Grant, you're making me cry, and that is not a good look on me. But I have to say this. You are amazing."

He looked uncomfortable. "Thank you, but that's not why I shared that story. I'm trying to explain why food is so important to me. I want to design recipes that every palate can enjoy, even the most sensitive ones. There's enough variety out there to please everyone. We just have to take the time to create it."

Carly wanted to say so much more, but she knew it would make him feel self-conscious. "Just promise me one thing. You won't ever stop playing the cello."

He reached over and touched Carly's wrist. "I promise. I won't ever stop playing the cello."

"Good."

Grant stood and set the chair back in place. "But I'm going to be a chef."

CHAPTER SEVENTEEN

GRANT LEFT SHORTLY AFTER THAT. HE AND THE TWO FRIENDS he'd met on the green earlier had tickets to attend an outdoor music festival in Manchester. The twinkle in his eye as he was dashing out the door suggested it wasn't only the music he was looking forward to.

His dilemma over culinary school stuck in Carly's mind. No wonder he was working so hard to save money. His parents were taking a hard line, refusing to fund his culinary school tuition. But Grant was following his own personal dream, and Carly applauded him for his dedication. If only he and his folks could find some middle ground, it would be a win-win for all of them.

Carly was finishing up the final tasks of the day when Gina came in. She clutched Carly's basket under one arm. Hanging from her other shoulder was a black, suitcase-like contraption.

"Hey, I wondered where you were." Carly took the basket and set it on the counter.

"Got here as soon as I could. I had to load up my table and all my other junk and get it into my car first."

"How was business? Did you sell a lot of cards?"

Gina's brown eyes beamed. "Business was great. When people found out I did mail order, they were grabbing my business cards like they were free chocolate bars. First things first, though." She plunked her suitcase down on the nearest stool and unzipped the cover. She pulled out a clear plastic cup filled with sugary blue fluff, covered in plastic wrap. "I figured you didn't have time to stop for one, so I got this for you." She slid it across the counter.

"My cotton candy! Bless your sugary little heart." Carly tore off the plastic, plucked out a blob of the blue confection, popped it into her mouth, and then licked her fingers. "Yum. I'm saving the rest for later." She set the cup down on the counter.

"Now. As to the grilled cheeses." Gina plucked an envelope from the satchel. "Sold all of them, except for two." She gave Carly the money.

Carly peeked into the envelope. "You had two halves left?"

"I did not," Gina said. "There's a woman, a homeless veteran, who's been living out of her car. She has a job, and she's saving money to put a security deposit on an apartment. A few people have offered her a room in their home, no charge, but she refuses to accept what she thinks of as charity. She's a really nice woman, and I told her you'd want her to have the sandwich halves."

"That's a given," Carly said, disturbed to think of a veteran living out of her car. "When you see her, please tell her she can eat in here any time, at no charge."

"I don't think she'll accept, but you can tell her yourself," Gina said. "She'll be coming by to thank you any minute. Her name's Becca Avery. She wanted to go freshen up before she meets you."

"Um, this might sound kind of nosy, but…where does she freshen up?"

Gina closed her satchel and zipped it. "She works for a company called Knock-Out Dirt Commercial Cleaning and does night cleaning in some of the downtown office buildings. One of the buildings has a workout room the tenants can use during office hours, so her boss gave her carte blanche to use the shower and bathroom. She cleans it, so naturally she leaves it spotless."

"That's good." Carly felt relieved to hear that.

"She also has permission to park her car behind one of the

buildings across the green. And the owner told her she can use his facilities any time."

"I'm glad she's getting support from so many directions. Who owns the building where she parks?"

Gina smiled. "Ari Mitchell."

Carly felt that familiar flush creep up her neck. Was it noticeable? "Wow, that's...really nice of him."

She was grateful for the distraction when the door opened, and a young woman came in. Carly pegged her to be in her late twenties. Garbed in black shorts and a light green, U.S. Army tee, she wore her dark blond hair in a thick braid that trailed down her back.

Ramrod straight, the woman smiled and took a tentative step forward. "Is it okay if I come in?"

"Come on over, Becca, and meet Carly," Gina said, smiling at her. "Carly, this is Becca. Becca, Carly Hale, owner of this wonderful eatery."

The woman strode over, reached across the counter, and took Carly's hand in a firm grip. "You made my day with those delicious sandwiches. Thank you for your generosity."

"I'm glad you liked them, but that wasn't much food. Can I whip up a whole sandwich for you? I have cheddar, Havarti, swiss, provolone—"

"Honestly, I'm fine," Becca said, thwarting Carly's attempt to feed her. "But thank you for the offer."

Gina hoisted her black satchel onto her shoulder. "I wish I could stay, but I promised my dad I'd have dinner with him, and I'm already kinda late." Gina grinned and looked at Carly. "Ever since I told him that you and I reconnected, he's been asking for you. He said he misses those Saturday nights when he used to make his homemade pizza for us."

The happy memory made Carly smile. "I miss those times too. Tell him I hope to see him soon."

"I will. Later, guys." Gina bade them both goodbye and hustled out the door.

After Gina left, Becca stood there somewhat awkwardly. "Is there anything I can help you with?"

"No, but I do want to thank you for your service to me and to our country. Gina told me a little about your circumstances."

Becca gave her a crisp salute. "My pleasure." She pointed at a stool. "May I sit?"

"Absolutely. Would you like a soda? Or water?"

Becca smiled. "I wouldn't mind one of those bottles of root beer."

Carly fetched a bottle for her and set it on the counter. "Tell me about yourself. Are you from this area?"

"Northern Vermont," Becca said, unscrewing the cap. "A little farm town almost on the Canadian border." She took a long swig from her bottle.

"How long were you in the service?"

Becca set down her bottle. "Four years total, three of them in Afghanistan. I was lucky; I came back with all my parts intact. The unlucky part? After I got home, I found out my grandmother had died."

"Oh, Becca, I'm so sorry. Weren't you notified of her passing?"

She shook her head. "Gram was my only family. I found out she'd been put in a nursing home while I was gone, and her house was sold to pay for it."

Carly's heart broke for the young woman. Four years serving her country and she returned to find herself homeless. And without any family.

"Luckily, Gram had one of those big old Lincolns. It was her pride and joy. It's ancient, but it runs. Before she went into the nursing home, she asked her mechanic to hold onto it for me till I got home." She laughed. "The back seat's the size of an army transport plane, so it's comfortable sleeping in for now."

"But it won't be once the cold weather sets in," Carly said with concern.

"That's okay. I have a few aces up my sleeve. The Veterans' Employment and Training Service helped me find my current job. Doesn't pay a whole lot, but I opened a bank account and I've been stashing away my earnings."

A loud thump from the overhead apartment made them both jump, Becca more so than Carly. "Sorry, force of habit," Becca said. "I'm planning to go to school to become a certified nursing assistant, like the ones who took care of Gram in the nursing home. Those people are like angels on earth. But first I want to get a decent apartment. I'm pretty sure I can get tuition help through the GI Bill, but I want to get a computer first. So far I've been using the computers in the library."

"Gina tells me you know Ari Mitchell," Carly said, then wanted to kick herself. Was that a tiny worm of jealousy she'd detected creeping into her tone?

"Ari. Gosh, yes. What a great guy. He worked it out with Chief Holloway that it's okay for me to park the Lincoln behind his building and stay there overnight. So far, no one's objected. I know how to keep a low profile," she added with a chuckle.

A series of thumps, followed by a loud cry, echoed from above.

"Sounds like someone might need help," Becca said, one leg poised to leap off her stool.

"There's a tenant living above, a woman named Tiffany," Carly explained. "We'll have to go outside to get to her apartment. She has a separate entrance behind the building with its own staircase."

Becca bolted off her stool. "Then what are we waiting for? Let's go."

CHAPTER EIGHTEEN

FINDING THE DOOR LEADING TO TIFFANY'S PRIVATE ENTRYWAY unlocked, they bustled up the stairs, Becca taking the lead. At the top of a dark and somewhat musty-smelling staircase was a wooden door painted flamingo pink.

From behind the pink door, a colorful sampling of explicit curses melded with a series of crashing sounds. Becca knocked so hard on the door that Carly's heart jumped. "Tiffany? Are you all right in there?"

The noises abruptly ceased. Becca knocked again. "We're here to help, miss. Can we come in?"

They heard the sound of a lock disengaging, and then the pink door was suddenly wrenched open. Both Carly and Becca nearly tumbled into the room.

"Oh, it's you," Tiffany hissed at Carly. "What do you want? And who are you?" she snapped at Becca.

Annoyed by Tiffany's rudeness, Carly ignored the question. "You were making so much noise, we thought you were in trouble. We only came up to see if you needed help. From below, it sounded like a hippopotamus had escaped into your apartment."

Clad in jeweled flip-flops, red short-shorts, and an oversized white tee, Tiffany glared at Carly through bloodshot eyes. Her eyelids were puffy, her face bare of makeup. She looked as if she hadn't slept in days. A pricey-looking gold chain hung from around her neck. Two charms—one plain and one glittery—dangled at the cusp of her cleavage. "As you can see, I'm fine. So, is that all you wanted?"

A pang of sympathy ripped through Carly. Despite the crusty shell Tiffany was trying to project, it was evident she'd been shattered by Lyle's death. Once again, Carly wondered if she had friends or family close by to comfort her.

Becca stepped forward and held out her hand. "Miss, please let me introduce myself. I'm First Lieutenant Becca Avery, former U.S. Army. I'm a civilian now, but my training is sort of ingrained in me. I hope we didn't intrude on your privacy."

Tiffany looked at the proffered hand but made no move to shake it.

Becca dropped her hand and said, "If you're sure you're all right, we'll leave you in peace. For a while there, it sounded like a knock-down drag-out was going on in here." She gave Tiffany a disarming smile.

Carly shot a glance around the room. Aside from the piles of papers and magazines strewn all around, along with a massive television blasting some crime show, the room was surprisingly cozy. Painted a soft shade of rose, the walls were graced with delicate white flowers stenciled just below the ceiling. The furnishings were straight out of the 1950s, right down to the pink dinette set tucked into a corner under the window and the chrome and gold starburst clock on the wall. Along an original wall of exposed brick, a set of painted shelves boasted miniature figurines of women in fancy, old-style dress.

"This is…really nice," Carly said. She'd expected Tiffany to have stark, modern decor. Instead, it looked like a set from *I Love Lucy*. "Did someone build that shelving for you?"

"Lyle had someone do it. He wasn't that good with his hands." She smirked. "Well, except—"

"Spare me," Carly said, before she could elaborate.

Tiffany snatched up a remote control that had fallen to the floor. She jabbed at the buttons. "Do either of you know how to get rid of this stupid program Lyle was recording on my DVR?

He was obsessed with this dumb show about missing fugitives. I haven't been able to watch regular TV since he…" She shook her head and sniffled.

"May I?" Becca took the remote from her. She lowered the volume, then tapped at it for several seconds.

Carly couldn't help wondering: If Lyle had his own home, why didn't he record the program there? In fact, if he and Tiffany were so close, why hadn't she moved in with him instead of staying in her apartment?

While Becca toyed with the remote, Carly strolled over to examine the figurines. "Are these collectibles?" she asked Tiffany.

"Yeah, but they're not as valuable as the ones the cops confiscated during their search. Jerks."

"They searched your apartment?" Carly asked, surprised.

"And my car." Tiffany crossed her arms over her chest. "For God's sake, Carly, didn't you know? The spouse, or *almost* spouse in my case, is always a person of interest. They took my three Fashion Dames figurines because they were tall enough and heavy enough to…" Her eyes brimmed with tears as she fingered the trinkets hanging from around her neck. "As if I would ever, *ever* hurt Lyle."

Carly and Becca exchanged worried glances, then Carly went over and took Tiffany's arm, propelling her gently over to her sofa. "I'll bet you haven't eaten in a while. Can I get you something?"

"No. Everything tastes like sh—garbage to me. Besides, I'm running low on yogurt."

"You must eat more than yogurt. Would you like me to bring you a sandwich from my restaurant?"

"One of those fat-laden grilled cheese sandwiches?" she said tartly. "Good God, no. And you're wrong. I practically exist on yogurt. The only other thing I eat is salads, and only if they're made with baby spinach or mesclun greens."

Suppressing an eye roll, Carly slid onto the sofa beside her. "All right, fine, but I really need to ask you something. Tiffany, did you hear anything the night Lyle was killed? Voices? Cars coming and going?"

Tiffany's face went taut. "I heard Lyle leave the apartment. It was pretty late, a little after midnight. I was restless—I never sleep well—so I went to the window and looked outside. Lyle's car was in the lot, but there was another car too. I figured he was meeting some babe he'd dumped who was trying to get him back."

Some babe? Janet Moody?

"Did you see anyone?"

After a pause, she said, "No, but when I lifted the window, I heard Lyle talking to someone. They were on the other side of his car."

"Was the other voice male or female?"

Tiffany's damp eyes glittered with anger. "A woman. I'm pretty sure. I was so mad. We were engaged! Why was he meeting *anyone*?" She broke into a soft sob, then sniffled. "I took two sleeping pills and went back to bed. A few minutes later, I heard a car roar off."

"Did Lyle come back inside?"

"No. He never—" Her eyes watered again. "Those pills kicked in fast. It wasn't till I saw his car the next the morning I knew something was weird. That's when I went outside and—" She buried her face in her hands.

"Tiffany, what about the other car?" Carly asked gently. "Did it look familiar?"

"Not really. It was just a dark-colored car. Cars all look alike to me."

Carly was sure Suzanne drove a white Camry. Had the police taken note of that?

Becca set down the remote in front of the television, then came over and sat in an armless chair adjacent to the sofa.

Tiffany clutched at her charms again.

"Did Lyle give you that necklace?" Carly asked, peering more closely at it.

"I already had the chain. Lyle gave me the charms." She lifted one of them and held it out. About an inch wide, it was a diamond-encrusted key superimposed over a gold heart. It looked like a pricey piece.

"He told me this was the key to his heart. He told me not to let anyone see it yet. He wanted to wait until we officially announced our engagement."

Becca leaned forward for a better look. "Wow. That's beautiful."

"Gorgeous," Carly echoed. "What about the other one?"

Tiffany's eyes brightened. She lifted the shiny brass key and palmed it. "I know it doesn't look like much, but this one was supposed to be a surprise. I'm not sure what it goes to, but I think it's the key to the home we were going to build together."

"The real key?" Carly asked.

Tiffany looked perturbed by the question. "I doubt it. I think it was symbolic." She turned over the key. At the top, the word *hummingbird* was inscribed in tiny letters. "He told me to keep these together, close to my heart." She pressed it to her lips as if it were a precious gem.

Something about the key bothered Carly. In no way did it resemble a house key. Nor was it an item of jewelry.

"Hummingbird," Carly said. "Does that have a special meaning?"

"*No.* Does it have to?" Tiffany spat at her.

"Sorry. I was just asking."

Tiffany sat up straighter and tossed back her hair. "By the way, I've given it a lot of thought, and I decided that your waitress didn't kill Lyle. Even if she is a witch. The more I thought about it, the more obvious it is who really killed him."

After a long silence, Carly prodded, "Was it the leasing manager?"

Tiffany looked sharply at her, but didn't respond. The flush in her cheeks told Carly that her guess had been right on target.

"For the love of butterflies in January, Tiffany, if you know who it was, you need to tell the police."

"That's not going to happen. First off, I don't have actual proof. Second, I'd be putting my life in danger if I did. As soon as Lyle's estate gets transferred to me, I'm bailing from this boring town. Let the cops figure it out themselves."

That was an interesting comment for a couple of reasons, Carly thought. For starters, why did she think Lyle's estate, whatever that consisted of, was now hers? They hadn't gotten married yet, and Lyle had an actual heir—his half brother Matt. Also, wouldn't a woman who loved Lyle enough to marry him want his killer arrested for the crime?

Another thing: Hadn't Tiffany been the one who wanted desperately to open a boutique in downtown Balsam Dell? Who thought the space Carly's restaurant occupied would be the ideal location for it?

"I'll open my boutique somewhere else," Tiffany said, as if she'd tuned in to Carly's thoughts. "Someplace where women actually care about fashion."

Carly looked down at her own ensemble, a blue, short-sleeved jersey tee over white denim capris. She wouldn't be heading down a catwalk any time soon.

"Tiffany," Carly asked quietly, "are you saying that Lyle left everything he owned to you?" As motives went, that was a fairly powerful one.

For a long moment, Tiffany remained silent. Finally, she said in a shaky voice, "I was supposed to get everything. *Everything.* Lyle promised me!" She shot off the sofa and stalked around the room. "He told me that since we were getting married, he was going to make out a will leaving all his worldly goods to me. He'd already been to the lawyer to go over the details." Her voice rose. "But when I called the lawyer yesterday, he said Lyle never got over there to finalize the will. And without proper execution, that's what he called it, it wasn't a valid document."

Carly sat quietly, thinking. How much of an "estate" had Lyle owned? She glanced around. "Is that why this stuff is scattered all over? You're looking for a will?"

"You're pretty sharp, aren't you? Lyle was always doodling on paper. He'd write stuff or print stuff, then stick it in one of his magazines. I thought maybe he'd written out a will or a draft of one. If he did, I haven't found it. *Yet.*" She kicked at a stack of magazines that had tipped over on the floor.

The wheels in Carly's head turned. Lyle couldn't have known that his death was imminent. But he might have suspected that someone was angry enough to harm him. Still, even if that were the case, signing a will was probably low on his to-do list, despite his looming marriage to Tiffany. Would he have taken the trouble to write out a will in longhand, as Tiffany seemed to think? Somehow, Carly couldn't picture it. The Lyle she remembered was too self-centered to spend any time on a task like that. More likely he'd have left it in his lawyer's hands.

Which, it appeared, is exactly what he did. Except that he didn't follow through with signing it.

With a sigh, Carly rose from the sofa. "As long as you're okay, we'll go. Just be careful, okay?" she said to Tiffany.

Tiffany didn't react. Her eyes had glazed over.

Carly waved a hand in front of her. "Tiffany, did you hear me? Becca and I are leaving."

Tiffany swiveled her head toward Carly. "Yes, sorry, I did hear you." She turned and looked at the television, then back at Becca. "You fixed it. Thank you. If I had to watch that stupid fugitive program for one more minute, I was going to toss the TV through the window!"

Something about Tiffany's reaction made Carly immensely

sad. She seemed unaccustomed to having anyone come to her aid. Was she as friendless as Carly imagined, or did she shun most people by choice?

Becca went over to shake Tiffany's hand, and this time Tiffany accepted it. "If there's anything else I can do," Becca said, "Carly knows how to find me."

Tiffany gave her a sly look. "Do you know how to pick locks?" she asked. "Because what I really want is to get into Lyle's house and look for a will."

Carly gawked at her. "Wait a minute. You mean you don't even have a key to Lyle's house?"

CHAPTER NINETEEN

"THANK YOU FOR GOING UP TO TIFFANY'S WITH ME," CARLY said after they were back inside the restaurant. "I'm not sure I'd have had the courage to do it on my own. With all that noise going on, I probably would have called 911."

"I'm glad I was here to help."

"She was sure thrilled when you deprogrammed that DVR for her," Carly said. "Good job, by the way. I'm kind of a techno-idiot myself. I would've been useless."

"I was the go-to gal in my platoon for stuff like that," Becca said with a bashful smile.

"Come on in the kitchen," Carly said. "I'm going to make you a sandwich before you go. I won't grill it, so you can eat it whenever you get hungry."

"Carly, honestly—"

"No arguments. What do you like? I have cheddar, swiss, Havarti, provolone—"

Becca threw up her hands and laughed. "Okay. I give up. I'd love a swiss on rye bread with loads of mustard."

"Ham?"

"Can't go wrong with ham," Becca said with authority.

They padded into the kitchen. Carly made up a plump ham and swiss sandwich, added a generous helping of mustard, and packed it in an airtight container to keep it fresh. She removed two bottles of water from the fridge and put everything in a paper takeout bag. "Do you want an ice pack?" Carly asked her.

"Thanks, but I have a cooler in the car. This is really nice of you, Carly."

Carly wanted neither thanks nor praise. What she wanted was an explanation for why a woman who'd served her country was living out of her car in a parking lot. She knew Becca's fierce pride was partly to blame, but still, it wasn't right.

"Around here, we help each other," Carly said, giving the bag to Becca.

"Thanks. Didn't you think it was strange," Becca asked, as Carly wiped down the cutting board, "that Tiffany didn't have a key to her own fiancé's home? I mean, why wouldn't he have given her one?"

"I don't know, but I nearly got my head bitten off when I asked her about it, didn't I?"

"You came close," Becca said, chuckling. "But I wonder why the question set her off like that. You almost lost the tip of your nose when she slammed the door in your face."

"The more I think about it," Carly mused, "the more all of her reactions seemed off to me. I'm beginning to think there was more to that relationship than met the eye." She slid the cutting board onto a shelf under the workstation.

"Since I didn't know either of them, I can't comment on that," Becca said. "But I sensed more anger than grief coming from her. On the other hand, anger is one of the stages of grief, so maybe that's where she's at right now. Who are we to judge, right?"

Carly hadn't thought of it that way.

"As for that poor murdered man," Becca continued, "I don't want to speak ill of him—he's not exactly here to defend himself. But those piles of magazines and newspapers he left all over would have personally driven me nuts. I'd have given him twenty-four hours to get rid of them, and after that they'd be on their way to the recycling station."

They walked over to the swinging doors, and Carly snapped off the light switch.

"Hey, can I use the facilities before we leave?" Becca asked, pushing through the door.

"Sure thing. Right around the corner to the left."

Carly dug out her key and waited for Becca near the back door. Her body—and her brain—both needed a break. She was on mental overload from everything she'd learned in the span of a day, especially from Tiffany Spencer.

When Becca returned, they went out through the rear door. Carly locked up, and together they ambled toward her Corolla. A light breeze cooled Carly's skin, and goosebumps pimpled her arms. It felt wonderful.

Carly took a deep breath and slowly released it. The air still bore aromatic remnants from the food carts that had peddled goodies on the green. From all outward appearances, the season's first Saturday on the Green had been a rousing success. Next Saturday, she'd make it a point to spend a little more time there. If Suzanne came back to work, the eatery would have enough coverage to spare her for a half hour or so.

If Suzanne came back.

"Nickel for your thoughts."

After a few seconds, Carly realized her mind had drifted. "Oh, sorry. I was just thinking about everything. Can I give you a lift over to your—" She felt silly saying 'your place,' since Becca lived in an old Lincoln. "Over to where you're parked?"

Becca grinned. "Nah. It's practically across the street. I am glad it cooled down some, though. It'll be comfortable sleeping tonight." She held up the bag Carly had given her. "And I've got a delicious snack to help send me to la-la land."

Carly was liking Becca more and more. She was strong and independent, yet also kind and capable.

"Well, Carly," Becca said, a smile sliding across her face, "meeting you has been a distinct pleasure." She offered her hand, and Carly returned her firm handshake. "Thanks again for the sandwich. I'll make quick work of it later, for sure."

"Oh, gosh, you're welcome," Carly said, "but it's only a sandwich."

"Best kind of food, in my book." Becca's smile faded. She glanced upward at the building, where Tiffany's apartment overlooked the parking lot. A light shone from the window. Even in the light of day, it seemed unusually bright.

Becca spoke softly. "I feel bad for that poor woman upstairs, Carly. She's got some issues. I can see it in her eyes."

"I know," Carly quietly agreed. She couldn't see if Tiffany's window was open, and she didn't want their voices to carry. "She lost the man she loved, and in a horrible way. In the blink of an eye, her entire future collapsed."

The same way mine did the night Daniel was killed...

Instead of responding, Becca turned and fixed her gaze on the area around the dumpster. She looked as if she wanted to say something else about Tiffany, but instead she lifted a hand in a tiny salute. "I'm sure our paths will cross again, Carly. Have a good night."

"Becca, wait." Carly fished her notepad and a pen out of her tote. "Do you have a cell phone?"

"Right now, I don't," Becca said.

"That's okay. Take my number anyway, just in case you ever need something after the restaurant's closed. There's a pay phone in front of the town hall." She smiled. "It's probably one of the few pay phones left in Vermont."

Becca took the slip of paper from her, clearly moved by the gesture. "Thanks, Carly. I'm sure I won't need to bother you, but it's good to have, just in case."

Carly watched Becca jog off, then opened her car door and dropped onto the front seat. She pulled the door closed and locked it immediately, something she didn't normally do. Her nerves felt as if they'd been scraped raw by a serrated knife.

Lyle's killer was still out there. Until now, it hadn't occurred to Carly that she herself might be in danger. Were Grant and

Suzanne also at risk? Did the murder have something to do with her restaurant?

Anxious to get home to her own comfy apartment, Carly swerved out of the parking lot. As she idled at the traffic signal, she glanced across the green. A light was on in only one of the shops, but she couldn't see which one. She inched her car forward to get a better angle.

The lights were on in Mitchell Electric.

She didn't know why it bothered her, but it did.

CHAPTER TWENTY

THE MOMENT CARLY STEPPED INSIDE HER APARTMENT, SHE locked the door and flipped on all the lights. She went into the kitchen and poured herself a glass of iced tea, emptying the bottle. Her supplies were running low. She hadn't shopped for groceries for almost two weeks. With Sunday being her one day off, she'd make it a point to get to the market tomorrow and stock up on staples.

It was after 8:00, so a light supper would be just the ticket. Unfortunately, she couldn't think of a single thing she felt like eating. With a diet that tilted heavily toward the dairy segment of the food wheel, she made a conscious effort to eat a salad two or three nights a week. This evening, however, nothing about the word *salad* held the slightest bit of appeal.

Carly made do with a spotted banana and the cup of cotton candy Gina had bought her. The banana was mushy, the cotton candy a delight. She was tempted to pour herself a short glass of wine, but a few gremlins from Joyce's bold red port still lingered in her head—reminding her of that awful headache the port had given her.

After finishing her meal, such as it was, Carly turned on the TV and plopped onto the sofa. The attack of nerves she'd suffered earlier was growing worse instead of better. She needed to relax, to find something to take her mind off her worries, at least for a few hours.

Carly surfed absently through the channels, hoping to land on a comedy—anything to take her mind off her gloomy thoughts. She didn't want anything that smacked of mystery or murder; she'd had enough of that lately. She had almost given up finding a show she liked when one of those drama-filled disaster movies filled the screen.

Snow everywhere, avalanche style. A rescue team, racing against time...

Carly's heartbeat spiked. Her breath halted in her throat. Her mind skidded backward, to that agonizing January night when a patrol car pulled into their driveway at 3:30 a.m. The grave look on the officer's face told her all she needed to know. She'd dropped to the floor in a sobbing heap, awakening on her sofa the next morning. Someone had given her a sedative and tucked a quilt around her, but she never remembered who it was.

A lineman for the power company, Daniel had returned home late from work the prior evening, half-frozen and bleary-eyed after a sixteen-hour stint restoring downed power lines. The hard-hitting January snowstorm had left thousands in the dark. A family that lived on a remote country road had been calling the power company repeatedly, begging to have their electricity restored. The family's dad, who was on disability, had a pregnant wife and two little kids. They had a wood stove, but their wood supply had dwindled to a few skimpy logs.

Daniel had heard about the family from a fellow lineman. Without giving it a second thought, he'd loaded wood into the bed of his pickup the moment he got home. Recognizing his exhaustion, Carly begged him to wait until morning, but Daniel couldn't get those little kids out of his head. He kissed Carly goodbye, teased her about keeping the bed warm, and promised to be home in a few hours. That was the last time Carly ever saw him. She later learned that his pickup, too heavily laden with wood, had skidded out of control on an ice-covered bridge. The vehicle had rolled over and tumbled down an embankment.

In her dreams—or rather, her nightmares—she'd imagined his death in a thousand different ways, each more heartrending than the last. Though nearly eighteen months had elapsed since Daniel's passing, the memory of that night was so clear in Carly's mind it might have happened the day before.

She sat up straight and turned off the television, her face damp with tears. She retrieved her laptop from her bedroom, carried it back to the sofa, and powered it on. The person at the center of her current nightmare was Lyle Bagley. The first time she'd Googled him, she'd come up with a whole lot of nothing. Maybe she needed to dig deeper.

Once again, she typed his name into the search box and hit Enter. The same few links popped up. She tried using "L Bagley," but that brought up even fewer useful links, along with a slew of unrelated ones.

She searched Pine Grove Mobile Home Park, and a website popped up. The park was depicted as an idyllic community, with lush greenery all around and pristine mobile homes flanked by flowering shrubs. Photos of residents chatting around a communal barbecue gave the impression of a fun-filled environment where every neighbor was a friend. None of it resembled the run-down place Gina had described.

And nowhere on the site was Lyle's name mentioned.

The landlord was listed, not surprisingly, as *Pine Grove Management*. Below that was a contact number, with no name attached. Carly would bet her favorite pair of flip-flops that the number went directly to Janet Moody. Didn't Gina say she lived in Carly's neighborhood? In the house with the painted giraffe out front?

Before shutting down her laptop, Carly searched one more name: Hummingbird. Tiffany claimed the word meant nothing to her, but Carly wasn't so sure.

It took only seconds for the screen to fill with page after page of links. There were dozens of sites relating to the tiny, migratory birds; there was even a Hummingbird Society.

But no Hummingbird key.

Carly put away her laptop.

She was half tempted to text her sister to see if she was free for a chat. Years earlier they'd devised a system, mostly for Norah's benefit. If Norah was available, Carly's phone would ring within seconds. If not, Norah would text a series of hearts, meaning *can't talk now, tell you all the juicy stuff later!*

Carly decided to wait. She was too exhausted for one of Norah's exuberant speeches tonight, anyway.

She turned off the air conditioner and opened her bedroom window. The night air had cooled. The soothing, chirping sounds of a summer night filtered through the screen, caressing her ears.

Before she turned off her light, she checked the messages on her cell. It was odd she hadn't heard from her mom in a few days, but Carly was sure there was a good reason. Maybe Gary had suffered a setback with his broken elbow, and she'd had to play nursemaid.

Another person who'd gone silent was Don Frasco. Had the chief warned him to mind his own business and let the police investigate Lyle's murder?

One thing Don had accomplished—he'd supplied some useful intel on Matt Bagley, including his whereabouts. If Matt's churlish attitude had been any indication, he hadn't cared a whit about his half brother. He was in town for the Caddy. Nothing more.

And what about Tiffany? One thing had stood out from Carly's conversation with her. The car she saw that night was dark, not white, like Suzanne's.

Should Tiffany be moved into the "suspect" category? It seemed to Carly she'd been more concerned with inheriting Lyle's estate than she had with losing the man she loved.

Too tired to think anymore, Carly crawled into bed and shut

off her bedside lamp. The last sound she heard as she drifted off to sleep were the gorgeous notes of Pachelbel's Canon in D Major, played on the cello by one amazing young man.

CHAPTER TWENTY-ONE

Carly awoke Sunday morning to a cloudless blue sky and a lemon-yellow sun. After a shower and a quick meal of toast and coffee, she pulled on a pair of white jersey capris and a periwinkle tee imprinted with tiny seahorses. She shoved her feet into her favorite flats, tousled her still-damp chestnut waves with her fingers, and grabbed her sunglasses from her tote. Then she headed outside for a walk that she hoped, fingers crossed, would lead her to Janet Moody's house.

"Hey, there, you're looking perky today!" Arlene Timson was on the front porch, her face half-hidden by an oversized pair of sunglasses and a straw hat that dipped low over her brow. Water dribbled from the multiple pots of pink petunias hanging over the railing of the porch.

"Hi, Arlene," Carly said in a cheerful voice. "I'm taking my first walk of the season. I've been so bad about getting any exercise!"

"Tell me about it," Arlene said dryly. She paused to look at Carly, the metal watering can in her hand poised over one of the hanging pots. "I have to say there, you're looking darn cute in that T-shirt. That color's adorable on you. Headed any place in particular?"

Slightly embarrassed by Arlene's overblown praise, Carly said, "Nah. Just around the neighborhood. How are you and Joyce doing? I haven't seen you in a few days."

"We're doing," Arlene said, then lowered her voice. "Joyce had a rough day yesterday. That's how the MS is sometimes. Poor gal. I hate seeing her out of sorts like that."

Carly sagged. "Gee, I'm sorry to hear that. Is there anything I can do?"

"Nothing, except show up for our Sunday Scrabble game," Arlene reminded. She looked out toward the road, then back at Carly. "Joyce always looks forward to that."

Shoot. Carly had almost forgotten. Every Sunday afternoon, the three of them played Scrabble on Joyce's kitchen table. Carly enjoyed the games, but she did it more for Joyce's sake than for her own. Joyce got out so infrequently these days that Carly knew their weekly games brightened her Sundays.

"I'll be there," she promised. "See you later!"

Carly dashed down the front walk before Arlene could detain her any longer. No doubt the woman was lonely with only Joyce for a constant companion, but sometimes she was a bit much. Even so, Joyce was fortunate to have a caretaker as devoted as Arlene.

She took a right at the foot of the driveway and headed up the street. Breathing in lungfuls of the fresh morning air, she felt her doom-and-gloom hangover from the evening before flitter away into the ozone.

A few minutes later, Carly turned right on Elm. She could already see Janet's house at the next corner—a small white bungalow with a busy front yard.

Carly slowed her pace. She'd been hoping to catch Janet puttering in her yard, but she didn't see any sign of her.

She continued to meander slowly until she reached Janet's front walk. A white mailbox sat atop a thick wooden post, the name *MOODY* imprinted on the side. The path leading to the bungalow's shallow front steps was a series of flat, bright-painted stones, each one depicting a different species of flower. The artwork on them was impressive.

On either side of the walkway were large, oval flower beds. Edged in brick, one was slightly larger than the other. A profusion of colors—reds, violets, yellows, and pinks—competed for glory within the carefully tended beds.

Janet herself was nowhere in sight, although a small black sedan sat in the driveway. Was she inside her house, mourning the loss of the man with whom Gina claimed she'd been obsessed? The only visible inhabitant was the three-foot-tall painted giraffe that stood guard at the foot of the steps.

When a door slammed at the back of the house, Carly's heart nearly catapulted through her windpipe. Without warning, Janet appeared from around the corner of the bungalow, a garden shovel clutched in her hand.

Carly must have stood out like a bullfrog on a wedding cake because the moment Janet spotted her, she halted in her tracks. Carly offered a friendly wave and a bright smile, but the woman striding toward her returned neither.

Janet sported a wary expression and a purple visor that matched her snug-fitting shorts. Her sleeveless white, boat-neck top accentuated her deep tan. She pulled a pair of leopard-print sunglasses from one of her pockets and shoved them on her face. "Can I help you?" she said when she was a short distance from Carly.

"I was just admiring your flowers," Carly said lightly, as if she'd accidentally stumbled upon the scene.

"Thank you." Janet's tone relaxed, and then, "Do I know you? You look familiar."

Carly laughed. "It so funny you said that. I think I remember you from school. Weren't you in Norah Hale's class? I'm Carly, her sister. You're Janet, right?"

"Right," she muttered. "I remember Norah Hale. Pretty, kind of boy crazy." She curled her lip with distaste.

"I guess she was a typical teen," Carly said in defense of her sister. Before Janet could diss Norah further, she blurted, "Those purple flowers, are they irises? They're spectacular!"

Janet swerved her head around briefly, then eyed Carly with

suspicion. "Yeah, they are. Now I remember where I heard your name recently. Don't you own the grilled cheese place?"

"I do," Carly said.

Janet's face froze. She'd obviously made the connection. The parking lot behind Carly's restaurant was where Lyle had met his unfortunate demise. Despite Janet's eyes being hidden behind sunglasses, her features were clearly etched in pain.

"Are you okay?" Carly asked, stepping forward into the yard. In the next instant, her shoe caught the edge of one of the flat stones. She sailed forward, arms flailing, then dropped like a boulder onto the pathway.

"Geez, be careful!" Dropping her shovel, Janet hauled up Carly by one arm, not letting go until she was back on her feet.

"I'm fine. I'm okay," Carly said, wincing from Janet's iron grasp.

"Now your hand's bleeding," Janet griped, as if Carly had singlehandedly brought down all of civilization. "You'd better come inside for a Band-Aid."

Carly brushed herself off, then examined her scraped palm. The blood was minimal, but it stung like the devil. "Sorry about that, Janet. I should have looked where I was going." She tried to sound contrite, but inwardly she was doing a fist pump. Her clumsy move had given her the perfect excuse for getting inside Janet's home.

"Come on."

Janet led Carly into the house. She directed her to a small office off to the right, where a laptop and an overflowing wire basket sat atop a battered oak desk. On the wall above the desk was an imposing portrait of a white-haired gent, a handlebar mustache curling around his cheeks and a roguish glint in his eye. Adjacent to the desk was a three-drawer file cabinet, and in a far corner was a copy machine that looked like a relic from the 1990s.

Janet grabbed her desk chair and rolled it toward Carly. "Sit there," she said, whipping off her sunglasses. "I'll be right back."

"Thanks." Holding her injured hand aloft, Carly sat down. As soon as Janet was out of sight, she swiveled around and used her heels to propel herself over to the desk. On the laptop, the screen saver showed a sea of wildflowers stretching across a country pasture. Carly was tempted to tap a key to see what might pop up in its place, but if Janet caught her, she'd be toast.

Instead, she peeked into the wire basket, which was piled high with correspondence. At the top was a handwritten letter addressed to Pine Grove Management. Carly tilted her ear toward the door. Hearing nothing, she snatched up the letter and began reading.

Dear Pine Grove Management,
   This is my third request. Next time I go to the Board of Health. There is a huge rodent problem that you are ignoring, and I can't deal with it any longer. I had three mice in my unit in one week, and I keep a neat, clean home. Please note, sir, I will not pay my rent until this matter is addressed. Yours truly...

Carly tossed the letter back on the heap, and not a moment too soon—or maybe a second too late. Janet stood stiffly in the doorway, glaring at her. "Have fun reading my mail?"

A rush of heat flooded Carly's neck and slithered into her cheeks. "I'm-I'm sorry. I didn't mean to pry. I was just...filling the time."

Lips pressed in a hard line, Janet came at her with a gauze pad and a box of Band-Aids in one hand and a bottle of clear liquid in the other. Feeling like a kid scolded by the school principal, Carly gingerly held out her hand. She cringed when Janet tugged the cap off the bottle. She swallowed. "Is that—"

"Don't worry, it's not alcohol. It's sterile water." Bending over, Janet squeezed some of the liquid onto the gauze and pressed it, firmly, to her palm. She swabbed it gently, then tossed the gauze into the wastebasket.

Carly bit her lip. Hadn't she read a mystery once where some-one was poisoned this way? "I probably don't need a Band-Aid," she said.

Ignoring her, Janet tore the wrapper off a large Band-Aid, then applied it expertly to the wound. "You need to protect the skin till you get home," she said. "You can take it off there if you want."

"Thanks, Janet." Carly flashed her a grateful smile. "I didn't mean to cause you so much trouble."

"Yeah, yeah. Don't sweat it. Besides, I don't need anyone suing me for falling in my yard."

I'd never do that, Carly wanted to say, but instead blurted, "Janet, I'm so sorry about Lyle. You worked for him, didn't you?"

Janet blinked a few times, then swallowed, her expression mor-phing into one of unfathomable grief. "Worked for him? I'd have given my *life* for him." She sucked in a shaky breath and then her entire body erupted into harsh, bone-racking sobs. Carly rose and tried to wrap her in a hug, but Janet shook her off.

After a few minutes, when Janet's crying had subsided, Carly pushed her gently onto the desk chair. She located a box of tissues and handed it to her.

Janet snagged a tissue and blew her nose loudly, then crum-pled the tissue in her fist. "You have no idea," she said raggedly, "how close we were before that...that skinny bimbo came onto the scene." She tossed the tissue into the basket, and her gray eyes darkened with fury. "I fought his battles for him, I evicted tenants so down on their luck they had no place else to go, all so he'd real-ize how indispensable I was. How much he needed me."

Carly winced. Did Lyle care so little about his tenants that he'd tossed them out on the street?

"I'm sure he appreciated—"

"Appreciated?" Janet screeched. She reached inside her sleeve-less tee and yanked out a gold chain. At the end was a round, diamond-encrusted watch, the face encircled by blue enamel. The detail was exquisite. "See this?" She shook the watch in Carly's face. "Does an antique Cartier pendant watch say I appreciate you?" she spat out. "No. It says *I love you.*" Her hands shook. Fresh tears flooded her cheeks, and she blotted them with her tanned knuckles.

"It's absolutely beautiful. Did Lyle give you that for a special occasion?"

Janet's face turned a mottled shade of red. "He gave me this a few months ago, when he finally came to his senses and realized he loved me. He wasn't good at communicating with words—that wasn't his strong suit—so he did it with a special gift. It's just the way he was." Pouting like a first grader, she shoved the watch back inside her shirt, then changed her mind and lifted it back out. After pressing it lovingly to her lips, she rested it on her chest. "He didn't want *her* to know he gave it to me. That's why he told me not to wear it in public. I guess it doesn't matter now, does it?"

"I guess not," Carly agreed, "and anyway, it's too lovely to hide. I'm sure Lyle would want you to wear it where everyone can admire it."

An anguished smile touched Janet's lips. "Do you think so?"

Who knows? Carly thought. She was only trying to make Janet feel better. "Of course, he would. He gave it to you, didn't he?"

Not that Janet's reasoning made any sense. If Lyle had loved her enough to give her an expensive watch, why had he taken up with Tiffany?

"That witch never loved him," Janet went on, nearly spitting the words. "She only wanted him to build her a boutique so she could flaunt it all over town that she owned a business. She used him, Carly." Her eyes took on a savage gleam.

"When did Lyle tell you he and Tiffany were engaged?" Carly asked her.

"He never really did. I had to hear it from one of the gossips at my hair salon!"

"Is that when you smashed Tiffany's taillights?"

"How did you—" Janet's shoulders drooped. "When I heard about the engagement, I saw every shade of red in the spectrum. First thing I did was question Lyle. He finally admitted it was true, but it was like pulling antlers off a moose to get him to admit it."

"How did you react?"

Janet closed her eyes and tilted her head toward the ceiling. "I bawled my eyes out, that's what I did. I told him marrying that gold digger would be a huge mistake, but he just stood there like a lump, staring at me as if I'd lost my mind. After he left, I tried to pull myself together, but I couldn't. I knew that bimbo worked at the outlets, so I drove there the next afternoon. I found that red car she drives and beat the crap out of her taillights."

And let the air out of her tires.

Janet twisted her lips into a disgusted frown. "I knew I was in trouble the minute I looked up and saw the security cameras. They were *everywhere*. The mall cops caught up with me the next day, but Lyle persuaded them not to report it to the real cops. He wanted it kept quiet, so he paid the damages. He said it reflected badly on him, since I worked for him. He got his girlfriend to agree not to press charges."

Naturally. It was all about him.

Carly pushed out a sigh. She knew she was riding her luck close to the edge, but this might be her last chance to talk openly with Janet. "Janet, after Lyle's death, did the police talk to you?" When Janet shot her an odd look, she said quickly, "They usually talk to people who were closest to the...you know, deceased, just in case they knew something that might help them solve the crime." *That's what they did on television, anyway. Who knew about real life?*

Janet's eyes had gone glassy. She nodded mechanically. "The police questioned me twice, but I told them I didn't know anything." Her gaze shifted sharply to the overflowing basket, then back at Carly.

Carly squeezed Janet's shoulder. "Again, I'm so sorry about Lyle," she said genuinely. "Do you have any idea who might have wanted to harm him?"

Janet snorted and rolled her eyes. "I can probably name a dozen people. Most of them live at the mobile home park I manage for him."

"Did you tell that to the police?"

"Of course, I did," Janet snarled. "Do I look like a moron?"

"Sorry. I didn't mean to imply anything." Carly had obviously overstayed her welcome, which had been dubious to start with. "I'll leave you alone now. Thank you for the first aid. If you're ever in the mood for a gooey, delicious grilled cheese, please stop by the restaurant, okay? My treat." She offered a genuine smile, and this time Janet returned it.

"Thanks. I might just do that." Janet hauled herself out of the chair. "Come on. I'll walk you outside."

At Carly's suggestion they exchanged cell phone numbers. On the way out, she noticed a vintage-looking wooden coatrack just inside the entrance to the office. Below a set of elegantly curved arms designed to hold hats and coats was a circular rail for umbrellas. The rack was bare, save for a heavy wooden cane resting in the umbrella section. The cane's highly polished grip resembled an eagle's head. If Carly had to guess, she'd say it was solid brass.

"That cane is so unusual," Carly said. "Is it antique?"

"My grandfather's," Janet said, by way of explanation. "We lost him three years ago."

"I'm sorry," Carly murmured.

They went outside, where the temperature had jumped upward at least five degrees since they first went into the house.

"Gonna be another broiler," Janet said and slipped on her sunglasses.

Carly picked her way cautiously over the flat-stone path, this time watching every step. "Did you paint all these stones?"

"I did," Janet said.

"Well, you're an amazing artist."

Carly knew when she was being hurried along, but another question suddenly occurred to her. When they reached the mailbox, she turned to Janet and said, "Will you continue to manage the mobile home park?"

Janet's features seemed to shrink. "I don't know. I guess that depends."

"On what?" Carly asked.

"On who ends up inheriting Lyle's estate."

CHAPTER TWENTY-TWO

LYLE'S ESTATE.

The words rattled around in Carly's head as she retraced her route toward home.

What *did* Lyle's estate consist of? Was there a way she could find out who his legal heirs were? Surely Matt was one, but were there others?

Carly chided herself for not having checked into it sooner. After all, Lyle's real estate included her eatery, and her eatery was her livelihood. She needed to be more proactive for her own sake.

Tomorrow was Monday. She vowed to find out who Lyle's attorney was and pay them a visit.

That decided, Carly paused on the sidewalk. She'd intentionally left her cell in the apartment so she could enjoy her walk without interruption. Now she was beginning to feel lost without it. Another one of her mom's warnings rang in her ears: *Never go anywhere without your phone. You never know when you'll have an emergency!*

Should she go home or get a bit more exercise? Distance wise, she hadn't walked all that far. She'd spent most of her time inside Janet's home.

In a way, Carly felt bad for Janet, despite her brittle personality. Deep in her heart, the woman had adored Lyle. His death left a massive hole in her life.

According to Janet, she'd been crushed when she learned about his engagement to Tiffany. Had it pushed her over the edge? *If I can't have you, then no one can.* It was an ancient motive, as cliché as they get.

But it happened.

Carly was deciding whether to head home or continue in the opposite direction when a thirtysomething woman with a black ponytail came bounding along the sidewalk toward her. Two dogs scampered ahead of her. A larger one with golden fur and a smaller dog that looked exactly like—

Carly's heart jumped. "Dr. Anne! I'm so glad to see you."

"Carly? I thought that was you." Expertly juggling her two leashes, the chief's daughter, Anne, beamed at her and then wrapped her in a one-armed hug. "Hey, I got your message yesterday. I started to call you back, but then I got interrupted with an emergency and it slipped my mind."

Carly stooped down, and the little Morkie leaped into her arms. "You adopted Havarti. I'm so happy!"

The veterinarian laughed. "Wait a minute. I didn't adopt him. I just haven't sent him to the shelter yet, so I'm giving him some exercise. He's such a good boy, aren't you, Havarti?" she cooed to the pup. "He loves my boy Fritzie."

Disappointed, Carly gave Fritzie a tickle under his chin. "Oh. I thought maybe Havarti was so cute you couldn't resist him."

"Every dog I treat is too cute to resist," Dr. Anne said sweetly, "but I can only adopt so many. This little guy obviously adores you. Sure you won't change your mind?"

Carly's heart sank. "I can't, Dr. Anne. I wish I could."

"There are ways to make it work, you know. Think about it, okay?"

They hugged again, and the veterinarian strode off. Havarti turned and whined at Carly before trotting alongside his companion.

Carly continued along Main Street, regret weighing on her.

When she reached the entrance to Ledyard Park, she paused.

She looked out over the grassy incline, at the crest of which was a white gazebo with a wide terra cotta roof. Beyond that was an area set out only for kids, where they could swing on the swing sets, slide down chutes, and build sandcastles in a community sandbox.

A wistful smile touched Carly's lips. She and Norah had played there as kids—Carly more so than Norah, who hated getting her sneakers dirty. One of the few memories Carly had of her dad was of him pushing them on the swings, higher and higher, his soft laughter coasting on the air until he caught each of them in his arms. Whenever Carly tried picturing him, the only image that emerged was a blur of thick dark hair and a grizzled beard.

Carly was seven and Norah was nine when he passed, their mom only in her midthirties. He'd been a Vietnam vet, much older than her mom. His own parents had never been part of his life, and therefore never part of Carly's. Paul Hale's wife and daughters had been his entire world.

Pushing away the memory, Carly walked a little farther. She cast her gaze over the area where several benches sat around a shallow fountain. Water spewed in graceful arcs from a pair of carved dolphins that had been captured by the sculptor in midleap.

Only two benches were occupied. A pair of elderly women sat at one, their knitting bags open before them. Opposite them, a man hunkered over a magazine, a bottle on the bench beside him. Something about his profile looked familiar. She moved closer, and she realized it was Matt Bagley.

A short distance ahead was the paved trail that led up the hill to the fountain. Carly made quick work of climbing the path. A little out of breath when she reached the crest, she slogged over to where Matt was sitting with a magazine propped over one crossed leg.

"Hi, there!" She dropped onto the bench beside him.

Matt jerked his head sharply, then glowered at her from beneath his green ball cap. "What are you doing here?"

"Well, that's a pleasant greeting." Carly forced a smile,

determined to remain upbeat. "I'm getting some exercise, that's what I'm doing. Sunday is my one day off and Vermont summers are short, so I want to enjoy this gorgeous morning." Carly tilted her head and peeked at his glossy mag. This one appeared to be a lawn care catalog. "Whatcha reading?"

"Is there any way you could make like a banana and split?" Matt said through clenched teeth.

Carly made a funny face. "Gee, I haven't heard that one in a while."

It was then she noticed the earbud stuck in his ear, and his cell phone beside him on the opposite side of the bench.

"I'm listening to an audiobook, if you don't mind, and I can't do it with you jabbering at me."

"You're listening to an audiobook while you're reading a magazine?"

He shot her a look. "Yeah, as you chicks like to say, I'm *multi*tasking."

Carly stifled the retort that hovered on her lips. "What kind of audiobook?"

Matt threw up his arms. "On operating a small business, okay? Now leave so I can finish this session."

Undeterred, Carly said, "What kind of small business do you want to operate?"

His narrow jaw tightened. "I don't want to start one. I want to take over one of the businesses my brother owned. *Half* brother, I should say. Not that he ever acted like a brother."

"You two weren't close?"

"The only thing we had in common was my dad. Dad was a jerk and a schemer, but"—Matt swallowed—"he was good to me. He didn't call me *loser* the way my mom did. He taught me a lot about cars. And regardless of what Lyle claimed, that Caddy was mine. Dad gave it to me." His jabbed a finger at his chest, and his eyes flared.

A knot formed in Carly's stomach. If everything Matt said was true, he didn't have much of a childhood. She felt for him, despite the massive chip on his shoulder.

"I'm sorry, Matt. Life isn't always fair."

"Yeah, like you'd know."

Carly whirled on the bench and faced him. "I lost my husband when his pickup skidded over an icy bridge. He was thirty-two years old, the same age I am now. He was bringing wood in the dead of winter to a family desperate for help." She nearly choked getting the words out, but Matt had ignited her temper and now she couldn't stop. "How's that for fair?"

Matt's mouth opened slightly, and his thin face flushed. "Sorry. I didn't know," he mumbled.

Carly pushed her hair away from her face. "And I didn't mean to snap at you. All I'm saying is, at one time or another we all face hardships. No one is immune."

Matt blinked a few times and looked off into the distance. "What's weird is that Lyle and me used to be close. After Dad died, he promised to start a business with me. Supposedly, he was just waiting for me to graduate high school. What a crock that turned out to be."

Pretty much what Gina had told her. Lyle had let his little brother down.

"Then he had the flippin' gall to drive off with the Caddy. He knew it was mine, but he didn't care. When I told him Dad promised it to me, he said Dad never told him that."

Carly waited a beat. "I'm sure that was disappointing. Did… Lyle's attorney say anything to you about the car?"

If he thought her question was an odd segue in the conversation, he didn't let on. "Nope. Nothing. I drove by Lyle's house yesterday. The Caddy's still sitting in the driveway. If I had an extra key, I'd take the flippin' thing and go. Far as I know, Lyle had both keys. The cops probably have them now."

Interesting point, Carly thought. Presumably, Lyle's keys were with him when he was murdered—maybe on his key ring. If there was an extra key to the Caddy, it was probably inside his house.

"I suppose Lyle's house is all locked up," she said with a probing sigh. She thought about Tiffany wanting to get inside to search for a will.

"Yeah, it is. Tight as a drum. I used to have a key, but he changed the locks."

So you tried, Carly thought. "I guess I should head home. One thing I meant to ask you, Matt. What do you do? I mean, for work."

"God, woman. You are relentless. I work for a private auto repair shop. Sometimes I fix cars, sometimes I detail them. You satisfied now?"

Well, no. I really want to know if you murdered your brother.

The sun had risen higher, warming her arms and face. By the time she got home, she'd probably be drenched in sweat, not to mention sunburned.

She rose off the bench. "I've invaded your space and I'm really sorry. I'll leave you to your lessons."

"Good." Then, "Wait. I wanna say one last thing."

This time Carly kept her lips buttoned.

"That sandwich I got at your place the other day? It was the best flippin' grilled cheese I ever ate in my life."

CHAPTER TWENTY-THREE

"*B-I-S-C-U-I-T.* Biscuit!" Arlene wiggled side to side in her kitchen chair and did a little victory dance.

Carly rested her chin on her cupped hands and studied the Scrabble board. "You do it every week, Arlene. Joyce and I don't stand a prayer."

"Hey, speak for yourself." Joyce gave Carly a playful tap on the arm. "I won three weeks ago, remember?"

"Ah, that's right. If I'm not mistaken, the word you won with was 'zealous.' But you lucked out with that triple word score."

"Maybe, but I still won." Joyce let out a faux cackle. "Now, anyone up for another slice of Arlene's homemade blueberry pie?" She swigged down the remains of her pink lemonade and plunked the glass on the table.

Carly patted her stomach. "I'd love one if I could squeeze it in, but I'm already stuffed to the earlobes. By the way, that pie was delish, Arlene. You could start your own bakery!"

"So glad you liked it." Arlene's plain face split into a wide grin. "It's a tad too early in the season for fresh blueberries, but the frozen ones we buy are straight from Maine. Right, Joyce?"

Joyce nodded distractedly, her gaze traveling to the window that overlooked the backyard. "That's right."

"Are you still having your groceries delivered?" Carly asked them.

"It's the best way," Arlene said with a heavy sigh. She rubbed the side of her eye. "These days, I don't like leaving Joyce alone any more than I have to."

"Oh, I'm fine." Joyce waved a hand. "But truly, Arlene is so on top of things. Back in May, she even ordered a kit for her car—a portable snow shovel and a windshield scraper. Just in case we have an early snowstorm," she added with a wink.

Arlene blushed and smiled. "I believe in being prepared."

"And," Joyce went on, "she took an online haircutting class so I won't have to make the trip to the salon every few months. By the way, Carly, did you notice my new do? Arlene cut it yesterday." Joyce swung her head left and right, her shortened gray coils doing a slight bounce.

"I did," Carly said, smiling at her. "Nice job, Arlene. I should ask you to cut mine. I'm *sooo* overdue for a trim."

"Any time. You name the day." Arlene mimed cutting hair with an imaginary pair of shears, then her overplucked eyebrows dipped toward her nose. "Truth be told, there's another reason why I'm learning to do more things from home now. I—" Her eyes welled. "It's so embarrassing, I shouldn't even tell you."

Carly looked at Arlene with concern. "Are you okay?"

"Oh, I'm fine. It's just—"

"Carly's one of us girls, Arlene," Joyce said benignly. "If we can't confide in our best buds, who can we confide in? Right, Carly?"

"That's right," Carly said, although she'd never thought of Arlene as a "best bud."

"Besides, it was an accident," Joyce said. "Could have happened to anyone."

Arlene looked at Joyce, then sucked in a shaky breath. "I know." She turned to Carly. "A few months ago, I went to Telly's Market to buy groceries. Joyce had been having a rough week. I wanted to stock up on things so I wouldn't have to go out again for a while. After I loaded the bags into my car that day, I realized I'd been gone over an hour and a half. I called Joyce to let her know I was on my way home, and when she didn't answer, I panicked."

"I'd dozed off in my chair," Joyce explained, "and by the time I heard the phone, I couldn't move fast enough to get to it."

"Anyway," Arlene went on, "I was so worried about Joyce that I backed out of the parking space too fast, and wham! I backed right into the car that was driving behind me." Arlene wrung her hands. "I was so mortified. I'm usually such a careful driver. I got out of my car to apologize and to exchange insurance information, but the guy I'd hit was already in my face, shrieking at me like I'd caused a fifty-car pileup."

"That's terrible. It sounds like he totally overreacted. No one got hurt, right?"

"No, but my rear fender put a dent in that old Caddy he was driving. To me it was barely noticeable; it only left a scratch on my car. But he acted as though I'd severed his car in half!"

Wait a minute. Old Caddy? That was waaay too much of a coincidence.

"I was scared out of my wits. I got so rattled I accidentally knocked my own sunglasses off. He raised his fists at me, and just when I thought he was going to sock me, he moved closer and stared hard into my face. He got this…this evil grin and said, 'You just bought yourself a whole lot of trouble,' and then he called me the b-word. Next thing I know, he's pulling his phone out of his pocket and taking pictures of me!"

"Horrible man," Joyce muttered, flicking another glance at the window.

"I was shaking so bad I could barely find my insurance card. He took a picture of it, then got in that stupid Caddy and drove off. I think he followed me, though. On the way home, I was sure I saw him in my rearview mirror." Arlene hugged herself and rubbed her arms.

"She was so upset when she got home that afternoon, Carly. She couldn't eat the rest of the day." Joyce's eyes filled with such compassion that it wrung Carly's heart.

Carly got up from her chair and squeezed Arlene in a reassuring hug. "Don't beat yourself up over a fender bender. No one even got hurt. Did you ever get the driver's name?"

"*Ohh*, yes. He couldn't wait to make a claim on my insurance. Oh, Carly, it was that awful Lyle Bagley. He's the one whose car I hit!"

I knew it. The old Caddy was a dead giveaway.

In the next instant, Arlene's face shuttled downward into a saggy frown. "Oh boy," she said in a thin voice. "Here I am trashing a man who was just murdered. That makes me an awful person, too, doesn't it?" Her lips quivered, and her wide-set eyes filled with tears.

"Of course it doesn't," Carly and Joyce said almost in the same breath.

"Listen, darlin'," Joyce said, "Lyle Bagley probably had so many enemies that the police don't know where to begin looking for his killer. If it gets it off your chest to trash him a little, so be it. I've got no issue with that." She gave a sharp nod as if to emphasize her point.

"And I agree with Joyce," Carly piped in. "Not that Lyle deserved to be murdered—no one does—but I'm guessing he made a lot of questionable choices. Maybe one of those choices got him killed."

Arlene seemed to take comfort from that. "You're probably right." She flashed a tiny smile.

"I always remember what my grandmother used to say," Joyce put in, winking at Carly. "What goes around comes back around to bite you in the arse."

Carly giggled, and Arlene's face brightened. "You're both so wonderful." Arlene reached for Carly's hand and squeezed it. "I'm glad you're in my life."

"Then what are we waiting for?" Joyce slapped her hand on the table. "I'll have another slice of that blueberry pie, missy. And this time add a scoop of ice cream!"

CHAPTER TWENTY-FOUR

CARLY POLITELY DECLINED A SECOND HELPING OF PIE, although she accepted a small scoop of vanilla ice cream. Afterward, she thanked the women for a fun game of Scrabble and wished them both a pleasant evening. She was almost out the door when Arlene padded after her on quiet, slippered feet. "Carly," she whispered, "got a minute?"

"Um, sure." Carly halted in the doorway.

"Let's go in the hall." Arlene made a *shushing* sign with her finger to her lips and followed Carly into the vestibule.

"Is anything wrong?"

Arlene sighed and crossed her arms over her chest. "I've been concerned about Joyce lately, more so than usual. More often than not, she's tired. She's been sleeping later and later every morning."

"That does sound worrisome. Have you spoken to her doctor about it?"

"Not to the doctor, but I spoke with the nurse practitioner," Arlene huffed. "She adjusted one of her medications and prescribed some vitamins, but none of it seems to be helping. The nurse practitioner thinks Joyce might be suffering from depression. I'm beginning to agree."

Carly's heart plummeted. "Then she needs to see the doctor. Have you made her an appointment?"

"She has an appointment, but it's not for several weeks. That's how far in advance her doctor's booking patients." Arlene shook her head, her forehead creased with worry. "I'm sort of at a loss, and as her caretaker I feel responsible. I'm not sure where to go from here."

"Everything you're saying concerns me too," Carly said, although something about the diagnosis of depression wasn't ringing true. "She seemed in good spirits when we were playing Scrabble today. And she sure put away that blueberry pie like it was nobody's business."

Arlene smiled. "I always try to make her favorites to cheer her up. As for her being in good spirits, she makes a special effort when you're here, Carly."

"Oh boy." Carly rolled her shoulders, which had gotten stiff from sitting so long. "Is there anything I can do? Anything that would help?"

"Not that I can think of. I wanted you to be aware, that's all. Please don't tell her I talked to you about this, okay? She'd be horribly embarrassed, and I wouldn't hurt her feelings for anything. She's about the kindest woman in the world."

"I know she is," Carly said, a wave of sadness rolling over her. "No worries. I'm glad you let me know. Please, *please* let me know if I can help in any way, okay?"

"I sure will, and thanks for listening." Arlene gave Carly an awkward hug, pressed a finger to her closed lips, and scurried back inside Joyce's apartment.

Once inside her own apartment, Carly sank onto her sofa and rested her head back. Her mind filled with so many thoughts at once. She didn't know how to begin filtering them.

Joyce.

Carly wished there was a way she could help her, but she honestly didn't know where to begin. It sounded, from what Arlene had revealed, that Joyce needed medical help now, not several weeks from now when her doctor was available.

As for Arlene, she was one of the most selfless people Carly had ever met. Did she ever get weary from caring for Joyce 24/7? Did she ever take time off for herself? Now that Carly thought about it, Arlene had looked a bit drawn today. Was the isolation getting to both of them?

Maybe Carly could do something special for the two of them. Something that would cheer up Joyce and give Arlene a break at the same time.

She was turning ideas over in her head when her cell rang. "Mom!" she yelled into the phone.

"Oh, I'm so glad you answered," Rhonda said. "I thought you might be too busy. How are you, honey?"

"I'm good, Mom. It's so great to hear your voice. How are you? How's Gary?"

A long-suffering sigh came through the phone. "I'm fine, but Gary's being a total pill. He wants to go back out on that sailboat again, and I told him no, that his broken elbow from his last sailing excursion hasn't even healed yet. Stubborn old pimple-popper. That's exactly what I called him too—a stubborn old pimple-popper."

Carly giggled. Gary Clark had been retired for so long, she'd almost forgotten he'd once been a practicing dermatologist. "What did he say?"

"Oh, he backpedaled on that idea, real quick. I think the look on my face scared him into last week."

"I'm familiar with that look," Carly said dryly.

"Enough about Gary. Honey, are you really okay? From what I've read on the internet, the police still haven't made an arrest in Lyle Bagley's murder."

Carly went into the kitchen and opened the fridge. She didn't want to tell her mom that Suzanne was still their prime suspect and that her eatery's future was in limbo. "I know, but they'll probably make one soon. Have you heard anything from Norah?" She pulled out a bottle of water and closed the door with her knee.

"No, and that's another thing. Even when she travels, she

usually texts me at least once a day. I haven't gotten a text from her in three days. What could she and that new beau be so involved in that they can't take two minutes to send me a text?"

"I'm not even going to hazard a guess on that one, Mom. She's an adult, remember?" Carly teased.

"Very funny." Rhonda blew out a sigh of annoyance.

A sudden lump clogged Carly's throat. A tsunami of longing rushed over her, nearly drowning her in the realization of how much she missed her mom. Why did her mom have to move so far away? What was so great about Florida, anyway?

"I know you, Carly Hale," her mom said quietly. "You're dealing with too much right now, aren't you? I can hear it in your voice."

Carly squashed a tear with her palm. "Okay, you're right. I'm dealing with a lot, but that's life. Good days and bad days, right? Everything will work out, Mom. I promise."

A crash sounded in the background, followed by a yelp.

"Oh Lord, honey, I have to run now so I can go kill Gary. I think he knocked over my planter trying to fix it. We'll talk again soon, okay? I love you." Her voice choked.

Carly made kissy noises into the phone, then disconnected.

She tossed her cell phone on the kitchen table, swallowed a mouthful of water, then gazed out through her kitchen's sole window into Joyce's backyard. A stockade fence ran along both sides, with a row of dense juniper hedges forming the rear boundary. A maple tree, lush with greenery, dominated the yard, its leaves swaying slightly in the late-afternoon breeze. Near the fence, a wooden picnic table rested crookedly in the grass.

Carly headed outside, down the front steps, and then along the concrete walkway to the backyard. She laughed as a pair of gray squirrels chased each other around the trunk of the maple, then skittered into the upper branches. Ambling over to check out the picnic table, she was disappointed to find it soiled and grimy, spotted with bird droppings and squashed berries. How long had it been since anyone used it? A robin flew out of nowhere and flitted overhead, landing on top of the fence. He watched Carly for a few seconds, then darted off into the tree.

Her ideas coalescing, Carly began planning a picnic of sorts for Joyce and Arlene.

Joyce had told Carly on several occasions that she'd love to sample one of her grilled cheese concoctions fresh off the grill, while the cheese was still melty and the sandwich sizzling hot. If Carly set up her own portable grill in her apartment, she could prepare the sandwiches and dash outside with them. As for dessert—oh, she could think of so many sweet treats to offer! She cast a glance over the picnic table, her lips curving into a grin as she imagined it covered with bowls of food, plates of grilled cheese sandwiches, and pitchers of refreshing drinks atop a festive tablecloth.

The first thing she'd do was give the picnic table a thorough cleaning, both the tabletop and the bench seats. She could pick up an inexpensive plastic cover at a discount store, with napkins and paper plates to match. With Carly's schedule, the picnic would have to be on a Sunday. If she planned it right, she might be able to pull it off on the following Sunday—exactly seven days from now.

Maybe she could persuade Gina to join them, and possibly even Grant. Something told her that Joyce needed to see fresh faces, meet new people.

According to Carly's mom, Joyce had once been an active volunteer in the community. After her diagnosis of MS, however, she was forced to stop driving. Eventually, she needed in-home care.

A pang of sorrow went straight to Carly's gut. The Joyce she knew now bore little resemblance to the woman her mom had described. Though Joyce was fortunate to have Arlene as her caretaker, she was too isolated, too removed from the everyday activities she'd enjoyed before the illness confined her to a wheelchair. Carly was more determined than ever to plan a special day for her.

Excited about her idea, Carly started to head inside. She wanted to jot down her thoughts before she forgot any of the details.

As she turned toward the walkway, something at the foot of the maple tree caught her attention. She squinted to get a better look, but all she could see was a small gray lump. Using tiny steps, she inched a bit closer, stopping abruptly when she realized what it was. A furry gray squirrel lay huddled at the trunk of the tree. As Carly approached, the squirrel blinked but didn't move. One leg looked out of place.

Poor thing. Had it fallen out of the tree? Whatever happened, the creature clearly needed help.

The minute she got inside she was going to call Animal Control. Or should she call Dr. Anne? No, Animal Control was more accustomed to dealing with wildlife, especially injured animals. Maybe they could help, or at least determine if it needed help.

Her mood dampened, she headed back inside. She glanced up at the house. From the first floor corner window, her landlady stared out at her. Carly smiled and waved, and Joyce halfheartedly returned the gesture.

But her expression was as grim as a boneyard.

CHAPTER TWENTY-FIVE

CARLY CLIMBED THE STAIRS TO HER APARTMENT AND immediately called Animal Control. They promised to send someone by as soon as possible.

Pushing it out of her mind, Carly focused on pleasanter things. She located a blank pad and a pen, plunked herself onto a kitchen chair, and began scribbling down her ideas. She divided the page into two columns: menu suggestions and grocery list. When she was through, she chuckled at both lists. They were so long she'd filled two entire pages.

With today being her last free day until next week, she decided to take a drive to the dollar store. She could pick up a plastic tablecloth, napkins, and paper plates for the picnic, which would give her a head start on supplies. After that, she'd stop at Telly's Market for groceries and sundries and stock her shelves for the next few weeks.

Before she jumped in her car, she tapped on Joyce's door. Arlene answered, and Carly gave her the news about the squirrel.

"I didn't want you to worry if you saw the Animal Control van drive in," Carly told her. "I'm going out for a while to do some shopping, so I wanted to let you know, just in case they stop by while I'm gone."

Arlene's eyes widened in distress, and she clutched the door frame. "Oh my gosh, I'm so glad you noticed the poor little dear. I hope it'll be okay. What made you go into the backyard?"

"Oh, just getting some fresh air. You know, taking a break from the air-conditioning." Carly smiled and felt her cheeks flush from the fib. She hated lying, but in this case she felt justified. She was planning a fun surprise for the ladies and didn't want to spoil it by dropping any hints.

~

When Carly returned home a few hours later, she found a note taped to her door. *Spoke to owner's caretaker, and squirrel was removed. Will be taken to state wildlife refuge for rehabilitation of broken femur.* It was signed by B. Briggs, Animal Control Division, Balsam Dell Police. The officer's cell number was printed at the bottom.

Grateful the little squirrel was in caring hands, Carly removed the note from the door and went inside her apartment.

Carly put away all her groceries and other purchases. The apartment was slightly warm but still comfortable. She'd been testing the different settings on her new air conditioner and was finally getting the hang of it.

One glance into the bathroom mirror told her she'd gotten quite a bit of color while she was out. Her face was pink, as were her arms and the front of her legs. And if she didn't get a haircut soon, she was going to start resembling a sheepdog.

The day had turned out crazy, she thought, resting her head back on one of her throw pillows. Her encounter with Janet Moody had added another layer to the mystery of Lyle's horrible demise.

A woman scorned.

The words jumped into Carly's head as Janet's face flashed before her. For years, Janet had clung to the delusion Lyle secretly adored her. She'd convinced herself that one day he'd come to his senses, sweep her into his arms, and declare his undying love. When she learned the truth, she'd been crushed beyond reason. Her initial reaction was to vandalize Tiffany's car, but had she done even worse? Had she made Lyle pay the ultimate price for his perceived betrayal?

In some ways, Matt Bagley was an even sadder figure. He'd hung his hopes on the shaky hook that was his half brother. When that hook loosened and fell to the ground, Matt's dreams for his future went with it. For most of his adult life, his love/hate relationship with Lyle had tainted his emotions. But which emotion ruled—the love or the hate?

Her mind overflowing with unanswered questions, Carly curled up on the sofa and closed her eyes. She wasn't sure how long she dozed, but at the sound of someone pounding on her door, she jerked awake.

She sat up and rubbed her eyes. *What time was it?*

"Carly?" a woman's voice called through the door.

Carly jumped to her feet, unlocked her door, and whipped it open. "Gina! I thought I recognized your voice. Why didn't you tell me you were coming over?"

Gina stepped inside. She looked chic in a crisp yellow blouse, a denim skirt, and platform espadrilles. "How can I surprise you if I call you first, silly?" She held up a square pink box that looked suspiciously like a bakery box.

"You didn't," Carly gasped. "Is that from Sissy's?" Sissy's Bakery had been one of their favorite hangouts when they were in high school.

"Of course it is!"

Carly pulled Gina inside and locked the door behind her. "Let's go in the kitchen."

"This place is adorable," Gina said, swerving her gaze all around.

Carly was already at the kitchen table, cutting the string on the box. She opened the cover and squealed. "Raspberry swirl brownies. They're the absolute best."

"I know, right?" Gina looked all around the kitchen.

Carly removed two sandwich plates from the cupboard. "Thanks. I totally lucked out. Plus, my landlord is Joyce Katso, and she's the best. I think she remembered Mom from her library days." Carly poured each of them a glass of iced tea and sat down.

"How's Joyce doing?" Gina plucked one of the oversized brownies from the box. "I always used to see her at the market or in the pharmacy, but she hasn't been around lately."

Carly grabbed a brownie for herself and bit off a large corner. "Unfortunately, with her MS, she doesn't get out much."

"That's a shame," Gina gulped down a mouthful of iced tea.

"Hey, do you want to help me cheer her up with a backyard picnic?" Carly explained her plan to serve grilled cheese sandwiches and other goodies to Joyce and Arlene on the picnic table the following Sunday.

"That sounds like fun. Count me in." Gina licked raspberry cream off her fingers.

"You were telling me the other day that your dad had health issues," Carly said.

Gina sighed. "Last year he was diagnosed with type two diabetes. His circulation is lousy. He feels bad about selling the house, but he needs the money for his new place. It's brand new and gorgeous, but…" Her eyes watered, and she shook her head.

"But it will break his heart to give up the house he raised you in," Carly finished, reading Gina's mind.

"Exactly. We still have a few months before we have to move, but in the meantime, I need to find an apartment. If you hear of anything that won't cost a queen's ransom, will you let me know?"

"Of course I will."

Gina sat back and blew out a breath. "After we talked the other day, I couldn't stop thinking about how devastated you must have felt after your husband died."

Devastated didn't begin to describe Carly's agony during those weeks after Daniel's death. She'd shuffled around in a daze, barely eating, sleep her only escape from the searing pain of her loss. Then spring arrived, the trees began to bud, and fresh grass sprang up along the roadways. Carly finally realized what she couldn't let go of: the anger. Anger still as fresh and raw as it had been the night that police car pulled into their driveway and shattered her world.

If she was ever going to get past it, she had to go to the source. She had to confront the family that had cost Daniel his life. She found their address—their surname was Auberge. When she reached the two-story clapboard house, she parked her Corolla in the rutted driveway. Blood pulsing through her veins at race-car speed, she clambered up a set of concrete steps and rang the bell. After a minute or so a young woman came to the door. She had dark gray eyes, curly brown hair, and a smile so trusting it made Carly's stomach throb. An infant girl with chubby pink cheeks was nestled in the crook of her arm. "Hi, can I help you?"

Carly gave her name, and the woman clapped a hand over her mouth. "Oh my, please, *please* come in." She pushed open the door and Carly stepped inside. "Give me a minute to put Danielle in her crib and I'll be right back."

The woman dashed off and returned a minute later. By then, hot tears were streaming down Carly's cheeks. "You named her Danielle."

"We named her after a hero," the woman acknowledged and crushed Carly in a tearful hug. "I'm Glenda, by the way. My husband isn't home, but he'll be sorry he missed you."

Over tea and homemade banana cookies, they talked about that night. After Daniel's tragic accident, the Auberges' neighbors had pitched in with food and essentials to ease their struggles through the winter. Glenda had suffered nightmares for weeks, but eventually they subsided. But not a day passed that she didn't think about Daniel and the sacrifice he'd made for her family.

On the drive home, Carly felt a sense of peace fall over her. Despite knowing the risks that fateful night, and over Carly's protests, Daniel had made a choice. To do otherwise would have gone completely against his nature. With the past in focus, Carly began formulating a plan for her future.

"Carly?" Gina jiggled her arm. "You're lost in thought, aren't you?"

"Sorry. I did get lost for a minute."

"No, I'm the one who should be sorry. I didn't mean to bring up bad memories. It's just...I wish I'd been there for you, you know?" Gina blinked back tears.

I do too, Carly thought. She clasped her friend's fingers for a brief moment, then released them. "It's okay, Gina. You're here now, and that's what counts, right?"

Gina gave her a half smile. "I guess so."

Not wanting to dwell on the past any longer, Carly filled her in on her conversations with both Janet and Matt earlier in the day. "So, what do you think?" she finished. "Who's at the top of your suspect list?"

Gina crossed her arms over her chest. "Between those two? Probably Janet, but my sense is that it's neither of them. No, someone else got ticked off enough to do away with Lyle. He was a pro at pushing people's buttons."

"Janet said any number of tenants at the mobile home park might have had it in for him," Carly suggested.

"True, but murder is a big leap from being a disgruntled tenant. I can't help wondering if the killer *intended* to murder Lyle, or if he or she only wanted to threaten him but carried the attack too far."

Carly had never thought of that. Identifying the murder weapon would help, for sure. So far, the police hadn't reported finding it.

"What about Tiffany?" Carly asked her.

"As a suspect?" Gina shrugged. "I hadn't thought of her, but she was closest to Lyle. Maybe they had a blowup that night, and she chased him into the parking lot. Who knows?"

"I almost forget to tell you." Carly gave Gina a recap of her and

Becca's jaunt up to Tiffany's apartment the night before after they heard all the crashing noises.

"So, Lyle left his garbage all over her place too. When we were married, he had magazines stacked everywhere. Never wanted to throw them away. I used to sneak them into the trash can, but he always fished them out. Sounds like Tiffany was already getting a taste of his hoarding habits."

"There was a tiny part of me that felt sorry for her," Carly said, swiping crumbs from the table into her hands and onto her empty plate. "She seems kind of friendless."

Gina made a face. "There's probably a reason for that."

"Becca, on the other hand, is a total sweetheart. I just hate the idea of her living in her car."

"Becca's okay," Gina said. "She can take care of herself. She'll find a better place before you know it."

Carly bit her lip. "I hope so. Hey, on another subject," she said slyly. "Is there anyone special in your life right now?"

"Oh, you slipped that in so cleverly," Gina scolded playfully. "There is someone, but so far neither of us has acted on it. He's still smarting from a relationship that ended badly, so he's not ready to take the plunge. We're friends for now, but I can tell he's interested."

"Well, you know the old saying," Carly offered with a wink. "Slow and steady wins the race."

"Yeah, maybe." Gina's full cheeks flushed a bright pink.

Carly wiped her lips with a napkin. "I have to ask you, how do you know so much about everyone in town? You seem to be an inexhaustible source of information."

Gina laughed. "Do you remember my aunt Lil? The one who used to read palms?"

"Oh boy, do I ever! She read my palm when I was in the seventh grade. Told me I was destined for greatness and that I'd never marry. My mother was furious."

Gina groaned. "God, I'd forgotten that. Luckily, she gave up the palm reading."

"What is Lil now, in her late seventies?"

"No one knows, but she's at least that. These days she has purple hair and works as a hair washer at the Happy Clipper salon. Boy, is that place a hotbed of gossip. Aunt Lil finds out things about people they didn't even know about themselves. A lot of my intel comes from her, but Dad picks up tidbits from his old gang at the fire department too."

"I can only imagine," Carly said.

"And since Lil has the hearing of a bat, she picks up on every conversation going on simultaneously in that salon. I swear, the woman could spy for the FBI. Janet Moody's been getting her hair done there for years. According to Aunt Lil, Janet pours out all her troubles, in excruciating detail, while she's having her hair washed."

"Interesting," Carly said. "Joyce's caretaker, Arlene, offered to trim my hair. She took an online course in haircutting so Joyce wouldn't have to make trips to the salon."

"No offense to Arlene, but you should really go to my gal, Ladybug Ellis, for a cut and style. She's excellent."

"Her name's Ladybug?"

"Her hair's flaming red, so everyone calls her that. Do you have any free time this week for a trim?"

"I get into the restaurant around eight or eight-thirty, and I don't leave till after seven."

Gina retrieved her cell phone from her pocket and tapped out a quick text. A minute later she smiled. "Ladybug can take you at quarter to eight tomorrow morning. Shall I confirm it?"

"That would be wonderful. I'm starting to look pretty shaggy." She smiled. "And since I'm the boss, it's okay if I get to the eatery a bit later than usual."

After they cleaned up the table, Carly found her notepad. They divided up tasks for Sunday's picnic.

"Gina, I'm really excited that you're helping me with this." Carly smiled at her friend. "I know it's only grilled cheese sandwiches, but I want to make it special for Joyce."

"First off, there's no such thing as *only* grilled cheese sandwiches," Gina corrected. "Second, I'm loving all this. It's sort of like the old days, you know?"

After they completed their list-making, Gina checked her cell phone. A smile touched her lips, and her cheeks reddened.

"Anyone special?" Carly teased.

"No, just the usual. It's getting late, though. I'm gonna head home before Dad sends out the cavalry. You know how he worries. Hey, you better put some cream on that sunburn," Gina said, pointing at Carly's arms.

"I will. Don't worry." Carly didn't think her sunburn was that bad, but she'd take Gina's advice anyway.

They hugged goodbye, and Gina promised to stop into the restaurant during the week.

After Gina left, Carly called it a night. The following day was the beginning of her work week. She was tempted to text Suzanne and beg her to return, but she decided to wait until morning.

Carly was shutting off the air conditioner when her cell pinged with a text. She frowned when she saw the readout on the screen: *No Caller ID*. She tapped open the message.

> U don't know how to mind your own business, do U?
> Better start, before it's 2 late.

CHAPTER TWENTY-SIX

THE MOMENT CARLY STEPPED INSIDE THE HAPPY CLIPPER ON Monday morning, her spirits rose. The bright yellow walls and hanging, tulip-shaped lights gave the salon a welcoming vibe. A receptionist who looked no more than thirteen flashed a chartreuse-lipped smile at Carly.

"Hi! Are you here for Ladybug?"

"I am," Carly said. "She was kind enough to squeeze me in early for a wash and a trim."

The receptionist crooked a finger. "Follow me. She's not in yet, but she'll be here any minute. Lil will do your wash first."

Carly trailed her into a small room at the back, where a petite, elderly woman with lavender hair and pink plastic earrings was wiping down a sink with a sponge. When she saw Carly, she dropped the sponge and threw her skinny arms around her. "Carly Hale. Gina told me you were comin' in. I haven't seen you in an elephant's age! How ya doin', doll?"

"I'm doing fine," Carly said. "You look great!"

Lil fluffed her lilac hair and jutted out a bony hip. "Why, thank you. I do my best." She tossed a plastic cape over Carly and instructed her to lean back in the sink.

"I'm so glad the salon could accommodate me this early," Carly said.

"Well, we take good care of our customers. We know everyone has crazy schedules, and we try to work around them."

After a few minutes of idle chatter about Gina, Carly's eatery, and the world in general, Lil sprayed lukewarm water over Carly's hair. "Gina tells me you're investigatin' her ex-husband's murder," the elderly woman blurted.

Carly cringed, and in a quieter voice said, "Not exactly, but I've been chatting with people who were close to him. I understand his manager, Janet, comes in here quite a bit."

"Oh, she sure does. Gets her hair cut once a month, like clockwork. Truth be told, I think she was always primping for her boss, if you get my meanin'." She squirted a blob of shampoo onto Carly's head. "Won't need to do that no more. But murder's a terrible thing, no matter who the victim is, right? Even if Lyle Bagley was a scuzzy worm."

"I heard Janet was crazy about him."

"Oh ho! You heard right, lady," Lil said, massaging Carly's head. "She'd have married him in an instant, if he'd asked her." She paused. "I actually used to like Janet. Felt sorry for her, in fact, until something happened a few days ago that really bothered me."

"What was that?"

"Well, after I put the cape on her, she leaned back in the sink and the necklace she was wearin' fell backward on her neck. Man, you should've seen it. A blue watch with a fancy face and diamonds all around the edge. She tucked it back in her bosom real fast when she realized it'd fallen out." She tapped Carly's shoulder. "Wouldn't have bothered me, except that I'd seen that pendant before. *On someone else,*" she added meaningfully.

That got Carly's attention. "Who else did you see it on?"

"That hoity-toity Mrs. Dobson, that's who," Lil said crisply. "'Course Mrs. D. never wears it when she's gettin' her hair done. She takes it off and sticks it in a velvet pouch, then puts it back on after Ladybug gets her all spiffed up. Funny thing is, she hasn't worn it for a few months. I didn't think much of it till I saw that one on Janet."

Carly's ears perked. Was it the same pendant watch Janet had been wearing yesterday? The one she claimed Lyle had given her?

"Do you think it's the same pendant? It might be a replica."

Lil snorted. "Maybe, but I'd bet my next paycheck it was the same one. You'd have to see it to know what I mean."

I did see it, Carly thought. "Does Janet get her hair done the same day as Mrs. Dobson?"

Lil shut off the water and toweled Carly's head. "No. Mrs. D. has a standing appointment every Tuesday, but Janet comes on Wednesday. So, if Janet pinched it, when did she do it? That's what I can't figure out."

"Lil, did you call Mrs. Dobson to ask if her pendant was missing?"

Lil blew out a coffee-laced breath. "Not yet. I been debatin' with myself what to do. What would you do?"

"I'm not sure." Carly sat up straight and hopped off her chair. "Maybe the next time Mrs. D. comes in, you could ask her why she's not wearing her pendant watch. If she says it was stolen…"

"Then I'll be forced to tell her what I saw." Lil grinned. "I'm glad I told you about it. I feel better now." Her gaze softened. "Gina told me about you losin' your fella, Carly. I'm awful sorry."

"Thank you. He was a good man."

Lil squeezed both of Carly's hands in her wrinkled ones. "It was sure good to see you, again. And you got real pretty hair, you know that? After Ladybug gets through with it, you're gonna look totally *adorbs*."

CHAPTER TWENTY-SEVEN

LADYBUG TURNED OUT TO BE A SHEER DELIGHT, OR A *SHEAR* delight, as Carly thought of her. Within twenty minutes, she'd transformed Carly's overgrown, chestnut waves into soft, short rings that framed her face. If Carly ever got the chance to shop again, she'd make sure to treat herself to a pair of earrings to show off her new do.

Unlocking the back door to the eatery, she felt a sudden chill race down her spine. That creepy text message from the night before had invaded her dreams, chopping up her sleep into small, fitful chunks. Was someone watching her? Someone who wasn't happy with the questions she'd been asking?

She hurried inside, locked the door quickly, then flipped on the lights. After stashing her tote in her desk, she returned to the dining room and turned on the air conditioning. Another humid day was predicted, and she intended to stay inside as much as possible. Gina was right—she'd gotten more sun the day before than she realized. Her skin was now tender to the touch.

Carly put on the coffee and waited for it to brew.

You don't know how to mind your own business, do you? Better start, before it's too late.

The message had been partially in text speak, but the meaning was clear. Someone didn't like Carly poking into Lyle's murder.

When the coffee was ready, she poured herself a mugful, inhaling the fragrant aroma. Carly knew coffee made some people jittery, but for her it had the opposite effect. Coffee relaxed her, gave her a sense of calm, a feeling she could attack any challenges that crossed her path and kick them soundly to the curb.

Skipping her usual breakfast sandwich, she began prepping for the day. She'd barely begun wiping down the tables when a loud knock at the back door nearly made her drop her spray bottle.

She tiptoed toward the door, listened for a moment, then called out, "Who is it?"

"Carly, it's Colm. I have your bread delivery."

At the sound of Colm Hardy's familiar voice, Carly tapped her chest in relief. Of course. Monday was bread delivery day. How could she have spaced on that? She opened the door and held it for him so he could maneuver his dolly over the threshold. "Colm, I'm so sorry. My mind was in a thousand places."

"No problem," he said, wheeling a metal dolly laden with cardboard boxes through the doorway. He pushed his black-rimmed glasses farther onto his nose and followed her into the kitchen. "It's already so humid out my glasses keep falling," he chuckled.

"I know what you mean. It's supposed to be another steamer."

Carly helped him unload the contents of the boxes and then examined the packing slip. "Looks good, Colm. Next week I might order a few extra loaves of rye."

"Works for us. By the way, Sara told me she talked to you the other day about Bagley. Piece of work, that guy was." His expression soured, and he leaned one arm on the dolly.

Carly's heartbeat quickened. "Sara said you were tempted to confront him after he cheated her. I can understand how angry you must have been."

He laughed. "I wanted to punch the guy's lights out, but you know Sara—all peace, love, and flowers. For her sake, I left him alone. Probably just as well, or the police might be questioning me about his murder," he joked. "But I gotta tell you, Carly, Sara was relieved when her sister moved out of that place. Lori said some weird guy had started hanging around there on weekends. Thin face, piercing eyes. No one knew who he was, but he always acted like he belonged there. Drove an old Chevy with New York tags."

Carly gasped, her thoughts traveling immediately to Matt Bagley. "Did Lori say what color the car was?"

"Not really, but Sara saw it one day. I think she said it was a metallic gray. She made a mental note of it, just in case anything ever happened. So anyway, the guy would poke around the property for a few hours, then take off, but he always came back the next weekend. Gave Lori the willies."

From Colm's description, it sounded like Matt Bagley. A zing of alarm shot through Carly. "No one ever questioned him?"

"Not that I know of." He glanced at his watch. "Shoot, I'd better get going. Sara will chew out my behind if I don't make my deliveries on time." He snapped his fingers. "Oh Lordy, I almost forgot. She gave me a loaf of bread she wanted you to try. Can you come out to the truck with me?"

Carly's heart tripped. "Um, sure." Carly felt her pocket for her cell phone, just to be sure it was there, which it was. There was no reason to be nervous about Colm, except that he'd nursed a grudge against Lyle.

Colm's white van was parked behind Carly's and Tiffany's cars. He loaded the dolly into the back, then reached into a cardboard box and pulled out a white bag.

"It's cranberry-pecan," Colm explained, handing it to Carly. "Might not work for grilled cheese, but Sara's been experimenting with different versions and she wants your opinion. Once she perfects it, she's going to add it to her repertoire."

Carly peeked inside the bag at the crusty brown loaf. "Wow, it looks delicious. I can't wait to try it. Thank Sara for me, okay?"

"You got it, Carly." He slammed shut the rear doors of his van, and with a wave of his hand, he zoomed off.

Carly hurried back inside, making sure the door was locked behind her. As she carried the loaf into the kitchen, she couldn't help speculating as to why Matt Bagley would've been hanging around the mobile home park on weekends.

Wait.

Hadn't Matt told her he wanted to take over one of Lyle's businesses? What if the business he wanted to take over was the mobile home park? If so, it sounded as if he'd been checking out the place for quite some time, long before Lyle was murdered.

Carly slid the loaf of cranberry-pecan bread out of the bag and onto her cutting board. With her serrated knife, she sliced off a thick end, then cut a sliver from that. She popped the sliver into her mouth. The blend of tart cranberries and sweet pecans made her taste buds dance a tango on her tongue.

Carly smiled down at the loaf. Might not work for grilled cheese?

We'll just see about that.

~

Carly was stashing loaves of bread into the freezer when her cell pinged with another text. Her heart racing, she tapped it open.

> Carly, can you let me in? I'm at the back door.

Yes! It was Suzanne.

She raced into the dining room and flung open the door. "Suzanne, I'm so happy to see you!"

The moment Suzanne stepped into the dining room her face brightened. "Not as happy as I am," she said wryly. "Is it okay if I work today? I'd like to work till closing, if that's okay. I could use the extra dough."

"Okay if you work?" Carly threw her arms around her. "Is it okay if I win the Vermont Powerball?"

Suzanne gave a slight laugh, and Carly took a step back and

looked at her. Her eyes were slightly droopy with fatigue, but she didn't look as tense as she had a few days earlier.

"Coffee," Suzanne said, scurrying behind the counter. She poured herself a steaming cup and took a long sip. "Hey, you got your hair cut. It's cute."

"Thanks. What made you decide to come in?"

Suzanne stared down at her mug. "Jake and I were talking," she said quietly. "We both agreed that my staying home was only making me look guilty, so…" She held out a hand. "Here I am. Until the cops haul me away, I'm yours."

"So, you and Jake are talking?"

Suzanne made a face. "Well, we have a kid together, so we sort of have to." Her cheeks reddened. "Actually, he's been okay lately. Working a lot. *Not* gambling, according to him. Time will tell, I guess. I'm not getting my hopes up."

Carly decided not to comment. If Suzanne and Jake were working things out, she didn't want to break the spell.

"One good thing. I got my wheels back," Suzanne said. "The only thing the police wouldn't return to me was the key to the restaurant."

That was a surprise. If Suzanne was their top suspect, why would they return her car to her?

"That's okay. I'll have a new one made. Did the police confiscate anything from your car?"

Suzanne took another sip of her coffee. "No, nothing. Jake did a dumb thing, though. He told the police he was with me that night, that I stayed at his apartment all night."

Carly's eyes widened. "He gave you a false alibi."

"Exactly. I set them straight, but now Jake is in trouble. I don't think they'll press charges, but he sure didn't help matters."

Carly didn't know what to say, so she said nothing. She was so happy to have Suzanne back!

After Suzanne finished her coffee, they both got busy preparing for the lunch crowd. At 11:00 a.m. on the dot, Carly opened up. Before long, customers began streaming in. Many had Carly's yellow coupons in hand, which meant Grant had done a thorough job distributing them.

The coupons reminded Carly that she hadn't heard from Don Frasco in a few days. Not that she was complaining, but his sudden silence made her a little nervous.

"What's with those yellow coupons?" Suzanne asked, after delivering two Smoky Steals the Bacon sandwiches to a couple in the rear booth.

"Long story, but I had them made up so I could check out someone who's staying at the Peacock."

Suzanne's eyes widened. "Whoa. You can tell me about it at the break."

Lunch was busier than ever. Suzanne had returned to being her cheery self as she scribbled out orders, delivered sandwich plates, and chatted up customers as if each was a special old friend. It made Carly's heart soar to see her back in the swing of things.

A little after 1:30, Ari Mitchell came in. He took a seat at the counter, and once again that familiar flush crept into Carly's cheeks. She prayed it wasn't noticeable, but she suspected her face was flashing like a neon sign.

She realized he was staring at her. "Carly, you look…lovely," Ari said, his dark-brown eyes drinking in her face. "I mean, not that you don't normally, but your hair… It looks especially nice today."

If Carly was blushing before, she was probably strawberry red now. "Thanks. I had it cut this morning. What can I get for you today?" Her gaze slid to his muscular, suntanned arms, and her heart skipped a little. Without asking, she poured him a coffee and set it down in front of him.

"Thanks, you read my mind. I think I'll have the Vermont Classic. It's a cheddar kind of day."

A cheddar kind of day. What did that mean? Was he as self-conscious as she was?

"You got it." She moved to the side and began preparing his sandwich, adding an extra slice of cheddar to increase the melt factor.

"Looks like you got a bit of sun over the weekend." He took a sip from his mug.

"I did," she said, buttering one side of his sandwich. She flipped it onto the grill, buttered the top side, and weighted it with a grill press. "Yesterday was a great day for a walk, so I decided to explore my neighborhood. I ended up getting more sun than I realized."

Sheesh, could I sound any more boring?

To Carly's relief, three teenaged boys wearing red ball caps came in. Hadn't the trio been in a few days earlier? They clomped into a booth with all the grace of a herd of moose. Carly waved to them, smiling at their animated chatter as Suzanne took their orders. Carly flipped over Ari's sandwich to grill the other side.

"Isn't that Mr. M?" one of the boys called.

The three bolted out of the booth. Wearing huge grins, they came over and surrounded Ari. "We thought that was you," the tallest of the three said.

"Hey, guys!" Ari smiled at them.

Carly watched them curiously. She wondered how they knew him.

"Carly," Ari said, pointing a finger at each of the boys, "this is Ethan, Chris, and Logan. Boys, Carly is the owner of this fine establishment. She makes the best grilled cheese sandwiches on the planet."

"Hey," each of them mumbled by way of greeting.

Ari turned on his stool to talk to the boys. "All set for the game tonight?"

"Yup," one of them said, his eyes lighting up.

Carly slid Ari's sandwich onto a plate, added a cup of tomato soup along with pickles and chips, then set it down in front of him. Gooey, warm cheddar leaked from the edges. She felt like biting off a chunk herself.

"Whoa, now that's a grilled cheese," Ari said, his grin wide.

One of the boys leaned over Ari's shoulder. "Aw man, that looks sick. I hope ours come out like that."

"Your sandwiches will be just as *sick*," Carly said with a chuckle. "I promise."

"See you tonight, Mr. M!" they called out, trudging back to their booth.

Carly refilled Ari's coffee. "Friends of yours?"

He nodded. "They're great kids. I coach their summer softball league." He bit off a corner of his sandwich. "Mmm, this is definitely sick," he said, grinning after he swallowed. "Um, Carly, after the boys are through, would you give me their bills to pay? I'd like to treat them."

"Gotcha." She gave him a thumbs up. *What a nice gesture.*

She prepared the boys' sandwiches, piling them with extra cheese the way she'd done with Ari's. When their plates were ready, she signaled Suzanne.

Groans of pleasure rose from the booth as Suzanne set down their lunch plates. Watching the boys attack their meals, Carly felt a surge of pride. This was why she'd returned to Balsam Dell, why she opened the eatery she'd always dreamed of. Watching customers bubble with joy over her grilled cheese sandwiches was the best high she could imagine.

All the more reason to find Lyle's killer and rescue her livelihood.

When Grant arrived, his eyes sparked with delight at the sight of Suzanne. The women went into the kitchen for a break while Grant made them a Farmhouse Cheddar Sleeps with the Fishes to share.

As they ate, Carly gave Suzanne a recap of what she'd uncovered over the past few days.

"I've got to find out who Lyle's lawyer is and talk to him," Carly said, popping a stray blob of tuna into her mouth. "If we knew who stands to inherit Lyle's estate... Oh, wait a minute." She looked at Suzanne. "Why am I such a dolt? Tiffany knows who the lawyer is! She's already talked to him."

Suzanne looked doubtful. "Yeah, but would the lawyer even tell you anything? Isn't stuff like that supposed to be confidential?"

"Maybe." Carly chewed her lip. "Since Lyle's dead, I'm not sure."

Grant pushed through the kitchen door and headed to the fridge. He pulled out a container of washed lettuce, then went over to the women. In a quiet voice he said, "Guess who's sitting in the back booth, scarfing down a grilled cheese with the gusto of a running back?"

Carly exchanged glances with Suzanne. "I give up."

"Tiffany Spencer."

CHAPTER TWENTY-EIGHT

"ENJOYING YOUR SANDWICH?" CARLY USED THE CHEERIEST voice she could muster as she approached Tiffany's booth. For someone who'd claimed she existed on yogurt and salads, Tiffany was doing an admirable job of putting away a grilled cheddar on asiago bread along with a mound of potato chips.

"Trying to," Tiffany said, glaring at Carly over a mug of coffee. Her eyes were clear, her makeup applied to perfection. Her blond hair, cut in an asymmetric style, was fluffed around her face. A dramatic change from a few days ago. One thing hadn't changed: the two keys dangling from around her neck still nested in the crook of her cleavage.

"May I sit?" Carly asked.

Tiffany shrugged. "It's your restaurant."

Carly slid onto the bench seat opposite her. "I wondered if you've heard anything new from the police."

Tiffany rolled a pair of eyes that sported a tad too much mascara. "This might surprise you, but the police don't exactly share with me."

"Have you shared your theory with them? About the killer?"

Tiffany picked up a grilled cheese half. "No, because I changed my mind. I have no idea who it is." She bit off a large chunk of her sandwich and chewed in a most unladylike fashion.

"Really?" Carly blew out a frustrated breath. The woman was maddening. Was she playing games, or had she honestly changed her mind about the killer's identity?

"What I want," Tiffany said, jabbing a manicured fingernail at Carly, "is to get into Lyle's house. If he wrote something that said he was leaving his estate to me, then that's the only place it could be."

"But why do you think he did that?" To Carly, it simply wasn't logical.

"I told you, because he wrote down everything! He was always scribbling in notebooks or on notepads."

Carly still wasn't convinced, but then another thought struck her. "Tiffany, were you *ever* in Lyle's house?"

Tiffany averted her eyes. "I was only there twice. Except for Lyle's bedroom, it's kind of a pit. Both times I spent the night, but I barely slept. And get your mind out of the gutter," she added with annoyance. "That's not why. Lyle insisted on keeping the outside light on. It was right below the bedroom window, and it was so bright I couldn't sleep."

"Why wouldn't he turn it off?"

"Who knows? Lyle had a lot of quirks. But it ticked me off because he knew I had sleep issues. It's one of the reasons I moved into this building, because the downtown is so quiet at night."

Hmm, that was interesting. Carly's gaze went to Tiffany's hanging keys. "And he definitely never gave you a house key?"

Tiffany shook her head. "All I have are these stupid things." She picked them up and let them flop back onto her chest. In the next instant, her face went rigid. "Wait a minute. *Wait. A. Minute.* When you said that just now, it made me remember something. The first time I went to Lyle's with him, a few months ago, he was locked out. I can't remember why, but all of a sudden, a light bulb seemed to go off in his head. He reached under the wheel well of that dumb Caddy and pulled off one of those magnetic key holders."

Carly felt her pulse jolt. "And his house key was there?"

Tiffany's eyes sparked with triumph. "Exactly. If it's still there, and I'll bet it is, I'm going inside that house."

"I'm not sure that's a great idea," Carly cautioned. "Aren't you worried someone might see you? And remember, the police haven't arrested anyone for the murder yet. It could be dangerous."

Tiffany seemed to mull that possibility. "I'll wait till it's dark. And I'll bring a flashlight, so I won't have to turn on any lights."

"If you're determined to do this," Carly advised, "then I think you should go before dark. Who knows? The police might even be watching the house. A car turning into the driveway before it gets dark will look a lot less suspicious than one driving in after sundown. Besides, if you get there before dark, you'll have enough daylight to look around and won't need a flashlight."

With a purse of her lips, Tiffany fingered her dangling keys. "I have to admit, you've got a point." She narrowed her gaze at Carly. "You sound like you've done this before."

Carly stifled a smile. The day she and Gina kidnapped the frogs from the high school science lab, Gina had suggested sneaking into the school after dark to steal the amphibians. Carly, however, saw the flaw in that plan. After dark they'd have to jimmy open a window, plus they'd probably set off an alarm or be caught on camera. Instead, they carried out their plan in broad daylight, right after the last class got out. No one suspected the shoe boxes they were carrying contained anything other than school supplies.

"Not exactly, but it makes sense, doesn't it? In fact…" Carly paused, giving her brain a moment to ponder the possibilities. If Tiffany were to find the key in the Caddy's wheel well and use it to gain access, then she wouldn't be entering illegally. If anyone asked, she was simply going in to retrieve some personal things. Since she and Lyle had been engaged, it made perfect sense.

And this might be Carly's only chance to get into Lyle's house to do a little spying.

"Tiffany, I don't think you should go into the house alone. If I go with you, we can look for Lyle's notes together. Two sets of hands, and eyes, are better than one, right?"

Tiffany eyed her critically. "Possibly. What's in it for you?"

"Nothing, except maybe to find something that'll clear Suzanne's name. She's still under suspicion, even if she's not in police custody." Carly intentionally used buzzwords she'd heard on TV crime shows, hoping Tiffany would buy her argument.

Tiffany's expression seemed to soften while she considered the idea. "I guess it could work. What time would we leave?"

"I can't leave the restaurant until after seven. Why don't we meet in the parking lot at seven-thirty? It doesn't get dark till about nine, so that should give us time to search Lyle's place. *If* we get in, that is."

Tiffany shoved the last bite of her sandwich into her mouth and nodded as she chewed. She swallowed and said, "Okay. You got a deal." She wiped her lips and tossed down her napkin.

"Before you go, I have one more question. You mentioned before that you spoke to Lyle's attorney. It is someone in town?"

"It's a guy he knew from high school. Brad Gearhart. His office is in Bennington."

Brad Gearhart. Carly remembered him. In school he was the quintessential nerd, but he was smart and studious and never missed a day of class.

"What do I owe you for the sandwich?" Tiffany asked.

"Nothing. It's my treat. See you out back at seven-thirty then?"

Without another word, Tiffany nodded and slid off the bench seat. She smiled at Grant and snubbed Suzanne as she strode through the eatery's front entrance, a swirl of floral perfume trailing in her wake.

Around 4:30 p.m. the eatery got busy again. Officer Palmer came in, this time without his pal Kevin O'Toole. He ate his Vermont Classic in silence, perusing a folded newspaper as he did so. After he paid his bill, he waved at Carly and said, "You pick up that dog yet?"

She laughed and shook her head as he walked outside into the humid afternoon.

They worked steadily until a little after 6:00, when things quieted down.

"If you don't mind, I think I'll take off," Suzanne said wearily. "I guess I'm not used to working a full day."

"You look tired. Go home and rest," Carly told her.

Suzanne hugged her. "Thanks for believing in me. Let's hope this nightmare is over soon."

Grant waited on a few stragglers while Carly took over the grill. After the last customer left, they scrubbed the booths and the counter. Carly was tempted to tell Grant to leave early so she could meet Tiffany in the parking lot, but she didn't want to arouse his suspicions. To her relief, he headed for the door right at seven. "I'm going to catch Ari's game at the school," he said. "It's the first game of the summer season."

"Which school?" Carly asked him.

"The Berrybain School. It's for so-called 'at-risk' boys, but I hate labels like that. It's like saying these kids aren't as good as kids in regular schools." His dark-brown eyes flared.

Carly saw his point about labeling people. "Have a good time. Tell Ari I say hi!"

Grant smiled. "Thanks. I'll tell him."

Locking the door after him, Carly groaned. *Why did I say that? Now Grant will think I'm crushing on Ari, which I'm not. I'm definitely not.*

Carly removed her apron, tossed it into the bin, and dug her cell out of her tote. It would be folly to accompany Tiffany to Lyle's without letting someone know. Someone she absolutely trusted.

She shot off a quick text to Gina, explaining her plan. Gina responded instantly.

Be careful! Why don't U wait till after dark?

Giggling to herself, Carly responded: Remember the frogs. She was rewarded with a laughing emoticon.

Before shutting off the lights, Carly grabbed a handful of vinyl gloves from the box beneath the counter. Shoving them into the pocket of her denim skirt, she headed for the back door.

There was one potential drawback to Carly's plan: the possibility that Tiffany was the killer. Her gut instinct told her otherwise, but still, she had to consider it.

At 7:20, Carly stepped outside into the parking lot and locked the door behind her. Tiffany was already there, sitting in her red Nissan with her hands planted on the steering wheel. She powered her window halfway down. "Get in."

In that moment, Carly made a decision. "I'll follow you in my car," she said. "Lead the way."

CHAPTER TWENTY-NINE

LYLE'S HOME WAS ON A WINDING, HEAVILY WOODED ROAD OFF the main drag, four miles or so from downtown Balsam Dell. Carly followed Tiffany's Nissan around to the back of the modest white house. Instead of driving up behind Tiffany's car, she parked off to the side of the sizable paved driveway, where she could make a quick exit if she had to.

The house itself was unimpressive. White aluminum siding, no shutters, the barest of landscaping—not a shrub in sight. A dense thicket of towering pines hugged the yard on all three sides. If Lyle had wanted privacy, he couldn't have done any better.

The Caddy was there. Carly wondered why Lyle had left his vintage vehicle in the driveway instead of in the one-car garage, where it would be protected from the elements.

Because he thought he'd be coming home again...

Maybe Lyle hadn't been the nicest guy around, but he didn't deserve to die a horrible death by someone else's hand. It would be a huge relief, for everyone, once his killer was in police custody.

Wasting no time, Tiffany was already out of her car and stomping over to the Caddy in surprisingly sensible shoes. She'd changed into comfy-looking jersey shorts with a matching top, and she'd shoved her blond hair back from her face with a plastic hairband. She was dressed for battle, in a manner of speaking. A battle to gain control of Lyle's estate.

Tiffany reached under the Caddy's wheel well and felt around, her face lighting up with elation as she pulled out a black rectangular box. She waved an impatient hand at Carly. "Let's go," she mouthed.

Carly followed Tiffany, and they scurried up a set of shallow steps onto the narrow back porch. Tiffany stuck the key into the brass door lock and jiggled it, cursing when it didn't budge. On the fourth try, after a few kicks from the toe of Tiffany's loafer, the door burst open and they went inside Lyle's kitchen.

The musty smell hit Carly like a hammer blow to the nose. The house needed some serious airing out. The white fridge and matching stove looked older than the Caddy, and the Formica countertop was warped. Two cabinet doors hung crookedly. It would have been easy to tighten the hinges, but Lyle obviously hadn't bothered with aesthetic details.

The kitchen's two window shades had been pulled low, making the room dim. Tiffany grabbed the crocheted rings at the bottom of each and sent both shades flying upward. Dust motes danced in the fading light of day.

"There, that's better," Tiffany said, then sneezed twice.

"Before we go any further—" Carly retrieved two sets of vinyl gloves from her pocket and gave a pair to Tiffany. "I know you've been here before, but I haven't. I thought these might come in handy."

"Smart thinking," Tiffany said, a touch of admiration in her voice. She began humming a tune that sounded vaguely familiar.

Carly put on her own gloves and waited for instructions.

"I'll start in the kitchen," Tiffany said. She explained to Carly where the living room and bedrooms were located—one bedroom down and two up. Carly reluctantly agreed to search upstairs while Tiffany worked the lower level.

"Is there a basement?" Carly asked, hoping the answer was no.

"There is, but Lyle never went down there. He was afraid of cellars, terrified he might see a mouse. Now remember, we're looking for written material. Notebooks, loose sheets, whatever. Yell down to me if you find anything."

"I don't suppose we'll be lucky enough to find a laptop?" Carly asked, already dreading the search. She had no idea Lyle's home would be so grimy and dusty.

"No, he used his cell phone for everything. Come on, let's get started while there's still some daylight. Otherwise, I'm turning on my flashlight."

"Wait a minute. Let's think about this. Maybe we should both start downstairs, then work our way up together," Carly suggested, feeling her nerves jangle. The thought of going upstairs alone was beginning to creep her out.

"You're the one who wanted to come with me," Tiffany snarled.

Carly couldn't deny that.

"Oh, all right," Tiffany relented, aiming a painted fingernail at a doorway off to the right. "Start in that bedroom, and then we'll both go upstairs."

Carly moved gingerly into the room Tiffany had indicated. It contained a bed, a bureau, a closet boasting piles of athletic shoes, and not much else. The bureau was filled with socks and unmentionables of a masculine variety—thank heaven she was wearing gloves—but nothing resembling paper. Minutes later, Carly returned to the living room.

A sofa, a glass coffee table, a wooden cabinet, and a flat-screen TV were about all the room consisted of. How did Lyle live like this? It didn't seem at all like a home. A sickening thought gripped Carly by the throat, squeezing some scary thoughts into her brain.

What if this was a drug house? What if Lyle had used it for drug trafficking, hence the lack of any creature comforts?

The driveway, she'd noted, looked recently paved. Had Lyle enlarged the parking area to accommodate drug dealers or buyers coming and going at all hours?

"Tiffany, I think we should go. I'm getting a bad feeling."

"Tough. You're the one who insisted on coming, and I'm not leaving until we've searched every square inch." Tiffany was on her knees, humming that same tune as she rummaged beneath the cushions of a sagging, wine-colored sofa.

Carly suddenly remembered the song. In fact, hadn't she heard it somewhere recently? "That's an old one."

Tiffany shot her a dark look. "I'm not in the mood for guessing games. What's an old one?"

"That song. 'Lola.' I just realized what you were singing. My husband always liked it. He'd pretend he was playing the opening guitar riff."

Tiffany twisted her full lips in disgust. "Well, I hate that stupid song. Right before Lyle...you know, he was singing it all the time. Made me nuts, plus he had a horrible singing voice. I hope it's not permanently stuck in my head. If you catch me humming it again, slap me, okay?"

"Gladly," Carly said, only half joking.

"Oomph," Tiffany grunted, tossing sofa cushions onto the floor. She held up her gloved fingers and wiggled them. "I'm glad you thought to bring these. There's enough crap under these cushions to start my own toxic waste site."

It was nearly 8:30 by the time they finished searching downstairs. Although the sun had yet to set, nightfall was rapidly approaching.

A sudden, muffled thump echoed from a far corner of the house.

"Did you hear that?" Carly said, grabbing Tiffany's arm. "It came from upstairs."

Tiffany shook her off. She cocked one ear and listened for several seconds. "It was your imagination," she scoffed. "Let's get going and finish the upstairs. Even I'm starting to get unnerved."

The staircase leading to the upper floor was covered in cheap brown carpeting. Once again, Carly followed behind Tiffany as they trudged up the stairs. She was beginning to feel like an obedient dog, following its mistress toward disaster.

When they entered what had to be the master bedroom, Carly's mouth opened in shock. The carpeting was plush and clean, the king-size bed covered with a gold and black brocade bedspread that matched the heavy drapes. The dark, cherrywood furniture was solid and gorgeous—the polar opposite of the junky pieces that populated the downstairs.

Carly walked over to the nearest window and pulled aside the curtain. They were directly above the driveway, she realized. Lyle would've had a perfect view of anyone coming in.

"It's too dark in here," Tiffany griped. "Open that other—"

Another thump, louder this time, made them both freeze in their tracks.

"Okay, that time I heard it," Tiffany said, sounding frightened for the first time. "It's coming from the other bedroom."

Carly pulled her cell out of her other pocket. "That's it. I'm calling nine—"

"No!" Tiffany grasped Carly's wrist. "Let's wait till we're out of here, and then we'll make an anonymous call."

A series of thumps, accompanied by a high-pitched squeal, made them gasp simultaneously.

Someone's in that room. Someone needs help.

Mentally kicking herself for not having brought along a weapon of some sort, Carly tiptoed cautiously into the other bedroom. The room was empty, save for a long metal clothing rack shoved against one wall. The rack, which was on wheels, was packed tightly with shirts and coats.

Thump.

The sound came from behind the rack. Her heart slamming her chest, Carly located a wall switch and flicked it on. A sickly yellow light sprang to life overhead. She tugged on one end of the clothing rack and dragged it away from the wall, revealing a closet door.

Carly looked at Tiffany, whose face had gone rigid. One hand on the doorknob, Carly opened the door, stumbled backward, and screamed.

A man was crumpled on the floor, his hands behind his back. A burlap sack was tied around his neck. Cringing with dread, Carly stooped down and fumbled with the rope until she was able to wrest the sack off the man's head.

Don Frasco lay scrunched on the closet floor, his eyes wide with terror, his mouth sealed shut with duct tape.

"Call 911," Carly ordered Tiffany in a no-nonsense tone. She pinched one end of the duct tape and tore it off. Don let out a shriek, his eyes watering from the pain. Then he turned on his side so Carly could untie his hands, which were bound with rope tied into about a thousand knots.

"Don, what the heck happened?" Carly demanded, helping him to a sitting position. "Are you all right?"

Sucking in a series of noisy gasps, he finally caught his breath. "Gotta...bathroom."

He crawled out of the closet, tottered to his feet, and ran unsteadily down the hallway.

Carly rose and grasped Tiffany's skinny arms. "Tiffany, did you call the police yet?"

But Tiffany wasn't listening, because her gaze had homed in on the back of the closet. She was staring at the steel door to a walk-in safe.

On the front of the safe, the image of a bird had been artfully etched into the door. Wings aloft, its long beak dipping into the mouth of a trumpet-shaped flower, it was a bird anyone would recognize.

A hummingbird.

CHAPTER THIRTY

TIFFANY WRENCHED THE CHAIN OFF FROM AROUND HER NECK and shoved the hummingbird key into the safe's lock. Carly's breath halted in her throat as Tiffany pulled open the safe door.

They both went dead silent. The safe was lined with steep shelves, atop which were treasures and jewels of every nature. Porcelain figurines, paintings, diamond bracelets, watches, earrings. High-end stuff, for sure. No costume pieces here.

The burglaries Chief Holloway had mentioned to Carly—the ones that had been baffling the police for months—were these the stolen goods? Is that what they were staring at? If so, it meant Lyle had been up to his ears in the thefts.

Her hand trembling, Carly pulled her own cell out of her pocket and called 911. Offering few details, she reported only that they'd found a man tied up in a closet in Lyle Bagley's home. The operator tried pelting her with questions, but Carly quickly disconnected.

Don shuffled up behind them holding a hand towel, his hair and face damp. "Sorry if I smell. I had to throw up. God, how did you ever find me? I thought I was a dead man!"

Ignoring his question, Carly demanded, "How did you get here? How long have you been here? Who did this to you?"

Still shaky, Don sat on the floor and stretched out his legs. His face looked almost bloodless. "About four o'clock this afternoon, I saw my boss behind one of the downtown office buildings loading stuff into his trunk. He was acting weird, jittery, so I followed him.

I couldn't believe it when he turned into Bagley's driveway! I knew I was onto something big. I saw him let himself in here with a key, so as soon as he was out of sight I snuck in and hid in the broom closet. After I heard him leave, I thought I was safe. Suddenly he was on me, shoving me against the wall and tossing that sack over my head. I think I passed out for a few minutes. When I came to, I knew I was in major trouble. If you hadn't found me…" He pulled in a ragged breath.

Carly scrubbed her eyes with her fingers. "Let's back up," she said. "Who's your boss? I thought you worked for yourself?"

Don's eyes widened in fear. "I–I didn't say boss. I said a *guy*. You heard me wrong."

Carly looked over at Tiffany, who was still staring into the safe. Blue lights flashed in the window, casting eerie, jagged shadows over the room.

"Don, you clearly said boss. Now what's going on? Tell me who it was."

The downstairs door slammed open. Moments later, three police officers, led by Chief Holloway, pounded up the stairs.

"Carly," the chief said, "is everyone all right?" He went over and rested a hand on her shoulder.

"Everyone's okay, but Don said his boss attacked him."

"I didn't say boss!" Don protested.

"It's okay, Carly," Holloway said evenly. "We'll take it from here."

As Chief Holloway stooped to examine Don, one of the officers went over to the closet. The officer sidled in next to Tiffany, who still hadn't moved, and shone his flashlight into the safe. "Hey, Chief. Get a load of this."

The chief went over to take a gander. When he saw the contents of the safe, his jaw dropped open in shock. "Well, I'll be a son of a—"

"*Noooooo*," Tiffany cried, dropping to her knees in the closet.

She pounded the floor with her fists. "That lowlife. That... liar!" she shrieked, pointing a finger into the safe. "That's Mrs. Chadwick's anniversary ring. I recognize it. She showed it to me right after her husband bought it for her in London. The sapphire is extremely rare. It's worth tens of thousands of dollars!"

Lifting a screaming Tiffany gently but firmly off the floor, the chief steered her out of the closet. "I'm calling for a crime scene team," he said to the officers. "Take these three and separate them. Don needs to go to the hospital to be checked out first, but the women need to be detained for questioning."

Feeling numb with both horror and disbelief, Carly allowed herself to be escorted downstairs. Tiffany remained upstairs, presumably in Lyle's bedroom. Don looked immensely relieved when the ambulance arrived and he was promptly wheeled out on a stretcher.

After two hours of questioning by three different detectives, Carly was finally allowed to leave. They offered her a ride, but she insisted she was fine to drive.

The realization that Lyle had been involved in so many burglaries still rocked her to the core.

Another disturbing thought gripped Carly. Had Don been an accomplice in the burglaries? Or had he just stumbled into the nightmare by being nosy and careless at the same time?

CHAPTER THIRTY-ONE

THE NEXT MORNING, NEWS OF THE DISCOVERY OF THE STOLEN items was all over town. Everyone who came into the restaurant was gossiping about it.

To Carly's relief, word hadn't gotten out that she'd been at Lyle's home when the stash was found. The police were keeping everything tightly under wraps. Carly prayed to the angels and to her lucky stars that a few loose lips wouldn't sink her ship.

Several times that morning she'd tried reaching Don Frasco, with no luck. In desperation she'd called the chief, who admitted that Frasco was currently MIA. Don had insisted on being examined at the hospital before he would agree to talk. Once in an exam room, he managed to sneak out through a rear entrance. He hadn't been seen since. The police retrieved his car, so they were working on the assumption he couldn't have gotten far.

"Based on what you told the detectives," Chief Holloway had told her, "we're trying to find out who his boss is. If he really has one. If he contacts you, Carly, I need to know, pronto. Frasco might be up to his eyeballs in this mess. Whatever the case, he can identify his assailant."

"Of course," she promised, her heart heavy. Don was a pest, for sure, but she didn't want to think of him as a crook.

Carly was grateful when Suzanne showed up early again. They worked through the busy lunch crunch like robots on speed. When they finally had a lull, Carly told Suzanne about her involvement in the escapade the previous evening.

Suzanne looked horrified. "Carly, you could have been killed. Don't you ever do anything like that again!"

"I'm not planning on it, but right now it's Don I'm worried about. I called him a bunch of times, but he doesn't answer."

"Poor kid." Suzanne bit down on her lower lip. "He never seems to get a break. When I was working at Dot's Diggity Dogs, he had a part-time job in the kitchen, washing dishes. I knew he wanted everyone to think of him as a reporter, but I guess he needed the money. He said he was happy to wash dishes because no one would see him in the kitchen."

Carly frowned. "I never knew that."

"One day I was slinging dogs when I heard this loud crash from the kitchen. I ran in and found Don on the floor surrounded by broken dishes. He'd slipped and fallen on the wet floor. Turned out the owner's son, who was a nasty little weasel, had squirted dish liquid all over the floor on purpose. The owner was ready to fire Don when I stepped in and told him the truth. Poor Don. In his misguided loyalty, he was trying to cover up for the jerk who'd booby-trapped him."

The story made Carly feel even worse. She now understood why Don had been so defensive of Suzanne. Plus, it convinced her even further that Don had a second job. The question was: Where, and with whom?

"I sure hope he's all right," Carly said, tapping his number again on her phone. She looked at Suzanne and shook her head. "Voice mail."

Grant, bless him, also showed up early. "Everyone hear the news?" he said, putting on his apron in the kitchen.

"Ohhh, yes," Suzanne replied, fetching a package of napkins from the supply shelf.

Carly gave him a rundown of her role in the recovery of the burgled items, ending with Don Frasco being missing.

Grant smacked his forehead. "Carly, why didn't you tell me

where you were going? I'd have offered to go with you. Or better yet, talked you out of it."

"Exactly why I didn't want you to know," she said, warmed by his concern. "Besides, you'd have missed Ari's game. How was that, by the way?"

"It was great." Grant grinned. "Ari's team won with a ninth-inning home run. You should go next week!" His ears suddenly perked. "Customers," he said and dashed through the swinging door. Suzanne followed behind him with the napkins.

Saved by the bell.

Taking a breather, Carly sat at her desk, her mind revolving like a frazzled planet around a rapidly scorching sun.

If her assumption was correct, she'd come close to encountering Lyle's killer the night before. The thought made her stomach do a backflip. At the same time, she was thankful she and Tiffany had gotten there in time to rescue Don. How long could he have survived like that? Did his attacker mean to kill him or only frighten him?

Suzanne burst through the swinging door carrying the portable landline phone. "Someone for you, Carly. Says his name is Brad Gearhart."

Brad Gearhart. Lyle's attorney!

"Thanks." Carly grabbed the phone from her. "This is Carly Hale. Can I help you?"

"Carly Hale," he said, a smile evident in his voice. "I remember you from high school. Other than the obvious, how are things going?"

They chatted for a few minutes, and then he said, "Listen, I know you're probably going nuts worrying about your restaurant, so I wanted to give you an update. Since Lyle Bagley passed without leaving a will, I've been appointed personal representative of his estate. Even though, on paper, he bought your building at foreclosure, he only made the minimum down payment.

Until his estate is settled, the renovations he planned are on hold indefinitely."

Carly gasped out a breath of relief. "That's such good news. So, I have a little more time?"

"You do, but you probably won't need it. I have an interested buyer, a reputable real estate group that wants to assume Lyle's purchase and sale agreement with the lender. If the deal goes through, they'll reimburse the estate for the down payment and take over the purchase. Here's the best part—they have no interest in renovating the building. They want you to stay right where you are and keep on bringing in those lovely rent monies."

Carly laughed, a lump of sheer relief filling her throat. "That's wonderful news, but I have one last question. Since Lyle never signed a will, who inherits his estate?" She'd assumed all along it was Matt but wanted confirmation.

Brad chuckled. "I'm not at liberty yet to name names, but you can Google it yourself. Just look for Vermont laws of intestacy."

She thanked him again and disconnected, feeling more buoyant than she had in days.

Wasting no time, Carly did the Google search Brad had suggested. It took only a few minutes to find the information she needed.

Just as Carly suspected, since Lyle had neither a spouse nor any children, his estate would go to his sole heir—who, in Lyle's case, was his brother, Matt Bagley.

CHAPTER THIRTY-TWO

THE EATERY REMAINED BUSY ALMOST UNTIL CLOSING TIME.
Not only the usual locals, but so many fresh faces came in to enjoy
Carly's grilled cheese concoctions that it gave her spirits a major
lift.

The summer months were going to be good for business, she
decided. Maybe she and Grant could put their heads together and
design some new sandwiches for the season. Locally grown tomatoes, spinach, and fresh basil came to mind, but there were other
summer veggies and herbs that could be incorporated into their
grilled cheese recipes. She still had Sara Hardy's cranberry-pecan
loaf to experiment with. With everything else going on, she'd stuck
the loaf in the freezer for future use.

Carly noted, with a twinge of disappointment, that Ari Mitchell
hadn't come in all day. Had he gotten wind of her role in last night's
police bust and figured she was too crazy to bother with? Or was
he sick enough of grilled cheese sandwiches that he'd opted for a
different lunch?

Right on time at 7:00 p.m., they closed the eatery. Grant had
plans with his musical buddies for the evening. Suzanne was
having pizza with her son and her ex, which delighted Carly.

Before they left, Carly gave them the good news from Lyle's
attorney. They danced in a circle and hugged each other, then
went their separate ways.

Earlier in the day, Carly'd had a lengthy conversation with
Gina. She'd given her friend only brief highlights of her harrowing

evening at Lyle's. They'd agreed to get together as soon as they were both free to firm up plans for Sunday's picnic. Gina was seeing a movie that evening with her boyfriend-who-wasn't-yet-a-boyfriend. She offered to ditch him and spend time with Carly instead, but Carly adamantly refused. As much as she'd have loved Gina's company, she didn't want to spoil her plans.

Driving home, Carly was overcome by a wave of loneliness she hadn't felt since those early days after losing Daniel. Everyone close to her had plans for the evening, either that or someone to go home to. Carly had no one, not even a sweet little dog with adorable brown eyes, and whose fault was that?

She was almost home when a thought jolted her.

Janet's pendant watch.

Carly was certain the watch had been one of the stolen items. But why had Lyle given it to Janet? Did he hope to soften the blow before delivering the bombshell about his engagement to Tiffany?

Lyle had told Tiffany not to wear her diamond-encrusted key in public. And he'd told Janet not to wear her Cartier watch where anyone, especially Tiffany, might see it. The reason was now glaringly obvious.

Instead of turning into her own driveway, Carly drove directly to Janet's house. If Janet hadn't figured it out already, she needed to know.

She parked behind Janet's car and shut off her engine. Moments later, Janet appeared in the doorway. Her expression was so morose that Carly's first instinct was to run up to her and wrap her in a hug. Instead, she said, "How are you doing?"

"How do you think?" Janet snapped, then her shoulders slumped. Her eyes looked bleary, her lids puffy from crying.

"Can I come in for a minute?"

With a distraught look, Janet opened the door and beckoned Carly into her office. She didn't offer her a seat, so Carly stood. Glancing around, Carly felt as if something was missing. What was it?

"The cops sent two detectives here yesterday." Janet grabbed a tissue and blew her nose loudly. "They think I knew about those stolen goods, but I didn't!"

"I'm sorry, Janet. I know this will sound blunt, but I have to ask you. Did you show them the Cartier watch Lyle gave you?"

Janet's face went gray, and she dropped onto her chair. "Yes. I turned it over to them. They confirmed it was one of the stolen items. They went through some of my files, but they're coming back tomorrow. They said if I didn't allow them access to my computer, they'd get a warrant to audit my accounts. Carly, I swear, I didn't know a thing about any burglaries! What if I get arrested?"

"I know it's scary, but try to stay calm," Carly advised. "The best thing you can do is tell the truth."

"As soon as I heard the news, I knew," Janet choked out, covering her face with her hands. "Oh God, Carly, how could he do that? How could Lyle have been so deceitful? And how could I have been so blind?"

"He fooled at lot of people. Don't beat yourself up."

Janet's voice hitched. "That day, when he gave me that watch, I truly believed it was a declaration of love. My God, what else could it be? The watch looked like he'd paid a small fortune for it. I poured my heart out to him, Carly. I told him how I'd adored him for years, how I'd fantasized about our future together. I told him I was so ready to give him every last ounce of my love, with my whole heart. I—I was so sure he'd tell me the same thing."

Oh, Janet.

"Instead, you know what he did? He *laughed* at me. He ruffled my hair, like I was a pet dog, and called me his 'dependable little clerk.' The second he left, I ran in the bathroom and threw up my guts. I cried for two whole days. I could barely get out of bed."

Carly's stomach churned. After all Janet's years of devotion,

Lyle's callous rejection must have been unbearable. To compound the hurt, he announced his engagement to Tiffany soon afterward. Was it enough to push Janet over the edge and murder him?

Janet's expression was hollow, her eyes swollen and red. "God, what a fool I must look like. Everyone in town's going to hear about it."

"What people think doesn't matter," Carly soothed. "Only the truth does."

Fresh tears bubbled out of Janet. "Yeah. Whatever."

"I'll leave you alone now," Carly said, "but please call me if you need anything, okay?"

On the way out, Carly glanced at the empty coatrack. That's what was missing! "Where's your grandfather's cane?"

Janet jerked her head up. "It's in the back seat of my car. I'm taking it to an antiques dealer to get it appraised, just in case I decide to sell it. Since my whole life is going down the hopper, I might need the money."

"That's a good idea. At least you'll know what it's worth."

Janet stared at her. "Um, Carly," she said suddenly. "Didn't you promise me a free grilled cheese sandwich?"

The question startled Carly. "I sure did. Stop in the restaurant any time for it."

"The thing is," Janet said, "I don't really want to go out in public yet. I don't suppose you could drop it off to me after you leave the restaurant tomorrow? That way I can have it with a glass of wine."

It was an odd request, and an inconvenient one for Carly. But given Janet's sad state of affairs, she was willing to honor it.

"Sure, that would be okay. How does a grilled cheddar and bacon sound?"

"That would be awesome."

"Great. I'll drop it off on my way home tomorrow, say, seven-thirtyish?"

Janet agreed, and Carly hurried out the door. As she approached

Janet's vehicle, she slowed her pace. Was the cane really on Janet's back seat, or had Janet hidden it from the police?

"Ouch," Carly squawked. Listing sideways, she leaned one hand against Janet's car and pulled off her denim flat. Standing on one foot, she shook out her shoe, peering into Janet's car as she did so.

"Rock in my shoe," Carly said, waving it before slipping it back on. "See you tomorrow!"

She'd just confirmed one thing. The cane wasn't on Janet's back seat.

CHAPTER THIRTY-THREE

DESPITE THE EXCELLENT NEWS SHE'D GOTTEN FROM LYLE'S attorney, the next morning Carly felt irritable and out of sorts. Not long after they opened at 11:00, the eatery became extremely busy.

Suzanne had flown through the door two minutes before they opened, her cheeks rosy and her hair wavier than usual. Carly suspected a certain *almost*-ex was responsible, but she minded her own business and refrained from commenting.

One thing had nagged at Carly all morning—the cane missing from Janet's umbrella stand. Had Janet hidden it from the detectives so they wouldn't suspect she'd used it as a murder weapon and confiscate it?

Carly already regretted her promise to deliver an after-hours grilled cheese to Janet. *What was I thinking? How did I get roped into that?*

Around 1:30, Ari came in. At the sight of him, Carly felt her pulse race. He took a seat at the counter, his kind smile and warm brown gaze brightening the dining room. His curly hair was neatly trimmed, and his muscular arms even more tanned than before.

"Hey, I heard your team won." She poured him a fresh coffee.

He laughed. "It was great. Ethan slammed a home run into left field at the top of the ninth. Put us ahead by two. I took the boys out for hot wings afterward. They had a blast."

"Hot wings. I haven't had those in, like, forever!"

"Then you should join us some time." His dark-brown eyes

gripped hers. They didn't let go until she turned away to prepare his Farmhouse Cheddar Sleeps with the Fishes.

She'd just slid his sandwich onto a plate when Becca Avery came in. Carly hadn't seen her since Saturday. Becca waved to Ari, then signaled to Carly that she needed to talk to her.

Feeling mildly annoyed at the intrusion, Carly held up a finger, then finished adding the extras to Ari's plate. She went around the counter to where Becca was standing.

"Hey, I know you're super busy," Becca said quietly, "but I really need you to come with me for fifteen minutes."

"Fifteen minutes? Becca, I can't. Grant doesn't get in till three, and I can't leave Suzanne alone. What's this about?"

Becca blew out a breath. "It's about Don Frasco."

~

Grant arrived a few minutes early, and Suzanne agreed to work until Carly returned from her clandestine meeting. Supplying few details, she assured them the meeting would be short and that there was no cause for concern.

When she reached the address Becca had given her, which was only a short walk from her restaurant, Carly recognized the building. Three stories high, the red brick structure had been a crumbling old schoolhouse, until one of the big insurance conglomerates purchased it and restored it to its former glory.

A blast of cool air smacked Carly's face as she stepped into the lobby. The floors were marble, the walls a series of murals of landmark Vermont scenes. The elevator off to the right was an old-fashioned contraption, its vintage brass doors restored to their original gleaming beauty.

Carly rode the elevator to the second floor, her heart slamming her chest. The building was quiet—too quiet for her liking. Didn't anyone work in this place?

Stepping off the elevator, she walked down a carpeted hallway until she stood before the door labeled 202. Bending her head, she listened for a moment, then tapped the door lightly. The door opened a crack, and then a powerful arm reached out, gripped her wrist, and pulled her inside.

Carly cried out and tried to resist until Becca Avery placed a firm hand over her mouth. "It's all right, Carly. You're not in danger, but we need to be quiet, okay?"

Anger surging through her veins, Carly nodded. Becca carefully removed her hand from Carly's mouth and made a *shushing* motion with her finger.

Her breath coming in gasps, Carly found herself in an empty office. The floor was bare concrete and the room devoid of furnishings. The vertical blinds on the room's sole window were open only enough to let in a smidge of ambient light.

"What is going on, Becca?" Carly demanded in a harsh whisper. "Why all this high drama? You scared me half to death. Now tell me where Don is before I call the police."

Her face somber, Becca opened the door to an adjacent room and beckoned Carly over. The room was windowless, smaller than the outer room and illuminated by overhead fluorescents. Seated on a chair before an old school desk was Don Frasco, looking as beaten down as she'd ever seen him. His eyes were hollow, his face a ghostly white. A small wastebasket beside him was piled with sandwich wrappers and empty root beer cans. Next to that was a white Styrofoam cooler.

Carly staggered slightly from the shock of what she was seeing, then shoved her hand into her tote and dug out her phone.

"Carly, wait!" Don pleaded. "Don't call the police. Let me explain first."

Shaking with anger, Carly gripped her phone. "You both have two minutes to spill your guts before I call Chief Holloway."

CHAPTER THIRTY-FOUR

BECCA REACHED INTO A CLOSET FOR A FOLDING CHAIR AND plopped it down in front of Don. "Sit," she told Carly, who glared at her before dropping onto the seat.

"I work for an outfit called Knock-Out Dirt Commercial Cleaning," Becca explained. "Don works three nights a week with me. He needs the extra dough. Right, Don?"

Don nodded miserably.

"We clean offices in this building and in a few others. This suite is on tap to be renovated, which is why it's making a convenient hideout, for now."

"Before you go any further, who's your boss?" Carly demanded. "I'm sick of all the subterfuge."

Don looked at Becca, then back at Carly. "It's Kevin O'Toole."

"A.k.a. the snake dude," Becca said darkly.

Kevin O'Toole.

Carly felt her world do a seismic shift. She took in a few deep breaths to regain her bearings. "Did he kill Lyle?"

"We don't have the answer to that," Becca admitted.

"Then for the love of daisies in December, why didn't you go to the police right away?" Carly fumed. "If O'Toole murdered Lyle, he's probably halfway to Alaska by now."

Don's face collapsed. "It's my fault. I made Becca promise not to tell the cops until I was sure I could get protection. O'Toole is a dangerous dude, Carly. I've seen his dark side, and it ain't pretty. If he knew where I was right now, my life would be worth about four cents."

Carly was still furious. "All right. Tell me what happened. From the beginning."

Don leaned forward. "Monday night when I was coming to work, I saw O'Toole remove stuff from one of the vacant offices and load it into his trunk. He kept looking over his shoulder, like he was afraid of being seen. I was sure he was up to no good, so I followed him. When I saw him turn into Lyle Bagley's driveway, I was psyched. I parked up the road and doubled back on foot to see if I could figure out what he was doing."

"By the way, how did you know that was Lyle's house?" Carly challenged.

"Are you kidding? After Bagley was murdered, I drove past there about a thousand times. I was hoping to see something that would help the cops."

Carly wanted to scream. "Okay, so, when you saw O'Toole's car drive in, you didn't think to call the police?"

"No, because I didn't have proof of anything, not yet. If he had anything to do with killing Bagley, I wanted to find some evidence first."

Carly shook her head.

"His car was parked behind the house, so I knew he must've gone inside. When I peeked through the window and didn't see him, I went in and hid in a downstairs closet. I could hear him stomping around upstairs. About ten minutes later I heard him storm out of the house."

Carly nodded. "Then what?"

"I waited a few minutes, then went upstairs to look around. That's when he hit me from behind, slapped tape over my mouth, and tossed that sack over my head. When I came to, I was on the floor with my hands tied behind me, and I could barely breathe. I like, panicked, totally. I thought sure I was going to die there. The creep stole my camera too."

"He locked the door when he left," Carly mused, remembering

how Tiffany had struggled with the key to gain access. "It was a miracle Tiffany remembered where the spare key was. You lucked out, Don."

"I know," he said in a wobbly voice. "You guys saved my life."

Carly shivered. If she and Tiffany hadn't gone into Lyle's house that night, Don undoubtedly would have perished in that airless closet. The thought made her insides twist into knots.

"Carly, will you go to Chief Holloway for me and run interference?" Don begged. "I'll tell them what I know, as long as I'm promised protection. Remember, O'Toole left me in that closet to die."

Carly shuddered. "I know."

She tried to remember when O'Toole was last in her restaurant, but her memory failed her. Once the discovery of the stolen goods was plastered all over the news, he'd have known Don could ID him. He was probably in hiding. Either that or he left the state altogether and was heading for parts unknown.

"We really need your help," Becca said in a subdued tone. "I'm sorry we didn't come clean right away, but if Don turns himself in to the police, do you think they'll agree to protect him until O'Toole is in custody?"

"You're asking the wrong person," Carly said, "but I'm willing to make a call. I hope you both realize," she added testily, "that O'Toole is probably a thousand miles away by now because of your delay."

Becca's face fell. "I'm sorry. But I gave my word to Don, and I don't break my promises."

Carly sighed. "Don, do you have your phone?"

"Yeah, but I turned it off so the police couldn't track me."

"Then you need to turn it on and make sure it's charged so I can contact you. I'll call the chief as soon as I get back, so be prepared to come forward. Is that understood?"

Don nodded. "Understood."

"I'll stay right here until he's safely in the hands of the police," Becca said, with a nod at Carly. "And I give you my word—nothing bad is going to happen on my watch."

~

When Carly got back to the restaurant, business had quieted down. Normally, she and Suzanne would split a grilled cheese for lunch, but she was too wired to think about eating. She promised to fill in Suzanne and Grant on what was happening, but first she needed to contact the chief.

From her desk in the kitchen, she called Chief Holloway. She filled him in on her meeting with Don and Becca, then waited for a verbal explosion. To her relief, he muttered only a few expletives.

"I'm sending out officers right now to look for O'Toole," he said tightly. "I'll pick up Frasco myself, and he'd better still be there. How did you get involved with this, Carly?"

"I guess because I'm one of the few people Don trusts. Remember, O'Toole left him to die in that closet. Tiffany and I were the ones who found him."

After she disconnected, she Googled O'Toole. It was too common a name to bring up anything useful, so instead she plugged in the business name. The website for Knock-Out Dirt Commercial Cleaning was garish and busy, boasting 5-star reviews and an impressive client list.

Knock-Out. K.O. Kevin O'Toole. Kevin had obviously used his initials in creating the business name.

Carly searched a few more variations. When a second site popped up, her heart almost flew out of her chest.

Knock-Em Out Dead Pest Control was another one of O'Toole's businesses. The website depicted cartoon images of dead bugs and assorted rodents, with a heavily tattooed assassin gloating over their strewn corpses. It reminded her of that horrible snake etched into O'Toole's arm.

Something tickled Carly's brain. She called the chief again. "Chief, I have a question. When you investigated the homes that were burglarized, did you ask the homeowners if they'd had any recent services?"

The chief sounded annoyed. "Of course, we did. It was a dead end. One of them had recently hired a cleaning company, and another one used a pest control service, but that was it. Carly, what's this about?"

"Chief, except for the homeowner who used a pest control service, please contact them all again and ask them the same question. Tell them, this time, to tell the truth."

"Only if you tell me why."

"Because I think all of them used a pest control service owned by Kevin O'Toole. And I think they were too embarrassed to admit their high-end, well-maintained homes had been overrun with rodents."

When closing time rolled around, Suzanne, Grant, and Carly left together, and Carly locked up the eatery. She noticed that Tiffany's car was in the parking lot.

In Carly's mind, there were still a few puzzle pieces that weren't fitting together.

For starters, Tiffany had been sure she heard a woman's voice behind the building the night Lyle was murdered. So how did Kevin O'Toole fit into the scenario? Had he been there that night too? Maybe as a silent accomplice? If so, who was the woman?

As for Matt Bagley, he stood to gain everything from Lyle's death. The question was: Had he been aware of that? Or was the coveted vintage Caddy motive enough for him to murder his brother?

Janet was the true wild card. Her admission that she vandalized Tiffany's car, combined with her utter despair at being rejected by

Lyle, suggested an unstable personality. And where was her grandfather's cane, the one she claimed was in her back seat? Did she hide it because she knew the brass head bore traces of Lyle's blood?

Carly needed to talk to Tiffany again.

CHAPTER THIRTY-FIVE

CARLY SCURRIED UP TIFFANY'S STAIRCASE AND KNOCKED ON the pink door. She heard a crashing sound right before Tiffany whipped open the door. "Not you again."

"Gee, thanks. That was just the greeting I was hoping for. Can I come in?"

Tiffany's face was damp with perspiration, her blond hair like a fright wig. The chain that normally hung around her neck was noticeably absent. "Suit yourself. What do I care?"

Carly glanced around at the chaos. Boxes were stacked haphazardly atop one another. A heavy green trash bag hung open, piles of magazines spilling out from it.

"Are you moving?" Carly asked her.

"Good guess, Einstein. Why else would this junk be all over the place?" She stomped her foot, and then her face collapsed, fat tears streaming down her cheeks.

Carly took her by the arm and steered her over to the sofa. She found a box of tissues and sat down beside her, distributing the tissues as needed until Tiffany's sobs finally dried up and she blew her nose.

"M-my life is in the crapper, Carly," Tiffany stuttered out. "Lyle left me with nothing. Even that diamond key he gave me was stolen. He was a lousy piece of trash, and now I'm paying the price!"

"Listen to me," Carly said. "Do you know that you saved a life Monday night? If you hadn't been so hell-bent on getting into Lyle's house, Don Frasco would have suffocated in that closet."

Tiffany sniffled and gaped at her.

"Things happen for a reason, Tiffany. I know everything looks horrible right now, but you're a strong woman. You'll get past this and you'll be so much better for it. Why are you moving out?"

"Because there are too many reminders here," she blubbered. "Right now, I'm probably the town laughingstock."

"I don't agree," Carly said, then softened her tone. "Will you answer a serious question for me?"

Tiffany splayed her fingers over her bare neck. "I guess."

Carly hesitated, then plunged forward. "Were you in love with Lyle?"

Tiffany lowered her eyes, then shook her head. "You want the truth? I was in love with what he could do for me. I wanted people to respect me, not just to see me as some pretty, airheaded bimbo."

"I'm sure no one ever thought that." It was a tiny fib, but Carly wanted to spare Tiffany's feelings. She knew people often harbored unfair biases against women as stunning as she was.

"I have a knack for styles and trends, Carly." Tiffany's eyes glistened. "I know what looks good on people and what doesn't. My boutique was going to be a fabulous shop, where women would ask for my help and value my opinions. I wanted to be the go-to person when someone had a special occasion and needed fashion advice. Some of the most well-heeled women in this town had already promised to be regular customers." She blotted her eyes with a tissue.

"And I'm sure they will, once you find a new location."

"It's too late for that. I'm moving in with a friend in Manchester until I can find another quiet apartment. I don't have the money to open a boutique."

"I'm sorry to hear that." Carly folded her hands in her lap. "Tiffany, that night, the night Lyle was murdered, you were probably the closest thing to being a witness."

Her face went taut. "So? What are you getting at?"

"Is there anything you didn't tell me? Anything else you can remember? You said you heard voices outside, and that one of them was a woman's."

She shrugged. "I told the police all that."

"What about Kevin O'Toole? Did you know he and Lyle were involved in the burglaries?"

"I swear, Carly, I never even met O'Toole. If I'd known Lyle was hiding stolen goods, I'd have been long gone. And yes, I told the police that too."

"Is there anything you didn't tell them?"

Tiffany twisted her fingers. "I didn't tell them about the fight Lyle and I had that night," she murmured. "I was afraid if I did, they'd think I killed him."

"What did you fight about?"

"About what a blowhard he was, always making up crap to make himself look good. I was so tired of it. I was sick of always having to stroke his ego."

"What did he make up?"

Tiffany rolled her eyes at the ceiling. "That night, he told me he was onto something big. Something that was going to put this boring little berg in the news. When I asked what it was, he laughed and started singing that stupid song again. Then he said I'd find out when the time was right. He said stuff like that all the time. You can't imagine how irritating it was." Tiffany rubbed her eyes with her finger.

That marriage would never have lasted, Carly thought, flicking her gaze around the apartment. "Is there anything I can do to help right now?"

Tiffany grabbed another tissue and swiped it over her nose. "No, not unless you want to take those stupid magazines to be recycled. I know everyone thinks I'm an airhead, but I know enough to recycle."

"You're not an airhead, and stop putting yourself down." Carly rose and went over to the trash bag. Stacks of magazines had dribbled out and were fanned out on the floor. She was stuffing them back inside the bag when something caught her eye. Tucked between the pages of a yachting magazine were several sheets of paper. They looked like copies of news articles printed off the internet. The words "fugitive" and "robbery" leaped out at her from one of the headlines.

"Tiffany, there's other stuff in here besides magazines, like papers and folders. Did you look through all of it?"

"I did. I'm telling you, there was no will. Just all that fugitive garbage Lyle was obsessed with."

Carly crammed the magazines back into the bag and lugged them toward the door. "Tiffany, listen to me. I want you to be extra careful, okay? Whoever attacked Don Frasco is still out there, and he's dangerous. Can you stay with your friend in Manchester tonight?"

"I could, but if a man attacked Frasco, then I'm not worried."

"Why not?"

"Because I know what I heard that night, and it wasn't a man's voice. I'm more convinced than ever that Lyle was murdered by a woman."

~

Carly had finished loading the trash bags into her car when her cell pinged with a text: Are you coming with my sandwich or not?

Oh no. She'd totally forgotten about the sandwich she promised to deliver to Janet. She felt like kicking herself for making the promise in the first place.

Tiffany was dead sure Lyle's killer had been female, and Janet was the poster girl for a woman scorned. All the more reason to postpone the sandwich until the killer was in police custody.

She punched in Janet's number and got her voice mail. "Hey,

Janet, it's Carly. Sorry about the sandwich. I've been unavoidably detained, so I'll have to give you a rain check. Talk to you soon. Bye."

Janet would probably be angry with the lame excuse, but Carly vowed to make it up to her another time. *If* she was innocent.

Ten minutes later, Carly swung into her driveway and parked beside Arlene's Fiesta. She lugged the bag of magazines upstairs to her apartment. After locking the door, she tossed her tote on the sofa and dragged the bag over with her. Something about those internet printouts nagged at Carly. Why had Lyle hidden them inside a magazine? She was pulling them out and stacking them on her ottoman when her cell rang.

"Guess who we just arrested?" Chief Holloway's grin came through loud and clear.

Carly crossed her fingers. "Kevin O'Toole, I hope."

"Right on the money. He's been holed up at a motel in Shaftsbury since Monday night. He admitted conking Frasco on the head and stuffing him in that closet but swears he only wanted to scare him. He claims he went back a few hours later to let him out but panicked when he saw all the cop cars there. We're not buying it. He knew full well that Frasco was a liability and that he couldn't afford to keep him around."

Carly blew out a breath of relief. "I'm so glad he's in custody. Is Don at the police station now?"

"He is. As a material witness, he's going to have a lot of questions to answer, so he'll be here for a while. But he's safe; that's the main thing. We're charging O'Toole with the assault on Frasco, plus a slew of offenses related to the burglaries. Once the DA gets involved, it's likely they'll pin Bagley's murder on him too. There's a lot more to this case than I can reveal, but O'Toole was getting help from an unexpected source, I'm sorry to say."

Carly's pulse raced. "Really? Can you tell me what or who it was?"

"I can't," Holloway said with a sigh, "but it'll all come out soon enough."

Yet another piece of the puzzle, Carly mused. If only the chief wasn't so tight-lipped! But at least with O'Toole in custody, Don was safe now. And for that matter, so was Tiffany. "So, the police think O'Toole killed Lyle?"

"We do. O'Toole was doing the heavy work—the burglaries— and Bagley was supposed to be getting rid of the stolen goods and taking a cut of the proceeds. But Bagley was helping himself to more than his share, and O'Toole decided to teach him a lesson. That's our theory, anyway. O'Toole had gone over there several times to try to break into that safe, but he had no luck. Without a key, it was hopeless."

And all along, Tiffany had the key. She'd been at risk without ever realizing it.

The chief cleared his throat. "We, um, contacted the other homeowners, as you asked. You were right; all of them had recently used O'Toole's pest control service. They were too embarrassed to admit their high-end mansions were overrun with rodents, so they kept that little tidbit to themselves. How did you guess that?"

"O'Toole bragged about his pet boa constrictor one day," Carly told him, "and it struck me that he probably had to buy mice to feed the creepy thing." She shivered. "Which meant he knew exactly where to buy scads of mice he could release near the homes he wanted to burglarize. That gave him access to the houses he wanted to go back and steal from. Is that right?"

"You're a regular Miss Marple," the chief said wryly. "But in the future, let us do the investigating, okay? And, Carly, please don't share any of this. It'll be all over the news by tomorrow, but for now we'd like to work without the media breathing down our necks."

"You got it," Carly agreed. "Tell me, how did you find O'Toole so quickly?"

"That's one for the books. We planted an unmarked car in a hidden cubby across from his house, but we never really thought he'd show up. Unbelievably, he pulled into his driveway less than an hour later. But you'll never guess why he went back to his house."

"I'm afraid to ask."

The chief's laughter burst through the phone. "To feed his snake. He was worried because the poor reptile had missed his regular feeding time."

CHAPTER THIRTY-SIX

IT WAS NEARLY 8:00 P.M. AND CARLY HAD ONLY PICKED AT FOOD all day. She dropped a fruit tart into the toaster in the hopes of quieting the rumble in her stomach. Not a great supper, but it would keep her going while she checked out those internet articles. When the warm pastry was ready, she dropped it onto a plate and went into her living room.

She sat down on the floor next to the trash bag, then pulled out magazines two or three at a time and stacked them in piles on her ottoman. In the last stack, she noticed the edge of a folder sticking out from that same yachting magazine. When she pulled out the folder and opened it, her heart did a frog leap.

The folder contained printed articles about a 2003 bank robbery in Missouri. Two young men and their female accomplice had robbed a savings bank, killing a security guard in the process. Only one evaded capture.

Carly studied the grainy faces. One of the men was pudgy, and the other was light-haired and muscular with a thick beard.

She was skimming the article to see which robber evaded capture when a loud knock at her door startled her. She shoved the folder back inside the magazine. In her haste, she elbowed one of the piles, sending magazines toppling to the floor. Another pile avalanched atop that one. Muttering to herself, Carly stood and went over to answer the door.

"Who is it?" she called out, vowing to install a peephole.

"It's Arlene. I just have a quick question."

Irritated at the interruption, Carly glued on a smile and opened the door. "Hey, come on in. What can I do for you?"

Arlene scooted inside. Her T-shirt was chocolate stained. She'd no doubt been baking again. "Sorry to bug you, Carly, but I wanted to know if you had any news about the squirrel."

"I haven't heard anything since it was transferred to the wildlife rehabilitator. I've been occupied with other things," Carly said truthfully, "but if it'll make you feel better, I'll make a call in the morning." *Or you could do it yourself*, she thought with annoyance.

"Oh, that would be super. I've been worried sick ever since you found the poor thing. I hope they were able to fix that leg. Tell you the truth, Joyce was a bit annoyed with me because I didn't try to get help for the squirrel when it first fell out of the tree. She saw it out there struggling to walk, and it broke her heart."

"I'm sure we'll know something soon," Carly assured her, anxious to return to her mission.

Arlene's razor-sharp gaze scanned the apartment. "Oh my, looks like you've got a project going there."

Carly smiled. "Yeah, but I tipped everything over."

"It is a bit of a mess," Arlene said. "Why don't I help you straighten those."

"Arlene, it's fine; you don't need to—"

But Arlene wasn't listening. She went over and began picking up magazines and plunking them onto the ottoman. As she did, that same folder fell out and landed upside down on the floor. The articles slipped out. Arlene glanced at them before shoving them back inside the magazine.

"There, nice and neat again." Arlene's plain face was flushed.

"Thank you." Carly was trying to remain patient, but she was anxious to get back to the articles.

Arlene wrung her hands. "Actually, I have something else to ask you. I know it's late, and I can see you're eating a fruit thingy, but I wondered if I had a pizza delivered, would you split it with me and Joyce?" Her wide-set eyes pleaded with Carly.

Carly squelched a sigh. She hated to admit it, but a slice of pizza *would* hit the spot. And Joyce would probably enjoy the company. "Um, sure. That would be great."

"Excellent!" Arlene beamed. "I'll text you when it's here."

After Arlene left, Carly went into the bathroom to freshen up. Feeling grubby from handling the magazines, she wanted to wash her face and brush her hair. It seemed late for Joyce and Arlene to be eating pizza, but maybe Joyce hadn't been hungry earlier. Carly was more determined than ever to put together a fun-filled picnic for her on Sunday.

While Carly waited for Arlene's text, she went back to examine the photos of the robbers. Lyle had obviously saved the articles for a reason, but why?

She was studying the face of the bearded robber when her attention jumped to the woman standing beside him. The photo, captured as the robbers entered the bank, was fuzzy at best. But something about the woman's posture was eerily familiar.

Carly flipped to the next article, and her heart jolted. The mug shot of the female robber, who'd been twenty-three at the time, stared out from the page. Wide-set eyes, flattish lips, a wart near her right eye. But the nose was wrong; it had a tiny bump.

She read the robbers' names in the caption: Derwood Clapper, Edward Sherman, and Lola Bracken.

Lola Bracken. *Lola.*

Without warning, Carly's door burst open and the pages flew out of her hand. She turned to see Arlene standing in the doorway, a pizza box in one hand and a bottle of wine in the other. She'd slipped on a loose-fitting tunic over her T-shirt. A delicious, spicy aroma wafted from the box.

"Sorry." Arlene's face reddened. "I didn't mean to open the door so hard."

"That's okay." Carly swallowed. Why was she bringing the pizza here? "What about Joyce? Doesn't she want pizza?"

Arlene pressed her lips together, then said, "No, poor dear. She was super tired, so I gave her a sleeping pill and tucked her in for the night."

Something's off. Tired or not, Joyce would never pass up pizza.

Arlene sashayed into the living room. Her mouth twisted with annoyance as she glanced around for a place to set the box.

"Let's go in the kitchen," Carly said, every nerve on red alert. "It'll be easier to eat."

Arlene stared hard at the pages Carly had dropped. "No. I want to eat in here." She sidled around the sofa and plopped the pizza box onto the stacks of magazines. Though it landed crookedly, she made no move to straighten it.

Her mouth drier than the Mojave Desert, Carly said, "I'll get plates, napkins, and wineglasses."

Her limbs felt like boiled noodles as she stumbled into the kitchen. When she returned to the living room, Arlene was perched on the edge of the sofa. Carly handed her a wineglass and kept the other. "Need a corkscrew?" Carly asked her, keeping a fake smile glued to her face.

"I already opened the bottle," Arlene said flatly. She poured them each a glass of white wine and set her own glass on the floor.

Wine in hand, Carly bent over and opened the pizza box. "Gosh, I'm *so* glad you got pepperoni," she gushed. "It's my fave." She set her own wineglass on the table next to the rocking chair and handed out plates. When she reached into the box and pulled out a cheesy slice, the entire box, along with another stack of magazines, slid to the floor. Another set of papers fell out, and Carly's throat nearly slammed shut.

"My, I'm not having much luck today, am I?" Carly gave out a strangled laugh.

Arlene didn't respond. Her gaze was fixed on the enlarged photo gaping up at them from the floor.

When Carly bent to retrieve it, all feeling in her limbs drained southward. The photo was an age progression likeness of what the female robber, Lola Bracken, might look like today. Except for the bump on the nose, she was a dead ringer for Arlene.

"I'll clean up that stuff later," Carly warbled in a voice that sounded like someone else's. "For now, let's dig into this pizza, shall we?"

Arlene shook her head. "I'm afraid not, Carly." She reached into the pocket of her tunic, pulled out a handgun, and pointed it at her. "I wish you hadn't been so nosy. Don't you realize that getting rid of Lyle helped you too?"

Numb with dread, Carly said, "Lyle recognized you, didn't he? He must've seen you on that TV program, the one about fugitives from justice. After that, he checked you out on the internet and found all these articles."

Arlene's eyes glinted like hardened steel. "I was twenty-three, Carly. No one cared about me, until a smooth-talking dude with slick looks came along and made me believe I was his world. What he really wanted was a willing accomplice." Tears puddled in her lower lids. "He was the one who shot the guard, not me. No one was ever supposed to get hurt!"

"You were so young. Why didn't you turn yourself in? You'd be out of prison by now, and free."

The gun jiggled in Arlene's hand. "I was terrified, but I wasn't dumb. I knew what prisons were like. It was a miracle I got away. I found a doctor who fixed my nose and got rid of that awful wart. I lived in a couple different states, but when I found Joyce through the agency, I knew I hit pay dirt. New state, new life—it was a dream come true. Joyce was so kind, and she didn't ask a lot of questions. I take good care of her, Carly. I don't deserve to go to prison!"

Carly sucked in a slow breath. If she had any chance of getting out of this, she needed to keep her wits sharp. "When did Lyle recognize you?"

"It was that day I hit his stupid car and I took off my sunglasses. He found out where I lived and started leaving threatening notes on my car, telling me to pay up or else he'd turn me in for the reward. One day, he left me a burner phone and told me to use it to call him."

"Did he think you still had money from the robbery?"

"Yes, because I told him I did. I don't have a plug nickel, but I was stalling him until I could figure out what to do. I told him it would take a while to get to the cash. And then he got that other creep involved, and they tried to make me get rid of stolen jewelry."

"Other creep?"

"I never knew his name, only that Lyle called him K.O. Him and Bagley were partners in crime. They forced me to go to some sleazy pawnbroker and pretend a valuable ring was my dear, dead Aunt Matilda's. The guy was wise to me, though. Told me to get out or he'd sic the cops on me."

"Did Lyle tell this K.O. who you really were?"

"Unfortunately, yes. After I got rid of Bagley, K.O. kept calling my burner phone, telling me I better cooperate with him or else. I was ready to take care of him, too, if it came to that. I called him a few times, but he didn't call me back. He was playing games, trying to scare me."

A sudden memory came back at Carly. The last time Kevin had been in the restaurant, his cell phone had rung with a guitar riff that sounded strangely familiar. She realized now it was from "Lola." He'd declined the call, but it had to have been from Arlene.

Her hand shaking, Carly realized she was still holding her plate with the pizza slice. She set it down on the floor and stared at the woman aiming a gun at her. "It's time to turn yourself in, Arlene. I'm sure Joyce will vouch for what a wonderful caretaker you've been."

"Are you nuts?" Arlene howled. "You think the feds care about that? You know, you have some nerve. I did this partly to help you. That night, when you came downstairs crying in your beer about losing your lease? I knew then I couldn't go on letting him torture me any longer. I did it for you too, Carly, so you could keep your precious restaurant. When I was getting the birthday cake ready, I called him on my burner phone and arranged to meet him that night. I told him I had a cash down payment for him, plus I still had that ring I'd tried to fence. Believe me, he wanted that ring back real bad."

"What did you hit him with? The police never found the murder weapon."

Arlene's smile was chilling. "I told you I was prepared for a Vermont winter. I used my portable shovel. I had to hit him a few times, but I made sure he was dead before I bolted out of that parking lot." Her eyes glittered with righteous glee. "I had my gun with me, but I changed my mind about using it. Too noisy, and I was afraid someone would report the gunshot. Besides, slamming that scumbag in the head with my shovel was so satisfying. I love it when people get what they deserve, don't you?"

Carly tried to swallow, but her throat felt barricaded. "I never heard you leave or come back that night. I was so zonked out on Joyce's port wine."

"And on the sleeping pill I crushed into the frosting flower on your cake."

Carly gasped, remembering the throbbing headache she'd awakened with the following morning. "You drugged me?"

"I couldn't risk you waking up and seeing me leaving or coming home. Or seeing my car missing from the driveway." Arlene raised the gun and sighed heavily. "And I'm afraid I don't have time for any more chitchat." She pulled an amber pill bottle from her pocket and tossed it at Carly, but it landed on the floor. "Pick it up, Carly. Do this my way and it will be painless. You've been kind to me, and I don't want you to suffer."

Carly felt her blood chill. With a hand that felt like a Popsicle, she slowly reached down for the bottle.

"Now, open it and swallow them, *all* of them," Arlene said coldly. "You can wash them down a few at a time with wine while I watch."

Carly stared down at the pill bottle and shook her head.

"It's either that or the gun." Arlene's voice morphed into a singsong tone, and her eyes clouded. "You never got over your husband's death, did you Carly? You told me several times you thought about doing away with yourself."

"That's a lie, and you know it."

Arlene curled her lip. "What really set me off was when you called Animal Control about that stupid squirrel. Do you realize I had to answer the door when they showed up? You'd taken off to do your errands and I had to explain everything!"

"And that was a problem because…"

"Because after my nightmare encounter with Bagley, I didn't need to risk someone else recognizing me from that TV program. Remember that gangster from Boston who was on the lam for years? They caught him because someone recognized his girlfriend at a hair salon."

This can't be happening. I must be trapped in one of those crazy, never-ending dreams.

"You used your burner phone to send me that threatening text, didn't you?" Carly accused.

"I had to. You were poking your nose where it didn't belong, attracting more attention. I didn't need anyone else butting into our business. If I'd been smarter, I'd have gotten rid of you before, but I was being kind. Look where it got me."

She's deranged, Carly thought. *Totally off-kilter.*

With a sudden resolve, Carly flipped the cap off the pill bottle. "Okay, you win. I–I'll take the pills," she said meekly, pouring a few into her hand. She palmed them into her mouth and lifted her wineglass to her lips. In the next instant, she sprang out of her chair and threw the wine in Arlene's face.

Using a few nasty words Carly hadn't heard in a while, Arlene shrieked as she swiped the wine out of her eyes. Carly grabbed the wine bottle off the floor and swung it hard into the side of Arlene's head. The dull *thunk* of glass against skull made her cringe, but she spat out the pills, grabbed her keys off the hallway table, and raced out the door.

Moments later, Arlene came charging out the front door, the gun clutched in her hand. Carly jumped into her front seat, but before she could lock the doors, Arlene wrenched open the passenger door and dropped onto the seat beside her.

CHAPTER THIRTY-SEVEN

"GET BACK INSIDE," ARLENE ORDERED, POINTING THE HANDGUN at her.

"No." Carly's voice rattled. She glanced at her gas gauge. Her tank was about a quarter full. "You wouldn't dare shoot me in the car. My tank is full. If the bullet hits it by accident, you'll blow us both to smithereens."

With Arlene still screaming commands at her to get out of the car, Carly started her engine and backed out of the driveway. Mercifully, she didn't have to wait for any oncoming traffic.

"I said go back!" Arlene bellowed, jabbing the gun into Carly's side.

No! Carly screamed in her head. Turning back wasn't an option. Once they were alone, Arlene would kill her on the spot. Her only hope was to stall until she could figure out a way to get help.

Terror pulsing through every vein in her body, Carly tuned out Arlene's rants and headed toward town. Her fingers gripped the steering wheel so hard they felt like claws.

"I said turn *around*," Arlene shrieked. She poked the gun hard into Carly's ribs, planting the barrel firmly in her side.

Every nerve in her body quivering, Carly forced a calmness into her voice she didn't possess. "Arlene, listen to me. Killing me won't get you anywhere. The police will find you so fast you won't know what hit you, and you'll end up in prison for life. Let me go, and at least you'll have a chance of seeing the light of day again. I'll tell them how kind and caring you were to Joyce, how she'd never have survived without you."

Arlene pushed the gun harder, and Carly struggled not to squirm. "Nobody will give a crap about that, and you know it! You're just trying to save your sorry skin."

They were approaching the town center now, and the skies were growing dusky. At this time of night, the downtown shops were closed. Over to her left, opposite the town green, Carly spotted a light on in one of the storefront windows. Wasn't that Ari's shop? Staring at it a moment too long, she failed to notice the traffic signal up ahead had turned red. Carly slammed on her brake, sending Arlene slinging forward against the glove box.

"You dumb, stupid—" Her hair flying around her face like a wild mane, Arlene spewed a string of curses at her.

Decision time.

Carly inched her fingers toward her door handle, preparing to shove the gearshift into Park and make a fast escape.

In a split-second move that Carly barely registered, Arlene shifted the barrel of the gun from Carly's ribs to the side of her neck. "Where do you think you're going?" Arlene's voice was a deadly hiss.

A sob burst from Carly. She was trapped in a car with a madwoman—a madwoman with a gun. Why, *why* hadn't she run to a neighbor for help instead of hopping into her car?

She stole a glance at her captor, and what she saw curdled her blood. A sheen of pure insanity glimmered in Arlene's eyes. Her pupils were dilated, whether from panic or from the smack on the head Carly had given her—or both—she wasn't sure. Arlene swiveled her neck all around, and her eyes seemed to roll backward.

And then suddenly—a sliver of hope. Like a lake appearing in a barren desert, a familiar face emerged from around the street corner on Carly's left. It was Becca Avery, a brown grocery bag in her arms, walking in Carly's direction.

Becca was about twenty feet away when she spotted Carly's vehicle idling at the light. She lifted her hand in a wave and moved toward the edge of the sidewalk. With a furtive glance at Arlene, who was using her free hand to massage her temple, Carly peeled her flag decal off her window and flipped it around, pressing it against the glass. The stag's head that formed the peak of Vermont's coat of arms now hung upside down.

A car behind them beeped.

"The freaking light's green," Arlene growled, rubbing her temple with her free hand. "Now turn around and go home!"

Carly shot a glance at her rearview mirror and then released the brake, accelerating at a turtle's pace. The Balsam Dell police station was only a short distance ahead, and a few cars were behind her. Did she dare attempt a sudden turn into the entrance?

The thought had no sooner flitted through her mind when Arlene smacked her shoulder with the gun barrel. "You pull into that cop shop and I'll shoot the first one I see, and then I'll shoot you. Got it?"

Shivering, her mouth like cotton, Carly nodded. Arlene had killed once. She wouldn't hesitate to do it again to evade capture. Carly's only hope now was to continue driving until she ran out of gas—if Arlene let her live that long.

Her eyes on the road, her stomach somewhere around her tonsils, Carly continued along Route 7. Even with only a quarter tank of gas, she'd probably make it over the Massachusetts border before she ran out. In the meantime, she needed to keep Arlene distracted.

"I've got to hand it to you," Carly said, injecting false praise into her tone. "I get it now—why you taught yourself to cut hair, why you were having your groceries delivered. You were scared someone might recognize you, so you created your own little enclave. You, the dependable caregiver, Joyce the needy patient with enough money to support you both. It was a clever plan."

"I learned how to survive early on," Arlene sputtered. "My father flew the coop. My louse of a mother only cared about her boyfriends. The only one who cared about me was *me*." She rubbed her temple again and groaned. "And my head is throbbing from where you hit me. For that alone I should shoot you."

Carly's heart clenched. "I'm sorry I did that," she murmured, feigning remorse. "I think you have a concussion. Why don't I take you to the hospital so someone can look at it?"

"Yeah, you wish. Now turn around and go back to the apartment so I can finish this. I'll still let you use the sleeping pills if you go back now. Otherwise, we'll just pull over and—" She held up the gun for effect, but for the first time she looked uncertain. Her eyes were glassy, her grip on the gun shaky.

"Okay," Carly said meekly, having no intention of complying. "Just let me find a good place to turn around."

The sky was growing darker as night filtered in. Carly turned on her headlights, and Arlene flinched from the sudden flash of brightness. After that she went oddly quiet. But the fact that she held a loaded gun still posed a deadly threat.

The sudden, shrill whine of a siren made Carly jump in her seat. The sound grew louder until a glut of blue lights filled her car. A state trooper sped up beside her, then veered over in front of her as Carly squeezed her brakes hard. Arlene jerked forward and mumbled something, just as a second police car came up behind them, its lights flashing like a carnival ride.

"Pull over. *Now*," the male voice burst through a loudspeaker.

Her hands quaking, Carly pulled over to the side of the road and brought her Corolla to a jerky stop. In the next instant, her door was wrenched open. "Step out of the car," a grim-faced trooper ordered.

Carly complied instantly, then looked over to see Arlene being hauled out of the passenger side by two officers. As if she'd been jolted by a cattle prod, Arlene jerked to life, turning on the officers like a wild animal. Her obscenity-laced screams cut through the night as her hands were cuffed behind her. It took the strength of both troopers to propel her into the back of one of the police cars.

Once inside the car, Arlene bashed her head against the side window. She mouthed threats at Carly, her face twisted with rage. She let out one more shriek of fury before crumpling against the seat.

Her entire body trembling, Carly turned away. A female trooper remained with her. "She's a fugitive from justice," Carly explained. "Her real name is Lola Bracken. She's been on the run for a very long time. Oh, and she also killed Lyle Bagley." With that, Carly burst into tears.

Despite the balmy evening, the woman trooper draped a blanket over Carly's shoulders. "You're safe now, Ms. Hale. Tomorrow will be a busy day for you. Do you want to stay with a friend tonight?"

Carly wiped her tears away with her fingertips. "No, I need to go home. Joyce, my landlady, is alone and will need someone to stay with her. Arlene—Lola—was her caretaker."

"Fine, then—"

"I'll take her home." The deep voice, so warm and familiar, made Carly's arms tingle and her heart catch. Until now, she hadn't noticed the pickup that had pulled up behind the troopers or the man jogging toward them wearing a look of deep concern.

"A-Ari, what are you doing here?"

His face strained with worry, he said, "I was puttering in my shop when Becca came banging on my door. She was sure you were in trouble; she saw you turn your Vermont flag upside down. I called the police immediately."

The trooper smiled. "Ah, an upside-down flag—the universal signal of distress. It's supposed to be the American flag, but that's okay; you got your message across. Good thinking, Ms. Hale."

Carly's knees nearly buckled. "Becca's a veteran. I knew she'd get it. Thank you, Ari." To the trooper, she said, "So, I don't need to go to the police station?"

"You do, but for now we're letting you go home. We contacted Chief Holloway, and he gave it his blessing. He couldn't say enough about you, by the way."

"Enough good or enough bad?" Carly squeaked.

"Enough good. But you'll need to be interviewed first thing tomorrow, so get a good night's sleep." The trooper checked with her supervisor, and Ari was granted permission to drive Carly home.

"Wait a minute," Carly told the trooper. "Arlene needs to go to the hospital. I had to hit her with a wine bottle to get away."

"Don't worry. She's in good hands. The main thing is that you're okay."

Carly nodded, silently thanking Daniel—a former National Guardsman—for teaching her about the upside-down flag. In the next instant, Ari's muscular arm slipped around her shoulder. It felt warm and comforting and reassuring. She wanted to cry again, but instead, she leaned against him.

He helped her into his pickup and tucked the blanket around her. "Ready to go home?" he asked, snapping her seat belt into place. His dark eyes beamed at her, and she felt that increasingly familiar flutter in her chest.

"Oh, you bet I am. I can't get there fast enough."

CHAPTER THIRTY-EIGHT

"I SWEAR, THIS IS LIKE BEING BACK AT WOODSTOCK," JOYCE chortled, lifting a glass of mildly spiked lemonade to her lips. Garbed in her Woodstock fiftieth anniversary tee and rainbow-striped seersucker shorts, she looked more vibrant than Carly had ever seen her. And why not? Her backyard was teeming with friends who were laughing, eating, playing.

"Well, that was before my time, Joyce," Carly said, "but I'm happy you're enjoying the picnic."

Joyce reached over to squeeze Becca's hand. "And I don't know where I'd be without this beautiful lady. No more slacking off for me. Between my new exercises and my deep breathing, I'm feeling like a brand new gal."

Becca, sitting on a lawn chair with her legs stretched out, smiled at her new employer. Since the previous week, when she'd accepted the position as Joyce's live-in caretaker, both women had been thriving. Joyce was spending more time outdoors, and they'd both joined the library's book club.

Grant trotted over with a tray of mini hot dogs in puff pastry. "Try my dogs, Ms. Katso? I make my own spicy mustard."

"You betcha." With a wink at Grant, Joyce grabbed a few and set them on her paper plate. "And if there are any more of those grilled tomatoes, I'll take one of those too."

Becca and Carly each nabbed a mini dog and devoured them in two bites. Carly loved watching Grant dazzle everyone with his summer appetizers. Chef-wise, he was in his element. His folks were there, too, and Carly was delighted that the Robinsons had agreed to attend the picnic. An object that looked suspiciously like a violin case sat on the grass next to Grant's dad, Alvin Robinson. His mom, Raynelle, was the picture of casual elegance in a sleeveless white top over a pair of yellow flowered slacks. According to Grant, they were still pressuring him to study music in the fall, but for now they'd made their peace with his current choice.

"Speaking of dogs," Carly said, looking around the yard, "where's my Havarti?"

"He's playing Frisbee with Josh and his dad," Grant said. "They're having a blast."

Carly craned her neck and peeked around their guests toward the rear section of the yard. Her heart twisted at the sight of her sweet little pup leaping up to catch the Frisbee. Dr. Anne, instead of bringing him to a shelter, had kept him at her facility. She was counting on Carly coming to her senses and adopting him. Which is exactly what Carly did.

"I'm psyched about Suzanne, aren't you?" Grant leaned over and asked Carly.

"Totally. Keeping my fingers crossed for success."

Suzanne had agreed to a trial "unification" with Jake. His new job was paying well, and they'd rented a small house. From the genuine smiles on all their faces, Carly suspected the trial was working out.

After Arlene's arrest and the discovery that Kevin O'Toole had been the elusive burglar, the town had gone into a mild uproar. Given all the media attention, Carly had postponed the picnic until the following Sunday. The crisp blue skies and temps in the low eighties seemed almost special ordered.

Joyce had happily invested in a new grill. Ari, who offered to assemble it, had arrived early with Ethan, Chris, and Logan, and they'd expertly put it together.

Carly was thrilled Chief Holloway had taken a rare day off

to join them. He sat in a mesh chair next to Dr. Anne and Erika, enjoying a beer and a plate of Grant's mini dogs. A few days earlier, he'd given Carly an update on the law enforcement side of things. The details of O'Toole's cleverly wrought crimes boggled Carly's mind.

O'Toole had moved to Vermont from Kansas a few years earlier when he learned his cousin, Officer Palmer, was on the Balsam Dell Police Force. The two had never been close, but O'Toole knew that Palmer, as a teen, had been involved in a serious drunk driving accident. Due to Palmer's age at the time, the court records were sealed. Palmer's mistake was failing to disclose the incident on his application to the police force.

Although Palmer hadn't been involved in the burglaries, he'd been pressured—or rather blackmailed—by O'Toole to overlook or misplace evidence. O'Toole, meanwhile, had set up a tidy business for himself doing commercial cleaning, which earned him growing respect among the locals. His pest control gig was a clever sideline; it gave him valid entry into the finest homes in town.

Releasing scads of mice near the high-end mansions he'd targeted had been his ticket to getting pest control work. From there, he either copied a key or found other means of access. With his amiable, chatty style, it was easy to learn when homeowners would be on vacation or out of town.

The kink in O'Toole's plan had been Lyle, with whom he'd somehow hooked up during a card game. Lyle had agreed to help fence the stolen goods, hence the installation of the fancy vault. He'd given O'Toole a key to the house but refused to give him one to the safe. On nights when Lyle left on his outside light, O'Toole knew to stay away.

It soon became obvious that Lyle was cheating O'Toole, keeping some of the best items for himself. In retaliation, O'Toole let loose an army of mice at Lyle's mobile home park. As for Officer Palmer, he'd been fired and was facing charges. Carly felt a twinge of pity for him. Though he'd made some horrible choices, she couldn't help remembering how he'd encouraged her to adopt Havarti.

"What I can't fathom," Carly had asked the chief, "is why O'Toole didn't speak out sooner and turn Arlene into the authorities."

"Good question," the chief had responded. "He told us he was saving it for his ace in the hole. If he ever got nabbed for the burglaries, he was going to use it as a bargaining chip in a plea bargain deal. He didn't count on you turning her in first."

"Hey." The voice behind Carly made her turn around. Don Frasco was trudging toward her carrying a blue and white cooler.

Carly smiled at him. "Don, I'm so glad you're here. Is that root beer?"

"Yeah." He plunked the cooler down on the grass. "Since I drink so much of it, I figured I should bring some with me in case anyone else wanted it."

Carly had been thrilled that everyone had offered to contribute to the picnic goodies. "Why don't you put it on that table over there with the other soft drinks, then go ahead and mingle." She winked at him. "After all, you *are* a popular figure these days."

Flashing Carly a red-faced smile, Don loped over to the beverage table with his cooler. His unwitting role in putting O'Toole out of commission had made him somewhat of a local celebrity. Business owners all over town had been showering him with accolades and freebies. Best of all, orders for ads had been pouring in to the point he'd had to expand the length of his free paper.

Excusing herself, Carly went over to where Gina and her friend were sitting at the picnic table. "What's cooking? You guys enjoying the snacks?"

"Everything's awesome," said Gina's boyfriend-who-wasn't-yet-a-boyfriend. His name was Zach, he had startling green eyes, and he was gazing at Gina as if the earth revolved around her.

Carly suspected he wouldn't remain in "only a friend" territory for too much longer.

"You ready to start the sandwiches?" Gina asked. She'd placed two massive salad bowls, one green and one potato, in Carly's fridge. Once the sandwiches were on the grill, she and Zach were going to carry them out to the buffet table they'd set up on the grass. With so many more guests than originally planned, Carly had splurged on several new lawn chairs and two portable tables. All could be folded and stored in the cellar. If Carly's budding idea for an end-of-summer celebration came to fruition, they could easily be hauled out for another picnic.

Carly glanced around. It looked as if everyone had arrived. Her mom, who couldn't make the trip in time for the picnic, was flying in the next morning. Norah would be with her, and Carly couldn't wait to see them.

Carly felt someone's elbow jab her. "You daydreaming again?" Gina teased her.

"Sorry. I guess I was." Carly rose from the picnic bench. "I'll go find Grant so we can start putting the sandwiches together. He's making a special one for his folks. I can't wait to see their reaction! Give us ten minutes before you bring out the salads."

With Grant's help, Carly prepared a variety of sandwiches to please every palate. Grant had been eager to use Sara's cranberry-pecan loaf to make a specialty sandwich for his folks. With a layer of fig jam paired with brie and spinach, it was a sandwich not everyone would embrace. Grant, however, was sure it would please his mom and dad and couldn't wait for them to taste it.

When they were ready to roll, Grant carried the tray out to the yard and they began grilling. As sandwiches became ready, he sliced them each into four sections and set them out on trays. That way, guests could sample an assortment of grilled cheese delights.

Carly, with Havarti on the bench beside her, sat with Joyce and Becca at the picnic table, across from Gina, Zach, and Don.

Suzanne, her hubby, and her son Josh spread a blanket on the lawn where they could enjoy their eats as a family. The chief sat at one of the portable tables with Dr. Anne, Erika, Ari, and the Robinsons. Ari's helpers, who all wore grins the width of the Walloomsac River, had stretched out on the lawn with their plates stacked to the clouds with tasty food.

After everyone had pretty much stuffed themselves, Grant waved Carly over. She set Havarti on the grass and joined the Robinsons.

"Carly," Alvin Robinson said, dabbing his lips with a napkin. "I never thought a grilled cheese sandwich could be so special, until Grant made this one for us. Adding fig jam and spinach to a grilled cheese was genius. And that bread? It was absolute perfection!"

His wife smiled approvingly at Grant. "I totally agree. Our son never fails to surprise us with his culinary creations. Thank you for giving him a chance to experiment with his recipes."

"I'm lucky to have Grant in the restaurant," Carly said. "I do hope you'll stop in one day."

After Carly and Gina cleaned up the tables and separated the trash, the chief motioned Carly over for a private chat.

"Just wanted to let you know about Arlene," he said quietly. "She's been transferred to a federal facility, but she'll have to return to Vermont to stand trial for Bagley's murder. You'll be required to testify at the trial."

"I know," Carly said, dreading the day. "It's so sad. Arlene— Lola—had so many good qualities. If she'd turned herself in years ago, by now she'd probably be living a better life."

"Exactly."

Arlene's declaration that Joyce was depressed had been a total fabrication, designed to keep them both living a cloistered life-style. Terrified of being recognized again, she'd been determined to avoid leaving the house except when she absolutely had to.

"I heard Matt Bagley is going to take over Lyle's mobile home park," Carly said.

The chief gave a slight laugh. "With his brother gone, he's finally getting the chance to have a business of his own. He'd been scoping out that place for months, going there every weekend to see how he could improve the property. He couldn't afford to buy it outright from Lyle, but now everything that was Lyle's is his. Even the old house they grew up in."

"Did he finally get the Caddy?"

"Oh, he sure did. I think Matt's going to do okay once that chip falls off his shoulder. He's planning to live at the park as the on-site manager. Once he sells the old homestead, he's going to use the money to improve the place."

"I'm glad Janet Moody will still be the leasing manager," Carly said. "I'm even happier that she's not being charged with anything."

Three days before, Carly had finally delivered the grilled cheese sandwich she'd promised to Janet. Janet had invited her in for a glass of wine, but Carly had graciously declined.

The chief turned and looked toward Ari, who was sitting in a lawn chair with Havarti snugged to his chest. "I think your dog misses you," he said with a playful wink. "Better go grab him before Ari takes him home."

The chief strolled off, and Carly felt that familiar flush warm her cheeks. She turned and was walking toward Ari when Logan tapped her on the shoulder. "Ms. Hale? I, um, have the desserts ready to bring out. Is this a good time?"

The desserts! With everyone so stuffed, she'd almost forgotten. Logan, who'd gotten a summer job at Sissy's Bakery, had insisted on using his employee discount to buy sweets for the picnic. He'd left the covered trays in Ari's pickup.

"Oh, gosh, the desserts. Yes, this is the perfect time, Logan. Do you need my help?"

"Nah." A strand of his longish brown hair fell over one eye. "Chris'll help me, if he doesn't eat half of them first."

"Then go ahead and start serving."

"Oh, um, a lady with a red car just parked out front."

Red car? "Thanks, Logan."

Carly looked toward the driveway. Sure enough, Tiffany Spencer was striding toward her. Wearing a lovely green sundress that didn't come close to brushing her knees, she looked more relaxed than Carly had ever seen her.

"Tiffany, it's great to see you. You look beautiful."

"Thank you. I wanted to let you know, I'm cleared out of my apartment. Once it's cleaned and reno'd, it'll be available for rent."

Carly had learned a few days earlier that the real estate group Brad Gearhart had told her about had officially bought the building. Carly was offered a five-year lease with an option to extend. As for the apartment, she had the perfect tenant in mind.

"Thanks for letting me know," Carly said. "Did you find a new apartment?"

Tiffany's eyes danced. "I'm still working on a place to live, but I have fab news. Yolanda Breslin was so elated to have her diamond pendant back that she's going to help me open my boutique. She'll supply the financial backing *and* be a silent partner. I've already found a place in the new strip mall. It's an end unit and it's absolutely ideal."

Carly pressed her palms together. "I am so happy for you. Let me know when you open, okay? I'll be one of your first customers!"

"I will."

"Would you like to stay?" Carly asked her.

"I'd love to, but I'm meeting Yolanda for cocktails. Another time, maybe?"

Tiffany air-kissed Carly and then ambled toward her Nissan, leaving Carly feeling a bit lighter. The woman deserved a break, and she was finally getting one.

Musical sounds drifted into Carly's ears. She turned to see everyone gathered around Grant and his dad. Grant was plucking at his cello, while his dad sat with his violin perched on his shoulder.

Ari, holding Havarti, patted the lawn chair beside him and

grinned. Carly scooted over and sat down, taking her pup in her arms. "Thanks," she whispered.

"We'll begin with a little Vivaldi," Alvin Robinson announced, winking at his son.

And the music began, lush and gorgeous and fabulous. Everyone's gazes were riveted on the musicians. Some, including Joyce, had tears in their eyes.

After the duo played a series of classical numbers, Carly thought the concert was over. Until Grant and his dad broke into a round of old-style rock, from the Beatles to Metallica to Prince. Everyone roared with delight, and some sang along to the tunes.

In a flash of inspiration, the perfect name for Grant's specialty sandwich popped into Carly's head: Vermont Jammin'.

As the warm sun cast shadows on the lawn, Grant and his dad packed up their instruments. Suzanne hugged Carly and then left with her family, while the boys cleaned up the remaining trash. When the tables were wiped clean, Zach helped Ari fold them and carry them into the cellar.

Grant's face was glowing as he hugged Carly. "Mom and Dad had a *great* afternoon," he told her.

After the picnic wound down and the guests went home, Ari and his softball buds remained. The boys sat on the grass around Joyce while she regaled them with tales from Woodstock.

Ethan looked enraptured. "Like, you saw Jimi Hendrix in person? That is so *sick!*"

Carly murmured to Joyce, "Sick is a good thing."

Joyce chuckled. "Oh, then it was definitely sick."

Ari finally rounded up the boys, stating they were overstaying their welcome. Carly promised them an end-of-summer bash, which elicited hoots and hollers from the teens.

"Thanks for everything," Carly said quietly to Ari. With Havarti in her arms, she walked him out to his pickup. "We couldn't have done any of this without you."

"Not true, but I'll accept the compliment." Smiling, he kissed her lightly on the cheek, and Carly felt a zing of electricity. "See you tomorrow, Carly."

I hope so.

Hugging Havarti, Carly went back into the yard, over to Joyce and Becca. "I don't think this day could have been any more perfect, do you?"

Becca laughed and wrested Havarti from her grip. "Au contraire, as my grandmother would say. Look behind you."

Carly swung around. Her mom and her sister were rushing at her like a pair of overcaffeinated linebackers. "Mom! Norah!"

"I got an earlier flight!" her mom screamed. "Norah picked me up in Albany!"

They crushed Carly in a hug, and all three cried.

This is what it's like to be home, Carly thought. *Truly home, where everyone is where they should be.*

Read on for a look at Linda Reilly's
next cheesy mystery

NO PARM NO FOUL

A Grilled Cheese Mystery

LINDA REILLY

CHAPTER ONE

GRANT ROBINSON SWEPT THROUGH THE FRONT DOOR OF Carly's Grilled Cheese Eatery and scooted behind the counter. "It's over, Carly. I finally did it. I gave my notice at the sub shop."

The grilled cheese Carly Hale was flipping did a slight wobble. Grant, the twenty-year-old food aficionado who'd been Carly's part-time grill cook since she first opened, also worked part time at Sub-a-Dub-Sub, a sandwich shop located across the town square. Or rather, he *had* worked there.

Carly shifted the grilled cheese back onto her spatula, then placed it, butter side down, on the grill. "Wow, you really went through with it. What did Mr. Menard say? Was he upset?"

"Upset? From the steam coming out of his ears, I'd say he was like a water heater about to burst."

Using her spatula, Carly slid the Sweddar Weather—a grilled Swiss and cheddar on marble rye—onto her cutting board. She sliced it in half, transferred it to a plate, and added chips and pickles to the dish, along with a cup of tomato soup. The heady aroma of melted cheese and butter-grilled bread never failed to delight her. It was the primary reason she'd returned to her hometown of Balsam Dell, Vermont and opened her grilled cheese eatery. She'd taken over the space where a failing, decades-old ice cream parlor had finally gone belly up.

The other factor that prompted her return to her hometown was the death of her husband two years earlier. To escape the memories and start a new life for herself, she came home, as she thought of it, and opened her dream business. Sharing her favorite comfort food and earning a living from it was the best of both worlds.

Carly glanced around the dining room. At a bit past 2:00, only one booth was taken. Its sole occupant was Steve Perlman, a forty-something man sporting rimless eyeglasses, a paperback book in front of him. Mr. P., as Carly referred to him, had been one of her high school teachers. Physics, her least favorite subject, she recalled with a shudder. But he'd been an earnest young man then, passionate about science as well as a good teacher. When he spotted Grant, he waved. Grant returned the gesture with a big smile.

Carly had opened her eatery earlier in the year, and though summer had brought in visitors galore, it was autumn that was proving to be her busiest season. While leaf-peepers descended on the town in droves, it was the high school that was turning out to be her best source of customers. The kids, and even some teachers, had been invading her restaurant daily after the last bell rang. They scarfed down grilled cheese sandwiches and cheesy dippers with gusto while they droned on about the disgusting food in the school cafeteria.

"You can tell me all about it later," Carly told Grant. "Go put on your apron. You can give me a break before the hungry hordes come in, okay? Suzanne had to leave early for a meeting with Josh's teacher."

Suzanne Rivers was Carly's other server. With a son in fourth grade, Suzanne normally worked from 11:00 a.m. to 3:00 p.m. so she could be home for Josh after school. Lately she'd been putting in some extra hours to help Carly get through the midday rush. It helped that Josh had signed up for a few after-school programs, so on most days it worked out perfectly.

"Say no more." Grant hustled through the swinging door that led into the kitchen. He returned moments later wearing a crisp apron and vinyl gloves.

Carly delivered the sandwich plate to her sole customer. "There you go, Mr. P. Need a coffee warm up?"

"I'd love one." He picked up a sandwich half and aimed it toward his mouth. "And Carly, please stop calling me Mr. P. It's been a long time since you were in my physics class. 'Steve' will do just fine."

"Force of habit," Carly said with a smile. She returned and refilled his mug. "By the way, how did you manage to beat the kids here today? School doesn't get out till two-thirty."

Steve swallowed a bite of his sandwich. "I had a doctor appointment, so I took the afternoon off." He winked at her. "Good excuse, right? Plus, it gave me a chance to pick up a few sci-fi books from the library. I read at least three a week."

"Ah. Got it." She smiled as if to assure him his secret was safe with her.

Carly went back behind the counter. Grant looked dismayed as he wiped down the grill.

Carly knew him so well. She was sure he felt both guilt and relief at having ditched his job at the sub shop. The owner's lackadaisical approach to food hygiene had, apparently, finally pushed him over the edge. Although Grant had only recently turned twenty, he was more mature than most thirty-year-olds and had a passion for all things culinary. He was also a gifted cellist, but to his musical parents' dismay, he was determined to become a chef.

With Grant's help, Carly had added some inspired new sandwiches to their grilled cheese menu, including their most recent offering—Brie-ng on the Apples, Granny! The new autumn sandwich was made by grilling creamy Brie, thin-sliced Granny Smith apples, and cherry relish between slices of raisin bread. After its debut in early September, it quickly became an eatery favorite.

Grant had also helped her design their entry in the town's annual Halloween Scary-Licious Smorgasbord competition, which was only two days away. *Yikes*. Aside from supplying light sticks to kids for trick-or-treat night, it was Balsam Dell's only concession to Halloween.

It would be Carly's first time participating in the event, and she was feeling more excited as the day approached. The competition, sponsored by the town's recreation department, was held every year on the Saturday before Halloween. Tables were set up on the town green, and local restaurants gave out samples of their creepy culinary creations. Attendees voted—one vote per ticket. After all votes were tallied, the winner was awarded a $500 cash prize, along with the coveted plaque engraved with the restaurant's name. Carly had already chosen a spot for the plaque, should it be awarded to her eatery.

"Carly, we're probably gonna be mobbed soon, so I'll tell you what happened real quick." Grant winced, then spoke in a low voice. "Mr. Menard is blaming you for my quitting. He thinks you put me up to squealing on him to the board of health."

"But…but…I would never do that! I would never try to influence you." She tried to keep her tone quiet, but she knew she'd hit a few high notes. Still, she was both aghast and furious at the man's accusations.

"I told him that. I defended you to the moon, but he kept ranting right over me." Grant shook his head. He looked worried. "At one point I got scared his heart would give out. He takes medication for it, even though he's only in his forties. His face got bright red, and he stumbled backward. His daughter Holly made him sit down and take a pill of some sort. She said he has angina."

"I'm sorry to hear that," Carly said. "I hope he's getting the proper care for it. But it doesn't give him the right to attack my character."

"It's weird," Grant said, looking puzzled. "He was blaming you more than he was me. Almost like…like he had a vendetta against you."

"I'm sure he was only lashing out," Carly said. "No doubt he's bummed about losing you right before the Halloween competition, but he has his daughter to help him. Once he calms down, he'll see that you had every right to give your notice, and to tip off the board of health. Maybe it'll inspire him to clean up his act, right?"

Grant looked unsure. "Yeah, maybe."

"Hey, now that you're here, do you mind if I pop into the kitchen for a few? I need to make a call about my Halloween costume. I'm having it specially made for Saturday!"

"Take your time. I'll handle things here." He gave her a half-hearted smile.

Carly headed into her commercial kitchen. She fixed herself a quick cup of tea with one of the pumpkin spice teabags she'd bought earlier in the week. Though coffee was her normal comfort drink of choice, the Halloween season seemed to inspire cravings for anything pumpkin-flavored.

She sat with her mug at the pine desk beneath the window that overlooked the small parking lot behind the eatery. Only four months earlier, she'd found a body out there. With her help, the murderer had been caught. Nonetheless, she hoped never to see a body again. Pushing away the memory, she grabbed her cell phone and tapped a saved number.

"Miranda Busey. Can I help you?" came a squeaky, tired-sounding voice.

She sounded so young. Carly could hardly believe Miranda was a twenty-two-year-old student who was taking design classes in college. "Hi, Miranda, it's Carly Hale. I'm just checking on my costume. Can I pick it up tonight?"

Carly and the man she'd been seeing, local electrician Ari Mitchell, were attending the Scary-Licious Smorgasbord competition dressed as Morticia and Gomez Addams. Ari's costume was finished, but Carly's required a slinky, lacy stretch of fabric over a full-length, gauzy black dress.

A long silence followed. "Miranda?" Carly prodded.

Miranda groaned. "Carly, I am so, *so* sorry. I was putting the zipper in the back of the lace overlay when my hand slipped and I tore the whole thing. I was so exhausted. I was practically seeing double. I was up almost all last night, sewing."

Carly's stomach dropped. She'd been counting on being Morticia to Ari's Gomez. With his dark eyes and neatly-trimmed mustache, he fit the part perfectly—and much more handsomely than any Gomez she'd ever seen.

"It…it can't be fixed?" Carly swallowed.

"Unfortunately, no. I had to send away for that lace fabric. Even if I had more of it, I'm jammed up the wazoo with more jobs to finish. I guess I took on more than I could handle."

"Can I wear the dress without the lace?"

"Only if you want the entire world to see your underwear." Miranda hesitated. "There's one thing I can offer, but I'm not sure you'll like it. I made a darling lady vampire costume for a customer who changed her mind. It's kind of a pale gray, with a filmy cape that extends out like bat wings. I think it'll fit you, and it's super pretty. Wanna try it?"

Carly was positive she didn't want the entire world to see her underwear. "Sure. I'll stop by after work and try it on."

Disappointed, Carly gulped the rest of her tea and returned to the dining room. As if a magic door had opened, in the short time she'd been gone nearly every booth had filled. The high school contingent had arrived.

A sudden burst of gratitude filled her.

With every passing week, her restaurant was gaining popularity. Only recently, an informal newspaper poll voted it one of the "coziest eateries" in southern Vermont. She had to admit, she agreed. With its exposed, pale brick walls, vinyl aqua booths, and chrome-edged counter lined with stools, it was exactly the way she'd hoped it would look when she first imagined the concept. In every booth, a vintage tomato soup can filled with faux flowers of the season graced the table. October's flowers were orange and yellow mums.

If she won the competition, it would add another feather to her culinary cap, so to speak. With luck, that would translate to an increase in business. It would be a perfect way to usher in the start of the holiday season.

Ferris Menard had won the competition the past three years in a row, according to Grant. It made Carly even more determined to emerge as this year's winner.

At one of the rear booths, a former middle school classmate of Carly's—Stanley Henderson—sat with books and notebooks spread over the table. These days he was preparing for the Realtor's exam and enjoyed reviewing his study notes while he scarfed down a sandwich and a cola. His current job as a guidance counselor at the high school was no longer "floating his boat," as he'd put it. He wanted to make his own hours and be his own boss, not to mention earn some serious commissions selling homes.

When he caught Carly's glance, he gave her a wide, pleasant wave. "Hi, Stan," she mouthed, then went behind the counter.

In the booth behind Stan's, Evelyn Fitch, a retired English teacher, sat with a book of crossword puzzles and a pink notepad. Carly had never had her as a teacher—she'd retired about ten years too early. Now somewhere in her eighties, Ms. Fitch spent at least three afternoons a week enjoying a late lunch of a Vermont Classic—sharp cheddar on country white bread—while she pored over a puzzle. "It's both my lunch and dinner," she'd told Carly one day, "which is why I always come here midafternoon." Carly suspected it was more a case of the lonely Ms. Fitch enjoying being around loads of people, but she'd told her, "Good plan," and let it go at that.

Carly's heart skipped when she saw Ari seated on one of the stools. She went over and leaned toward him. "Hey."

"Hey yourself." His smile warmed her, and she felt her cheeks grow pink. She gave him the bad news about the Morticia costume.

Ari reached over and squeezed her wrist. "Don't worry. It'll be fine," he soothed. "Actually, I'm sort of anxious, now, to see you in that lady vampire dress." His throaty voice and stark gaze made her heart leap skyward again.

Carly grinned, and in the next moment the door to the restaurant swung open, hard. Ferris Menard stormed in, his blond brush cut gelled into porcupine quills, his face a scary shade of red. "Carly Hale," he boomed. He looked around, spotted her, and strode over to the counter. "Yeah, you. I heard about your little sabotage ploy. Well, it won't work—do you hear me?"

As if someone had turned off a switch, the dining room instantly quieted. Stunned by the verbal assault, Carly took a step backward. Grant, who had the protective instincts of a mother grizzly, moved to stand in front of her. "Mr. Menard," he said quietly, "what are you doing here?"

"My beef isn't with you, Grant. I know she put you up to it!"

"But—"

Carly shifted around Grant to face the man. "Ferris," she said tightly, "I will thank you to behave courteously in my establishment. Otherwise, you need to leave. Is that clear?"

"Oh, yeah? Well, I'll thank *you* to stop trying to ruin me." His small blue eyes blazed with fury. "I got a little visit from the health inspector this afternoon, but you already knew that, didn't you, *Miss Hale*. Unfortunately for you, I run a clean, sanitary operation. Oh sure, I got cited for one dumb thing, but it was ridiculously minor. As for this place"—his lip curled as his gaze flickered around the dining room—"suffice it to say, you wouldn't know an aged cheddar from a bale of hay. You're a fraud, and I'm going to prove it."

In the next instant, Stanley Henderson shot out of his booth and strode toward Menard, one fist curled at his side. Steve Perlman was right at his heels, and between the two of them, they blocked Menard's view of Carly.

With a shake of his head, Ari slid quietly off his stool. He went over to Menard and took him firmly by the arm, propelling him toward the door. "Time for you to go, Ferris."

Feigning bravado, Menard stumbled sideways a step, trying unsuccessfully to extract himself from Ari's grip. "Let go of me," he hissed. Spittle formed on his lips, and he swiped at it with his free hand.

"Wait a minute, Ari." Carly circled around all of them and moved to stand directly in front of Menard. "Ferris, I did nothing to sabotage you, as you put it. But if you ever come in here and accuse me again, you can expect a visit from Chief Holloway. Is that clear?" She turned to her would-be protectors. "Stanley, all of you, go back to your seats. I appreciate your help, but I can handle this myself. Besides, Ferris is leaving now. Aren't you, Ferris?"

The rage in Menard's expression was so dense it could have been sliced up and served on a buttered biscuit. Stan flinched, and Steve took a step backward.

Menard wrenched his arm away from Ari, who was edging him closer to the door. Then, with a shake of his fist, he stalked outside into the crisp October day.

CHAPTER TWO

"It was so embarrassing," Carly groaned to her bestie, Gina Tomasso. "First Ferris verbally attacking me, and then Stanley and Mr. P.—Steve—jumping out of their seats to come to my rescue, like I was some damsel in distress. I swear, if they'd had pitchforks and torches, they'd have chased Ferris into the street, like the villagers who went after the Frankenstein monster."

Carly was seated at Gina's kitchen table in the apartment upstairs from her restaurant. She'd stopped in after closing time to give her friend the lowdown on the day's events. Glancing around, she saw that Gina's digs were really shaping up. Though she'd moved in only five weeks earlier, Gina was filling it with every 1960s artifact she could find. Gina's mom, who'd died when she was nine, had loved the decor of that decade. Carly suspected that her friend was sub-consciously choosing furnishings that would've pleased her.

Gina chuckled. "Well, at least they had your back, right? Gotta give them credit for that."

"They did," Carly admitted, "and I felt bad afterward for scolding them. I apologized later to both of them, but they waved it off. Truth be told, I was relieved when Ari escorted Ferris to the door."

"It just infuriates me," Gina said darkly, "to think that Menard barged in like that and caused a scene in front of all your customers. Personally, I'd have wanted to sock him in the snout."

"I draw the line at fisticuffs," Carly said dryly, "but don't think

I wasn't tempted. Now, though, I'm almost dreading the competition on Saturday."

"Why? You didn't do anything wrong."

"I know, but now it feels like there's a dark cloud hanging over me in the shape of an angry Ferris Menard." With a slight shiver, Carly plucked a handful of candy corn from Gina's candy dish and funneled them into her mouth. "You should've heard the sarcasm in his voice when he called me *Miss Hale*. It's obvious he doesn't approve of a woman not taking her husband's name."

Gina waved a dismissive hand. "Don't let him intimidate you. Every year, Ferris Menard enters the same thing in the competition, with only a slight variation. I'm *so* over his sub sandwiches shaped like monsters."

Carly had heard about Ferris's triumphs. For the past three years in a row, he'd won the Scary-Licious competition with sub sandwiches resembling reptiles and zombies, complete with edible eyeballs. His sub shop was known for its special blend of dressing, created by Menard himself. It was used on all the cold subs they served.

Carly's own entry was going to be eye-catching, delicious, and tangy to the third power, as Grant had put it. In addition to her scrumptious grilled cheese, he'd created two dipping sauces—a ghoul green and a blood red—both of which would be presented in hollowed out pumpkins.

Gina set her jaw and tucked a dark-brown curl behind her ear. "If I were you, I'd just let Menard stew in his own juices. Or rather," she snickered, "in his own oil and vinegar dressing, which he thinks is so special. Anyway, just cross the jerk off your list of worries."

"I know you're right, Gina. It's just—"

"It's just that men are pros at making women feel guilty," Gina interrupted tartly. "You remember my ex-husband?"

Oh, Carly surely did. He was the body she'd found in her parking lot at the beginning of the summer.

In fact, it was only after the discovery of Lyle's body that Carly's defunct friendship with Gina had been reignited. In high school, the girls had been almost inseparable—until a huge misunderstanding over Lyle's pursuit of Gina had severed their friendship. Gina had married Lyle straight out of high school but divorced him three years later. By then Carly was living with her husband, Daniel, in northern Vermont—a good two-hour plus ride from Balsam Dell. Neither woman had attempted to contact the other, a mistake they now both regretted.

These days, having resolved their conflict, their friendship was stronger than ever.

"Well, that was one of Lyle's specialties," Gina went on. "That and cheating. Are you sure you don't want a cup of coffee?"

"No, thanks. I have to stop by Miranda's and try on the lady vampire costume. Plus, I have a dog at home who doesn't tolerate tardiness." She grinned at the thought of Havarti, her sweet little Morkie, rushing to the door to greet her. Half Yorkie and half Maltese, he was perky and funny and perpetually ready to shower everyone he encountered with kisses.

"I thought Becca took him outside during the day?"

Becca Avery, an army veteran, was the live-in caretaker for Carly's landlady, Joyce Katso. The pair lived in the apartment downstairs from Carly in Joyce's two-family home.

"She does, but Havarti has a sense of timing like you wouldn't believe. If I'm ten minutes later than usual, he does a circular dance around my feet and barks at my shoes."

Gina giggled. "I love that dog."

Carly glanced at the tangerine-colored Lucite clock on Gina's wall. "Hey, I've really gotta run." She hoisted her pumpkin-themed tote bag—a gift from Ari—onto her shoulder and rose. As she did, a folded slip of pink paper fell out of an outer pocket. Smiling, she picked it up and handed it to Gina. "Look at the note that adorable Evelyn Fitch left in her booth this afternoon after she paid her bill."

Gina unfolded the paper and read: "'Carly's food is tempting and tasty. Always stuffed with melted cheese. Remnants of cheddar sizzle and brown. Leaving a flavor so unimaginably fine. You'll return again for more.'" Gina's face softened. "Aw, it almost sounds like a poem." She raised a dramatic hand to her heart. "Ode to Carly's Grilled Cheese." She grinned, then tucked the note back into Carly's bag. "You really do have a loyal posse of customers."

"On a different subject, are you seeing Zach tonight?" Carly asked her in a teasing voice.

Gina and Zach Bartlett had been an item for about four months. His job as an account manager for a national delivery service kept him on the road a lot, but he and Gina managed to see each other every chance they got. So far, they seemed to be nuts about each other.

A fierce blush colored Gina's round cheeks. "Can't. I've got a custom order for shower invitations that has me burning the midnight oil."

Gina owned a shop aptly dubbed What a Card—a gorgeous card shop located opposite the town green in the next block. Having mastered the technique of quilling, Gina was constantly filling demands for her custom-made cards—especially shower and wedding invitations. Carly worried that sometimes she took on too much work, but Gina never complained, even when she had grueling deadlines.

"So anyway, tomorrow night," Gina explained, "Zach and I are gonna see some new scary movie. I hope I don't scream as loud as I did at the last one. I felt like a total wuss."

"Not to worry. I'm sure Zach'll save you from any zombies."

"Are you kidding? He screamed louder than I did."

Carly laughed. "Later!" She waved and bounded down the stairs and outside to car.

~

The lady vampire dress fit Carly to a tee. And, she had to admit, added a touch of sex appeal without her having to work for it. The pale gray satin hugged her form without being overly snug. When she extended her arms upward, the filmy cape swept around her like shimmering bat wings.

To help her celebrate her first year entering the competition, Ari had bought her a pair of sterling silver spider web earrings. More whimsical than creepy, they would work just as well for a lady vampire as they would for Morticia. The fact that they were a gift from Ari made them that much more special.

Carly carefully removed the dress and slipped it over a hanger. She hung it in her closet—away from Havarti's curious black nose and prying paws. A pleasant little zing of electricity went through her.

Which was appropriate, she thought with a tiny smile. Something told her that Ari, her very own electrician, was also going to feel a zing when he saw her.

Something told her Ari's eyes were going to pop when he saw her in it.

Carly's thoughts drifted to her first husband, Daniel Brownell, who'd died in a tragic accident in January of the previous year. Daniel'd been working as a lineman for the power company and Carly as the restaurant manager at a historic inn. Exhausted after returning home from an eighteen-hour shift repairing downed lines, Daniel had made a fateful decision—to deliver firewood to a family in desperate need. Over Carly's pleas to wait until morning, he'd loaded his pickup, promised to return soon, and drove off into the snowstorm.

That was the last time Carly saw him. His truck, over-burdened with logs, had skidded off an ice-covered bridge and tumbled down an embankment.

After months of moving robotically through her daily tasks, including her job at the Ivory Swan Inn, she made the decision to return to her hometown. A prime commercial space in the heart of the quaint downtown had become available, and it was time, she'd decided, to invest in her longtime dream of opening a grilled cheese eatery.

As for Ari, the fact that he was kind and caring and infinitely patient added several checkmarks to his "plus" column. If Ari had any serious faults, they hadn't yet bubbled to the surface.

Carly had just fed Havarti his evening meal of kibble when her cell rang.

"Hey, Mom!"

"What's this I hear about Ferris Menard harassing you this afternoon?"

"Wow, not even a 'hello' first?"

Rhonda Hale Clark and her hubby, Gary, had made Carly's life complete when they left Florida at the end of the summer and moved back to Vermont—permanently. The bugs, the occasional stray alligator, and the ceaseless air conditioning had finally gotten to Rhonda. When she announced to Gary they were moving back home, he'd smiled and replied, "Anything you say, dear."

"I'm sorry, honey." Rhonda puffed out a breath. "But I saw blood red when I heard from Evelyn Fitch's daughter what happened today! She volunteers with me at the library, you know. By the way, she told me how much her mom loves eating at your place."

"Evelyn's one of my favorites." With her free hand, Carly removed a bottle of apple cider from her fridge. "She wrote me a darling note today."

"That's lovely, but do you want me to have a word with Ferris? I'm pretty handy at putting the fear of eternal damnation into people."

"As Norah and I well know," Carly said wryly. Norah was Carly's older sister by two years, and they'd both experienced the force of their mom's scare tactics. "Honestly, don't worry about it, Mom. I'm not giving it a second thought. Really."

"Harrumph! That's a fib and you know it."

After several minutes of cajoling, Carly managed to soothe her mom's nerves. She was taking a sip of the sweet, delicious cider when she heard the rumble of a noisy car engine outside in her driveway.

Carly hurried over to her front window, Havarti trotting at her heels. She peered out into the dark. In the driveway, Becca Avery's massive, vintage Lincoln hunkered like a primitive beast to the right of Carly's green Corolla. Behind Carly's vehicle, a smallish car idled loudly. Maybe Becca and Joyce had ordered takeout, Carly thought, and the delivery person had a defective muffler.

Carly watched for another minute or so. When no one came out of the house, she slipped on her jacket, then headed down the stairs and out the front door.

The night air was cold and crisp, redolent of decaying leaves and chimney smoke. She'd barely reached the bottom step when the porch light snapped on. Seconds later a car door slammed, and the noisy vehicle backed out of the driveway with a roar. Then it turned and barreled toward the center of town at a seriously fast clip.

Flashlight in hand, Becca hurried up beside Carly. An army veteran, she was always on high alert to anything happening in the neighborhood.

"Who was that?" Becca asked her, scanning the area with the beam from her flashlight.

"I don't have a clue. I thought maybe someone was delivering takeout to you and Joyce." Carly rubbed her arms and shivered.

Becca shook her head. "We had takeout last night. Whoever that was, they should invest in a new muffler," she said tartly. She took in a long, deep breath, then jogged over to the back of Carly's vehicle. Carly followed her.

"I knew I smelled paint. Look at this," Becca said, aiming her beam at Carly's trunk.

"Oh!" Carly gasped.

The image of a grinning skull gleamed with fresh, sparkly white paint. Tiny curlicues around the hollowed-out eyes suggested the skull was supposed to be female. At the bottom of the image, the paint had dribbled off. The artist probably panicked when the porch light went on and fled before he, or she, got caught.

Carly's heart hammered her rib cage. Who would do something like this?

The name dropped into her head without a second's hesitation. *Ferris Menard.* Did he even know where she lived?

Probably. Since her return a year earlier, she'd learned that nothing much stayed private. Balsam Dell was a small, close-knit community. Most everyone in town knew Carly rented the top floor of Joyce Katso's home. And since the house had been in the Katso family since the early 1900s, Joyce was somewhat of a local fixture.

"You need to report this, Carly." Becca's expression was somber.

"Do you really think so? What if it was just a prank?" she offered weakly. "Halloween *is* only four days away."

"Maybe, but—" Becca shook her head and slung an arm loosely around Carly's shoulder. "But it's better to be safe than sorry, right?" Her words were heavy with meaning. Becca was no doubt remembering Carly's near fatal encounter with a killer four months earlier.

"You're right," Carly agreed with a sigh.

Becca called the police from her cell, then took a few pictures of the graffiti. She texted the pics to Carly, and a few minutes later a patrol car swung in. The officer took statements from both women and promised to file a report. He didn't offer much in the way of hope that they'd nab the vandal. The loud engine was probably the best clue, so he advised them to keep their ears peeled for any such vehicles. Before he left, he snapped a photo of the offending image with his phone. "Looks like water-based paint," he said before he left. "It should come right off with some nail polish remover."

After Carly thanked Becca for her help, she bade her good night. Luckily, she had a half-filled bottle of nail polish remover in her bathroom cabinet. She made quick work of eradicating the gruesome image, which came off more easily than she'd anticipated.

She'd purposely stopped herself from telling Becca about the confrontation with Ferris in her restaurant that afternoon. Why drag anyone else into her pool of worries? Taking care of Joyce, who was challenged with MS, and studying to earn a degree as a licensed nursing assistant, kept Becca busy enough.

After securely locking her apartment door, Carly swept Havarti into her arms. "Well," she told him wearily, "I don't think much more could happen today, do you?" Havarti licked her nose in response.

When her cell rang, she set Havarti on the sofa. She smiled at the name on the screen. "Hey, Suzanne, what's up?"

"Oh, Carly, I hate to tell you this. I fell and sprained my ankle this afternoon when I was helping Jake put up a curtain rod in the bathroom. The doctor said I need to stay off it for a week!"

Carly flopped onto the sofa next to Havarti, squelching the urge to scream. After offering Suzanne healing hugs and instructing her to take proper care of herself, she disconnected the call.

First Ferris's verbal attack, then the graffiti painted on her car, and now Suzanne's accident.

If the universe was trying to mess with her head, it was doing one heck of a good job.

CHAPTER THREE

CARLY HAD AWAKENED TO A PERFECT SATURDAY MORNING—
at least as far as the Scary-Licious Smorgasbord was concerned.
Clear blue skies and wispy clouds heralded a dry, sunny autumn day.

The competition would begin at 11:00 and end at 3:00. That
gave the judges sufficient time to tally the votes and announce the
winner before dark, which was slipping in earlier every day.

Halloween season was, by far, Carly's favorite time of year.
For her, it was a surefire "treat" before the days grew shorter and
colder. She was anxious to see all the costumes people would be
wearing. Her own costume was hanging in the coat closet. As soon
as she and Grant were ready to set up on the green, she'd slip into
the restroom and put it on.

Grant had agreed to meet her at the restaurant at 8:00 a.m.
sharp to help prepare for the event. Judging from past years, he'd
estimated they'd need about two hundred fifty of the mini sandwiches they'd be grilling throughout the competition. Not only
would each one be made with pumpkin bread—it would also be
pumpkin-shaped. Carly's mom had donated one of the cookie cut-
ters from her vast collection.

"This bread is fantastic," Grant said. "There's only a touch of
pumpkin, so it's not sweet and it doesn't overpower the cheese.
And the pale gold color is perfect."

Sara Hardy, the bread baker who supplied all the artisan breads
for Carly's eatery, had created the pumpkin bread recipe especially
for her.

"I'm really going to miss my mom," Carly said with a sigh, glancing at her mom's cookie cutter as she removed Grant's homemade dips from the commercial fridge. "Gary's favorite niece is getting married this afternoon, so it's not like she can skip the wedding."

"Lousy timing, but I'm sure they'll enjoy the wedding. I wonder how Suzanne is doing," he said, feeding chunks of extra sharp orange cheddar into a shredder. They'd decided to use shredded cheese, not only for ease of preparation but for faster melting. "Is she taking pain medication for her ankle?"

"Only ibuprofen." Carly set two hollowed out pumpkins on the worktable in the kitchen. Grant had carved faces in each—one scary and one smiley. He'd prepared a guacamole dip for the scary pumpkin and a spicy marinara for the smiley one. "Her ankle's not so much painful as it is annoying. She has to wear one of those clunky orthopedic boots."

"Oh boy. She must hate that."

"She's not a happy camper, as they say."

Over the summer, Suzanne had reunited with her almost ex-husband, and their marriage was on a path to healing. Recently, they'd rented a house that they hoped eventually to buy.

Carly set a glass bowl in each of the pumpkins. "I'm thinking we should keep the reserves of our dipping sauces in our fridge. When we start to get low, one of us can run across the street for more. Gina said she and Zach can act as gofers."

"Gina's a sweetheart. Is she home?"

"No. I think she stayed at Zach's last night. I meant to ask you, Grant. Did you help Ferris Menard last year when he entered his sub sandwiches in the competition?"

"Yeah." Grant made a face. "Even though he won, it was a nightmare getting ready for it. That whole week we were prepping for it, he was constantly screaming orders at me and Holly—that's his daughter. Made us both crazy."

"Any idea what he's making this year?"

"He's doing another version of the dragon bites he did last year. Only this time he's using wraps instead of sub rolls. And, of course, his *famous* dressing." Grant's words held a touch of sarcasm.

"You don't think they'll be good?"

"It's not that. Mr. Menard's been acting *really* weird for the last few weeks. On a good day he's like a grenade ready to explode, but lately it's been different. Something's definitely bugging him. Even his daughter's been tiptoeing around him."

Carly wondered if that explained Ferris's outburst on Thursday. "Do you regret quitting?"

"No way. Don't even think that, Carly. I'm *so* glad I'm out of there."

When the preparations were done, Carly headed in first to don her costume.

Grant grinned when he saw Lady Dracula emerge. "My gosh, you look so cool, Carly. You even drew bite marks on your neck!"

She'd also brushed baby powder over her face and neck to simulate an "undead" look. On one side of her neck, she'd drawn two "bloody" holes with lip liner, and she'd outlined her lips in black.

"Thanks. I like it too." She especially loved the spider web earrings Ari had bought for her.

When it was Grant's turn to change, Carly gasped. Atop his short dreads he'd attached a curly black wig that trailed down his back, a la Prince. Over a ruffled white shirt, he wore a long purple coat, with black leather pants and boots completing the look.

"You look amazing," Carly squealed. "Straight out of *Purple Rain!*"

By the time they packed up their food and supplies and reached their assigned spot on the town green, Ari had already set up their table. *Reliable and efficient,* Carly thought. *Another checkmark in the plus column.*

He'd also set up the large, portable griddle they'd be using. When he saw Carly approaching, his eyes danced. "Bless my soul, you are the prettiest vampire I've ever seen." He came over and squeezed her in a firm hug, holding her for a beat longer than usual. Then he planted a featherlight kiss on her powdered cheek.

"Thank you, Ari," she said, hoping the flush in her cheeks wouldn't bleed through the baby powder. She took a step back and stared at him. "And you—you switched costumes! How did you find a vampire getup so fast?"

"It's actually only a cape with a turned-up collar. The black pants are mine. I called three costume places until I finally lucked out. One of them still had a few vampire capes in stock." He grinned, and his brown-eyed gaze burned into hers. "Now you and I are an authentic undead couple."

Something in his tone made Carly's insides go all squiggly. She was impressed that he'd taken time from his busy schedule to hunt down a costume that would complement hers.

That "plus" column just keeps growing…

By 11:00, the town green was bustling with goblins, ghosts, princesses, and wizards. Thirteen local restaurant owners were participating in the competition. The tables were set up in neat rows on the green. A large placard attached to the front of each one advertised the name of the eatery, along with its assigned number. Carly's number was 12—the month of her mom's birthday. She hoped it would bring her good luck.

Gina showed up with Zach shortly after 11:00. Dressed as plain M&M's and peanut M&M's, they bustled around Carly and Grant's table, taking turns with Ari at cleaning up used plates, emptying trash, and replenishing supplies.

"These things are like, ridiculous," Gina gushed, rescuing a blob of gooey orange cheddar from her cheesy pumpkin-shaped sandwich. "I'd better not eat any more or you'll run out."

Carly smiled at her friend and slid another grilled cheese onto an orange paper plate. The line at her table ebbed and flowed, but she and Grant managed to keep up with the demand without any serious backups.

"This is *so* much more fun than last year," Grant said, piling shredded cheese onto a row of cutouts. He glanced up to see a young, full-figured woman with blond sausage curls waving at him from a few feet away. Over a frilly, long-sleeved white blouse, she wore a flouncy blue jumper. Her feet were clad in black leather patents so shiny they gleamed in the sunlight. She twisted her hands nervously.

"Oh, hi, Holly." He gave her a polite smile.

Holly. So this was Ferris's daughter.

"Hey, Grant." Avoiding eye contact with Carly, the young woman stared hungrily at the offerings on their table.

A tiny hobgoblin of suspicion slithered into Carly's brain. Was the woman spying for her dad? Or did she genuinely come over only to say hello to Grant?

Seeing Holly's glum expression, Carly instantly felt bad. "Would you like to try one?" She slid a cheesy sandwich onto a paper plate.

With a nod, Holly accepted the treat, then snagged a condiment cup filled with "guts" dip—a.k.a. guacamole—from a tray. Her blue eyes widened after the first bite.

"This is awesome." She swallowed another huge bite, then turned and shot a quick, worried look behind her. "Grant, I have to go. If you want to come back, Dad says all is forgiven, okay?"

Grant looked pained. "Holly, I can't." He turned his attention back to the grill. "I–I have to work now. Sorry."

Holly's face fell. Clutching the meager remains of her cheesy pumpkin, she dashed off into the throng.

So that was her mission, Carly thought with annoyance. *To lure Grant back into the fold.*

They continued grilling and serving, and Carly was pleased to see a few of her regulars stroll over to her table. Evelyn Fitch came by and introduced her daughter, Lydia, an attractive brunette who was a younger version of her mom. Both women sported cat ears, and they each taste-tested a cheesy grilled pumpkin. "The best so far!" Evelyn pronounced, with a resounding thumbs-up.

Carly leaned toward Evelyn and said quietly, "Thank you for the note you left. I loved it."

Evelyn beamed and ambled off with her arm looped through her daughter's. Moments later, Stan Henderson, dressed as a roguish pirate, waved at Carly as he approached her table. "Whoa. I knew you'd have the best treats!" His eager smile faltered a bit when Ari came up behind Carly. "Hey, Ari, how's it going?"

"Great, Stan. Enjoying the festivities?"

"Aw, you bet. This is one of my favorite days of the year. Can I cheat and have two?"

"Not a problem," Carly said, handing him a plate.

Accepting his double order, Stan looked like a kid who'd just been given carte blanche to plunder a candy store. He swallowed a huge bite, his eyes closed in apparent bliss. When he opened them again his smile was wide, his hazel-eyed gaze locked on Carly. "These are going to win, Carly. Hands down."

"I hope so, Stan. Keep your fingers crossed for me."

Moments after Stan walked away, Carly spotted Don Frasco. Don was the sole owner of the Balsam Dell Weekly, a free paper that published more ads than news. He'd earned some recognition early in the summer for his role in putting away a local crime ring. He sported an auburn goatee that matched his eyes and an old-style fedora with a large "Press Pass" pinned to it covered his red hair.

"Hey," he said, snapping a photo of her and Grant. "Nice spread. Too bad I hate cheese."

Too bad indeed, Carly thought dryly as he moved on. One thing about Don, he was blunt with his opinions.

Carly was pleased when Suzanne's husband and son came by to sample her offerings. She greeted them warmly and handed each a sandwich.

"Mom is like, so bummed that she couldn't make it here," Josh mumbled over a mouthful of melted cheese.

"How's she doing today?" Carly asked them.

"Better," Jake Rivers said, "but she's cursing herself for being a klutz. Her words, not mine," he added quickly. "She's worried about how you guys'll be able to handle the restaurant without her."

"Not that we won't miss her, but we'll be fine," Carly assured him. "Tell her to stop worrying and stay off her ankle so she can feel better soon."

In truth, it was going to be a challenge for her and Grant to do everything without Suzanne. Carly was half tempted to contact a temp agency to see if they could send in a ringer for a few days.

By 2:30, things had quieted down. The noise level had dropped from a jumbled cacophony to a low drone. Either everyone had eaten their fill, or the chilly air was sending them inside to warm up. Carly noticed a short line at the ballot box, where participants were dropping in their votes.

Like most of the other restaurateurs who participated in the competition, Carly had closed her eatery for the entire day. After the winner was announced, they'd pack up their table and return any perishables to the restaurant, and then everyone could go home. She and Ari had a quiet evening planned—Chinese food at her apartment, followed by a classic horror movie And, with any luck, they'd be popping open the bottle of champagne she'd stashed in the fridge to celebrate her eatery's win.

Grant had packed up the remaining supplies—they'd brought more than they needed—and he and Ari began lugging them back to the eatery. Carly was getting antsy for the judges to tally the votes and announce this year's winner. Each person who paid for a ticket was entitled to one vote. Votes were deposited in a tamper-proof box and would be counted promptly at 3:00 p.m.

Carly was also itching to know how Ferris Menard's dragon

bites looked and tasted. For obvious reasons, she didn't dare go within twenty feet of his table. And he no doubt knew that Gina and Carly were best buds.

Hmm…

Gina came over and whispered to Carly, "I'm taking a quick bathroom break. Need anything before I go?"

"No, but is Zach up for a little spying? I want to see what Menard is giving out."

Gina grinned. "Say no more."

Ten minutes later, a triumphant Zach strolled casually back to Carly's table carrying a greasy white paper plate. "Got one." Taking her and Gina aside, he lifted a napkin off his plate. "Way too oily, and wraps don't really slay me. But the cold cuts are good, sliced thin the way I like them, and this one's packed with mozzarella. The edible eyeballs"—he shrugged—"nothing special. Anyone can hollow out an olive to make an eyeball."

Without tasting it, Carly had to agree. The visual was nothing to write home about, and in her mind, a greasy plate was far from appetizing. "What about the salad dressing?" she pressed.

"Again, it's good, but I wouldn't give it a ringing endorsement."

"Which is interesting," Gina pointed out. "Because I heard that Menard's soon-to-be-ex-wife started bottling the stuff and selling it under her own brand. Supposedly, she tweaked the formula to make it spicier. *And*…get this. She made a deal to sell the modified recipe to a boutique spice company. For some pretty serious bucks too."

"Really?" Carly marveled at friend's never-ending supply of local intel. "Gina, where do you hear this stuff?"

"Same place as usual. My aunt Lil at the Happy Clipper."

Carly smiled as she mulled over this latest bit of news. A hair washer at the local beauty salon, Gina's elderly, lavender-haired aunt collected more tidbits of information than an FBI bugging device. "I can't imagine that Ferris is too thrilled about *that* development."

"According to Portia, he's furious over it. Portia's his almost-ex," Gina explained. "I think— Uh oh." She swallowed. "Speak of the devil. And I do mean that literally."

A man wearing red devil's horns came barreling in Carly's direction. Ferris Menard's face, nearly the same shade of scarlet as his long, flowing cape, was contorted with anger.

"Why you little witch," he said ferociously. "Sending your minion"—he aimed a thumb at Zach—"to steal my food so you could analyze it? You are the lowest of the low, you know that?" He used a few expletives that sent Carly reeling.

Zach moved in closer to Menard. "First of all," he said, his voice deceivingly soft, "no one *stole* your food. I sampled your dragon bites as part of the competition. I paid for my ticket and I'm entitled to one vote, which means I get to taste the entries. And second, if you ever use language like that again in the presence of either of these women, you are going to be very, very sorry."

Carly stared at Zach. When had the mild-mannered account manager grown fangs?

"It's all right, Zach," Carly said evenly, refusing to be baited by Menard. "He knows full well he sent his daughter over to spy on me too."

"The reason my daughter came over here," he sniped, "was to say hi to Grant. That's *it*. And she only ate one of those leaky pumpkin things to be polite."

Leaky pumpkin things? Like the one she practically inhaled?

In the next instant, Ari and Grant came up behind the women. Ari's dark brown eyes blazed, and his smile was anything but cordial. "I see you're overstepping your bounds again, Ferris. Do you need an escort back to your table?"

Menard glared at Ari but didn't respond.

Carly took a step closer to her nemesis. Flashing him the sincerest smile she could muster, she said, "The votes will be counted soon, Ferris. If you win, I will personally come over and congratulate you. If I happen to win, I'd like you to do the same for me. Deal?" She held out one hand as a gesture of good will.

He glared at her proffered hand as if it were a dead rat. Then he told her to go to a hot place, turned on his heel, and stomped back over to his table.

~

By 3:10, the crowd was buzzing with anticipation. Gina frowned up at the makeshift podium where the town's recreation director, Teresa Gray, was deep in conversation with a bespectacled young man. "I wonder what's taking so long," Gina groused to Carly. "By now they've usually announced the winner."

"Patience," Carly teased her friend.

The mic squeaked. Everyone's eyes went to the podium. Ms. Gray, her expression oddly blank, spoke in an even tone. "Good afternoon, everyone. I would first like to extend a huge *thank you* to everyone who participated in this year's Halloween competition—not only the chefs but those of you who purchased tickets and voted. We saw some wonderful offerings and tasted some mighty delicious treats this year, didn't we?" She paused for a brief clapping of hands and a handful of cheers. "Best of all, we raised over one thousand dollars, five hundred of which will be awarded to the winner. The remainder will be gifted to local food banks. As for this year's winner—"

Grant grinned over at Carly with crossed fingers.

"We have counted the votes. *Twice*," Ms. Gray emphasized. "Unfortunately, due to a mix-up, we are not yet ready to announce the winner."

"*What?*" Gina blurted.

A nervous hum went through the crowd. "Whaddya mean, mix-up?" someone squawked.

Carly caught Ari's worried look and said, "Has this ever happened before?"

"Not since I've been attending."

Ms. Gray fingered the mic nervously. "We hope to have an announcement by later this evening. Please check our Facebook event page for updates. Thank you." She turned and scurried away as if she'd spotted a mouse.

Grumbles and moans rose from all the people who'd gathered to hear the winner's name. Carly didn't know how to process what had just happened. Her first year entering the competition and they'd encountered a glitch.

Don Frasco came up next to Ari and Carly, his eyes glittering. "Don't say where you heard it," he said, "but the reason they can't announce the winner is that someone stuffed the ballot box with illegal votes."

Carly's mouth opened, but nothing came out. Though she knew it sounded crazy, she couldn't help wondering if her first entry into the competition had brought bad luck to the entire town.

CHAPTER FOUR

"MY FIRST COMPETITION, AND IT WAS RIGGED," CARLY GROANED to Ari. She slipped a tiny bit of chicken, *sans* the fried coating, to the little dog gazing up at her with pleading brown eyes.

They were at Carly's apartment, picking at the remains of their Chinese food feast. Carly had changed out of her lady vampire costume into a fuzzy-knit, pumpkin-colored sweater and black jeans. Ari had removed his Dracula cape and stashed it in the back of his pickup.

In keeping with their usual practice of cost sharing, Ari had treated to the crab Rangoon, the sweet and sour chicken, the vegetable lo mein, and the pork fried rice, while Carly had contributed a bottle of chilled sauvignon blanc. In spite of the delicious meal, not to mention the charming company, she felt decidedly out of sorts.

Ari gave her a sympathetic look. "I know it's disappointing, honey, but eventually they'll straighten it out. Once they do, I'm willing to bet they'll find out that you won." He gave her a smile clearly meant to be encouraging, but Carly's heart felt heavy.

An hour earlier, she'd gotten a call from the recreation director further explaining the situation. During the counting of the votes, they'd discovered the number of votes removed from the ballot box had exceeded, by a total of eleven, the number of tickets sold. At this stage, it was impossible to determine which were the illegal votes, but they were determined to resolve the mystery. Those eleven votes had pushed Sub-a-Dub-Sub into the winner's category, but it was unclear if those were the phony votes. The cheater, whoever it was, had used a photocopier to reproduce the original ballot and print out additional ones. Unfortunately, it had been easy to do. The original votes had been printed on plain white paper.

"Ms. Gray said they don't have any idea who did this," Carly had told Ari. "Not yet, anyway. They're going to start an investigation. She's confident they'll figure out who the culprit is, but I'm not so sure."

Ari reached over and wrapped his hand around hers. "The organizers have always done a great job, Carly. I'd be willing to bet it won't take them long to figure out who tried to cheat. Someone must have seen the fraudster copy that ballot. Maybe in the library or in a local office somewhere. Who knows? Menard himself might have a copier in his restaurant."

Carly made a scrunched-up face, then gave up a reluctant smile. "I know. I'm being a whiny baby, aren't it?"

"Not in the least. You have every right to be ticked off." He leaned over and kissed her nose, then delivered his empty plate to the sink and returned for hers.

"Ms. Gray said they're going to examine every vote to see if they can figure out which are the bogus ones."

Together cleaned up the rest of the dishes and put the leftovers in the fridge. After finishing off the wine, they shared a humongous, mummy-shaped frosted sugar cookie from Sissy's Bakery. In keeping with the theme, they curled up together on Carly's sofa and watched the 1959 version of *The Mummy*. Havarti, acting as a mini chaperone, nestled between them. Despite rolling their eyes at the cornier parts of the movie, they agreed it had undeniable vintage appeal.

After they watched the highlights of the eleven o'clock news, Ari wrapped Carly in a massive hug and bade her goodnight. "I had a wonderful day and a terrific evening," he told her huskily. "But you're super tired. I can see it in those beautiful green eyes."

Carly smiled at him and stroked his cheek with the back of

her fingers. "I can't deny that. It's been a day, hasn't it? Thanks for everything, Ari."

"No thanks are needed. I'll call you in the morning, okay? Maybe by then we'll have some answers."

Carly leaned into him for another long kiss, then reluctantly closed the door, locking it behind him.

She was trying mightily to take Ari's advice and trust in the process, but it wasn't easy. The idea that someone would attempt to skew the results of the competition still felt like a sliver of wood wedged under her thumbnail.

Was Menard involved?

It was hard to believe he wasn't.

"Things will look brighter in the morning," she told Havarti over a huge yawn. Only half believing it, she lifted him into her arms and squeezed him to her chest.

The dog gave her a quizzical look, then licked her cheek.

"Don't worry," she said. "Regardless of how it turns out, it won't affect your lifestyle. You'll still get everything your little canine heart desires."

~

The jingle of her cell phone jerked Carly out of a half sleep. Rolling to one side, she peered over Havarti's furry head and glanced at her bedside clock.

6:56 a.m.

Who in the name of galloping goldfish was calling her on a Sunday at this unforgiving hour?

She fumbled for the phone and blinked at it through filmy eyes. Rhonda Hale Clark's smiling visage beamed at her from the screen. Carly swiped open the call. "M-Mom?"

"He's dead," Rhonda bleated through the phone. "Ferris Menard is dead!"

Carly jerked upright. The sudden jolt sent Havarti scurrying off the bed. "What do you mean, he's dead? You mean dead as in, he didn't really win the competition?"

"I mean dead as in, he's never going to wake up again."

Carly sucked in a gasp. A lump landed in her gut like a block of lead.

"I'm heading over to your apartment now with breakfast. Norah's coming too. And you'd better get dressed. Chief Holloway will be right on my tail if he doesn't get there first."

"Wait a minute. What does Chief Holloway have to do with—" Before Carly could complete her question, her mom disconnected.

Ferris must have died from a heart attack, Carly reasoned. Hadn't Grant mentioned that he was on ticker medication?

Throwing on a pair of jeans and a warm sweatshirt, Carly hurried into the bathroom and scrubbed her face. After turning up the heat a notch, she headed into the kitchen. Havarti was wagging his tail as he danced around his food bowl, but first things first. She clipped on his leash, put on a warm jacket, and escorted him outside into the yard for a bathroom visit.

The early morning air was chilly, damp with a slight mist. Her head spun with questions: Was Menard really dead? Had his heart given out? Or had her mom gotten hold of some bad information?

Back in the kitchen, she poured kibble into Havarti's dish and replenished his water. At the sound of footsteps clomping up her stairs, she raced to her door. Luckily, she now had a peephole that allowed her to check out visitors. Ari had installed it over the summer after her encounter with a deadly killer.

She aimed an eyeball into the opening. "Thank goodness," Carly breathed, letting her mom and Norah in.

Rhonda Hale Clark, her brunette hair pulled back neatly from her face and secured with a decorative black comb, looked as crisp as ever at barely 7:00 in the morning. Over slenderizing black pants, she wore a lilac, cowl-neck sweater that brought out the sparkle in her green eyes. The sight of her never failed to give Carly a lump in her throat. After all those of years of her mom living in Florida, having her home again for good was the icing on the cake of Carly's life.

"Good morning, dear." Rhonda deposited a pink bakery box into Carly's hands. "Take these and set them out on a plate, would you please? Norah, bring the coffee into the kitchen."

Carly's sister, Norah, her usually perfect, gorgeously high-lighted blond hair a rumpled mess, looked as if she'd had about eight minutes sleep. With a roll of her bleary eyes, she threw an air kiss at Carly and shuffled past her and into the kitchen. In her hands she carried a cardboard holder with four covered cups tucked into the cutouts.

Four cups?

"Mom, what's going on?" They followed the trial of caffeine into the kitchen. "Is Ferris Menard really dead?"

Norah grimaced. "He'd better be, for Mom to get me up at this hour."

"Norah!" Carly's mom scolded. "That's a terrible thing to say."

Carly wanted to scream. "Will someone please fill me—" A knock at the door interrupted her. "Oh, for the love of daffodils in December, who's here now?" She went over to the door and pulled it open. "Oh, hi Chief."

Police Chief Fred Holloway removed his hat, displaying a head full of thick gray hair. "Good morning, Carly. May I come in?"

The chief was a longtime family friend. His wife, before she passed, had been in Rhonda's book club, and his daughter, Doctor Anne, was Havarti's veterinarian.

"Sure, why not?" She sighed. "My mom and sister are already here. I think they brought you a coffee."

"That's thoughtful of them." His face reddened. "I, um, called your mom first so I wouldn't have to alarm you with an early morning call."

Which made not an ounce of sense. Any early morning call would alarm her, regardless of the caller. "Chief, I need to know what happened."

They sat around Carly's table, each with a cup of steaming coffee. Only Norah, not a fan of breakfast, passed on the pink box full of doughnuts.

After fortifying himself with a long gulp of black coffee, the chief sighed. He reached down to pet Havarti, who was vigorously sniffing his knees. "I'm sorry to confirm that Ferris Menard is dead. His daughter found him this morning in the restaurant. He was on the floor, face up, clearly not breathing."

Carly shivered. "Oh, no, that's terrible news. Sadly, though, it doesn't surprise me. Grant told me Ferris was on heart medication. He obviously had cardiac issues."

The chief nodded slowly, but then his jaw hardened. "Which doesn't, I'm afraid, account for the steak knife that was found jabbed into his chest."

The chunk of cinnamon cruller Carly had just swallowed stopped in its tracks. She managed to choke it back with a slug of coffee, but it still felt lodged in her throat. She looked at everyone in horror. "Mom, did you know about this before you got here?"

"I did," Rhonda said quietly. "But I wanted Fred to be the one to tell you."

"Chief," Carly said with a gulp, "are you saying Ferris was murdered?"

"As best we can piece it together, it looks that way. Turns out Menard was taking medication for angina. His pill bottle, the one with his nitroglycerin tabs, was found on the floor, sitting upright, but out of his reach. One of the investigators has a working theory. He thinks that during his scuffle with the killer, Menard suffered an attack of angina and tried to get to his medication. The killer taunted him by setting it just out of his reach and waited until he...*expired* to stick the knife in his chest. It's only a theory, and at this stage we're far from proving it. There was one other critical finding, but we're not releasing that information."

"But why would the killer stab him if he was already dead?" Carly asked him.

RECIPES

AT CARLY'S GRILLED CHEESE EATERY, THE CUSTOMER RULES! Carly knows that everyone loves their grilled cheese their own way, and she strives to accommodate even the pickiest of eaters. (She used to be one herself!)

Grilled cheese sandwiches can be as simple or as complex as you like, but Carly starts with the basics and then builds from there depending on each customer's taste. While a few of her sandwiches have become her most popular, she encourages everyone to try their own variations. The beauty of a grilled cheese is its versatility.

Each recipe is for one sandwich, so simply multiply the ingredients by the number of people you're serving.

PARTY HAVARTI!

With its creamy, buttery flavor, Havarti makes for a delectable grilled cheese. Combine it with sourdough bread and you've got yourself one delicious meal.

Ingredients

salted butter, softened
2–3 slices Havarti cheese
2 slices sourdough bread
tomato slices (optional)

Directions

1. Butter one side of each slice of bread.

2. On the unbuttered side of one slice, stack your cheese slices and other ingredients; top with remaining slice, butter side up.

3. Grill in a cast-iron pan or nonstick skillet over medium heat for about 3 minutes. Because of its chewy consistency, sourdough bread can take a bit longer to achieve that wonderful golden hue. As you grill, press lightly with a spatula or grill press and then flip over and grill the other side for approximately 3 minutes. The outside should be golden and the cheese thoroughly melted.

4. Slice in half diagonally and serve with chips, pickles, tomato soup, or whatever else gladdens your taste buds!

SMOKY STEALS THE BACON

This simple recipe produces a grilled cheese that bacon lovers will add to their list of favorites!

Ingredients
    salted butter, softened
    2 slices asiago bread
    4–6 slices thin-sliced smoked gouda
    3–4 slices crispy cooked bacon
    parmesan cheese

Directions
1. Butter one side of each slice of bread.

2. On the unbuttered side of one slice, stack half the gouda slices; add the crispy bacon slices and then the remaining gouda. Top with the remaining bread slice, butter side up.

3. Sprinkle a generous layer of grated parmesan cheese in a cast-iron pan or nonstick skillet.

4. Grill over medium heat for about 3 minutes.

5. As you grill, press lightly with a spatula or grill press. Before flipping over to grill the remaining side, sprinkle another layer of parmesan cheese in the skillet and then grill the other side for approximately 3 minutes. The outside should be golden and the cheese thoroughly melted.

6. Slice in half diagonally and serve with chips, pickles, tomato soup, or whatever else makes your taste buds sing!

GRANT'S VERMONT JAMMIN'

When Grant wanted to create a special grilled cheese for his folks, he looked to their slightly eclectic tastes and created this delight.

Ingredients
salted butter, softened
2 slices cranberry-pecan bread
thick layer of soft brie cheese, rind removed (it will be spreadable)
1–2 tablespoons fig jam
spinach leaves (optional)

Directions
1. Butter one side of each slice of bread.

2. On the unbuttered side of one slice, spread the soft brie.

(You won't be able to resist sampling the creamy brie, so be sure to leave enough for your sandwich!)

3. On the unbuttered side of the remaining slice, spread a layer of the fig jam—whatever amount suits your taste.

4. If desired, top the jam with a few spinach leaves. (Be sure they're washed and dried.)

5. Top with the remaining bread slice, butter side up.

6. Grill in a cast-iron pan or nonstick skillet over medium heat for about 3 minutes. As you grill, press lightly with a spatula or grill press and then flip over and grill the other side for approximately 3 minutes. The outside should be golden and the cheese thoroughly melted.

7. Slice in half carefully. (It will be gooey!) Serve alone, with pear slices, or with whatever else tickles your palate!

CARLY'S GRILLED CHEESE TIPS:

- For better melting, room temperature cheese works best.

- Softened butter works best for spreading on the bread. Carly is generous with its application, but feel free to cut back to suit your taste.

ACKNOWLEDGMENTS

When I first envisioned a mystery series centered on a grilled cheese restaurant, I didn't know if anyone would want to read it. It was my fabulous agent, Jessica Faust, who embraced the idea and who guided, prodded, and encouraged me every step of the way. Thank you, Jessica, for helping me realize my own grilled cheese dream.

The folks at Sourcebooks have been nothing short of amazing. From the artwork to the marketing to the copyediting and so much more—you've all made me feel like a valued member of the team. Margaret Johnston, my superbly talented editor, offered insightful suggestions and revisions that made the story so much better. Margaret, I'm honored—and so very lucky—to have you in my corner.

Big hugs to Judy Jones and Jenny Kales for doing early read-throughs and offering targeted suggestions to those first drafts. In my book, you're both rock stars!

Huge thanks to my friends and colleagues at the Cozy Mystery Crew for your support, encouragement, and expert advice.

Last of all to Mom, who patiently helped me test out grilled cheese recipes. She made them for me when I was a kid, and...oh wait, she made one for me yesterday. Love you, Mom!

ABOUT THE AUTHOR

© Amelia Koziol

As a child, author Linda Reilly practically existed on grilled cheese sandwiches, and today, they remain her comfort food of choice. Raised in a sleepy town in the Berkshires of Massachusetts, she retired from the world of real estate closings and title examinations to spend more time writing mysteries. A member of Sisters in Crime, Mystery Writers of America, and Cat Writers' Association, Linda lives in southern New Hampshire with her husband and her cats. When she's not pounding away at her keyboard, she can usually be found prowling the shelves of a local bookstore or library hunting for a new adventure. Visit her on the web at lindasreilly.com or on Facebook at facebook.com/Lindasreillyauthor. She loves hearing from readers!